Also by
DD Barant

Back from the Undead

Better Off Undead

Killing Rocks

Death Blows

Dying Bites

UNDEAD
TO THE
WORLD

DD Barant

St. Martin's Paperbacks

This is a work of fiction. All of the characters, organizations, and events portrayed in this novel are either products of the author's imagination or are used fictitiously.

UNDEAD TO THE WORLD

Copyright © 2012 by DD Barant.

All rights reserved.

For information address St. Martin's Press, 175 Fifth Avenue, New York, NY 10010.

ISBN: 978-0-312-54507-9

Printed in the United States of America

St. Martin's Paperbacks edition / December 2012

St. Martin's Paperbacks are published by St. Martin's Press, 175 Fifth Avenue, New York, NY 10010.

10 9 8 7 6 5 4 3 2 1

ONE

My name is Jace Valchek, and I'm pretty sure I'm going insane.

Either that, or everything I know is wrong. I'm not the woman I think I am, the place I live isn't what I thought it was, and everyone I know is an imposter. What's really, truly, crazy, though, is that right now both of those ideas are running neck and neck in the what-do-I-believe race, and the fact that I'm seriously considering option two is really tipping the balance in favor of option one.

Bear with me, okay? Things are going to get really weird before I'm done, so I'm going to start slow, with just the basic facts. Here we go.

I live in a small town: Thropirelem, Kansas. If you live in a small town too, you know what I mean when I say that it manages to be completely mundane and boring and flat-out strange at the same time.

It's all about the people that live There, of course. The town itself is the definition of ordinary, but some of its residents are a little odd. And yes, I include myself in that category.

I'm thirty mumble mumble years old, single, reasonably attractive, and I work part-time at both the local diner and the hardware store. I briefly flirted with a career in law enforcement when I was younger, but I flunked the psychiatric evaluation. A few years after that, I flunked another psychiatric evaluation—also conducted by the state—but this time my failing grade briefly landed me in a locked ward. I'm much better now.

More or less.

I still have a fascination with the law—and psychology, for that matter—but that's under control. No, what's more troubling is my interest in a television show: *The Bloodhound Files.*

Okay, it's more like an obsession. I've never missed an episode. I own every season that's been released on DVD and have every comic, toy, and novelization. Or I did, until I had to get rid of it all as a condition of my release. At least I made some money on eBay.

I guess my problem started because of the heroine's name: Jace Red Dog. Jace (short for Jacinda) isn't a common name. And we're both tall brunettes, though she's got Native American blood and I'm from Spanish-Polish stock. But it wasn't her name or appearance I really identified with: it was her *style.* Red Dog kicks ass and speaks her mind, and nobody ever messes with her without regretting it. My kind of woman.

So much so that I kind of forgot who *I* was, for a while.

But I'm better now, right? All the doctors say so. I have a place of my own, employment, even a dog. I'm doing fine.

"How you doing?" Charlie asks.

"I'll be doing better with another beer," I say, and knock back what's in my glass. He nods and pours me a fresh one.

Charlie's my best friend, I guess. He owns and runs the local tavern, the Quarry, and spends most of his time behind the bar. He's a little older than me, ex-military, with the build and haircut to go with it. Green eyes, a square jaw, and a tan so dark you're not really sure of his ethnic background. Charlie's about the only person in town who doesn't seem to care about my stay in the nut hut; I guess that's why I spend so much time hanging around with him. Although the beer might have something to do with it, too.

"Hey," I say. I'm at my usual spot at the end of the bar, which always seems to be where the regulars in any given watering hole congregate. "I see you're keeping the rumors about you fat and healthy."

Charlie looks up from the book he's reading, some kind of oversized paperback edition of *The Wonderful Wizard of Oz.* "Hmm? What, that I raise and breed flying monkeys? I keep telling people, they're both males."

"That's what I mean, Dorothy. The only female anyone sees you with is me, and they're starting to wonder if I'm a tranny."

"The only tranny these people have ever been close to was the one bolted to the chassis of their car."

"Maybe. But people love to talk about what they don't know."

"Keeps their opinions from getting all muddled up with facts?"

"Usually. But that also means that the occasional fact tends to stand out, like the fact that the toughest guy in town likes to read about singing munchkins and rainbows."

"You're thinking of the musical. This is a *book,* see? No buttons, no batteries. The only noise it makes is when I roll it up and smack you with it."

"Ooh, how manly. Did the Wizard give you that courage, Mr. Lion?"

Charlie chuckles. "Nah, I've always had plenty of that. And please, let's not go for the obvious Scarecrow joke."

"You're right. That one's a no-brainer."

He winces, then shakes it off and goes on. "I've always identified with the Tin Woodsman, actually."

"What, the guy with the funnel on his head and no heart?"

"That's what he thought, but it turns out—"

"I know the story, okay? Everybody knows the story. I always thought they got that guy all wrong."

Charlie frowns. "All wrong? What do you mean, all wrong?"

"I mean, he was a guy made out of metal with no heart and an axe to grind—literally. Obvious precursor to the Terminator. Serial killer all the way."

Charlie sighs. "You do know this is a kid's book?"

"The Cowardly Lion? Furry fetish. Scarecrow? Anorexic bulimic. And don't get me started on Toto."

"I guess we're not in Kansas anymore. No, wait, we are." He tosses the book down. "I can see I'm not going to get much reading done with you around."

"Oh, don't mind me. I'm not terribly important, just a paying customer."

"Not so much . . ."

"Okay, so I'm a paying-sometime-in-the-near-future customer—"

The door opens, spilling late-afternoon sunlight into the bar. I squint and wince, only half joking. Charlie's place is called the Quarry, but it may as well be named the Cave; he likes things dim and shadowy, and I tend to agree. Bright lights make me think of hospital corridors.

Then I see who it is, and the wince threatens to turn into a grimace. Terrance—*never* Terry—Adams and his little pack of troublemakers. Every small town has them: people who spend all their time complaining about how much they hate it here, but never seem to get up the nerve to leave. They vent their unhappiness in a variety of mean and petty ways on those around them, and we do our best to grit our teeth and ignore them until they either grow up or wise up. Some never do.

They're all here, trooping in after him like loyal little soldiers: his wingman, Zev Kitson, a redhead who thinks practical jokes are the height of wit; Sally January, who rides a motorcycle and pretends she's tough; Neil Maigan, aspiring musician; and Alexis Adams, Terrance's first cousin and the town's one and only goth. Or punk. Or alternative-heavy metal-gangsta-rap-hippie, depending on her mood and the day of the week. Sometimes I think she just dresses in whatever's on top of the pile and applies her makeup in the dark—that being said, she's actually a halfway decent kid. I wish she'd spend less time with her waste-of-space cousin, though.

"Hey, hey, hey!" Terrance says when he spots me. "Look who's here! It's our local celebrity!"

"Well, somebody has to be Chief Loser Detector," I say. I point at Terrance and say, "Ding! Ding! Ding! Now look what you did—you made me go off."

Terrance is in his twenties and has the kind of rough good looks that means when he forgets to shave or comb his hair he actually gets better looking, which is win/win for him and an overall loss for standards of hygiene everywhere. His hair is brown and shaggy, his smile devilish, his eyes those of a puppy with a mean streak. I don't like him.

"Whoops!" he says, putting his hands up in mock horror. "Sure wouldn't want you to go *off*, Miss Blood Doggy. You might *shoot* me or something."

Zev laughs, a maniacal little giggle I think he does deliberately to get on people's nerves. "I think she's *already* a little off," he says. "Off her rocker, off her meds, awfully out of her awful little mind."

"Hey," Charlie says. "You want a beer?"

"Well," says Zev, rubbing his hands together, "I *am* a little dry—"

"Then stop flapping your lips," Charlie growls. "Or you'll stay that way." He doesn't even waste a glare; he gives Zev Ugly Look Number Two, which on the Charlie Allen scale means a flat glance implying more contempt than anger.

Zev grins back and says, "*Mucho* cervezas, por favor, garçon," then sits down on the stool next to me. Terrance plops himself down on the other side. I was hoping they'd head straight for their regular spot in the back by the pool table, but apparently they aren't done.

"What's the matter, Doggy?" Terrance says. "You seem a little cranky today. Your collar too tight?"

Both Alexis and Sally stay on their feet. Sally's dressed in her usual leathers, while Alexis has spiked her black hair straight up and applied enough eyeliner to shame a raccoon. "Come on," Sally says. "I wanna shoot some stick."

"So go," Terrance says. "I've got something I need to talk about with our local expert, here."

"Oh, now I'm an expert?" I say. I don't bother making eye contact with either of them, looking straight ahead.

"Sure. When it comes to weird, you know your stuff. I mean, that show you watch, it's all about weird stuff, right?"

I spare him a warning glance. "It's about a lot of things. The supernatural, serial killers, even parallel universes."

"Like I said—weird stuff. So I figured you'd be the person to ask about the Gallowsman."

"The what now?"

"Local spook story," Charlie says, sounding a little annoyed. "Kind of thing kids use to scare each other on camping trips."

"Oh, it's more than that," Terrance says. "Based on fact—everybody knows that. Edward Jump, his name was. Died right in the middle of the town square in 1799. My father showed me the town records."

Terrance's father is the mayor of Thropirelem, so I guess if anyone would have access to that kind of thing, he would. "Eddy Jump, huh? I'm guessing he didn't kick off from a heart attack."

Terrance grins. "Well, you got it half right. He did kick off, right through a trapdoor and down to the end of a rope. In fact, I'm told he did a whole lot of kicking—went on and on for a good ten minutes or so. Just wouldn't die."

"Doing the Hangman's Tango," says Zev, holding up a hand with two fingers dangling down. He twitches them back and forth frantically. "No noose is good noose . . ."

"So they hanged him," I say with a shrug. "What did he do, ogle a farmer's wife?"

Terrance shakes his head. "That's just it. He didn't do anything. Well, nothing criminal, anyway. Edward Jump was one of those guys who just couldn't catch a break; bad luck followed him like a dog chasing a pork chop on a string. First his crops failed. Then three of his kids got sick and died. His house burned down. Then his wife—who was pregnant at the time—got killed by a runaway horse, trampled to death right in the middle of the street. After that, he was pretty much a basket case."

"Let me guess. He snapped and went on a killing spree with an ax."

"Good guess, thank you for playing," says Zev. "But no."

"I told you, he didn't do anything," Terrance says. "He just sat in the town square, right by the spot where his wife died, and wept. Sunup to sundown. Old Edward had never been real popular with the townsfolk—kept to himself, had no friends—but they still tried to do right by him. Brought him food, tried to console him."

"Didn't work, though," says Zev. "Old Eddy bought a full-price ticket on the Boo-Hoo Express, and he wasn't getting off until the end of the line."

"It went on and on. Day after day. Started getting on people's nerves. So they tried to convince him to do it somewhere else. He wasn't interested. They didn't know what to do."

"Kind of like having a giant two-year-old throwing a permanent tantrum," says Zev. "After a while, you'll do just about anything to make it stop."

"They tried locking him up, but the sheriff couldn't stand the noise. They thought about starving him out, but that was just plain cruel."

"They were," says Zev, "at the end of their rope. Bet you saw that one coming." I don't bother replying.

"But then something happened," Terrance continues. "A woman disappeared in the middle of the night. And she just happened to be married to the man whose horse killed Edward Jump's wife.

"Some said she just ran off. Some said her husband did her in and laid the blame on Edward's shoulders. But Edward had no alibi—and let's face it, by that point they were just tired of the noise."

"Wait," I say. "Are you trying to tell me they executed him for *grieving?*"

Terrance takes a long sip of the beer Charlie's finally put down beside him. "No, they executed him for being a pain in the ass. For not *getting with the program.* You know what people in this town—hell, in any small town—are like. The nail that sticks up gets hammered down—and Edward Jump was one stubborn, heartbroken nail."

Zev slams his hand down on the bar. "So down he went! Ka-boom!"

"But before he did," says Terrance, "he stopped crying long enough to deliver his last words: 'The gallows is not a punishment. It is a release from pain.' And then he looked out over the whole town that had come to see him drop, and added, 'Soon that pain will be yours. And I will release you as you have released me.' "

I shiver involuntarily. Terrance may be a jerk, but he's a decent storyteller.

"That should have been the end of it," says Terrance. "But it wasn't."

"It was just the beginning," says Zev softly. I wait for the punchline, but it seems he's fresh out.

"It started with the man whose wife disappeared," Terrance continues. "He found his dog dead. Got herself tangled in some barbed wire, wound up with it wrapped around her neck. Strangled.

"Then his oldest son had an accident, fell in the river. When they found him, his face was almost black; he had weeds wound around his throat so tightly the townspeople had to cut them off. Then his daughter's first child was found dead in her crib with the blanket twisted around her neck . . ."

"That was when people started calling old Eddy the Gallowsman," Zev says. "You might wonder why he didn't just go straight after the man who'd falsely accused him—"

"He wanted him to suffer," I say. "The same way he'd suffered."

Terrance nods again, with a smile. "So the Gallowsman took away the guy's life, bit by bit, until he'd lost everything. Eventually they found the poor bastard hanging from an oak tree in his own backyard."

My throat's suddenly dry as an old bone—or rope. I signal Charlie for another beer. "Creepy story. What's it got to do with me?"

Terrance studies me for a second before answering. "They say the Gallowsman is the patron saint of people who hang themselves—especially those who do it in the woods. When someone's life gets so hard they just can't take it anymore, and they trudge out to the forest in the middle of the night with a rope in one hand and a chair in the other—well, that just calls to him. And once that noose tightens, once the body has stopped jerking and twitching and its shoes fall onto the mossy ground with two little thumps . . . that's when he comes. His spirit slips into the corpse like a thief putting on someone else's coat, and no matter how tight the knot was tied it just slithers apart like a snake stretching. And then, trailing the rope behind him, the Gallowsman goes in search of those who did the victim wrong—because when there's that much pain in someone's soul, there's always somebody who put it there."

Terrance's voice has gotten slower and quieter as he's been talking. It's an old trick to draw the listener's attention in—but it's old because it works.

"So here's where I thought you could settle a little dispute Zev and me been having. See, he thinks the Gallowsman just out-and-out kills people—that he can bring any kind of cable or cord to life and send it out to throttle his victims. Me, I think he's more subtle."

"How so?" I ask.

"He doesn't just kill for the sake of killing. He kills for *despair*. In his mind, there's only one victim, one person he's going after. He kills everyone that person cares about—but that's just a means to an end. He needs his victim to die by their *own* hand. To take them down so far they don't even know what up is. And to do that, he needs to do more than just murder; he needs to get up close and personal with the person he's targeting, to get right in their head. Whisper in their ear, point out just how bad things are." His voice is low, hypnotic, almost a whisper itself.

Red Dog's a profiler, so part of my obsession is—*was*—studying how people think. Everything Terrance is saying makes sense from a psychological point of view, and he's very good at focusing a listener's attention. A politician's son, for sure.

"Still not hearing a question."

"My question? I thought that was obvious." His smile is predatory. "What's it like, hearing those whispers? Do they sound like they're coming from inside your head, like you're just talking to yourself? Or is it an actual hallucination, a voice you can hear coming from a person you can't see?"

I don't say anything for a moment.

The strange thing is, I'm not even angry. I should be—it's what he wants, what he's trying to provoke—but I'm not, which I suppose is a victory of sorts. No, what I really want to do is answer his question honestly. I want to say, *No, that's not quite it. It's like hearing voices in another room, a mutter of conversation that suddenly sharpens into something meant for you. It's like hearing words in the rustle of trees or underneath the static from a radio. It's like the chaotic, random parts of the universe have suddenly snapped into a new alignment that's aimed right at you.*

What I say is, "I wouldn't know." I turn to look at him. "And if I did, I wouldn't tell you."

"Come on, guys," Alexis says. "Leave her alone."

"Good idea," says Charlie coldly. "Or find someplace else to drink."

"Hey," Zev says, grinning like a loon, "take it easy, big guy. We're just having a little fun—"

Charlie locks eyes with Zev. "Oh, *fun.* Why didn't you say so? I *like* fun. Want to see *my* idea of fun?"

Zev looks away first. "I'll pass."

Charlie turns to Terrance. "How about you?"

Terrance doesn't spook so easily. He meets Charlie's gaze calmly. "You know, I just might . . . but I'm kinda busy at the moment."

"My schedule's flexible."

"I'll keep that in mind."

Alexis sighs. "Geez, get a room already. Or an arena, or octamom or whatever."

Terrance blinks. Charlie frowns. Both of them give Alexis *WTF?* looks, which breaks the tension.

"I think you mean *octagon,* sweetie," I say.

"Whatevs." She turns and heads for their usual table. Sally follows, and after a second so does Zev.

Terrance drains his beer and sets the glass down in front of Charlie with a smile. "Bring us another round, will you?" he says. "Thanks." He saunters off.

"Don't let them get to you," Charlie says. "Small town bullies, you know? They don't have anything better to do."

"Yeah, I know. Nothing breeds mean like boredom and ignorance." I try to sound casual, but I feel a little light-headed. I should probably go home and take my medication, but I'm not going to give Terrance and his gang the satisfaction of driving me away.

But then I check my watch and realize what time it is. I finish my beer in a hurry, say, "I gotta go," and head for the door.

Charlie's no fool. He knows what's going on, but he doesn't try to stop me. "See you later," he calls after me.

"Count on it," I say.

I get in the door with plenty of time to spare, ten minutes at least. My dog, Galahad, greets me with lots of happy woofing and ankle licking. He's a Saint Bernard with a sunny disposition and a drizzly mouth—I don't need to water my plants, I just get Galahad to stand over them and drool. He's also extremely bright, so much so that I've offered to pay for driving lessons. He just sighs and rolls his eyes.

Eight o'clock, Friday night. Time for the latest episode of *The Bloodhound Files*.

I'm recording it, of course. I don't *have* to watch it live. Except I do.

I take my medication first, an antipsychotic called Erthybon. I'm not supposed to combine it with alcohol, but hey, I'm not supposed to be watching Jace Red Dog hunt down werewolves and vampires, either. You do what you have to.

I turn on the TV and get settled in on the couch, Gally lying beside me with his head on my lap. I used to put a towel over my thighs, but I eventually just gave up and learned to live with damp pants.

I can't really explain my fascination with the show. Yeah, I identify with the main character, but I was never all that interested in the supernatural before I started watching it. Maybe because it's really different from all the other occult TV shows out there: It takes place on a world where ninety-nine percent of the population are either vampires, werewolves, or golems. Jace is from a different reality—the normal one, I guess—but gets yanked across the dimensional divide to use her finely-honed profiling skills to hunt psychos with an aversion to sunlight and/or silver. I love the characters, but it's the world Jace lives in that really interests me—all the little details of an entire planet full of supernatural beings. I especially love the fake commercials, which is how the show usually starts.

"He's a vampire. She's a werewolf. Their best friend is a golem with a talent for getting into trouble. Tune in at nine on Thursday for *How I Bit Your Mother*—on the FANG Network!"

"Would if I could," I mutter.

It's pretty good, as episodes go. Jace is hunting some maniac who's killing werewolves with silver-tipped crossbow bolts. She's helped by a mysterious masked woman who's the head of a criminal gang, dresses like a pirate, and has a really cool submarine; she calls herself the Sword of Midnight, and carries a dual-bladed weapon that resembles two overlapping clock hands, one slightly shorter than the other.

For the next hour I'm enthralled. I resist the urge to take notes on the different criminology methods Jace uses, something I used to do compulsively. I don't touch the TV screen, even once. Overall, I'd say I'm doing well.

Right up until the end.

"I think it's clear where this is headed," Jace says. She and the Sword of Midnight are studying a table loaded down with ancient texts and scrolls.

"Yes," replies the S of M. "There's no room for doubt."

"Then there's only one man we can go to," says Jace.

"Longinus."

"What?" I blurt. I *know* that name. Old Man Longinus lives in a sprawling, rundown mansion on the edge of town, the kind of place the local kids dare each other to trick-or-treat at on Halloween. It's not exactly a common surname, either; I must have misheard it.

And then the Sword of Midnight turns and stares directly at the camera.

No—not at the camera. At *me*.

"That's who has all the answers, Jace," the Sword says. "That's where you have to go. *Seek Longinus.*"

The screen goes dark.

TWO

For a while, I just sit there on the couch and stare at the TV. I have the remote in my hand, but I'm sure I didn't use it to turn off the set.

Pretty sure.

Then again, I'm also "pretty sure" that someone on a TV show just spoke directly to me. Which puts a whole new spin on those two words, and possibly my brain.

Galahad whines. He knows I'm upset—he can always tell. Then he does something he's never done before: He grabs the remote out of my hand, springs off the couch, and sprints for his doggy door.

"Hey!" I say, too startled to be angry. I jump up and give chase.

I catch up with him in the back yard, where he's digging furiously. I watch, stunned, as he excavates a quick hole, drops the remote in, then fills it back up.

I stare at him, then glance up into the sky. Nope, no UFOs or angels. Too bad; if I'm going to lose my mind—again— I'd really appreciate a few special effects added to the mix. "After all," I say out loud, "if you're going to go crazy, you may as well go all the way."

No invisible people reply. I don't hear anything but crickets and somebody's badly maintained pickup in the distance. Ken Tanaka's, by the sound of it.

It's a nice night in September, the tail end of an Indian summer. The air is warm and a little dusty. I stand there for a while, hugging myself and just listening to the twilight sounds of a small town: children yelling and laughing in the distance, the bang of an old screen door, dogs barking. It's peaceful and serene and very, very ordinary.

I try desperately to savor it, but I just can't. It's wrong, it's all wrong.

And after a few minutes I sigh, dig up the remote, go back in the house and go to bed.

I'm working a breakfast/lunch shift at the diner the next day, so I crawl out from under the covers at an ungodly hour, stagger to the kitchen, and try to deal with the pre-coffee technology problem: you know, how to operate the necessary devices to make coffee before you've *had* coffee. The guy who invented the espresso machine was probably wired on three pots of dark roast at the time, but I'm guessing that for the first decade after coffee was discovered, people got up and blearily smashed some beans with a rock, then stuck the pulp in a cup of lukewarm water. They probably hit their fingers with the rock a few times, too.

Galahad watches me intently the whole time, like he always does. I don't know why he finds the process so fascinating—I tried giving him a little coffee once and he wouldn't go near it—but he does. I think he must have been a barista in another life.

Then it's off to Farmers Diner to bring other people their coffee. Yes, I know it looks like there should be an apostrophe somewhere near the end of that word, but that's how it's spelled on the sign and that's who generally eats there.

I'm not a morning person, but I do enjoy walking to work at this time. The sun's just starting to rise, the air has that damp, fresh smell to it, the dew glitters where the light hits it—it's nice. Not too many people are up, either, though I do nod hello to Brad Varney, our mailman. He's a big guy, hairless as an egg, and it looks like he forgot to wipe off that last bit of eyeliner he's wearing. I stop him and point it out with a smile, and he thanks me without a trace of embarrassment. Thropirelem may not have any transsexuals, but we do have at least one transvestite—a fact known only to Brad, me, and whomever he chats with online while wearing a cocktail dress and pearls. When he asked me how I'd found out, I told him not to worry; nobody else in town has my eye for psychological markers and incriminating details—like the lacy edge of a camisole peeking out from his open collar when he asked me to sign for a package.

By the time I get to work I've convinced myself that last night's cryptic message was just a coincidence. The Sword was talking to Red Dog, not me. Longinus is a weird name, granted, but I probably just misheard what she actually said—Ron Shyness or John Highness or something. I blame it on combining booze with my meds and shove it to the back of my brain, where it can play Parcheesi with all the other crazy ideas.

The diner used to be a Chinese restaurant, once upon a time, and it's still got the pagoda-style roof and carved dragons over the front door. It's not locked. It doesn't have as much window space as most diners, either, favoring small, rectangular panes set high in the wall. Inside, booths line most of three walls, with the door to the kitchen behind the counter and a few small tables in the center. There's an ancient jukebox that hasn't worked in years in one corner, and old-fashioned lights with green glass shades hanging from the ceiling over every booth.

I go in the back, drape my jacket over one of the chairs that function as our staff area, and say good morning to Therese. She and her husband, Phil, own the place; Therese does double duty as bookkeeper and waitress, while Phil handles most of the cooking. She's a stocky, good-natured woman with curly brown hair and laugh wrinkles around her eyes.

Phil, on the other hand, is living proof of the principle that opposites attract. Where Therese is friendly, he's grumpy. Where Therese is generous, he's suspicious. He's also short, balding, and Japanese.

"Morning, Phil," I say. He's already wearing a stained apron, and chopping onions. "How's things?"

He gives me a scowl. "Mr. Isamu."

"Excuse me?"

"I am your boss. You should address me as Mr. Isamu."

I force a smile. "Okay. How's things, Mr. Isamu?"

"Fine. Get to work." He turns back to his onions.

I resist the urge to flip him the finger, grab my apron, and stalk out of the kitchen. "He's in a mood," I say to Therese.

She nods, a worried look on her face. "I'm a little concerned, actually. I know he can be cranky, but this is different. Been going on for the last few days, getting worse and worse. He hardly eats, keeps staring off into space. It's like his mind is somewhere else."

"Well, wherever it is, I hope it has a nice vacation and comes back cheerful and rested."

"Arrested?" says a voice. I look up to see our first customer walk through the door: Deputy Quinn Silver. He's a Native American—though I don't know which tribe—and, of course, a regular. He once said to me that's he probably eaten more of our breakfasts than his own mother's, though he wouldn't say which he preferred. "Let's just say she thought rattlesnake was a fine substitute for bacon and leave it at that," he told me.

I get him some coffee and take his order. More customers trickle in, every one of whom I know by name. "Morning, Mayor," I say, filling his cup. "The usual?"

Mayor Leo Adams beams at me. "Thank you, Jace, that would be wonderful." Mayor Leo—that's what everyone calls him—beams a lot, which is probably one of the reasons he's had the job for so long. He's got a bit of a paunch, a wide smile, and two wiry tufts of gray hair that stick up on either side of a bald head; he looks a little like a retired clown.

"How about you, Mr. Falzone?" Today Mayor Leo's having breakfast with my other boss, the one that owns the hardware store.

"Please, Jace, I told you—call me Donny." His smile is as wide as the Mayor's, but there's a predatory gleam to it. Donny Falzone may be in his sixties, but he keeps his mane of silver hair immaculately groomed, the top two buttons on his shirts undone, and at least a pound and a half of gold jewelry on his neck and fingers. Like they say, there's no wolf like an old wolf. He's charming and polite, but I try not to bend over when he's around.

The men wait until I've left before resuming their conversation, and talk in low voices when they do. Donny's one of the town's movers and shakers, and always seems to have two or three people hanging around him at any given time. Every small town has one, I guess, a local dispenser of wisdom and advice to whom people naturally gravitate. I've always wondered why he's never run for mayor himself; I guess some people are just more comfortable behind the scenes.

It gets busier after that, but thankfully Terrance and his buddies prefer to sleep in. That's good; I'm not sure I can handle any more needling after what happened last night. My conviction that I was imagining things erodes over the course of the morning with little surges of memory. I keep seeing the Sword's eyes drilling into mine from behind that mask, staring right into my soul. Feeling that connection you get when someone does that to you face to face.

Now, here's the really weird part. I keep thinking, *Why her?*

The Sword of Midnight is a recurring but minor character. I've never felt any kind of deep link with her before. So why her and not Red Dog?

"Because insanity and consistency don't really get along," I mutter to myself. I'm out back in the alley on my break, chewing on a breakfast burrito and trying to convince myself I'm not relapsing. "In fact, they probably can't spend five minutes in the same room without one of them making a snotty remark and the other one pulling a knife."

But that's not strictly true, I argue back silently. *Madness, like everything else, tends to follow patterns. Those patterns might shift and change focus, but they're almost never completely random. So what's the pattern here? What am I trying to tell myself?*

My thoughts are interrupted by a wheezing old pickup pulling into the alley and parking next to the door. Ken Tanaka gets out and gives me a curt nod. I nod back. Ken and I dated briefly, but it didn't work out; he had certain old-fashioned ideas about how a woman was supposed to act around a man, and I had a wicked left hook. We try to be civil around each other, but he's not exactly one of my biggest fans.

I go inside and tell Therese the morning food delivery's here, then make the rounds with the coffee pot. A booth that was empty is now occupied by our local physician, Doctor Peter Adams, and a redheaded woman I don't know.

"Hey, Doctor Pete," I say. "Eggs over easy, hash browns, sausage, and sourdough toast?"

"Yes, please," he says with a smile. Doctor Pete is Terrance's twin brother, and about the only thing they have in common is their appearance. I have to admit to having a little crush on the Doc, though I've never done anything about it. With my judgment, I'd probably wind up dating Terrance by mistake.

"Hi," I say to the redhead. She's quite stunning, with the kind of alabaster complexion that looks ethereal instead of just pale. "You look familiar—haven't I seen you over by the school?"

She gives me a wide smile. "Yes, I've just started there.

Athena Shaker." She offers me her hand and I take it. Her grip is cool and strong.

"Jace Valchek. Welcome to town, Athena. What do you teach?"

"History and biology, mostly."

"Interesting mix."

She shrugs. "I like to know how things grow, I guess. In fact, I'm trying to get a community garden started down by the baseball field."

"Well, there's no shortage of farmers here; you'll get plenty of advice, if nothing else. What can I get for you?"

She orders a ham omelette and orange juice, then goes back to talking to Doctor Pete. I feel a twinge of envy, but push it away. About the only relationship I can handle right now is the one I have with Galahad, and maybe caffeine. No, definitely caffeine.

The hours plod by. People come and go. I take orders, bring food, clear away empty plates. I catch Phil giving me dark looks more than once, though I have no idea what I've done to piss him off.

And I can't stop thinking about what happened last night.

It's not just the TV thing, either. It's that story Terrance told. I know he was just trying to spook me, but he did a good job. I keep fixating on that one little detail about the suicide's shoes dropping when the body goes limp. What if they were wearing boots? Gumboots might fall off, but anything with laces wouldn't. And how about beforehand, when the body is kicking and twitching—hell, a shoe could go flying, land in the bushes where no one would find it. Then you'd have a corpse with a shoe missing, and that would probably confuse the hell out of anyone investigating the case.

Except there *is* no case. Just a headcase, named Jace. Who is losing the race to keep her sanity in place. Whee.

By the end of my shift I know I have to do something— anything—to get this out of my brain before it burrows in so deep it turns white and its eyes fall out. Unfortunately, about the only plan I can come up with is to give in and go see Old Man Longinus, who by all accounts is as receptive to visitors as an irritable whale is to a harpoon.

I go home first to walk Galahad and try to figure out my approach. "Hi, Mr. Longinus? I'm the local loon. I understand you're the local crank, and I was wondering if we could get together and maybe discuss mutual areas of interest."

Mmm. Needs work.

"Good afternoon, Mr. Longinus. A woman on TV with a sword informed me you have some answers, and I was hoping you might be willing to share them. No, I don't know what the questions are. Oh, that's down the street? Under the big neon sign reading CRAZY MOTEL—RUBBER ROOMS AVAILABLE, FREE DRY CLEANING OF STRAITJACKETS INCLUDED? Thank you *so* much, I'll be right back."

Big improvement. Should be tweaked a bit.

"MWAH-HA-HA-HA! My tinfoil hat pointed at your house! I like *frogs*! Would you like to floopa-floopa my gazinga-ding? No, sir, I am not phantasmagorical! Look, Ernest Hemingway eating a pickle!"

Much better. Or at least more accurate.

Galahad and I are on our regular route, down to the end of the street and then through a little patch of woods next to the grocery store, and I'm so lost in thought I'm not really paying attention. That's how I wind up getting trapped.

"Hello, Jace," says a raspy voice.

I blink and look up. Father Stone stands in front of me.

I'm not really sure what denomination he represents—the United Reformed Methodist Presbyterian Baptist Something, I think. He looks like a midget linebacker with a bad haircut and only seems to have one expression, like a robot that skimped on the options. That expression is supposed to be a friendly smile, but it seems about as genuine as something assembled by a taxidermist. He never wears anything but solid black with a little white collar, and it wouldn't surprise me to learn he sleeps in the same outfit.

"Uh, hello, Father," I say. "I'm just out walking my dog." It's a lame and obvious thing to say, but the man makes me nervous. He doesn't blink often enough.

"I see," he says, smiling. "How have you been, Jace? How are *things*?" He puts just the barest emphasis on the last word, but it makes it sound like he's enquiring about a family of monsters living in my basement.

"Things are fine," I say inanely. *No, no, they're not. Things are moaning and squelching and waving their tentacles like a squid trying to signal a waitress.*

"We haven't seen you in church lately," says a voice behind me. My eyes widen and my heart sinks. Never let them surround you.

"Oh, hi, Miss Selkirk," I say, turning. Miss Selkirk is a collection of wrinkles wrapped around a skeleton, with bright blue eyes and a mouth that wouldn't know what to do with a smile if one ever showed up—maybe she sold hers to Father Stone. That would explain a lot; it was probably a bad fit but he just jammed it in there anyway and now he can't get the damn thing to budge—

Shut *up*, brain.

"I've been . . . busy," I say. Actually, I've *never* been to Stone's church, but it seems unwise to bring that up now. They might insist on marching me down there for an inspection. "You know, with . . . stuff."

"Your soul is important," Miss Selkirk says. She's dressed in lime-green pants held up with an orange belt, a purple and pink striped blouse, white gloves, and a black hat with what appears to be a dead crow stuck in the band. "You should *take care* of it." She squints at me like a racoon sizing up a garbage can.

"I do," I say. "I have it sent out and cleaned regularly."

Neither of them react to this little gem in the slightest. "Come by any time," says Father Stone. Smiling.

"We'd love to have you," says Miss Selkirk. She sounds hungry.

"I'll think about it. But I just remembered—Galahad did his business back there and I forget to bring a plastic bag with me. Gotta go get one." I spin around and march away quickly, before one of them magically produces said item from under a hat or maybe a metal hatch in their chest.

I take Gally back home and consider my next move. I finally decide to wing it—I'll march up to Longinus's house, knock on the door, and just talk to the guy. Feel him out. If nothing else, I can always invite him to church.

I change my clothes first. Not sure why. Stretchy black pants, sneakers, black top. Your basic breaking-and-entering outfit, though I have no intention of burgling the place—all I want is to have a conversation. I tell myself that, over and over, the whole walk there.

Which doesn't take long. The Longinus place is on the edge of town, but Thropirelem isn't a big place—maybe a few hundred people, all told. Small towns are like islands, little pockets of habitation separated by plains or forests or mountains instead of water—but mostly just separated by distance. People say that distance has dwindled in the twenty-first century, shrunk by modern transportation and telecommunications into a single global village, but there are still plenty of places where you can expect to drive for an hour or more before you see another human face. That distance always has been—and always will be—a factor in how people who live there act and think; isolation always is.

Here that distance is mostly filled with wheat instead of water, vast rippling fields of pale yellow. The Longinus house perches at the edge of that grassy ocean like a rotting seaside warehouse, huge and ancient and dark. It's only three stories tall, but it seems taller. The wood is that rough gray that unpainted lumber turns into under the hot prairie sun, like petrified elephant hide. All the windows are shrouded by dark curtains, and the front porch has a tumbleweed stuck in one corner beside an old wooden chair; I can't help but think of the Gallowsman.

I force myself to mount the creaking steps. The front door is a huge slab of oak with a panel of stained glass at head height. The designs worked into the glass are disturbing, but I'm not sure why; there's just something about the angles that seem subtly off, like an optical illusion you don't quite get.

And the door's ajar.

Just a few inches, enough to show a narrow slit of darkness beside the jamb. I freeze with my hand up to knock, then rap gently on the glass. "Hello?" I say softly.

Stupid. What's the point in knocking and calling out if you do it quietly? I say in a louder voice, "Hello! Mr. Longinus?" and knock again, harder this time. Hard enough, in fact, that the door swings open wider.

Dark hallway. No sound. I see an old oval mirror in a silver frame on one wall and faded wallpaper in some kind of floral pattern behind it. A shapeless dark coat hangs from a peg beside the door, and a worn pair of boots sit underneath it.

I take a step inside. My nerves are screaming at me to just turn around and leave, but some other part of my brain has taken over; I find myself checking the edges of the door, looking down for footprints, even glancing toward the ceiling at the cracked and dirty light fixture. My right hand keeps drifting toward my left shoulder, like I'm going to pull something out of a breast pocket.

No, not a pocket. A holster.

"Cut it out, Jace," I mutter. "You read too many police procedurals." I don't even own a gun, let alone a holster.

But apparently deep down inside I'm convinced I have cop DNA, because instead of leaving and closing the door behind me—or calling a real police officer—I move farther down the hallway.

There's another door ajar at the end of it.

When I peer around the edge of that one, I see stairs leading down. Basement, of course. No trail of blood on the steps, but that would be overkill. Creepy old house, door open, basement. I'd have to be some kind of idiot to go down there, right?

I throw myself on the mercy of the court. About the only excuse I have is possible mental illness, which in retrospect is probably closer to an explanation than an excuse. Also convenient, and less insulting.

Down I go. The staircase is well lit and doesn't creak. The stairs go down and end at another door, which is kind of strange. This one looks like it was forged out of cast iron about two hundred years ago, and it's open too. There's an orangey, flickering light coming from the other side; I peer cautiously into the room.

I don't know what I expect to see, but it isn't this.

First impressions: big room, lots of black draperies hanging down. More candles than the bedroom of a teenage goth girl, all of them lit. Lots of cushions on the floor, but no other furniture except for a big-ass table at the far end of the room.

No, not a table. An altar.

That's what draws my attention and focuses it. Because the altar—a big chunk of square granite that looks as if it was carved right out of the bedrock—has a body on it. Male, dressed in a long black robe, with a face only an undertaker could love.

Old Man Longinus.

I don't hesitate. I walk forward and inspect the body. He's got a long, presumably ceremonial dagger sticking out of his chest, and no pulse. I don't touch anything else, not at first. Instead, I look around and try to figure out what happened.

That's when I notice the photos.

There are seven in all, and from the way three are positioned on the altar it looks as if Longinus was placing them in preparation for some sort of ritual when he was attacked. There are two more on the floor. I find the last one trapped beneath the body, the corner barely visible.

They're all of me.

Me in different emotional states—gesticulating in anger, weeping, laughing, even one where I seem to be having an orgasm.

"Double. You. Tee. *Eff*," I say.

I don't study the pics for long. They go in my pocket.

If there's one thing I've learned from my police-work research, it's that the person who discovers the body is often the perpetrator. That, plus my being in the house for no good reason plus the pictures plus history of medical-grade wackiness equals Jace in jail. No way. I may be crazy, but I'm not stupid.

Okay, I may be crazy *and* stupid, but at least I try to alternate. And right now, I'm going to go with the crazy option and try to puzzle out what the hell went on here.

I look around. The burning candles are massive things that could have been lit days ago. But I also see the remains of smaller candles that are no more than puddles of cold wax that have obviously burned all the way down. That would have taken a while; if Longinus lit them before he was killed, the murder probably took place some time ago, hours at the very least.

No signs of a break-in or a struggle, so Longinus probably knew the person who murdered him. Whoever did it was fast, strong, and confident—the knife is buried up to the hilt, and it looks like it punched right through the breastbone. You don't kill someone with a single thrust like that, from the front, unless you know exactly what you're doing. Maybe you've even done it before.

The body isn't restrained, and one leg is dangling off the side of the altar. Not a ritual posture, in other words. He might have been shoved backward and off his feet before the killing blow was delivered.

So he let someone in, someone he wasn't afraid of. He was in the middle of preparing his altar, and then he was abruptly attacked and killed, possibly with a weapon of opportunity.

The cushions bother me.

You don't just scatter a few throw pillows around a room like this to brighten it up. The pillows are there for people to sit—or, more likely, kneel—on while something vile and perverse happens on that altar.

The evidence seems conclusive. Longinus was running a sex club.

Why they picked me as their fetish object isn't clear, but maybe it was only Longinus himself who was fixated on me. I go searching for corroborating evidence, convinced I'll find a chest full of sex toys and illegal porn hidden behind one of the black draperies.

Not so much.

THREE

"Charlie? It's me."

"I know it's you, Jace. I know how to cast this wonderful magic spell, *call display*. It only works on a rare mystic artifact known as a cell phone, but fortunately I have one of those, too—"

"Shut up, bonehead. I have a problem."

"And a truly unique way of asking for assistance—"

"You know that old saying about good friends, and what they'll help you do?"

"You'll have to unvague that for me."

"A friend will help you move. A *good* friend—" I pause, and hold my breath.

"Where are you?"

"The creepiest house in town. In the basement."

"Stay there. Don't call anyone else. Give me ten—no, fifteen minutes."

"Okay."

He hangs up. I let out my breath slowly. *A good friend will help you move a body.*

It's funny. You'd think I'd be freaked out or in shock or something, but I'm not. In fact, I feel more normal and less anxious than I have in months. And considering what I found in my search of the basement, that makes no sense at all.

There was a chest, all right, but it didn't contain porn or kinky costumes or anything even vaguely phallic. What it held was a book. That's all, just one single book. It was thick and leather bound and written in a language I didn't understand.

But I did understand some of what was on the loose papers stuck between the pages. They were handwritten in English and made the crazy between my ears seem as mundane as a mud puddle.

Longinus was the head of a secret club, all right, but it was more culty than kinky. The kind of obscene he was into involved black magic, ritual sacrifice, and summoning some kind of entity. There were lots of drawings, but they were badly done and hard to understand. His penmanship left a lot to be desired, too.

Okay, so I'm not the only crazy person in my little corner of the world, and some of the people I've known for years apparently like to dress up like the Emperor in *Star Wars* and chant in a basement. Life is weird, I get that.

But according to Longinus's notes—which don't name any names, of course—some of the people in this town don't just worship an unholy evil.

Some of them are vampires. And some of them are werewolves.

That's about all I could glean from my first look at the notes. As for the book itself, I think it's what's called a grimoire, a book of spells. It's written in a language—and sometimes, an alphabet—I don't recognize, on pages of ancient parchment. The ink is a reddish brown.

And every now and then, in the middle of what I assume is some sort of enchantment, my name pops up. *Jace Valchek*, written in English, in that same red-brown ink. It looks like it was written a long time ago.

Charlie arrives, driving his '57 Chevy with the big-ass tail fins, painted midnight black to highlight all the chrome. He pulls around the side of the house, out of sight, and I hear a knock at the back door, which turns out to be in the kitchen. I find it and let him in.

He's wearing sneakers, an old pair of jeans, and a faded black T-shirt. He's got a large gym bag in one hand. "Are you okay?" are the first words out of his mouth.

"Yeah. It's Old Man Longinus who's not doing so good."

"Tell me what happened." Charlie seems to be taking this in stride, too, which only heightens the unreality. It almost feels like we're just delivering rehearsed lines, falling into familiar roles, like characters in a long-running TV show. . . .

I give my head a shake. "All right. Here's the situation." I give him a quick summary, leaving out what brought me here in the first place. I show him the book, the notes, and the photos, which he studies briefly but intently before handing them back. "Show me the body."

I take him to the basement. He studies the corpse, then puts down the gym bag and unzips it. He pulls out some kitchen gloves, a bottle of bleach, and a roll of paper towels. "First things first. Wipe down every surface you think you might have touched. Do the same for footprints you might have tracked in." He takes out a handful of black trash bags and a roll of duct tape. "I'm going to do a little gift wrapping."

"Charlie. Aren't you going to ask me the obvious question?"

He rolls his eyes. "Did you kill him?"

"No."

"Duh. Now get moving—we don't know how long we have."

And so, my very first disposal of a body—excuse me, a murder victim—proceeds with the fervent intensity of cleaning house before the in-laws show up. I erase all traces of Charlie's presence and my own, while Charlie bags the corpse. There's surprisingly little blood, and what there is seems to have flowed into a gutter built into the table for just that purpose. We sanitize everything with bleach.

The body goes into Charlie's trunk, along with the knife. "What are you going to do with it?" I ask him.

"Better you don't know," he says. "But don't worry—nobody's going to find it."

I nod. "Thank you," I say. "I don't know what I'd—"

"Go home. Don't talk to anyone. I'll come over tomorrow and we'll hash this all out, okay? It'll be all right."

I want to hug him, but I just nod. "Yeah. Okay."

He gets in and drives away, carefully.

I've got a lot to think about on the walk home.

"*Jace*!"

I jump three feet straight up and my eyeballs bug out six inches from my skull. Okay, not really, but that's what it feels like.

I'm a block away from my house. I've got the book—wrapped in a plastic shopping bag—clutched to my chest. And standing directly in front of me on the sidewalk, blocking my path, is Vince Shelly.

Vince is, not to put too fine a point on it, the town drunk. He's got a crappy little house I think he inherited and some sort of disability pension, which is enough to keep him inebriated pretty much all of the time. He's more into beer than the hard stuff, though, which means he's usually just wobbly as opposed to falling-down wasted. He's bald on top, with long, greasy gray hair to his shoulders, and a ridiculous pair of muttonchop whiskers that seem to go with the Harley-Davidson hoodie he's wearing, though I've never seen him on a bike. Stained gray sweatpants and scuffed loafers finish off the outfit, no doubt handy when you don't want to fiddle with anything as complicated as zippers or laces.

"Hey, Vince," I say. He's not all that bulky, but the way he's swaying from side to side keeps me from darting either way around him. "Uh, excuse me."

"Why? Did you fart?" He grins at me, blinking bloodshot eyes. "Fine evening, ain't it?"

"Sure."

"Yeah. Sure is." He's studying me like a drunken cat trying to focus on a mouse. "But you can never tell, right?"

"I—what?"

"Might not be so nice." He nods, giving me an exaggerated look of secrecy. "You look under things, they're not always nice at all. Sometimes they're *nasty*."

I stare at him. "What are you—are you trying to tell me something?"

He stares back. Suddenly he doesn't seem all that unsteady on his feet. "Maybe," he says. "Maybe I am."

We're frozen like that for a few seconds, just studying each other, until he abruptly says, "You like tattoos?"

I'm rapidly approaching non sequiter overload. "I . . . guess?"

He yanks up his sleeve. His arm is covered with tats of superheroes—Spider-man, Superman, Batman, the Hulk. Lots of others. It looks like a ten-year-old's idea of heaven. "Cool, huh?"

"Oh, absolutely."

He beams at me with pride. "I know. But lately, I've been having problems with 'em. See?" He points at a tattoo of Thor swinging his hammer. "They're *running*."

"From what?" I'm only half joking.

He shakes his head. "Not running away. The colors are bleeding out . . . see?" He points. I'm no expert, but some of the lines look a lot blurrier than others.

"Something's pushing the ink out," Vince says. "Something *underneath*. I don't know what it is yet, but I can feel it. *Inside* me."

"I . . . I have to go," I say, and push past him. Whatever it is inside him—other than Coors and cheap pizza—I just can't have this conversation right now. I need to get home, lock all the doors and windows, and hide in a pillow fort. With my dog.

Vince doesn't chase me, or say anything as I hurry away. I'm afraid to look back. I'm afraid he won't be there anymore. Or worse, that something else might be standing in his place.

When I get home, the very first thing I do is turn on the TV.

The second is to dig out my stash of *Bloodhound Files* DVDs from where I've hidden them under the fridge. Nobody looks under a fridge, unless they've desperate to add to their dust-bunny-and-moldy-Cheerios collection. I put a DVD in at random and hit PLAY.

While I'm doing this, Galahad regards me with a very concerned look on his face. I grab the remote before he tries to bury it again, and he lies down on the floor beside the couch with his chin on the floor as if to say *Oh, crap, here we go again.*

And then, as the opening music kicks in over the credits, I pull the grimoire out of the bag and sit down to take a long, hard look at it.

"Okay, Jace," I say out loud. "Let's get to work."

One of my favorite things about *The Bloodhound Files* is the golems.

Most people have heard of golems. They're basically men made from clay, sort of mineral-based Frankensteins brought to life with magic. That's the traditional kind, from Jewish mythology.

On the show, they've been updated; they're mass produced, made from sand poured into human-shaped, thick-skinned plastic bags, and animated by the life force of an animal. They come in a variety of colors, and are largely used for their muscle power.

There are no golems in Longinus's notes, or his supposed

book of spells. I find that oddly reassuring, though I'm not sure why.

But there is something else, something I missed on my first reading.

A drawing of a hangman's noose.

It's in the grimoire, which is somehow worse than being in the notes, but at least there's no mention of my name on that page. I just wish I knew what it meant—is it a reference to the Gallowsman, or are creepy drawings of nooses just the kind of thing that pop up in tomes like this, like doodles of a happy face in a kid's notebook?

I glance up at the TV screen. It's showing a fake commercial at the moment, coincidentally enough for a golem product. A smiling golem wearing boxer trunks is demonstrating a polish called Gleam Cream, which apparently gives your plastic skin the kind of supple, shiny, and clear appearance all golems desire. I guess you can sell anyone beauty products, if you try hard enough.

The doorbell rings. Galahad pads over and sniffs at the door, but he doesn't bark. He's pretty laid-back as far as being a watchdog goes. I hit PAUSE and open the door a crack, hoping it's Charlie.

It's not. It's one of my neighbors, a kid named Billy. He's around eleven and a born salesman.

"Hi, Jace!" he says with a big smile.

"Hi, Billy. I'm a little busy right now—"

"Too busy for chocolate?" He holds up a bar you could club someone to death with. Damn it, the kid knows my weakness.

"I'll get my wallet," I say.

Billy hangs out in the foyer with Gally as I scrounge up some cash. If he notices the paused image of Jace Red Dog on my TV, he doesn't comment on it.

"Here," I say, giving him a bill. "What'll that get me?"

He grins. "Two of these bad boys." He digs into his satchel and hands over the bars. Extra Dark—like I said, the kid knows me.

"Thanks. You're going to college on my dime, aren't you?"

"Maybe," he says with a shrug. "But what I really want to do is drive a truck."

I frown. *Déjà vu*, but not quite. Because . . .

"Thanks, Jace," he says. "See you later!"

It's gone. I wave goodbye as he trudges off down the sidewalk to his next sales pitch, and then I sink back into the couch.

Which is when I notice the screen is no longer frozen on an image of Red Dog.

The Sword of Midnight stares at me calmly, a digital on-screen statue. I pick up the remote, study her nervously, then unpause the image.

"Thanks," she says. "That's a weird feeling, you know? Like your whole body is on hold."

She's talking directly to me.

"You're welcome," I say.

I must sound a little stunned, because the Sword frowns and says, "Okay, Jace, get it together. Communicating like this isn't easy, and I can't do it for long. I need you to listen, resist making smart-ass remarks, and trust me, okay?"

"Uh-huh," I say faintly.

"First of all, you're not crazy. This isn't a hallucination, or a dream, or anything simulated by technology or magic. It's going to get strange before you're done, but it's all *real*. You with me?"

I swallow, and nod my head.

"Good. Because—*Jace, look out!*"

I scream and dive for the floor. Galahad starts barking. There's a sudden swell of dramatic music—

Wait.

I look up. The Sword and Red Dog are battling a vampire street gang that call themselves the Lugosis—they all wear black capes and talk in ridiculous accents. I watch the fight for a few seconds, but I've seen it a dozen times before.

"Um," I say. "Hello?"

No answer. I'm talking to a DVD.

"Now *that* is just goddamn annoying," I say. Gally comes over and licks my face in a vain attempt to put a positive spin on things.

I watch until I fall asleep, but the Sword doesn't talk to me again.

Not even at midnight.

I wake up the next morning on the couch in the blue glow of the TV. I yawn, turn it off, and do my best to pretend it's just another morning. I stash my DVDs—putting the grimoire and the notes in with them—shower, and get into some fresh clothes. I feed Galahad and pour coffee in me, then take him out for his morning walk.

Which is when normal crashes and burns.

I can see the flashing red and blue lights before I reach the end of the street. I wonder if something went wrong and Charlie's been arrested, but he lives in the opposite direction. The lights don't seem to be coming from anywhere near the Longinus house, either.

I walk toward them. I probably shouldn't, but I'm not the only one; a police car with its flashers going is a relatively rare sight in town, and I'm not the only citizen strolling down the sidewalk and trying to look casual.

The police car is blocking the entrance to the church's parking lot. A deputy is trying to keep people back, but it's impossible to hide what's dangling from the third-story eaves of the church.

It's Father Stone. And even from here, I can see the distinctive knot of a hangman's noose in the rope around his neck.

FOUR

There's a small knot—sorry, unfortunate choice of words—of people gathering on the sidewalk outside the church. I join them. Nobody's saying a word, we're just all standing there in shock.

"Folks, you should really go home," says the deputy. It's Quinn Silver, the guy I was serving coffee to this time yesterday. He was just another customer, then. Now, he's . . .

Someone who could send me to prison.

But none of us leave. We're hypnotized by the sight of the black-clad body, swaying and spinning in the wind. I wonder how he got up there—I don't see a ladder. Maybe there's a hatch in the roof.

"Awful," someone finally mutters.

Me, I can't stop looking at his shoes. I keep expecting them to fall off, but they don't. "Are those lace-ups or loafers?" I say. "I can't tell."

I get a glare from a woman in a jogging suit. *Uh-oh, what's the crazy lady going to say next?* "Well, I can't," I mutter. There, that'll show her.

Thropirelem has two police cars. The other one pulls up, with the town fire truck right behind it. The sheriff gets out and confers with the two volunteer firemen about exactly where he wants the ladder.

A few words here about the sheriff. He's the town's most eligible bachelor, and probably the only guy who could take Charlie in a fight. He grew up here but went to school back east, all on scholarships; his brain is apparently as muscular as the rest of him. He's a lot better than we deserve—though there are rumors that the reason he took a job in his hometown was because of some sort of trouble he got into while he was away. That's probably just the usual small-town whispering, but I do know you don't want to make him mad. I've seen him lay out a belligerent drunk with a single backhand slap, and the drunk wound up losing a tooth, too.

He doesn't much care for me, though. Too bad, in too many ways.

And then the sheriff spots me in the slowly increasing crowd. The look on his face is hard to read, but it's not the usual mild irritation or restrained tolerance. If I didn't know better, I'd say he looked confused.

Oh, wait. I don't know better. In fact, I don't know much of anything at this point, other than I'm looking at my second dead body in twenty-four hours. That, and—according to that always-reliable source of hard data, Voices from the TeeVee—all this is really happening. Whatever it is.

I tug on Galahad's leash and step forward. The sheriff sees me coming and tries to retreat behind the yellow tape that Deputy Silver's putting up, but he doesn't have it taut yet and Galahad and I just hop over.

"You can't come any closer, Ms. Valchek," he says. "This is a crime scene."

"Is it?" I say. "Looks like a suicide to me." I keep my voice low—I don't want this conversation broadcast all over the town grapevine.

"It's the subject of an ongoing investigation, which as far as you're concerned is the same thing." He's studying me intently as he talks—as if he's decided that if he has to talk to me, he's going to pay attention.

"Of course, if it was a suicide, you'd expect to find a ladder," I point out. "Since the fire truck's here, I guess you didn't. Is there a hatch in the roof? I don't see one."

"We don't know how he got up there. Not yet."

I'm looking up as we talk, taking advantage of being a little closer than the rest of the crowd, and now I can see that the other end of the rope is tied around a rafter at the corner of the roof. There's something strange about the knot, though.

"Any idea why he'd do such a thing?" I ask.

"I can't speculate at this point, Ms. Valchek. Now, please, step back behind the tape." He takes my elbow and leads me there as he talks, and there's nothing hesitant about his grip.

When the ladder's in place, the sheriff himself climbs up with a camera and takes lots of pictures. Then they rig a harness up to the body with a cable going over the top of the roof before they cut the rope and lower it to the ground. I'd really like a good look at that rope, but there's only one idea I can come up with to do so. It's both stupid and unlikely to work. But since it's all I've got . . .

I take Galahad down the sidewalk, about twenty feet away from the crowd. I lean down and whisper, "Gally. I need you to do something for me, okay? When I take off your leash, I want you to dash over there by the policemen and make a nuisance of yourself. Don't let them catch you. Run around, bark, paw at the ground. I'm going to call for you, but don't listen. After a few minutes, head for home. Do this, and I'll go out and buy you a steak."

Galahad looks at me with the same sort of undisguised affection he always does, and licks my hand. *Sure, Jace. Would you like me to stop off at the supermarket and pick up some milk on my way home, too?*

I sigh. Then I unclip his leash. I know he's just going to sit there until I start moving, at which point he might be motivated to go pee on a bush—

He takes off at high speed. Right toward the sheriff.

The sheriff isn't really paying attention, so Gally starts barking while he runs. It looks like Galahad might try to bowl him right over, but he darts to the left at the last second. Now he's on a collision course with the deputy kneeling next to the corpse.

"Hey!" the sheriff yells.

Me, I just stand there dumbfounded. Apparently Galahad has Lassie genes somewhere in his DNA.

"Valchek!" the sheriff snaps. "Control your damn dog!"

Galahad slams to a stop, but now he turns and starts digging like crazy. Sod and dirt spray in the direction of Father Stone's body, as if my dog's decided he needs to be buried *right now.* Gally pauses for a second, though, and looks at me. I swear the expression on his face reads *Well? What are you waiting for?*

I stride forward, shouting, "Galahad! Stop that right now!"

Gally lets me get close before bolting away again. I give chase, which brings me within a few feet of the body. As if reading my mind, Gally abruptly changes direction, giving me the opportunity to swerve and fake a fall.

"Ah," I say. "My *knee!*"

I pause, favoring one leg as I slowly pull myself up, studying the corpse as I do so. The face is horrible, but I'm actually more interested in the rope. It's thick, old, and grayish white, tied in the classic hangman's noose with—I assume, since I don't have time to count them—thirteen loops around the central cord.

But it's the other end, the one that was tied around the rafter, that's really interesting. Deputy Silver was about to stick it in a clear evidence bag when Galahad went into his routine, and right now it's lying on top of the bag while Silver tries to corral my wayward pet. It's tied in the most intricate knot I've ever seen. The thick rope weaves in and around itself in an almost organic way, reminding me of strands of muscle or a tangle of vines. The end is buried somewhere in the pattern, tucked in so cleverly I can't find it. It must have taken a long time to create.

And somehow, it was done around a solid piece of wood three stories above the ground, in plain sight.

I get to my feet, trying not to overdo the limp, and wave the leash at Galahad. "Go home!" I call out. "Go home, you bad-ass dog!"

I think he's having a little too much fun now, because he doesn't stop right away. Well, Lassie was a ham, too.

He finally makes a break for it, and I limp after him. "Sorry!" I call back over my shoulder.

I swear I can feel Sheriff Stoker's eyes on my back as I leave.

Charlie's waiting for me when I get home. He's sitting on my front steps with Galahad, looking relaxed and not at all like he's just disposed of a dead body.

"Hey," he says.

I stop and give him the quizzical eyebrow, a move I practiced as a snarky teenager and mastered as a snarky adult. "Hey? That's what I get, a *hey*?"

"Would you prefer a *hi*? The more formal *hello*? Or are you looking for something in, say, a *howdy-do*?"

I crank the eyebrow down a few notches. "If you ever *howdy-do* me, I'll be forced to reconsider our relationship in a more critical light."

"Duly noted."

"Anyway, I just thought *hey* was a little flip. You know, all things considered."

"If I took the time to consider all things, I'd never get anything done."

"That sounds like a quote."

"It is. You said it to me last week."

"Well, that makes me a genius and you a thief. Let's go inside and celebrate the great success we're enjoying in our respective fields."

We pull off our usual banter—it's practically a reflex, at this point—but there's a certain hesitation underneath it, a little strain from forcing ourselves to be so casual. As soon as we get indoors, we stop trying.

"Why are there cop cars down by the church? I saw them but I didn't stop."

I walk into the kitchen and unwrap the steak I picked up on the way home. We may be a small town, but our local butcher is top-notch—I think he knows all the cows he sells personally. "Father Stone apparently hanged himself from the eaves."

"What?"

"You heard me. Three stories up, no ladder around, no hatch in the roof. I walked up there with Gally and got a look as they cut him down—there was something really weird about the noose. Not the one around his neck, the one looped around the eaves. The knot was . . . I don't know, really intricate. Would have taken a long time to do."

Charlie sinks down onto my couch. "Damn. Guilt, you think?"

"One local religious leader kills another and then suicides out of remorse? Nice theory, but it leaves a few questions unanswered—like how he tied that damn knot without being seen, or even how he got up there in the first place."

Charlie leans forward, hands clasped, elbows on his knees. "He could have tied the knot in the middle of the night. Used a ladder that was taken away afterward by someone else."

"Okay, but why?"

He shrugs. "To make it seem mysterious? An act of God, maybe? Or maybe because a murder attracts more attention than a suicide, and Stone wanted Longinus's little cult exposed."

I put the steak in Galahad's bowl, which he promptly attacks. "One type of crazy bouncing off another? I guess that's possible—but you'd think Stone would leave something a little more incriminating behind."

"Maybe there's a note inside the church."

I nod. "Could be. In which case the police are going to be showing up on Longinus's doorstep really soon—and we just sanitized the crime scene."

Charlie looks up at me. "I know what we did."

"Yeah, but do you know *why* we did it?"

"Because you're the obvious prime suspect. Those photos and that book indicate Longinus had some kind of obsession with you. You have a history of violence and mental illness and you're the one who found the body. How am I doing?"

"Better than me. Are you sure I didn't kill him? 'Cause I'm starting to wonder."

"You been having blackouts?"

"No. Never."

"Then you didn't kill him. But there is one thing I'm a little unclear on."

"Shoot."

"Why were you there in the first place?"

"That's . . . complicated. I think you need to take another look at Longinus's notes, first." I pull them out from their hiding place and hand them over before sitting down beside Charlie on the couch.

I let him read them over himself, first. Then we go over them together, helping each other decipher bits of scrawled handwriting. He doesn't comment on any of it, just asks the occasional question about a specific word or letter he can't make out.

When we've gone through the whole thing, he puts down the notes and leans back. Frowns.

"So," I say.

"So," he says. "Longinus was a loony toon."

"Um," I say.

"Vampires? Werewolves? He really believed all that? Makes the Satanic cult part look almost rational."

"Yeah . . ."

"So why *were* you there, Jace?"

I look at Charlie. I take a deep breath, and then let it out. "Before I tell you, promise me one thing."

"What?"

"That if I'm locked up in the psych ward, you'll bring me food. *Good* food. The stuff they have stinks."

He doesn't hesitate. "I promise."

"You know that show I'm not supposed to watch anymore?"

I tell him the whole thing. About the first time the Sword of Midnight spoke to me, and the second. I tell him what she said, emphasizing the "this is all real" aspect. He listens, very carefully.

"And that's about it," I say. "I know how it sounds. I'm not going to try to convince you I'm not crazy, because I'm not sure myself. But at least you know I'm not lying, because who the hell would try to use a story like this to justify anything?"

He nods, slowly. "Hmmm. So, the next step is obvious."

"Oh, it is, is it? Enlighten me."

"We watch some *Bloodhound Files*. See if I see the same thing you do. And even if I don't, maybe you'll get another message."

"Wait. You're not seriously suggesting any of this is *real,* are you?"

"No. But the Sword of Midnight is—kind of—and the first piece of information she gave you was the trigger that kicked all this into motion. I think that's earned her further consideration as a source, don't you?"

"Sure. If, you know, I'm not batshit insane."

Charlie sighs. "You seem pretty rational to me. In fact, if anyone's getting closer and closer to an asylum it's yours truly—mainly because I can't handle you questioning your sanity every thirty seconds. Let's just pretend you're normal and proceed from there, okay? For my sake?"

I study him for a second. Suddenly I feel a whole lot better—because if someone as hardheaded and down-to-earth as Charlie is willing to take my side, then I must be better off than I thought. It's like my feet finally found solid ground to stand on.

"Okay," I say quietly. "No more crazy talk."

Galahad gives a little bark of encouragement, then goes back to devouring his steak.

I play the last few minutes of the episode where the Sword mentions Longinus right at the end. I'm tapping my fingers nervously on the side of the remote as the scene begins to play, sure that either she'll say something else or Charlie won't hear what I hear.

But it happens exactly the way I heard it the first time. And when I turn to look at Charlie, he nods. "Yeah. I heard it, too. But it's only one word—could be a coincidence."

"That's what I thought. But then the whole corpse/cult/pictures-of-Jace thing happened, and I kind of gave up on that."

"All right. Let's check out the DVD—the one with the explanation."

It's still in the player, so all I have to do is find the scene. I'm sure that this time, nothing weird will happen.

But I'm wrong again. The whole thing happens just like I remember it—including the two little gaps in her dialogue when I responded to what she was saying.

Charlie's leaning forward on the couch, frowning. He doesn't say anything, not at first.

"That's really weird," he finally says.

"You think?"

"She's talking directly to the camera, not anyone else in the scene. The break in the action makes no sense from a story point of view, not that I can see. Those pauses were when you answered her?"

"Yeah."

"I didn't see any signs of editing, either. No cutaways to another camera angle. It looks legit to me."

"So what does it mean?"

He leans back, puts one elbow on the back of the couch. "Well, two things come to mind. The first involves a vast conspiracy that includes the actors on the show, the evil cult that Longinus ran, and a part-time waitress. Frankly, it's not really holding together for me."

"Me either. What's the second?"

"That this is what it appears to be. Which isn't a lot better, because all it does is remove the Hollywood conspiracy angle and replace it with magic. Real, actual sorcery. Or some kind of advanced technology that imitates it—but then we're getting into science fiction territory as opposed to the supernatural. Aliens, time travel, top-secret government agencies, that sort of thing. Not really an improvement."

"You sure you don't want to reconsider the cee-arr-ay-zee-why thing?"

He gives me a look. "So let's stick with the magic explanation for now, all right? We've got a dead cult leader and a book of what seem to be spells."

"Plus a dead priest hanging from the roof of his own church, with no explanation of how he got there."

"I want to give something a try, all right? Go in the kitchen and stay there until I call you back."

"Why?"

"Just humor me."

I shrug and do what he says, taking the opportunity to make a fresh pot of coffee. Galahad comes in and watches me, as usual. I hear the DVD start up again, but it must be another scene—all I hear are sounds of combat and action music.

"Huh," Charlie says. "How about that . . . you can come back in."

I do. He's paused the DVD. "Well?"

"Hang on a sec." He hits PLAY.

The Sword of Midnight shows up and starts talking again. Same spiel. Charlie lets her finish, then hits STOP. "Yeah, that's pretty strange. . . ."

"What is? It's the same as before."

"Sure. As long as you're in the room. When you were in the kitchen, she didn't break the fourth wall. You came back, and she did."

"So . . ."

"So congratulations. You're not nuts. Oh, and apparently magic is real."

I sink down on the couch. My brain feels overloaded. Turns out *I'm* not crazy, the rest of the world is.

Magic. That's a big word. It covers everything from alchemy to Zeus, with a lot of stops in between. Does this mean leprechauns are real? Or Santa Claus? Or—

"Vampires," I say.

"*And* werewolves," Charlie adds.

"I used to think this was such a *nice* town."

"No, you didn't. You hate it here."

"Well, yeah, but that was *because* of all the niceness. The horrible, small-minded, boring . . . *man,* do I hate it here."

"That's nice." He smiles.

"Shut up. No, on second thought, keep talking—you're like a walking antidote to niceness. You're an irritation on two legs."

"Gee, thanks. Now, what are we going to do?"

"About the vampires and werewolves?" I get back on my feet, stalk into the kitchen, and pour two mugs of coffee. Take them back to the living room and hand Charlie one. "Well, let's see. We could go door to door with garlic, stakes, and silver crucifixes, or we could watch TV."

"Got any popcorn?"

"No, just coffee."

"Even better."

So we settle in for a *Bloodhound Files* marathon, but as it turns out we don't have to wait for very long. I choose episodes with the Sword of Midnight in them, naturally, and the first time she's on screen—in a scene where she's lurking in a darkened alley—she turns directly to us and says, "Good choice of episode. I don't interact with anyone else in this scene for another minute, and I think I can stretch that out by staying on the move. Who's the hunk?"

"Um," I say. "This is—"

"Jake," Charlie says. "Just call me Jake."

I frown, but don't contradict him. Charlie's instincts have been good so far. "Let's skip the formalities and get down to it, all right?" I say. "Vampires and werewolves—*go*."

"You've only got two to worry about: the master vampire and the alpha wolf. Kill the alpha before the next full moon and anyone he or she has bitten won't become a were. It doesn't work that way for pires, though—you've got to stop all of them or it could spread. That would be bad—right now, these two are the *only* two of their kind in your reality."

"My reality? What does *that* mean?"

"It means—"

"Hey!" a man's voice shouts. "There's someone out here!"

"Crap," the Sword sighs, and then she's fighting for her life.

Leaving me, presumably, to do the same.

That's where we stall out. We watch a bunch more episodes—all the ones with the Sword of Midnight in them—but she fails to strike up another conversation. Either she's said all she means to, which seems unlikely, or there's some kind of limit to when or how often she can communicate.

"Makes sense, kind of," Charlie says. "Magic always has arbitrary rules, doesn't it? Only three wishes, be home by midnight, never get them wet."

"That was *Gremlins*, Einstein."

"And don't tell them your true name—names have power, right? That's why I gave her an alias."

"Brilliant. Your use of a pretend monicker makes her ability to communicate from another dimension seem childish and pathetic. Next time, tell her your last name is Smith—that'll show her just how outclassed she really is."

"Another dimension, huh?"

"Reality, dimension, realm—whatever you want to call it, she ain't from around here. And apparently neither are werewolves or vampires, which I find oddly comforting."

"Sure. Because a whole *dimension* full of them is much less disturbing."

"As long as they stay there, yeah. But it looks like Longinus was issuing his own diplomatic visas."

Charlie shakes his head. "Maybe. But maybe he was trying to stop them, and that's why he was killed."

I hadn't thought of that. "I guess it's possible. But we still don't know what *I* have to do with all of this."

"Well, let's see. Sorcery, cult, altar, attractive young woman. I'm guessing human sacrifice."

"Terrific," I grumble. "I'm the extra who's supposed to die in the first scene. Nothing like knowing your place in the universe."

"This isn't television, Jace. It's extremely weird and I have *no* idea what we're going to do next, but this *is* happening. We've gotta deal with it."

He's right. And while I'm still a little freaked out, I don't feel like I'm going to have a breakdown. I can handle this. For the first time in a long time, things feel *right*.

"I know what we have to do," I say.

"What?"

I smile. "We find the trail. And then we follow it."

FIVE

"We need information," I tell Charlie. "On as many players as we can."

"Players?"

"People who are involved. Who was Longinus, and what was the purpose of his cult? Who are the other members? What was Father Stone's involvement?"

Charlie frowns at me. "I thought we were supposed to be hunting vampires and werewolves. And maybe whoever killed Longinus and Stone in the first place."

I'm on my feet. I'm moving, restless, but I feel like I need more caffeine. I head for the kitchen to rectify that, talking as I go. "Those are the ultimate answers we need, yes, but we need more than that. We have to understand the bigger picture—and what with magic and other realities and supernatural baddies, that picture's got to be pretty freaking huge. We go rampaging into the middle of it without any information, we're dead. Or undead. Or howling at the moon."

"Don't forget dangling at the end of a rope."

"Need a larger mug," I mutter. I find one and fill it. "Yeah. What about the Gallowsman? We haven't even considered that particular monstrosity yet."

"What, you think he's real, too? Come on, that's just a local urban myth—"

"Father Stone wound up hanging from the eaves of his own church under very mysterious circumstances. What we can decipher from Longinus's notes seems to indicate they were trying to invoke some kind of entity. What if it was the Gallowsman? What if that myth is based on fact?"

I stride back into the living room and grab my coat. "Let's go. We've got some research to do."

He shrugs and points at my laptop. "What, Google isn't good enough for you?"

"It's broken. We'll use the one down at the library."

We leave Galahad in the yard and walk into the center of town—thankfully, in the opposite direction from the church. Thropirelem's town square is picturesque, in an unimaginative sort of way, with a fountain, a statue, *and* a gazebo in the middle and plenty of brick storefronts loaded with gables and turrets and other architectural quaintness around the edges. There's a little park surrounding the gazebo, and a few weeping willows mourning over a single park bench.

It's a nice day, the first crispness of fall in the air, the turning leaves caught halfway between green and orange-red. A kid rides his bike past us, and an old couple nod at me as they stroll by going the other way. Nice, normal, mundane.

Except that old couple might have two black, hooded robes hanging in their closet. That kid might be running around on all fours come the next full moon, or sucking on someone's jugular. And the same goes for every single person I see on the street.

The library is one of the buildings fronting the square, a red brick structure with a peaked roof that looks like it could have once been a schoolhouse. The doors are large, old, and heavily varnished to a brown so dark it's almost black. We go inside.

The interior is considerably more modern. Fluorescent

lights hang from the ceiling, the carpet is a tasteful gray, and there's a computer workstation in the back. The librarian gives us an inquiring glance from her desk when we come in, which hardens to a barely tolerant stare when she recognizes me. Gretchen Peters is the kind of librarian who would gladly approve capital punishment for speaking above a whisper in her domain, and is about as welcoming as a cold shower. We've probably exchanged all of a dozen words, eleven of which were mine. Hers was "No."

We tiptoe to the back and see that no one's at the computer terminal. I use my library card to log us on and then we do a little surfing.

We find nothing.

Nothing on the Gallowsman. Nothing on the word at all.

"That's impossible," Charlie mutters. "It should show up on a dictionary site, at least. I mean, it's a real word, isn't it?"

"Far as I know." I stare at the monitor. *Zero matches for your search.* I've never seen that happen before, not for a single word. It's somehow far more creepy than Longinus's basement with its altar and black curtains.

"Maybe it's the computer," Charlie says. "Public access. It probably has some kind of content filter installed."

"For porn, sure. But this doesn't make any sense."

"You're right. We should ask the librarian."

I sigh. "Okay. But you do it—I don't think she likes me."

"Don't take it personally. I don't think she likes anyone."

We stroll over to her desk, where she's doing something with index cards. She looks up coolly after we've been standing there a moment. "Yes?"

"We're having a problem with the computer. It—well, it doesn't seem to recognize a particular word we're searching for."

"Which word would that be?"

Charlie glances at me, then back at Gretchen. "Gallowsman."

UNDEAD TO THE WORLD 53

Her face is impassive. "Yes. That word has been redacted. May I ask why you're searching for it?"

"Redacted?" I say. "What is this, a branch office of the CIA? It's a public library!" I realize my voice has gotten a little loud when she frowns at me.

"We're interested in local history," Charlie says. "There's supposed to be a legend about—"

"I'm familiar with the story. As are too many of the local children. The town would prefer that sort of thing not spread."

"So you've blocked access on one computer," I say. "Good job. I sure hope those new-fangled machines don't catch on, though. What if the town got a *second* one?"

She turns her head ever so slightly, refocusing her attention from Charlie to me. Her frown shifts to a very tiny smile that's somehow much more intimidating, and I suddenly feel like a bug under a magnifying glass.

"Not everything is available on the Internet, Ms. Valchek. Many historical documents never reach the digital realm. They stay locked up in basements and back rooms and old trunks, where only people like me even remember they still exist. That's why you should always treat librarians with respect; our kingdom may have shrunk, but we are still the gatekeepers to a great deal of knowledge."

For the first time, I hear the trace of an accent in her voice. British, of course. I wonder why I never noticed it before, then realize this is the longest conversation we've ever had.

"Duly noted," I say. "No disrespect intended. In fact, we could really use your help."

"Oh?"

"Town history," I say. "We need to know as much as possible about this place—when it was founded, significant events, things like that."

She peers at me skeptically. "And the Gallowsman?"

"We don't care about ghost stories," I say. "We need *facts*. Was there such an incident in the town's past? Who were the people involved? What *actually* happened? That's what we're interested in."

I can see by the look in her eye that I've got her attention. Scratch a small-town librarian and you'll usually find a local historian under the patina.

"I might be able to contribute to such an endeavor," she says. "Depending on your reasons for doing so."

I pause, thinking hard. "I'm writing a book," I say. "Not about the town specifically, or the Gallowsman. It's fiction. I'd make sure to mention you in the acknowledgments."

She nods, slowly. "All right. I'll see what I can do. Check back with me in a few days."

A few days? Half the town could have fangs by then. "Can you put a rush on that? My publisher is bugging me for an outline."

"Tomorrow at the soonest."

"Thanks," Charlie says. "We appreciate it."

He's already tugging on my elbow. I reluctantly let him lead me back out into the sunshine.

"You think she'll come up with anything?" Charlie asks.

"Oh, I think she will. The real question is, how much does she already know? That remark about books in old trunks hit a little too close to the mark. . . ."

Our second stop is a direct result of the first. We could just go back to Charlie's place and use his computer, but our visit to the library has made me realize three things: one, that the more rocks we kick over the more we're likely to learn; two, that rock kicking inevitably leads to pissing off something lethal lurking there; and three, that if we're going to go around pissing off venomous, lurking rock-dwellers we should really get as much bang for our buck as possible.

I expound this theory to Charlie as we walk. He seems less than impressed. "I thought we were going to keep this low-key."

"I'm not saying we get up on a soapbox in the town square,

Charlie. But sooner or later the cult is going to figure out that Longinus is dead and we're snooping around. Which is good, because that'll make them nervous."

"Nervous cultists are good? What's the weather like on your planet?"

"Kind of stabby, with increasing chances of monstrosity toward evening. Plus, we might see some light decapitation overnight."

"Uh-huh."

"Look, I have to see this guy anyway, about my laptop. He's really good with stuff like that, and I'm sure he'd be willing to help us out."

"Why?"

I hesitate. "Well . . . he's kind of got a crush on me."

"Which we are going to ruthlessly exploit?"

"We don't have *time* to ruth. *For* ruth. To be ruthing?"

We've arrived at our destination, a plain little white house tucked away behind the hardware store where I work part-time. I ring the doorbell.

"I don't know about this, Jace," Charlie says. "If this guy is in the cult, we're tipping them off. If he isn't, we might be putting him in danger."

"I'm just going to ask him to do a little web surfing, that's all—no one will even know he's doing it. Unless he's a cult member, in which case we'll have succeeded in telling them that they're being investigated. Which, naturally, will lead to a response, and then we can force them out into the open."

"You do realize you're supporting both sides of an argument. At the same time."

"Genius is the ability to hold two conflicting views simultaneously. No, wait, it isn't."

The door opens.

Damon Eisfanger looks surprised to see us—astonished, in fact. He's in his late teens or early twenties, a little pear-shaped, and an albino. Not the creepy, henchman-of-an-evil-organization kind of albino, though—more like a pink-eyed, white-haired, human incarnation of the Easter Bunny. Cute, in a harmless sort of way.

He stays well back from the door. Albinos have extremely sensitive eyes, and you never see Damon outside on a day like today. Even the lights in the diner are a little too bright for him—when he eats there, he usually wears sunglasses. Right now he's wearing a pair of baggy shorts, bedroom slippers, and a T-shirt with a picture of a velociraptor riding a Segway.

"Hi, Damon," I say. "Can we come in for a minute? I was wondering if you could help me out."

Damon blinks a few times, then says, "Uh, yeah, sure. What's up?"

We step inside and Charlie closes the door behind him. "Computer stuff, mostly. My laptop isn't working, for one thing."

"Okay. Well, I might be able to do something about that." He motions us to join him and walks down a hallway. The living room on the other end is a little claustrophobic— heavy drapes over all the windows—but neat and clean. Damon sits in a lounger, and Charlie and I take the couch. I'm careful not to sit too close to him.

"Nice shirt," Charlie says.

"Thanks. You said *mostly*. What else?"

I study him for a second before answering. He seems a lot less awkward than when he hangs out at the diner, where he makes small talk and pretends he isn't watching me. I guess home turf counts for a lot, especially when you spend as much time there as he does.

"Research," I say. "Internet research. I could do it myself, I guess, but I thought you'd be better at it. You could find stuff I couldn't."

Now he looks intrigued. "What kind of stuff?"

We give him the same spiel as Gretchen: town history, local lore, facts about the Gallowsman incident. But with Damon, I emphasize the supernatural angle a little more; he has the same affection I do for *The Bloodhound Files*—all right, maybe nobody has the same affection for it as I do—and that crosses over into other spooky subjects of interest. "Especially cults," I tell him. "Anything that might be connected to the Gallowsman legend or this area in particular."

If he's secretly a member himself, he's hiding it well; he doesn't look uncomfortable at all, just interested and excited. "Sure, I can do that. What's this all about?"

"We . . . can't really say," Charlie intones in a solemn voice. "Yet."

Eisfanger looks suitably impressed. Charlie's something of a local legend himself, and to somebody like Damon he's practically a deity of Cool. "Wow. NDA material, huh? Okay, I can get behind that. Can you let me know what's going on, uh, later?"

"Absolutely," Charlie says.

Damon beams. I suddenly feel like I just drove over a bunny.

"You can bring your laptop over whenever you want, too. Any idea what's wrong with it?"

"It, my dog, and a cup of coffee had an informal discussion. Things got acrimonious."

"Yeah, I can see how that might go. Hopefully it's not too major."

I get to my feet, and Charlie follows my lead. "Okay, then. We'll let you get to it. I'll bring my laptop by later, all right?"

"Sure." Damon shows us to the door, then stands back in the shadows as we leave. He seems a lot happier than when we showed up, but that just makes me feel guiltier.

"It's not like I'm leading him on," I mutter as we walk away. "I've never come within twenty yards of flirting with him."

"Not really your style," Charlie mutters back. "You're more the intimidation type. Probably threaten to take him to the beach or something."

"I'm going to pretend I didn't hear that."

"Good idea. I'll pretend I didn't say it."

We walk back downtown. I've set things in motion, but I'm really not sure what to do next. What would Jace Red Dog do?

She'd go looking for trouble.

Trouble, in this case, meaning anything out of the ordinary. Odd behavior, things missing or out of place. Anomalies. I suggest this to Charlie, who shrugs. "I guess. I mean, it's not like we can conduct a door-to-door search. But we could roam around on foot and keep our eyes open. There's not much real estate to cover, all told."

So we do. I don't know what we're looking for—men with five-o'clock shadows at eleven AM, furtive clusters of nervous-looking people, a double-parked hearse—but what we find is a lot of nothing. Houses, people, dogs, kids, cars. Small town America on a fall morning. I see one suspicious-looking house with cobwebby windows, then realize they're just getting an early jump on Halloween.

But it isn't what we see that's interesting. It's what we *hear*.

Raised voices, coming from the parking lot beside City Hall. An argument of some sort? Charlie and I glance at each other, then head in that direction while trying to look casual.

I recognize the voices as we get closer. It's Mayor Leo and his oldest son—Terrance.

"—I don't understand your attitude, not at all!" That's Mayor Leo. He's sounds angrier than I've ever heard him.

"Yeah, well, I don't *care* if you don't understand. We don't have much to talk about, okay? I do my thing, he does his. And we're both fine with it."

"You're wrong. Wrong! Family is important, it's *everything*—"

"Not to me! You've never gotten that! And the only reason family is so damn important to you is because *you're* king of the hill—just like you're the king of this crappy little town! Too bad *families* don't have elections—"

We round the corner just as a tremendous *BOOM!* thunders into the air. A large Dumpster rolls toward us, but it's not moving very fast; Charlie stops it with his foot.

I peer around it. Mayor Leo is standing there with one clenched fist held at waist level. Terrance glares at him from an arm's length away. "Maybe you should go have that looked at, Dad," he growls. "You know, by the son you actually have some respect for." He spins on his heel and stalks off, not even noticing us.

Mayor Leo does, though. He looks at me like he knew I was there the whole time. "Hello, Jace," he says, his voice a little sad. "I'm sorry you had to see that. It's difficult, sometimes, being a parent."

I straighten up and walk around the Dumpster toward him. "Sure, of course. We just heard the noise and thought we'd see—"

"My apologies. I got a little upset and kicked the Dumpster. Made a heck of a racket, didn't it?"

Charlie's standing beside me, now. "Yeah, kinda. You didn't hurt yourself, did you?"

"No, no, nothing like that." He looks a little embarrassed. "Just lost my cool for a moment. I'm fine. Actually, if you'll excuse me, I think I should try to go patch things up with Terrance. He gets his temper from me, I'm afraid."

"Yeah, no, go ahead."

He strides away. "Huh," Charlie murmurs. "That's a little unusual. Never seen Leo lose it before."

I walk over to the Dumpster. "That's not the only thing. Look at this."

I point to a dent in the thick metal of the side. "This seems fresh. See how the paint's flaked off at the impact point?"

Charlie studies it. "Points, you mean. Four of them."

"Yeah. Kind of high for a kick, too. But just about perfect for knuckles. . . ."

Charlie nods, slowly. "All of which should be currently broken, if he hit it hard enough to do this."

"He seem like a guy with a hand full of broken bones to you?"

"No. But he is a politician."

"I know. Question now is, what *else* is he?" I shake my head. "All right, we have our first official suspect. We should . . ."

"What? Shoot him with a silver bullet? Drive a stake through his heart? I have no idea where we could get that sort of ammunition, but we can pick up some stakes at the hardware store. You get an employee discount, right?"

I sigh. "I'm not suggesting we do anything rash. We don't know what this means—he was standing in direct sunlight so I doubt he's a vampire, but maybe he's not a werewolf, either. Maybe he's a cultist with some kind of magically enhanced strength."

"You mean like Samson? Great. All we have to do is convince him to get a haircut. Worst-case scenario, we ambush him with scissors and some mousse."

"Wow, you are *so* helpful. You should share your talents with the world—maybe you could start by giving swimming lessons to bricks."

"I don't swim."

"All the better. You could demonstrate what people shouldn't do. See all this thrashing and sinking and drowning? Don't do that."

"Duly noted. So what *should* we do?"

I'm already moving. "You were right about one thing—we need to stock up on supplies. Hardware is a good idea, but let's hit the grocery store first."

"For?"

"Garlic."

We head for the local supermarket, Lucky Foods. It's just off the town square—like most of the local businesses—but it seems to be closed. There's no explanatory sign on the door, either; I would have expected CLOSED DUE TO FAMILY EMERGENCY or BACK IN TEN MINUTES or something similar.

I walk up and peer through the glass plate of the front wall. Nothing but rows of stocked shelves and a deserted cashier station. I frown. "Something's not right," I say. "Jimmy wouldn't just close up shop like this, not without a note. He never takes a day off."

"True," Charlie says. "Let's check around the back."

There's a parking lot at the side of the store, and an alley at the rear. I can see Jimmy's truck parked there, right next to the loading bay. The rolling steel gate is pulled down, blocking off the back door, but it's not locked.

"Hello?" I call out. "Jimmy?"

No answer. I grab the bottom of the gate and tug. It rolls upward with a loud rattle.

"Jace," Charlie says, a warning in his voice.

"It's not breaking and entering if the door's open. Just entering."

"I don't think Jimmy will appreciate us just wandering into his closed place of business."

"I'm a concerned citizen checking upon one of my peers. Maybe he's inside and injured. Maybe he needs help."

"Maybe he's got a shotgun and an aversion to people disturbing his privacy."

But I'm already in the loading bay and reaching for the door handle. I don't have to look back; I know Charlie's right behind me.

The back door's not locked, either. I pull it open and look inside: nothing but a shadowy room, stacked high with cardboard boxes on wooden pallets. I can smell traces of rotting vegetation mixed with the syrupy sweetness of spilled pop. "Jimmy?"

Still no answer. But as I take a step inside, listening intently, I can tell there's someone here; I can feel the presence of another person close by, and it's not Charlie.

"Jimmy?" I call out again.

And then I hear a ragged whisper from somewhere in the darkness: "*Jaaaaaace . . .*"

I look for a light switch but can't find one. Charlie's right beside me now. "I think it came from over there. Jimmy? You okay?"

"Not . . . okay," the voice says weakly.

I feel my way into the darkness, running one hand along the stacked boxes and taking slow, careful steps. My foot encounters something sticky that tries to persuade my shoe to stay and visit. "Jimmy? We're coming, all right? Just hold on."

"Over here," the voice rasps. Either Jimmy has a nasty case of laryngitis or he doesn't have the strength to speak; I can barely hear him.

We find him in the far corner of the storeroom. Charlie's dug out his cell phone, and the glow of light shows us the body of Jimmy Zhang slumped against a crate of bananas, the front of his shopkeeper's apron soaked in crimson. I kneel beside him and he moves an arm feebly, showing me he's still alive. "Jimmy? My god, what happened?"

"Found me," he murmurs. His eyes are slits, barely open. "So happy you found me. Everything . . . fine now."

"If that's his blood, he's in shock," Charlie says. "I'm calling nine-one-one—"

"No, please," Jimmy says. His voice is so quiet I have to lean in to hear him. "No ambulance. Just need . . . just need—"

"What? What do you need, Jimmy?"

His eyes snap open. They look as if every capillary in them has exploded; the whites are now bloodred. He opens his mouth wide, and I can see two long, very sharp fangs jutting from under his pale lips.

"Just need a *drink*," he says.

SIX

I have Charlie to thank for my life. He grabs me by the collar and yanks me backward at the same instant that Jimmy lunges forward, and I go sprawling down the aisle on my butt. I don't have a real clear view of what happens next, but I can see the only light source in the room, Charlie's cell phone, go spinning wildly into the air. I hear a loud smack followed immediately by a thud, and then I'm in the dark.

With a vampire.

I scramble to my feet. *"Charlie!"*

"Get outside!" he shouts.

Outside. Sunlight. Right. I turn around and stumble toward the door, knowing that's our best chance. Strangely, every instinct I have is screaming for me to turn around and fight, but I know that's suicide. Charlie's got size, muscle, and Army Ranger training—I've got a smart mouth and a bad attitude. He stands a much better chance of holding off an undead shopkeeper than I do, and once I'm outside I'll have the advantage—

Uh-huh. So why am I suddenly running the wrong way?

Because, apparently, sometimes doing the unexpected is the best strategy. Even when it's stupid. I mean, running full tilt toward a supernatural monster is bad, but doing so in the dark borders on the insane—in fact, it's so close to the border there's a little guardhouse there, with a full-time customs officer and a duty-free shop where you can get strait-jackets at a killer discount.

My foot skids on the floor, and I go crashing to the ground again. Jace Valchek to the rescue, armed only with her deadly wit and astounding pratfall skills . . . but a second later someone trips over me, and by the disgruntled *unf*! I hear on impact, it's Charlie. Vampires don't generally *unf,* I don't think.

All of which sounds terrible, except immediately after the *unf* there's a scream, coming from behind me. Jimmy must have leaped for Charlie's throat, except Charlie—thanks to me—was no longer there, putting newbie neckbiter Jimmy in a much longer leap than he was expecting. His touchdown point seems to have been the patch of sunlight coming in through the open backdoor—but from the sounds of Chinese cursing that follow, I guess he didn't get a fatal dose.

And now he's between us and the exit.

"Head for the front," Charlie whispers, and then he's gone. For a big man, he can move pretty fast—not to mention quietly.

I'm alone again.

I understand why Charlie took off like that—our chances are better if we split up, and if we try to take Jimmy on head-to-head he'll probably overpower us—but for a second I feel kind of abandoned. I feel—

Zhang, hovering in midair, wearing a black three-piece suit. His skull glowing a faint green through his translucent flesh.

What?

I shake my head. Some kind of vivid hallucination? No. Not a hallucination. Something more familiar . . .

I don't have time to think about it, so I don't. I make a beeline for the swinging doors that lead out to the retail area, not bothering with subtlety; I just put my head down and charge right through.

This time I luck out and don't crash into anything, as the door opens onto the main aisle of the store. I skid to a stop before I smack into the plate-glass windows at the front, and whirl around to make sure Zhang isn't right behind me. Somehow, it's hard to think of him as "Jimmy" anymore.

Charlie darts through a moment later. Late afternoon sunshine is streaming through the windows, and we stand as close to them as we can. In the dim shadows at the back of the store, I can see the double doors swinging back and forth, squeaking softly as they slowly lose their momentum. I've heard that squeak a hundred times before while I was shopping, but right now it's the eeriest, creepiest sound in the world.

And then one of the doors stops on the backswing.

It's too far away and too dark to see, but I know four fingers must be clutching the edge of that door. Four pale fingers, stained with their own blood. I wonder how long Zhang was in there, how long ago he was bitten. From his condition, I'm guessing I was going to be his first meal as a creature of the night. I might still be.

"We need to get out of here," Charlie whispers.

"You think?" I whisper back.

"I *remember* you," Zhang croaks. "You. *Bloodhound.*"

I'm standing in bright sunshine, but it feels like someone just slid an icicle down my spine. Zhang still sounds like he has the world's worst sore throat, but that's not all that's changed. His diction, his *accent* is different; it's like he's an entirely new person. And the *venom* in his voice—he's way past angry, or even enraged.

Hatred. That's what I hear. Pure, black hatred.

Part of me wants to call back, to say *Of course you remember me—I've known you for years. I'm the one who always makes bad jokes about your zucchini. I'm the one who makes sure you stock those vegetarian TV dinners and then complain about how bad they are. I'm Jace.*

But I don't. Because part of me remembers *him*, too.

The person I remember didn't have a first name—just Mr. Zhang. He didn't own a grocery store and he didn't wear plaid shirts with the sleeves rolled up and I never joked with him about produce. Mr. Zhang was smooth and cold and powerful, and I'm pretty sure he sent me to hell once.

So I don't say anything. Because I'm also pretty sure he'd love to send me there again.

"Time to go," I say. There's a steam cleaner standing by the front door that you can rent by the hour or the day, and I pick it up. Make sure I've got a good grip on the handle.

"Jace," Charlie says. "What are you—"

"Hammer time," I say, which is a lame early nineties reference as well as a pun on an Olympic event, but I don't have time to explain either because I'm spinning around in a circle while holding onto the steam cleaner with both arms extended and then letting go.

SMASH!

We leap through the shattered window. By some utterly amazing piece of luck, absolutely no one's on the street to see us do this.

We don't stop running until we hit the town square. Then we slow to a trot, try to ignore the few stares we get, and stroll at a not-too-hasty-but-definitely-determined rate back to my place.

"That went well," Charlie says.

"Oh, absolutely. What was your favorite part? I can't choose—there were just so *many*."

"Well, tripping over you in the dark while being attacked by a bloodthirsty monster is in my top three."

"Oh, yeah."

"Then there's the part where the guy I've been buying breakfast cereal from for the past couple of years tries to turn me into a protein shake."

"Also a contender."

"And let's not forget the whole breaking out of a locked store and bolting away like—like—"

"Small children running from a clown? Japanese extras being chased by a guy in a lizard suit? Panic-stricken penguins fleeing from a crazed nun?"

He stops his pacing and studies me for a second. "You know, I may have to rethink the whole you're-not-crazy thing."

"I thought a little nuttiness might help derail you."

"Derail me? Why would you want to derail me?"

"Because until about ten minutes ago, you were the biggest bad-ass in town. Now we're hiding from the guy that sells us toilet paper. It's kind of a shock to the system."

He abruptly sits down on the couch. "Yeah. I guess. I mean—goddammit, that guy was a *vampire!*"

"Pretty much."

I watch him carefully. Me, I've lived with crazy for a while, so I'm sort of used to it; but a regular guy like Charlie, whose beliefs and values sit firmly on a foundation of stable assumptions about the world, isn't used to this sort of thing. He's just found out what he thought was bedrock is in fact quicksand, and he's struggling to keep from going under.

He shakes his head. "Up until now, I thought I was handling this pretty well. Evil cults, messages from other dimensions . . . but—but that guy was a goddamn *vampire!*"

"What gave it away? The blood-filled eyeballs, the overbite from hell, or the instant sunburn?"

Charlie glares at me. "I've never run from a fight in my life. Never. I *tried* to fight him. But it was like—like he was a *robot,* almost. Rubber over steel. Soft on the outside, but unbreakable underneath. Nothing I threw at him fazed him. And he was so *fast* . . . fast, and strong, and impossible to hurt. It's as if he were—like he was—"

"A goddamn vampire?"

"I need a drink."

"I need a distillery. But we'll both have to settle for this."

I grab a purple teddy bear from where it sits on the mantel and hand it to him.

"Thanks," he says wearily, "but I think I'm beyond being comforted by a stuffed animal."

"That's because you're not doing it right." I reach over and unscrew the bear's head, revealing a bottle sticking up from its neck like a glass spinal column. "You like scotch, right?"

"At this point, I like paint thinner." He lifts the bear and takes a slug, then considers the headless body in his hand. "Hey. That's pretty good."

"That's why it's stashed inside a plush toy. If I ever get burglarized, I want to be able to sit here and console myself with some quality booze. Now gimme—can't you tell he's a Share Bear?"

He passes it back to me and I take a pull. "Okay. Obviously, we need a plan."

"How about we sit here and drink until we pass out? That way, when he shows up after dark to drain us, we kill him with alcohol poisoning."

"Mmmmm—no. Unless we're drinking fermented garlic, I don't think that's gonna work. And the only source of garlic in town has just become inaccessable, anyway."

"We need to go back there, Jace. We can't let that thing kill or bite anyone—"

My phone chimes. I used to have a ringtone that played the theme music from *The Bloodhound Files,* but after my stay in the State Home for the Sanity Challenged I changed it to something a little less obsessy: Bauhaus's cheery little number "Bela Lugosi's Dead."

I pull out my phone, check the number. I don't recognize it, but it's local. I don't answer, though, just stare at the phone in my hand. Galahad whines.

"Aren't you going to get that?" Charlie asks.

I should, but I don't want to. I have the sudden, overwhelming feeling that it's going to be Zhang. *Hello, Jace. I just thought I'd let you know that I'm going to be paying you a visit tonight. And after that, you and I will be together for a long, long time. . . .*

I hit the TALK button and put the phone to my ear. "Hello?"

"Jace Valchek?" I don't immediately recognize the voice, but it sounds naggingly familiar—like getting a call from someone you haven't talked to in years.

"Speaking. Who's this?"

"You don't know me, Ms. Valchek, but please don't hang up—I'm not a telephone solicitor. I'm calling from a bed-and-breakfast in Thropirelem, and I was wondering if you might have a few minutes to meet with me."

"About what?"

"About certain events that are happening in your town. Unusual, even distressing events."

He sounds educated, confident, friendly without being overly familiar. Not a salesman—someone in authority. Somebody used to telling people what to do and having them obey.

"Can you be . . . a little more specific?"

"Not over the phone. But I'm sure you know what I'm talking about."

"Who *are* you?"

"I'm sorry; I should have introduced myself earlier. My name is David Cassiar."

Cassiar. Once again, I have the overwhelming feeling that I should know him—that I *do* know him, or at least who he is. "That name—I've heard it before."

"I have a certain reputation that surrounds me, but I assure you it's not deserved. Meet with me in person and you can see for yourself."

Now what? He sounds like he might have some answers—or at least be aware of what's going on—but I don't want him knowing where I live; I don't even want to be alone with him. "Okay, but it's got to be someplace public."

"How about a restaurant? I saw a diner on my way into town."

"Yeah, okay. When?"

"Let's say . . . eight o'clock?"

"Fine. I'll see you there."

I hit the OFF button, then stand there looking at my phone like maybe it'll tell me more if I wait long enough.

"Who was that?" Charlie asks.

"Some guy named David Cassiar. Says he knows about what's happening, wants to get together to talk about it. Supposed to meet him at the diner tonight."

"Jace, the only people who know about this are either bad guys or in another dimension. Guess which one he has to be?"

"I know, I know. But we're meeting in public, and I've got you as my ace in the hole. Besides, I don't want to be trapped at home after dark."

"Why not? We could barricade the doors and windows—I think I could make this place pretty defensible, actually. And don't vampires have to have an invitation to enter a house?"

I grab the bear from him and take another swig, then screw the head back on. "Maybe, maybe not. We can't take for granted that it works exactly like the movies—and even if it does, which movies? They all seem to play with the rules. Not that it matters."

"What do you mean?"

"It doesn't matter *how* defensible a place is, if it also happens to be on fire."

"Good point."

"Our best shot is to go on the offensive. Go back to Lucky Foods with some wooden stakes, whatever garlic I've got in my spice drawer, and maybe an axe. Chopping Zhang's head off should definitely slow him down."

Charlie nods slowly. "I'm with you. We prepare, we arm ourselves, we go back in. But before we do—you have any idea what Zhang meant when he said he *remembered* you?"

I think back to that moment. The image of Zhang hanging in the air, bones glowing through his flesh, comes back to me so vividly I almost gasp.

"No," I say carefully. "No, I don't."

"He called you *Bloodhound*, too."

"Everybody in town knows about my obsession, Charlie. I think he was just trying to freak me out. Or maybe that was vampire humor."

"If you say so. . . ."

There's a major flaw in our plan, of course. The window I smashed doesn't go unnoticed for long, and by the time we arrive with a bulging duffel bag slung over Charlie's shoulder, Sheriff Stoker is there, too.

"Jace. Charlie," he says. Yellow crime scene tape is already strung across the window. "Looks like we've got a regular crime wave happening."

"Hope nobody got hurt this time," I say.

"Just a steam cleaner." Stoker points to the machine lying on the sidewalk surrounded by shards of glass. "Funny thing is, it looks like this was pitched through the window from the inside."

"Ah, the wily steam cleaner," I say. "I've heard no prison can hold them."

"I'd say they broke in through the back," continues Stoker, "but the security gate was down and locked."

"Really?" Charlie says. "That's . . . unusual."

"That it is. I'd like to ask Jimmy Zhang about it, but nobody can reach him."

"What about his truck?" I ask. "I mean, has anybody seen it?"

"Well, it's not here. That's about all I know at the moment."

Sheriff Stoker regards both of us calmly. A little too calmly. Any second now he's going to ask us what's in the duffel bag.

"Don't suppose you two heard anything?" he asks.

"Us?" I say. "We just got here. When did this happen, anyway? We've been watching a movie for the last hour."

"Short movie."

"Crappy movie. We gave up and went for a walk."

He nods, slowly. "Well, it's a nice day for it. Enjoy." He turns around and walks back over to the window, kneeling to peer at something on the ground. I hope it's not a Jace-sized footprint.

"Let's go," I murmur to Charlie.

We cut through the parking lot and back to the alley. Sure enough, Zhang's truck is gone and the security gate is down and locked. "How'd he get away?" Charlie asks. "The sun's up—it's not even cloudy."

"I'm guessing he used some clever, high-tech vampy method to defeat that. Like, you know, a tarp over his head. Or maybe one of those newfangled umbrella gizmos."

Charlie grunts in annoyance. "Right. And now we have no idea where he's gone."

"Someplace dark, I'd guess. But yeah, there are all sorts of places he could hole up. So much for a preemptive strike."

"For our side, anyway."

I think about that. We've got hours to kill until our meeting with Cassiar . . . but there's only one bed-and-breakfast in town. "Maybe not. Maybe we just need to change targets."

"Sure. You know of another vampire in town, or are we hunting werewolves now? Because I'm a little low on silver."

I shake my head. "No, I'm thinking more along the lines of the mysterious Mr. Cassiar. We could surprise him with an unexpected visit at the B-and-B."

"I thought you wanted a public meet."

"That's the safe way to do it. But fortune favors the bold, right?"

"Fortune favors the survivors, Jace. They're the ones that are still around afterward to write down pithy little sayings and stick them in cookies so they can be quoted by people about to do stupid, dangerous things."

"Are you agreeing with me or not? I can't tell."

He sighs, and hefts the duffel bag on his shoulder into a more comfortable position. "Neither can I. Let's just go—if I haven't turned around by the time we get there, I guess I'm sticking around."

I grin. "Now you're talking."

The B-and-B is typical. Far *too* typical. In fact, if there were an ultimate example of a B-and-B, some kind of perfect, iconic version that exemplified not only everything Bed but also everything Breakfast, then this place looks like three of those smushed together. With extra gables sprinkled on top.

We stop in front and stare at it. "This place has always creeped me out," I say. "It's like that house on the hill Norman Bates lived in with his dead mother, only it's the house itself that's in drag."

"What? It's quaint."

"No, a dairy churn is quaint. This is quaint cubed, with cuteness bleeding from the edges. The frilly, frilly edges."

I don't really have to describe it, do I? Its curlicues have curlicues, like some kind of deranged Victorian fractal. Every surface that isn't a blinding white is a sunshiny yellow, and I know once we get inside we'll be overwhelmed by an overstuffed tidal wave of teddy bears, lace, and flower arrangements.

I grit my teeth. "No one said this was gonna be easy," I mutter, and march through the little white gate and up the porch steps.

I ring the doorbell. A tinny little version of Pachelbel's Canon plays somewhere inside. A moment later, the door opens with the tinkle of a little bell. The owner, Silas Bloom, stands there: He's a paunchy man with pale, shiny skin, thick-framed tortoiseshell glasses, and a pair of red suspenders holding up baggy tweed pants.

"Hello, Mr. Bloom. I was wondering if we could pay a visit to one of your guests."

Bloom squints at me suspiciously. "I don't have but one," he says. "Don't rightly know if he wants to be disturbed."

"Oh, he's expecting us," I say. "Mr. Cassiar, right?"

Bloom nods slowly. "Well . . . I suppose so. No visitors after nine o'clock, though."

I refrain from pointing out that it's mid-afternoon. "We won't be long."

"Upstairs, first bedroom on the right."

He steps aside just enough for us to squeeze by. For someone in the hospitality industry, he's not exactly welcoming. Maybe he misread the word as *hostility.*

The interior is about as bad as I expected: Doilies infest every surface like some kind of embroidered fungus, there are picture frames so ornate you can't even focus on whatever they're wrapped around, and the floral pattern of the wallpaper is dense enough to smell. Going up the staircase feels like wandering into an actual thicket; I almost expect some kind of woodland creature with huge cartoon eyes to burst out of the wall and demand I sing a song.

But we make it to the top without incident. "Ready for this?" I whisper to Charlie.

"No," Charlie says. "But since you're going to do it anyway . . ."

I knock on the door.

It opens.

SEVEN

David Cassiar is not what I expected.

He's much younger than I thought he'd be, for one thing—but that's only at first glance. When he smiles at me, the wrinkles around his eyes put him in his forties, not the twenty-something man I initially saw.

He's tall, well built, his skin that golden color you see in ads for tanning salons. He's blond, with deep blue eyes, and damned attractive in a daytime soap kind of way. He's wearing a white button-down shirt with the sleeves rolled up, tan pants, and no shoes at all.

"Well . . . hello, Jace," he says. "This is a surprise—but a welcome one. Come on in." He beckons me inside like it's pouring rain in the hallway. "And you are?" he asks Charlie, putting out his hand.

Charlie hesitates, then shakes it. "Charlie," he says gruffly.

"Nice to meet you. I'm David Cassiar—but I guess you already know that." He chuckles, then closes the door behind Charlie. "Please, have a seat."

I glance around the room. Four-poster bed, of course. Frilly quilt, frilly pillows. Several antique chairs that seem to have been upholstered in the wallpaper's inbred offspring and then doilyed to within an inch of their overstuffed lives. I shudder. "I'll stay on my feet, thanks."

Cassiar shrugs and sits down himself, crossing his legs casually. Charlie picks a chair and occupies it like it's enemy territory. He drops the duffel bag down between his knees.

"I assume you decided you'd rather have your questions answered now instead of later?" Cassiar asks.

"More or less," I say. "Okay, more more than less. You told me you knew what was going on in Thropirelem. What would that be, exactly?"

He looks at me steadily for a moment before answering. "Monsters, Ms. Valchek."

"Monsters," I say. I say it the way a farmer might say *gophers,* or a teenager might say *algebra.*

"Yes. I've been tracking a cult for some time now, and I have reason to believe they're based in your little town."

"Wait," Charlie says. "Tracking? Who tracks a cult?"

The faintest trace of a frown surfaces on Cassiar's face. "Well, I do. I'm sorry, I thought you were familiar with my work—or would have Googled me, at the very least."

"We've been having connection problems," I say. "Pretend we're Googling you right now—what's getting the most hits?"

"Probably my own Web site, Evilhunter. That's what I do, you see; I hunt monsters."

The phrase resonates in my head so strongly I can almost hear echoes. "You hunt monsters. Like a profiler?"

"No. I don't seek to understand evil—just to eradicate it. And the Gallows cult is one of the most evil groups I've ever encountered."

"Are you talking about the Gallowsman?" Charlie asks.

"Yes. You know it as a local legend, but it pops up all over the Midwest. Minor details change, but the central story is always the same. Local man named Jump—or Leap, or sometimes Hopper—has a run of horrible luck. Coldhearted villagers turn their backs on him, or execute him outright.

He promises to come back and share his pain with them. Then people start to die. There are many variations of how they die, but it's usually something bizarre or improbable and always involves strangulation. The only way to stop it is for someone to hang themselves on purpose—to show the Gallowsman that somebody understands his pain."

Terrance hadn't told me the last part; then again, maybe he hadn't known it. Or maybe he hadn't wanted to risk the guilt in case somebody found me hanging from the rod in my closet. "So if this is such a widespread story, then why is the cult based here?"

"Because all stories have some element of truth to them, or they die out. This is the town where the actual event took place, over two hundred years ago."

"Hold on," I say. "Let's go back to the whole I-hunt-monsters bit. For whom?"

"For the good of all."

"Oh? That must be hard to bill."

"I write books about my exploits. They generate enough income to keep me going."

What I wouldn't give for an Internet connection right now—I can smell scam all over this guy. "I hate to be picky, but I'm not sure you're really what we're looking for in a monster-hunter right now. Do you have a résumé you could leave with us?"

Cassiar sighs, uncrosses his legs, and leans forward. "I don't blame you for being skeptical, Ms. Valchek. Monsters, for the most part, are fiction. I've never come face-to-face with a vampire or a werewolf, though I have found evidence that suggests such creatures did once exist. And I believe they might again, if the Gallows cult has its way."

I pluck a porcelain knickknack from a shelf and toy with it. I'm not even sure what it's supposed to be—a puppy? A kitten? A horribly deformed duck? "If you don't hunt vampires or werewolves, what *do* you hunt? Sasquatches? The Loch Ness Monster?"

"Oh, I'm intimately familiar with the supernatural, Ms. Valchek. Demonic possession is all too real, as are malevolent spirits like poltergeists. But what the Gallows cult is trying to do is far worse; they're trying to drag something physical across the Great Divide. Not a spirit, not a nebulous entity, an actual *being*. In fact, they may have already succeeded—and it could lead to something utterly catastrophic."

"What, an evil undead hangman isn't bad enough?"

"He is only the first. Should the cult be able to bring him through, others may follow. As terrible as the Gallowsman is, his threat is nothing compared to monsters that could turn others into beings like them."

"Others. You're talking about the *V* and *W* words, right? Or should I throw a *Z* in there, too?"

He shakes his head gravely. "At this point, I don't know. But yes, vampires and werewolves are certainly possibilities. The living dead are less likely, for occult reasons that are difficult to explain—essentially, the Gallowsman already fulfills that role, which makes it difficult for anything similar to cross over without his active help."

Charlie nods. "And he doesn't play well with others. Luckily for us."

"Exactly."

I toy with the knickknack and don't say anything for a minute. I don't know what to think; Charlie clearly believes him, but I'm not so sure.

No, that's not quite it. Everything he's saying makes sense and fits with what we've discovered so far—it's the man himself I'm having trouble with. There's something off about him, something not quite right. It's like if I caught a glimpse of him out of the corner of my eye, I'd see someone else.

But so far, he seems to know more about the situation than we do, and that's worth a lot. "Tell me about the cult. Why are they doing this? What do they stand to gain?"

"Beyond occult power? The Gallowsman's a locus, not

just for despair but for bad luck itself, the swirling destructive side of chaos. Like a curse come to life."

"Doesn't sound as if he gets invited to a lot of parties. So why would the cult want him around?"

"When brought here by the death of a suicide, the Gallowsman has a specific purpose—to bring suffering to the one the suicide blames for their pain. But when there's no suicide, he has no focus. He can be directed by those that summoned him."

"Like a weapon," Charlie says.

"When needed, yes. But there is another very real, very tangible benefit to summoning the Gallowsman. He draws ill fortune and hopelessness to him—and *away* from those he is bound to."

I frown. "So he's like a giant four-leaf clover and supernatural Prozac, in handy two-legged form?"

Cassiar smiles. "I suppose. Who wouldn't want an endless supply of happiness and good luck? Especially when you could inflict the opposite on your enemies?"

He has a point. It's a little undefined for my tastes, but I'm getting the feeling that's how magic works—it's always a little fuzzy around the edges. "So as long as the Gallowsman hangs around—sorry—the cult does a happy dance and never rolls snake eyes. Not great for anyone hunting them, right? And speaking of which, *what does any of this have to do with me?*"

I didn't really intend to raise my voice like that, but I'm a little surprised at Cassiar's reaction. He looks . . . sad.

"Summoning an otherworldly entity always requires a sacrifice, but in the case of the Gallowsman, it's a little different. He's drawn to pain—emotional torment. From what I've been able to find out, you're supposed to be the source of that torment."

Well, that would explain the pictures. "So they're planning on using me as bait? Torture me and wait for the Gallowsman to show up?"

"I believe so, yes."

"Well then, I guess you don't have all the answers after all, Mr. Cassiar. Because unless our local pastor managed to hang himself from the eaves of a three-story building without a window or a ladder, the Gallowsman is already *here*. You were right about one thing, though—he didn't come alone. You want to meet a genuine, unalive vampire? Keep your eyes out for our local greengrocer, Jimmy Zhang—he's suddenly developed a real sweet tooth. If, you know, by sweet you mean blood and by tooth you mean teeth. And while none have actually shown up yet, I have it on good authority that the lupine contingent are going to be putting in an appearance, too."

I'm a little out of breath by the end, but once I started I couldn't stop. It was like I had this bizarre need to prove myself to him, as if we were comparing schizophrenic stories and mine just had to be crazier.

He regards me calmly. He looks more thoughtful than worried. "I see," he says at last. "It seems I've miscalculated the timing. Things are further along than I thought."

"You think?"

"Jace," Charlie says. "Calm down. What we've got to do is figure out how to handle this."

"Handle? Handle? We've got a demon with a rope fetish, a murderous cult, and half the cast of a horror movie, all inside the city limits of a town you can walk across in twenty minutes! And that's *if* you stop and talk to all the people you know along the way, only you won't because they might *eat you!*"

"Your friend Charlie is right, Jace. We need to find a way to quietly contain the situation—"

"Quiet? No, no, no. Quiet time is *over*. Now is wide-awake, the house is on fire and we need to *do* something time."

Charlie gives Cassiar a glance he thinks I don't notice. I do, but I don't bother responding. "You know what this is? This is that moment in the movie or book or comic where the good guys screw everything up. This is where they decide to take on the monster all by themselves. Well, sorry, but no goddamn way. We call in the authorities. We get lots of people with lots of equipment—giant crucifixes, automatic weapons loaded with silver bullets, all the garlic they can carry—and we blitz the whole town. Spotlights, teams of at least six, and nobody ever, ever, *ever* goes off on their own—"

"Jace," Charlie says gently. "This is a small town in the middle of nowhere. We've got a sheriff and one part-time deputy. We might be able to rustle up some guns, but we don't have any silver bullets or the know-how to make them."

"We'll ask the Internet! It knows *everything*!"

Charlie sighs. "Okay, sure. But how long is that going to take? Where are we going to get the equipment we'll need? You have a metal foundry in your basement you're not telling me about?"

I'm starting to run out of steam. "No. But—"

"The only people that are going to believe you are the ones who already know the truth. And they'll be the first ones to call you crazy."

Which everybody else will agree with. "Okay, but . . . we need *help*, Charlie. We're way out of our league, here. This is a league we didn't even know *existed* twenty-four hours ago, and now we're supposed to compete at a professional level? Let's at least try to sign up a few more players!"

Charlie thinks about it. "Like who?"

"How about the sheriff? He already knows something weird is going on. Maybe if we show him what we've found out so far—"

"I wouldn't recommend that," Cassiar says quietly.

"Why?" I demand.

"Because Sheriff Stoker is a high-ranking member of the Gallows cult. He is, in fact, their second-in-command."

* * *

It's funny, how the mind works.

You can load it up with all kinds of contradictory information, and it'll adapt. You can overload it with sensory input, and it'll adapt. You can deprive it of any input at all, and it'll adapt. It's based in three pounds of jellylike flesh that's mostly water, and is capable of producing art, mathematics, language, and emotion.

But it has its limits.

I thought I was doing fine. Supernatural beings, my TV talking to me, evil cults out for my blood . . . but somehow, the simple fact that Sheriff Stoker is one of the bad guys just stops me dead. I got used to the idea of reality not being trustworthy a while ago, but the notion that someone I respect—and yes, I do respect cops, believe it or not—is a genuine Bad Guy just knocks the wind out of me. It hits me on a much deeper level than a nasty revelation; it feels like a personal betrayal.

"I have to go," I say. My voice sounds flat and unreal, like a bad recording. I'm out of the room and halfway down the stairs before Charlie catches up with me. He doesn't try to stop me, just says, "Jace? Are you okay?"

"No," I say. My voice sounds puzzled, but a little relieved, too. I don't feel either of those things. "I need to go home."

"Okay, we can do that—"

"Alone, Charlie. I need to be alone." That isn't true, I *know* it isn't true, but I can't explain. Not even to Charlie. "Stay here, talk to Mr. Cassiar. See if you can come up with a plan."

"I don't think you being alone is such a good idea right now—"

I'm already out the front door and down the porch steps. "Come by before it gets dark. Zhang won't do anything before then."

"I . . . all right. Just be careful, okay?"

I nod, but don't look back. I need to go home.

I need my shows.

* * *

I remember.

I remember the last time I felt this way. It was when I had my breakdown, when they had to take me away in an ambulance and sedate me. That was the last time I felt this . . . shattered.

My memories of the event have always been fragmented. Little bits of broken-glass sharpness mixed into a thick, murky broth of amnesia, like a stew made of mirror shards and tapioca. I remember the jab of the needle. I remember the way the blood spurted when I broke the EMT's nose. I remember being very, very concerned that nobody touch the remote.

But I didn't remember the breakdown itself. Not until right now.

Everything's very far away. My thoughts are very loud, and I don't have a lot of control over them; they jump from subject to subject, memory and imagination blurring together, making random connections. A small, quiet part of me is watching this happen, like someone watching TV. That's the part that's in control of my body, making me walk to my house, unlock the door, breeze past Galahad, and unearth my stash. Not the regular one, under the fridge; my *secret* stash.

It consists of exactly one DVD in a paper envelope, and it's duct-taped to the underside of a bookshelf. It's the one I watched over and over again, the one that convinced me I was somebody else, the one I swore I'd never watch again.

It's also the very first time the Sword of Midnight shows up, though nobody knows who she is yet. I can't believe I forgot that.

I slip the disc into the machine, turn on the TV. Galahad is watching me with a worried look on his face, but I'm careful to keep the remote well away from him.

"You don't understand," I tell him. "This has . . . this has what I *need*."

I sit down on the couch. The remote feels impossibly heavy in my hand, like a gun. I find that strangely comforting.

I know why Cassiar's calculation was off, why the Gallowsman is already here. It's because of my breakdown. That was the emotional torment that drew him to my little town, and he's been here ever since. Waiting. Getting stronger. Sucking down everyone's despair and bad luck and storing it for later, for whatever purpose his master had in mind.

But his master is dead now. And I don't know what will happen next.

I hit PLAY.

"Coming up on *CSI: Transylvania* this week:"

Forensic Investigator Helsing kneels beside a headless corpse in the moonlight. CSI Larry Talbot stands behind him, hands in the pockets of his trenchcoat.

"Vic was decapitated with a silver-edged weapon," Talbot says.

"Yes, he was," Helsing murmurs. "But look at this—bite marks on the right breast, with scorching around the edges. Pre-mortem, and probably made by silver."

"Silver teeth? That would rule out a pire or a 'thrope."

"You'd think so. But obviously, *someone* has fangs for the mammaries. . . ."

The opening bars of *The Who's* "Behind Blue Eyes" swell, and then the scene cuts to the opening credits of *The Bloodhound Files*.

The world around me falls away. The colors on the monitor are richer, deeper than real life. The theme music, so familiar, so haunting, makes my heart ache. I go up and touch the warmth of the screen, willing the hardness of the glass to soften into a membrane I can push through. Tears run down my face.

I want to be there. I want to go *home*.

The Sword of Midnight is in the very first scene. She's stalking Jace, who knows somebody's following her. The Sword is perched on the edge of a rooftop, looking down at her quarry.

"Hello," I whisper.

The Sword turns, slowly, to face me. She looks solemn. "So you're finally watching it. I didn't think you were strong enough yet."

"I don't know if I am, either. But I have to *know*."

"Yes, you do. So go ahead and ask me."

I take a deep breath and let it out. "Who am I?"

"Your name is Jace Valchek. You used to be a criminal profiler for the FBI. You were taken from your world and into another one, where magic exists and vampires, werewolves, and golems make up ninety-nine percent of the population—"

"No," I whisper. "That's crazy. That's Jace Red Dog's story, not mine."

"Jace Red Dog is just a character on a TV show. You're not—you're real, you're *you*. She's the imposter, okay? Life imitates art, especially when alternate realities are involved. You *know* that."

"Parallel worlds. Each one a little different than the next. Worlds with different histories, different rules, right next to each other."

"Yes. That's it, exactly."

"You're not telling me everything. *That's* what I am, right? Some kind of alternate version of the real Jace Valchek? Some kind of, of *echo*?"

"No, Jace. There *are* alternate versions of you—though not as many as there used to be—but you're the one I just described. It's the world around you that's not the original."

"That doesn't make any sense."

She sighs. "Your mind has been messed with, Jace. Your memories. You're not from a small town in Kansas, and you're not crazy. You don't belong where you are—in fact, you're probably being given some sort of medication to keep you from getting sick as a result."

I think about the Erthybon. About how I feel disconnected and nauseous if I miss a dose. "So why am I here? How did I get here?"

"You were taken against your will, by a sorcerer. Jumping between parallel worlds is extremely difficult, but he manages it with ease. He's the one behind all this, Jace. He's been manipulating the situation from the very start."

"I see. So I'm really a kick-ass crime fighter. I don't really belong here. I'm being victimized by an evil sorcerer, and the medication I'm taking is part of the plot." I laugh, a little wildly. "God, it all fits together perfectly, doesn't it? Nothing's my fault, it's all this big, evil *conspiracy.* I'm not a pathetic little nutcase trapped in a small town; I'm a *hero!* And all I have to do is believe, right? Or do I have to flap my fairy wings together, too?"

"Jace. Look at me."

I do. She reaches up and starts to undo the buckles that hold her mask in place. "You don't have to believe, Jace. You just have to *remember.*"

The mask falls away.

I have to admit, I was halfway expecting her face to be my own. But it's not—it's a woman who looks familiar but I can't quite place. She pulls a dark wig off, too, revealing short, pixieish blonde hair. She studies me, then gives me an encouraging smile. "Know who I am?"

"You look sort of . . . I don't know. I'm not sure."

"Try to remember. Take however much time you need. This link is better than the previous ones, so I can keep my image on screen longer."

I study her. Something comes back to me, but it's blurry. After a second, I realize why, and grin. "We got drunk together, didn't we? Somewhere . . . somewhere with slot machines."

She grins back. "Yes. Out of all the bizarre experiences we shared, why am I not surprised that's the one you remember?"

And then the name claws its way out of my subconscious. "Azura? Your name is Azura?"

"Yes, Jace. I'm Azura. What else do you remember?"

There's another *A* word that's trying to break through. It almost sounds like Azura, but it's longer. And darker. "Asa . . . no. *Ahaseurus*."

The smile falls off Azura's face. "Yes. What do you remember about him?"

"He—hates me. Or loves me? And he's bad, bad news."

Now she looks grim. "He's obsessed with you, Jace. He's a sorcerer, very old, very powerful, from *my* world. He's the one who dragged you across the dimensional divide in the first place."

"Why?"

"Initially, for the NSA; they needed your skills. But Ahaseurus wanted you here for his own reasons." She pauses. "A multitude of alternate worlds mean a multitude of alternate yous—you get that, right?"

"Yeah, yeah. Red-headed me, President me, South-won-the-Civil-War shitkicker me. What am I, Human Sacrifice me?"

"No, Jace. They're all the human sacrifice version. You once explained to me exactly what constitutes a 'serial killer'; that's what Ahaseurus is. And his choice of victim is you—a different you in every world, but still you."

I stare at the screen. And then I lean back and laugh.

"I'm sorry," I say. "It's just—this is getting to be a little much, you know? I have an evil cult dumped in my lap, then vampires and lycanthropes, then alternate worlds . . . now you're adding a *magic serial killer* to the list? What's next? Are there some *gods* out there I've pissed off, too?"

Azura looks uncomfortable. "Well, not recently. . . ."

"Okay, enough is enough. Just just give me everything you got, all right? The whole ball of deranged wax. I think I'd prefer a big whack of insanity all at once instead of this constant drip, drip, drip of crazy."

"I wish I could, Jace. But I don't know much more. Ahaseurus kidnapped you and brought you to the world where you are now. He's got something big planned—he always does—and obviously he decided to get you out of the way first. I can't reach you physically; it takes a sizeable amount of sorcerous power just to contact you. But I do have one small consolation to offer."

"I get frequent flyer miles for travel to other realities?"

Her smile comes back. "No, just the opposite. You acquired the dimensional equivalent of jet lag when you were pulled here—returning to your own reality would have stolen years of your life. You don't look any older to me, which means Ahaseurus nullified that effect when he took you this time. It probably doesn't mean anything to you right now, but it's important; it means you can return to your home reality now without Ahaseurus's help."

"Sure, great, fantastic. Hey, did I lend you my ruby slippers at some point? 'Cause I can't find 'em anywhere."

"I'm doing the best I can from my end, Jace. We'll get you home, I promise."

"Home? Home? I can't even *remember* my home! I don't know who I am, I don't know what's *real* and what's *not*. All I've got is two lousy names, yours and the guy who got me into all this. And I don't even remember what he looks like!"

"Well, there I can help you out." She tosses her blond wig in the air, and it transforms into an eight-by-ten glossy hanging in midair. "As I said, I may not be able to be physically present, but information is the most important weapon—"

I gasp. It shouldn't come as a shock, it should have been obvious from the start, but the hook-nosed image glowering at me is someone I instantly recognize.

It's Old Man Longinus.

EIGHT

"So," I say carefully, "what would happen if this guy was, say, no longer in the picture?"

"What, you mean if he leaves the reality he's stranded you in? That's unlikely; from the information I've been able to gather, he appears to be concentrating his mystic resources there. In fact, it almost seems as if he's setting up some sort of power base—"

"No. I mean, yeah, I think he's definitely left this reality, but I doubt if he's coming back. Of course, I don't know how things work with evil wizards, so maybe I'm wrong—"

"Jace. Are you telling me Ahaseurus is *dead*?"

"Not in any legally binding confessional kind of way, no. Otherwise, pretty much."

Azura blinks. I notice for the first time just how large her eyes seem to be, almost cartoonish. "You killed him?"

"No! No, I definitely did not. But I did sort of discover his body—after you told me to '*seek Longinus*'. Which means you already know who he is and what happened—"

She puts up her hands. "I don't, I swear. That was our first contact, and the link wasn't strong—I didn't even *use* the name Longinus, it's just what came through. What I was *trying* to say was *see Ahaseurus truly* but dimensional boundaries are tricky; they can change things around—"

"*See Ahaseurus truly*? What does that even mean?"

She sighs. "It means that—from what I can tell from here—you're surrounded by illusion spells. Things, people, even your own memories have been tampered with. If I could get you to realize Ahaseurus was the one tampering with your senses, I knew you'd figure the rest out. You're like that."

"Thanks. I think. So, evil killer wizard guy—really dead? Or another illusion?"

"How'd he die?"

"Someone got all stabby on him."

She shrugs. "I don't know. If he is dead, some of his more recent spells should start unravelling—but he's a powerful mage. A lot of his work will be self-perpetuating. It's more likely to mutate without him around rather than just falling apart. Magic's like that."

I think about that for a moment. Ancient serial killer harboring a serious obsession with yours truly has stuck me in a little town in the middle of nowhere. In another dimension. In a place where I'm viewed as the local crazy, and where said killer has apparently summoned a demon that personifies despair. It's starting to all make sense, and not the kind I want.

"This place," I say. "He made it to torment me. I'm . . . I'm a rat in a cage, and he's a sadistic teenager with a can of lighter fluid and a book of matches. That's how a lot of serial killers start, you know."

"I know. You told me."

"He wasn't going to kill me. He was going to see just how far he could push me. How bad he could make things before I went over the edge." My voice is starting to tremble, just a little bit, and I hate the way it sounds. "This isn't a town. It's a dungeon, filled with torture devices and traps. I can't trust anyone, can I? Even you might be part of it."

Azura opens her mouth, then closes it again. She knows I'm right, and nothing she can say will change that.

At that precise second, I know she's on my side. It's pure gut instinct, nothing else, but it's all I have right now. "And apparently it gets worse. If he isn't dead, this is all part of his plan to screw with my mind—and there's nothing I can do about it. If he *is* dead, then all the stuff he set up to torment me is still in place—only now it's going to activate randomly and in unpredictable ways. Either way, I'm trapped in a maze full of booby traps and land mines. That about right?"

She nods mutely.

I cross my arms. "Goddammit," I say softly. "You know, whether they were real or not, I'm starting to miss the good old days on Ward C. . . ."

There's a knock at the door. I hit the pause button on the remote and jump up. "Charlie?"

"No," says a deep male voice. "It's Sheriff Stoker. You and I need to have a little talk, Jace. . . ."

I don't know what to do.

After a second, I decide to turn off the television. I don't know why, but I don't want Stoker to see Azura's face. I'm running on instinct now, and don't have time to question it.

I open the door. "Hello, Sheriff. What's this about?"

Stoker looks at me and smiles. Just a good old boy on his neighbor's front porch, dropping by to say hello. Sure. The brim of his hat cuts off the late-afternoon sun, putting his eyes in deep shadow. "Just a few details I need cleared up. Couple questions. Won't take long."

"Oh. Okay, come on in."

He nods his head as if I just asked a question. "Yeah. No, the thing is, it'd be better if we did this at the office. I've got some reference material there, didn't bring it with me. You don't mind, right?"

I blink. Reference material. Implying some sort of police database he needs to access, something he can't do in my house. It sounds very reasonable and I know it's a complete and utter fabrication.

"Sure," I say brightly. I grab my jacket, step outside, then close and lock the door. I can feel his eyes on me the whole time, that focused attention you give a perp when you think they might abruptly do something stupid. I've done it myself, more than once—

I give my head a little shake. *I've done what?*

"You all right?"

"Fine. Just a little dizzy."

We go out to his car, where he apologizes for making me ride in the back and makes a little joke about it. I pretend to laugh. Then we drive the few blocks to his "office."

It's a small town, so we don't have much of a police station. It's got an open-plan reception area up front and a locked door at the back. Behind that door are four small, thick-doored rooms that serve as cells; I know, because I've spent the night there. I don't even bother to act surprised when Stoker unlocks the door at the back and motions me through.

But apparently I'm wrong about the number of cells. When Stoker opens door number four, it shows me a slightly larger room, one with two chairs bolted to the floor and a table between them. I take a seat without being told. Stoker closes the door softly behind him and sits down across from me.

"Interview room, huh?" I say. "Didn't know you even had one."

"Had it put in recently. Got Bill Johnson to convert one of the cells. Gave me a good price on the drywall."

I nod. "Yeah, Bill does good work. Charlie got him to fix up that room over his garage."

Stoker doesn't reply to that. He's studying my face, my body language, trying to get a read on my mood. I don't bother trying to fool him—I've never been that good an actress.

I lean forward. "This is the part where you ask me, 'Jace, do you know why you're here?' "

"And do you?"

"Sure. You want me a little shaken up, a little intimidated. You know I have a tendency to motormouth, so you're going to encourage that. You'll be deliberately obtuse about what's going on, because my guesses will tell you more than asking direct questions. How am I doing so far?"

He just shrugs, which makes me chuckle.

"Here's what I think," I say. "I *am* shaken up. I *am* intimidated. You can see that, right? But not because I've done anything, or seen anything, or know anything. It's because I'm an ex–mental patient with documented authority issues, I forgot to take my medication today, and I just saw a really gruesome dead body. I'm not doing so well, okay?"

"Okay."

"So quit playing cop games and just ask me your damn questions. I don't have anything to hide except maybe the fact that I'm kinda nuts—no, wait, you already *know* that—so whatever this is about—"

"Maureen Selkirk is dead."

Where did that brick wall come from? I swear it wasn't there a second ago, and then . . . I blink, trying to process what he just said. "Who is what?"

"Maureen Selkirk. I believe you spoke to her and Father Stone shortly before he died."

"How—how did she die?"

"The same way Stone did. Technically."

"What's that mean?"

"It means she asphyxiated. Boy selling chocolate door to door found her in her living room with the power cord from her air conditoner tangled around her neck. She had it mounted up high, above her door."

"And you think—" I stop, swallow with a suddenly dry mouth. "You think I had something to do with it?"

"Right now, it looks like some kind of freak accident. But

we're still investigating—and you were apparently the last one to talk to Selkirk and Stone, according to the witnesses I've been able to track down. Mind telling me what you said?"

"Nothing. I mean, they invited me to attend services with them. That was about it."

"Uh-huh. Can you be a little more specific?"

I'm about to deliver a zinger out of sheer reflex—*What, you want me to identify the church? It's that pointy building with the oversized dinner bell mounted on the roof*—when I realize that's *exactly* what he's asking.

Not just which church. Which *religion*.

He stares at me calmly. I stare back. *Sheriff Stoker is second-in-command,* Cassiar said. Which means that with Longinus/Ahaseurus dead, I'm locked in a room with the current head of a cult dedicated to making my existence one of eternal suffering and despair.

And he wants to know if Stone and Selkirk spilled the beans.

"This Sunday," I hear myself say. "They invited me to services this Sunday. I told them I'd try to make it, but no promises."

He nods. "That all they said to you?"

"That's all I said to them. Then I made my excuses and left, because frankly I had no intention of showing up."

I'm thinking furiously while trying to look bored and impatient. *Internal power struggle? A schism in the Cult of Let's Bedevil Jace? Someone staged a coup and Stone and Selkirk sided with the wrong faction?*

If so, the prime suspect was sitting right across from me. Stoker kills the cult leader and assumes the mantle; Selkirk and Stone are murdered because they supported Longinus. So where does that leave me?

That depends on whether they still need me or not. If they do, they won't kill me. If they don't, I'm an expendable loose end.

"Have you seen Ahab Longinus lately?" Stoker asks.

"Who?" I say, trying to sound confused—and believe me, it isn't hard. Stoker's using a classic interrogation technique, hitting me with one revelation right on the heels of another, not giving me time to think. "I mean, who gives their kid a moniker like Ahab? Was his family Welsh or something?"

Now it's his turn to look confused. "Welsh?"

"I'm sorry. I should have said, 'from Wales.' "

He tries to recover. "Longinus. Lives at the edge of town in that big, ancient house?"

"Sorry, don't know the man. It is a man, right? 'Cause people will name their daughters anything these days. I met a kid the other day who, I swear, goes by 'Lumina'. I asked her if she was the two-door or four-door model and she just gave me a blank look."

"He seems to be missing."

"How can you tell?"

He frowns. He's lost control of the interview and isn't sure how to get it back. I don't give him the chance, either. "Who reported him missing, is what I'm asking."

"He hasn't been reported missing. His neighbors are concerned, that's all."

"Which neighbors?"

He ignores the question, which tells me there aren't any nosy neighbors—just someone very familiar with Longinus's basement and what goes on there. "Longinus spent a lot of his time with Selkirk and Stone. Did they ever talk to you about him?"

"No. You find Jimmy Zhang yet?"

"No. You have any ideas where he might be?"

A number of possibilities pop into my head—root cellars, the local graveyard, somebody's old fridge—but I keep them to myself. "Afraid not."

"He's probably out of town," Stoker says. "Turns out that broken window was just an accident; display fell over, is all."

He waits to see if I argue with that. Because he knows as

well as I do that even if that steam cleaner did somehow manage to launch itself through a plate glass window, the big red puddle he found in the back room of the grocery store wasn't from a broken ketchup bottle.

I smile. "Oh, good. A perfectly innocent, reasonable explanation. I thought there'd be one."

"There usually is," he says softly.

We regard each other silently for a moment.

"I'm just a wee bit worried about you, Jace," Stoker says at last. "All these events must be difficult for you."

"Definitely. I was really close to that steam cleaner. Oh, the times we had—"

"So I think it might be best if you took it easy for a while. Stay home. Watch TV. Relax." *Don't make trouble and keep out of my way.*

"Funny, that's exactly what I was going to do. Thanks for the reminder." *I'll do whatever I want and you can go to hell.*

He gets to his feet. "I'll take you home. Drop in on you from time to time, make sure you're doing all right." *I'm watching you.*

"Thanks. I appreciate that." *See previous comment.*

I stand up. "Okay, then. Let's go."

He takes me home. The minute his car is out of sight, I turn around and leave. Not so much because I've got someplace to go as because I hate being told what to do.

The sun's pretty low on the horizon.

I head for the diner. I don't work tonight, but it's familiar and well lit and presumably safe. If Zhang decides to attack me there, at least I can throw some garlic salt in his face.

The diner isn't open twenty-four/seven, and in fact closes every day between two and four; people who want someplace to sit down on their coffee break head over to the hardware store, where Don Prince always has a pot on that time of day. It's close to five now, so the first of the dinner crowd will be filtering in any minute. I step inside and look around—only one of the booths is occupied, but all I can see is the back of someone's head. I take a seat at the counter and call out, "Therese? Got a hungry customer, sweetie."

No answer. Must be in the john or out back. I don't bother calling out for Phil; I don't need him snapping at me right now.

"She's not here." Phil's voice, surly as ever. Not coming from the kitchen, though—he's the one in the booth. That's a little weird; he doesn't like to sit out front with the customers. Usually, he takes his meal breaks in the kitchen.

"Oh," I say. "Well, can I get you to make me a grilled cheese? I'm starving."

I expect him to either complain about me interrupting his break or give me a chilly silence while he complies, but he doesn't do either. Instead, he laughs.

"You want me to make you a meal? Sure. I'd be *happy* to."

Uh-oh. I turn to look at my boss.

He looks just like my boss usually does—no fangs, no red eyes, no sudden eruptions of fur. He's wearing a long, stained cook's apron and has a cup of coffee in front of him.

But somehow, he seems different.

"But first, we should talk. Okay?" he says. He smiles and motions me over with a friendly nod of his head.

I get to my feet, slowly. He waits, patiently. Not threatening, not menacing, just waiting. Trying to keep my paranoia under control, I walk over and sit down on the other side of the booth. He's probably just going to fire me, which is why he looks so cheerful.

He studies me for a second. "Jace—how long have we known each other?"

"Well, I've been working here for about four months—"

"No. Before that."

"I guess I didn't really know you before that."

He shakes his head, still smiling. "No, of course not. Why would you? It's a small town, there's only one restaurant, you like to eat out . . . we must have run into each other hundreds of times, don't you think?"

Where is he going with this? "I'm sorry—I don't understand."

"Did you grow up here, Jace?"

It's a simple question. And after a long, confused moment, I realize I don't know the answer.

When he sees the look on my face, he nods. Still smiling, but looking a little more . . . satisfied. "Ah. You don't remember. I myself cannot remember when I got here, though it seems as if I've been here forever. But before I was here, I was . . . nowhere. My childhood, my youth—all a mystery. But I only realized this in the last few days. It was as though there were some sort of mirrored barrier in my mind, one that not only blocked any attempts at recall but deflected even the idea of trying."

He falls silent, staring at me intently. It's the longest speech I've ever heard out of his mouth, and it doesn't sound like him at all.

"You said, 'were'. Does that mean this barrier is gone?"

"Not exactly. It has become less substantial, though, more like a thick veil than glass. I can sometimes pierce it if I concentrate hard enough—it is weakening, I think. For the longest time, though, there were only two memories that came through clearly."

"What—what were they?"

"The first was falling," he says. His voice is hard, deliberate. "Falling endlessly through infinite space, between distant and unknown constellations. Plummeting into a vast, frozen silence."

"Wow. Sounds like you grew up on a space station. Or fell off one." I try to keep my own tone light—there's an intensity in his voice I don't like.

"The other was you. Jace Valchek. The Bloodhound."

"That's—that's just a TV show—"

"No. It is who you are. It is *what* you are. It has been hidden from you, just as my true identity has been hidden from me. But as I am clearly the stronger willed of us, I have regained my self-awareness first."

I swallow. "That's, uh, terrific. I'm glad you're clearing up that whole invisible-amnesia thing—"

"Surely you have recovered some of your memories, too?"

I hesitate, not sure how to react. According to Azura, my memories *have* been tampered with, though she didn't say anything about other people. Maybe Phil can help me get my brain working right again.

"I might be remembering a few things," I hedge. "Like . . . this town isn't quite what it seems to be. Know what I'm talking about?"

He makes a dismissive gesture. "This town is not important. It is a distraction, here only to occupy our attention. We are all that matter."

Phil's gone from cranky to arrogant; I can't say it's an improvement, but I don't feel like arguing with him. "Let's say you're right. Why us, Phil? Why are we so important?" I already know the answer to why I'm here, but I'm hoping his newly inflated ego will insist he talk about himself.

"I was wondering that myself," he says. "And then an old acquaintance dropped by and altered my perspective. By *we*, you see, I mean more than simply you and I. There is at least one other in this banal little village who is more than he seems."

And then the capillaries in his eyes begin to get bigger. The veins widen as they fill, spreading like a bloodstain soaking through paper. In seconds both his irises are a bright crimson, and when he speaks I can see how his incisors have gotten longer and sharper. "*Jimmy Zhang.*"

He's so fast, I don't even see him move—but suddenly he's got a hand wrapped around my throat. "It's really a shame," he hisses, "that you're so blithely ignorant of who you truly are. You're like a tiger that's been declawed, defanged, and blinded. Killing you will afford me little pleasure."

He grins, showing me just how long his new fangs are. "But I'm going to anyway. . . ."

NINE

I'm dead.

I know I'm dead. He's got me. I can't believe I'm not even wearing a crucifix—I could have *made* one in about thirty seconds with two pencils and a rubber band. But no, I had to have my emotional meltdown and abandon Charlie with all our monster-hunting gear, then throw my rebellious little hissy-fit after Stoker dropped me off. God, I'm so stupid I *deserve* to die.

Which is good, because I'm about to.

"I know *exactly* who I am, Ms. Valchek," my erstwhile employer says. "My name is Hondo Isamu. I am *oyabun* of the Sapporo yakuza clan. I am one thousand, four hundred and seventy-two years old, and in all that time no one has caused me more displeasure than you and your cohorts."

Cohorts? I have cohorts? Some part of my brain that isn't slowly dying from a lack of oxygen is gibbering at me frantically. I really wish it would slow down, because I can't understand most of what it's saying. Something about screaming eskimos?

"I am a patient man," Isamu says softly. "To kill a hated enemy once they are in your power is not something that should be done in haste. I would much prefer to kill you by inches, over many months. But I find myself trapped in a strange place, without access to my usual resources. Thus, I shall restrict myself to getting the necessary information from you to escape. Answer swiftly, and you will die the same way."

He favors me with another smile. "But you shall refuse, of course. The Bloodhound is not so easily broken. My inquiries will be met with your usual jibes, and I will respond accordingly. Though much less verbally."

He tosses me aside. One handed, off balance, and seated, he still manages to lift me out of my seat and pitch me over the counter eight feet away with little discernable effort. I think he was aiming for the counter itself—which would have really hurt—and actually misjudged his own strength.

I sail across the Formica and smash into the wall just below the pick-up window—hitting hard enough to make the order bell give off a tinny little ring—before falling to the floor behind the counter. I'm a little shaken up and my shoulder hurts, but I don't think anything's broken. Yet.

There's a mop in a bucket beside me. I grab the handle of the mop and use it to haul myself upright, pretending I'm more hurt than I actually am. I'm not surprised when Isamu lands on the counter in front of me as agilely as a cat. I keep a firm grip on the mop.

He grabs me with both hands—by my shirt this time—lifting my feet off the ground. "You disappoint me, Bloodhound. I remember you being quite the wit." He actually pauses, waiting for my reply.

"Please don't kill me," I whisper.

His lip curls in disgust. "Can it be? As much as I detest you, I must admit that I always held your fiery spirit in high regard. To kill you now seems . . . unworthy. I want you to perish cursing my name, Bloodhound. To die as the warrior you are, not some pathetic waitress. Perhaps you need further encouragement. . . ."

He throws me again, this time back toward the booths.

I land on top of a table and smack my head against the wall pretty hard—but the mop stays in my hand.

Pain throbs through my skull. My shoulder aches. He's not going to stop until I'm unconscious, and then he'll rip open my throat and gorge himself while I bleed out.

The *fuck* he will.

There's a steel post jutting up from the corner of the booth, with a few metal pegs near the top to hang coats or hats from. I get a firm grip on the mop's handle and swing it as hard as I can at the post, the point of impact just above the mop's head. Thankfully, the bucket was half full of water and the mop head is soaking wet; the weight adds enough kinetic energy to snap the wooden handle near the bottom. Dirty suds spray through the air and spatter against the counter.

Now I have a spear. A *wooden* spear.

The booth tables are bolted to the floor, so they're nice and sturdy. I get to my feet on the tabletop, holding my improvised weapon in both hands. From his perch on the counter, Isamu grins at me. "Ah. Does the Bloodhound bare her fangs at last?"

I shift my grip, spreading my hands farther apart. I bring the mop handle down and my knee up, snapping the handle into two equal lengths. I drop into a combat stance, one in each hand. "*Now* I've got fangs. And they're a lot longer than yours, Yak-boy."

I'm back.

It's that sudden, and that complete. I know who I am. I know where I came from. I know who my friends are, and who Isamu is.

But most of all, I know what I can *do*.

A little voice is talking in the back of my head. But it isn't whispering *You must be crazy* or *This isn't really happening* or *You're out of your depth*. In fact, it isn't whispering at all. It's too *gleeful* for that.

And what it's saying is: *Please do something stupid please do something stupid, please please PLEASE leap toward*

me like a big, overconfident moron so I can introduce a
stake to your left ventricle while you're still hanging in mid-
air like an idiot balloon.

Hello, brain. I missed you.

But Isamu doesn't do that. He just jumps down from the
counter, then unties his apron and pulls it off. He's wearing
a blue Mickey Mouse T-shirt underneath. "Come on, then,"
he says, gesturing. "We shall see if you are as formidable as
you believe yourself to be—"

I run.

Well, *jump* might be more accurate. And not toward
Isamu, either; I'm traveling over the line of booths, using the
tops of the seats and the tables as stepping stones. Staying
on the high ground, but forcing Isamu to either follow or try
to block me. I know how fast pires are, but Isamu—*this* version of Isamu—is newly minted; despite his claims of remembering exactly who he is, he's still getting used to his
increased abilities. The two conditions contradict each other,
sure, but that's how magic usually *works*.

Hello, magic. I still hate you.

But at least I *understand* you. Okay, not really, but enough
to know a few basic guidelines—including that different
realities often have different magical rules. For instance, in
Thropirelem lycanthropes have no problem with religious
items like holy water; in fact, the Catholic Church is mostly
made up of thropes. I asked about that once, and nobody
could give me a satisfactory answer; the best guess was that
once there were more supernaturals than human beings, faith-
based weaponry was no longer effective against creatures of
the night.

But according to Azura, this world doesn't *have* its own
thropes. Or pires.

I get to the end of the booths. Isamu, as I expected, keeps
pace with me. We're in the corner now, where there's a little
alcove formed by the dead jukebox and the far wall.

"I'm going to turn you into what you fear and hate most," Isamu growls. "A monster, just like me."

"Yeah? Cross your heart?"

I bring the two sticks together into a very familiar shape. Isamu's reaction is everything I hoped for: he howls, throws his arms up as if blinded and staggers backward into the little alcove. "Noooo!" he screeches. "What—what are you *doing*? What *is* that? *Keep it away from me!*"

I hop down from the table, forcing him even farther back. I know that the instant my two sticks stop forming a crucifix he's going to attack. I know he's about to shove the jukebox out of his way or try to leapfrog right over me. I know he's much faster than me.

And because I know all these things, I don't hesitate.

The jagged end of the first stick goes into his right eye. The other stabs into his chest, sliding under the breastbone and directly through his heart.

On Thropirelem, a pire's body instantly becomes its true age, either rotting away or crumbling into dust. I'm not sure how things work here, but I'm a little surprised when Isamu bursts into flames. I step back, leaving my improvised *escrima* sticks where they are.

"*Escrima*," I say to myself softly as I watch Isamu's burning corpse slump to the floor. "Not screaming eskimo. *Escrima*."

Then I get a fire extinguisher and put out the flaming heap of bones that used to be my boss. I consider making a bad pun about him being the one getting fired, and decide I'm above that sort of thing.

Besides, Charlie isn't here.

I remember Thropirelem. Not everything, but . . .

I remember watching crowds of drunken thropes partying in the streets during their monthly celebration while I drank scotch on a rooftop patio under a full moon.

I remember babysitting a three-month-old pire baby and feeding her bottles of pink milk.

I remember swing dancing with a golem in a pin striped suit and stealing his fedora halfway through.

I remember pire businessmen wearing smoked goggles, calfskin gloves, and full face masks as they strolled through the financial district at high noon.

I remember when my dog-were would turn into a paunchy, middle-aged man when the sun went down, and how he still liked to lick people's faces.

I remember all the people who have tried to kill me, or worse.

I remember my partner.

I remember the man who loves me.

And I decide I should really go see him before I do anything else.

Jimmy Zhang is still lurking out there somewhere, and it's full dark now. I don't care. I find a broom in the back and do the same thing to it I did to the mop, then hide the pieces in the sleeves of my jacket. If Zhang jumps me, he's in for a big surprise.

It's strange how empty the place is. This time of day I'd expect to find Mayor Leo, Joe Silver, or Don Prince here, at the very least. I wonder where Therese is.

I wonder where everyone is.

The streets are empty, too. I look up into the sky and realize that a huge, dark mass of clouds has bloomed there like a malignant growth. Kansas thunderstorms can be loud, drenching, violent things, and I really don't want to get caught outside in one.

Sure. Except I've never been in one before, have I?

I stop for a second, dizzy with cognitive dissonance. I can clearly remember many such storms, the sound of the rain hammering at the roof and walls, the ear-splitting crack of the thunder, the veins of lightning sparking across the sky. I'll bet those memories are real enough; they're just not *mine*. Stolen by Ahaseurus from some other Jace, I'll bet, and stuck in my head to convince me I was someone I wasn't. If Ahaseurus weren't already dead, I'd kill him all over again.

I hurry toward the B&B, keeping a wary eye out for Zhang. When I knew him, he was the head of a Chinese Triad based out of Vancouver and a powerful shaman; I had no idea what abilities, if any, he retained in this world.

I charge into the house without knocking and sprint up the stairs. The door to Cassiar's room is closed; I pause, then knock. "Dav—Cassiar? Are you there?"

"Just a moment." There's the sound of a lock disengaging and the door opens. Cassiar looks at me quizzically. "Ah, Ms. Valchek. How are you—"

I grab him and kiss him.

When you do that to someone, there's always a moment of shock. Most people freeze up. Then they respond, either negatively or positively.

Cassiar's reaction is . . . cautious. Willing, but tentative. More polite than passionate.

I break the kiss, pull back, and study his face. He blinks at me, clearly nonplussed. I sigh and slip past him into the room.

"That was . . . unexpected," he says, closing the door. "Jace, are you—"

"I'm fine," I say. "The question is, how are you? Or rather, *who* are you?"

"I'm exactly who I said I am: David Cassiar. I can show you identification—"

"Your name isn't Cassiar, it's Cassius. Your memories have been tampered with, just like mine. You're not a monster-hunter, you're the head of the National Security Agency on an alternate world. And a centuries-old vampire."

To his credit, he doesn't try to edge closer to the door. But he doesn't abruptly straighten up with a surge of realization, either. Instead, he studies me carefully, then glances to the side with a look of consideration on his face. "That's an intriguing scenario," he says. "Can you provide me with some hard data for corroboration?"

Damn it, that's *exactly* what Cassius would say.

"We had a relationship?" he asks.

"Yes! What do you remember—"

"That's deduction, not recall. Attractive women rarely show up at my door and throw themselves into my arms without good reason." He smiles. "Tell me more."

"Okay. Here goes." I sit down on the edge of the bed, hoping he'll join me, but he stays on his feet. Not a good sign. I take a deep breath, and then try to sum it up for him in a way that won't sound completely schizophrenic. "You and I are from a parallel world. You're my boss and my lover. The head of the cult you're tracking? He's actually a sorcerer named Ahaseurus. He kidnapped both of us and brought us here, mainly to torture me. Everything you said about the Gallowsman is still true, but the reason Longinus—Ahaseurus, I mean—picked *me* as his victim is because he well and truly hates me."

"I see. And why am I here?"

"Bait. See, you were on Ahaseurus's trail when he captured you. He wanted me to come after you, which I did—but I didn't have any more luck than you did. He tampered with our memories, so we're not even aware of the cage he's put us in."

He nods. "If I were the head of the NSA, I would have access to considerable resources, wouldn't I? It's difficult to believe I would let myself be trapped like that."

"You were off the grid. Hunting Ahaseurus for me, not the NSA. He was the only one who could get me back to my native reality—I'm not from the same world as you are. I started having weird dreams, which were you trying to contact me from *this* reality. That's the last clear memory I have. I don't remember what I did to find you, or how Ahaseurus captured me. But I do know that most of my memories of this town are false; I didn't grow up here, I'm not even *from* Kansas."

"And you know this how?"

I tell him about Azura. And my magic TV. And my fry cook boss who's really a vampire yakuza gangster, or was until I killed him with a mop handle. It sounds crazier and crazier, until even I'm having a hard time believing it. "Look, I know how it sounds. I know that the simplest and easiest explanation is that I'm just nuts, a delusional woman with an elaborate fantasy. But you *know* the Gallowsman is real. You said you've seen evidence that pires and thropes — sorry, vampires and werewolves—used to exist on this world. Is it so hard to believe someone might have found a way to bring them back?"

He's quiet for a moment. Thinking. "No, it isn't," he finally says. "Until now, I suppose I've always thought of the supernatural in terms of less physical dimensions, like the astral plane or spiritual realms. But actual, concrete, alternate realities . . . It's a lot to take in. I'm willing to consider that what you say is accurate, but there's one point I'm having trouble with."

My heart sinks. "Which is?"

"You say you've recovered your true memories—"

"Some. Not all."

"Why haven't I?" He shakes his head. "I'm sorry, Jace. I don't feel as if my life has been a lie, or that I've ever been anyone other than myself. A life which includes, by the way, a considerable amount of time spent in direct sunlight. If I were truly an ancient 'pire,' as you say, how could that be? Wouldn't a being as old and presumably experienced as that be harder to fool?"

I hate to admit it, but he's got some good points. And so far, none of them are on the ends of his teeth. "I needed a powerful emotional shock to wake me up; I thought the same might apply to you."

"Ergo the kiss."

"Yeah. It was worth a shot—believe it or not, I used the same trick to save your life once. And as far as the sunlight thing goes . . ." I touch the back of my head and wince. "Both the pires I've encountered so far seem to have been human until recently. Maybe that's my unreliable memory, too— but I don't think so. They both *acted* like newbies, like they weren't used to their new abilities and limitations yet. But at the same time, they were clearly recovering older, suppressed memories."

"An interesting contradiction."

It's not the only one, either. What I don't tell him is that Azura claimed Ahaseurus only brought a single pire and a single thrope across the dimensional divide with him: the master vampire and the alpha wolf, supposedly to create more like them.

Which suggests the master vampire is Cassius.

He's definitely masterly, and I know he was in Ahaseurus's clutches. But that's actually a vote *against* the idea— because, as Cassiar himself just said, a pire as old and cunning as he supposedly is would be difficult to brainwash. I've been inside Cassius's mind, and I know how formidable his mental prowess is; the only reason I was ever able to slip past his defenses was due to highly unusual circumstances.

"I don't know what the answer is," I admit. "The rules seem to be different here, too. On the *real* Thropirelem, there's no such thing as a 'master' vampire. I guess after centuries of propagation, whatever control the first pire exerted over those he turned got so attentuated it just faded away. But this place seems to have different supernatural restrictions. . . ."

An idea occurs to me. A very simple, obvious idea. I let my hands droop down, so both my improvised stakes fall out of my sleeves and into my hands. "Tell me, Mr. Cassiar, what do you think of . . . *this!*"

I bring both sticks up sharply, one across the other in a cross shape.

Cassiar stares at them. At me. Then he takes a step closer—and makes the same sign with his own arms.

"I think," he says gently, "that I'm not a vampire."

I sigh and lower the stakes. "Well, the lack of horrified screaming would seem to support that point of view. . . ."

He lowers his arms. "Your theory has some holes in it, it would seem."

"It's not a *theory*. It's like—" Something Azura said comes back to me. "Illusion spells. Azura said I was surrounded by illusion spells. Which means *everything* is suspect. Maybe you're not Cassius after all. You could be some kind of decoy."

"That makes it even more difficult—if not impossible—to prove what you're saying. If you can't trust your memory *or* your senses, what's left?"

"Thanks," I say bitterly. "I really needed to hear that right now. Of course, that doesn't mean there's any actual connection between what I'm hearing and what's actually being said. Or done. Or *anything*. For all I know, I'm just a brain in a jar, watching movies through the wires stuck in my cerebral cortex."

"In that case, I must be in the jar next to you."

"Terrific. Maybe we can admire each other's lobes."

I press my palms against my forehead. "No. No, I'm not going down that path again. Reality is more than just a concept. I'm here, I'm *me,* and I'm going to figure a way out of this mess."

"I'm sure you will. I'll help in any way I can."

I look up. "Charlie. I need Charlie. I left him with you—did he say where he was going?"

"To his bar. But Jace . . ." Cassiar pauses. "If I'm not who you think I am, then who is Charlie supposed to be?"

"My partner," I say as I stand. "Come hell, high water, or the apocalypse."

I stride toward the door. "Don't go anywhere. I'll be back."

I've got a little time to think as I walk from the bed and breakfast to the Quarry. About the cage I'm trapped in, and how many levels it might have.

Level One: Insanity. If I think I'm crazy, it makes me doubt everything I do, every decision I make. Slows me down, makes me less effective.

Level Two: False Memories. Everything I thought I knew about myself, my surroundings, my friends and enemies: all suspect. Hard to make deductions based on false data.

Level Three: Illusion. A combination of Levels One and Two. Can't trust appearances or events; more doubt, more unreliability, more confusion.

Level Four: Deliberate Manipulation. This is the level where Ahaseurus was going to get all his jollies. He could tweak any situation, any encounter, for maximum effect. Make me think my enemies were my friends, my friends my enemies. Fire up my paranoia, press down on my despair, and take my psyche out for a spin. He could have constructed all sorts of scenarios designed to hammer my emotions into any shape he wanted.

But not anymore.

I'm starting to think he must really be dead. If there's one thing the organized type of serial killer needs, it's control: control over his victim, control over the media, control over those hunting him. I can't see any reason for Ahaseurus to give that up—yet here I am, in more-or-less full possession of my faculties once more.

But then I think of what Isamu said to me: *I want you to perish cursing my name, Bloodhound. To die as the warrior you are, not some pathetic waitress.* Is that what's going on? Is Ahaseurus going to pull some last-minute switch, let me have some sort of carefully planned artificial victory, then step out of the shadows and laugh at me?

An even worse thought follows that one. Has he *already* done that? How many times? Am I just trotting through the maze for the hundredth go-round, my memories wiped each time I get to the exit? *Groundhog Day* as psychological torture porn?

It doesn't matter. Even if the game is rigged, I still have to play; I still have to win. There's no other option. The real question is: Who are the other players?

Who *is* Charlie Allen?

Charlie Aleph, I know. He's my partner, my enforcer, my best friend. He's three hundred pounds of black volcanic sand poured into a human-shaped plastic bag and animated by the spirit of a long-dead Tyrannosaurus rex. He's a streetwise, sarcastic war vet with a gift for police work, a lethal throwing arm, and a love for the clothing styles of the 1940s. He's a hell of a dancer.

But that's the Charlie of Thropirelem-the-World. The Charlie I know here is . . . what?

Human, for one thing. Sarcastic, definitely. Also a war veteran. His sense of style is drastically different from the lem I know, and I have no idea if he dances like Fred Astaire or Pee-wee Herman.

But I trust him. And Azura. Again, I'm going on nothing but gut instinct . . . but right now, that seems to be the most reliable source of information I've got. And if I'm wrong, I am so totally, completely hooped that nothing else really matters.

I get to the Quarry. I pause outside, looking around. I haven't seen anybody on the streets. Maybe they're all inside, dressed in black robes, with a big banner that reads SUR-PRISE! adorned with bunches of skull-shaped balloons. Sure, why not.

I open the door and step inside.

The place looks the same as it always does. It's not

completely empty—there are a few farmers at a back table, and the local plumber at the bar nursing a beer—but no crowds of bad guys lying in wait. Charlie's behind the bar, talking to Bob, his relief bartender. Bob's nodding and grinning, and Charlie's shrugging while he talks, a "what are you gonna do?" look on his face.

I walk up and take a seat. Bob spares me a slightly curious glance, nods, then walks to the far end of the bar and starts slicing up some limes.

"You all right?" Charlie asks in a low voice. "I thought you were going to hole up at home."

"And I thought I was going to grow up to be a ballerina who lived on the moon. Life's full of disappointment."

"Seriously, Jace, you're in real danger out on the street—"

"Oh, you have *no* idea. And don't ever, *ever* let me catch you using the phrase 'at least things can't get any worse.' "

I bring him up to speed. Stoker's interrogation. Isamu's attack. Me realizing who I really am. Cassiar and what I told him.

When I'm finished, he reaches under the bar and pulls out a bottle. No label, more dirty than dusty, metal screw top. He slides two shotglasses over, opens the bottle, and fills each of them to the top. Whatever it is, it looks like water and smells like tractor fuel. He downs his with a grimace.

"Is the other one for me?"

"No." He downs the second shot, then refills both glasses. "These are."

I slam the first one down. It's sort of like setting yourself on fire, then jumping into the Arctic ocean. Intense pain, then everything goes numb. I take advantage of the anesthetic effect to down the second one which makes it all the way to my stomach before detonating. By then the first one has eaten through my throat and most of my spinal column, so the pain never makes it to my brain.

"Ack-*Ack-ACK*," I say.

"Yeah, that's the usual reaction." He stares at me moodily. I don't know *which* mood, exactly, but there's definitely a mood going on. "So. You're not . . . you."

"Sure I am. In fact, I'm *more* me. The me you know? That's *me,* except less neurotic and more homicidal."

"I'm not sure that's an improvement."

"Okay, badly phrased. Let me put it this way: I have the same values, the same sense of humor, the same temper—but more confidence. Less self-doubt. I *know* who I am and what I can do, and I don't give a damn what other people think."

"You never did," Charlie says softly. "No matter what they said about you. Even when you were doubting yourself, you didn't pay much attention to other people's opinions. One of the things about you I always found . . . I dunno. Intriguing, I guess. How you could be so strong willed but so paranoid at the same time."

"Well, now you know the answer. Congratulations—you're at least a thousand points and a bonus round ahead of me."

He shakes his head. "I don't think so. I've been keeping up so far, but—what exactly are you saying? That the whole *town* isn't real? That none of us are? 'Cause I gotta tell you, I don't *feel* like an illusion."

"That's not it," I say wearily. "It wouldn't be as satisfying to Ahaseurus if it wasn't real. It's just that some things have been . . . altered, I guess. Changed to fit whatever twisted script he's written for me."

"Okay, so how do we figure out what's been changed?"

I think about that. "I'm . . . not sure it's *we,* Charlie. I think it's just *I.* I can recognize parts of my own history that have been woven into this place, but you don't have anything to compare against. Except—well, apparently, with Ahaseurus dead, the spells are going to start unravelling."

"Unravelling? Like a sweater?"

"Yeah, like a sweater. A big, magical memory sweater, knitted by pure evil."

He frowns. "Knitted by pure evil? I'm having a hard time with that concept."

I sigh, and put my head down on my arms. "I know. Not one of my best."

"I mean, I know this is a bad situation. I know it's serious. But *knitted by pure evil*? My brain doesn't know how to interpret that. It's trying, but—"

"Knitting. Grandmothers. Rocking chairs."

"And kittens, playing with yarn. You ever try to imagine evil kittens? Or evil yarn? I think I'm getting a headache."

"You've already got one. Its name is Jace Valchek."

"That's funny," says a voice behind me. "I've got a pain with the same name, only it's not in my head."

I glance over my shoulder. Terrance. Just what I need. He's wearing a leather motorcycle jacket over a grease-stained T-shirt, but—despite what he just said—he doesn't seem as cocky as usual. "Hey, Valchek," he says. "Got a minute?"

"Got a whole bunch. You can't have any."

"Geez, lighten up, okay? I just need to ask you a quick question. In private?" He gives me an "aw, c'mon" look; I'm always amazed at how many jerks think they can just flip a switch and suddenly you're supposed to forget all the times they abused you.

But right now, I need all the information I can get, and Terrance coming to me for help is an interesting development in and of itself. I slide off my bar stool and walk over to a table. "Sit," I say.

He does. Now he looks troubled, and more than a little unsure. "It's about my brother," he says.

"The doc? What about him?"

"Well—"

And that's as far as he gets, because the door opens and Sheriff Stoker strides in. He heads straight for Terrance.

"Terrance Adams," the sheriff snaps. "On your feet, son. You're under arrest."

Terrance is staring at Stoker in complete confusion. "What? What for?"

"Suspicion of murder, Mr. Adams. Now are you getting to your feet or am I going to help you?"

Terrance gets up. Stoker handcuffs him briskly and professionally, then marches him outside.

Charlie and I stare at each other.

"You know, you're bad for business, too," Charlie says.

TEN

I figure it's time to gather the troops—such as they are.

Right now, the only person I really trust is Charlie, but I can't afford to turn down Casssiar's offer of help. Charlie's already arranged for Bob to fill in for him. We jump in Charlie's car, drive over to the B&B, and get Cassiar. Then we head for Charlie's place.

We pass the diner on the way. The lights are out, the closed sign on the door. With a chill, I realize that someone must have found the burned corpse that used to be my boss—and instead of calling the cops, had shut down and locked up the diner instead. Was Zhang in there right now, red eyes peering out from between the blinds at us? Or had someone else cleaned up, the same way Charlie and I had cleaned up at the Longinus house?

I glance at Charlie, who gives me a grim look in return. He's thinking the same thing I am, but he isn't sure what to say in front of Cassiar.

Charlie's place is a double-wide trailer at the end of Third Street, with a gravel pad for a yard. I've been here before, but never really felt comfortable inside; Charlie keeps the place to a military standard of cleanliness and order, which seems unnatural to me. The kitchen and bathroom are so clean it's like he's never used them . . .

I didn't tell Charlie who he was to me. Or what. It seemed easier to leave that part out, somehow—along with all the myriad details of life in a world where only one percent of the population was human. It'd just be information overload.

We weren't *there,* anyway; we were *here.* And *here* had enough problems of its own, thank you.

Charlie's living room is sparse and utilitarian: a sofa, a coffee table, two armchairs. Two walls are taken up by bookcases, and he has an ancient stereo with a working turntable and numerous stacked milk crates filled with records: jazz and blues, mostly, with some Latin stuff, too. That fits neatly with the memories of *my* Charlie—only the music of Thropirelem rarely matched up with the music of my world. Different species might produce similar technologies, but cultural variance guaranteed their art would be highly divergent.

I realize I'm lecturing myself, a habit from my early days as a federal agent—a trick I used to pump up my confidence. It was an activity that corroded over time, becoming less about recalling information and more about making cynical observations, but I guess I feel the need for the reassurance of hard facts; in some ways, this is just like getting out of the academy. I have to prove myself all over again.

Charlie offers us beers; Cassiar politely declines, and I gratefully accept. Charlie gets them while Cassiar and I choose seats. He opts for the end of the couch, and I take an armchair. Charlie hands me my beer and picks the other armchair.

We study one another in silence for a moment.

"Okay," I say. "Here it is in a nutshell. This town is going to do its best to try to kill us. Oh, it might only cripple me, since its ultimate purpose is more about making me suffer than expire, but you two are definitely going to die. Charlie, you were my partner. Cassiar, you were my lover. I'm not stupid; I can practically see the bull's-eyes painted on your foreheads. I say we get in Charlie's car, *right now,* and get as far away from this place as we can. Sound good?"

"And then what?" Charlie says. "I live here, Jace. I own a business. I can't just . . . run away."

"Sure you can. And Cassiar, you've only been in town for a few days. There's nothing stopping you from leaving, right? Why don't we just relocate to wherever it is you live and consider this problem from a safe distance?"

Cassiar nods. "That would seem to be the most prudent course of action," he says. "But before we leave, I have to ask you one question."

"Go ahead."

He spreads his hands. "What good is a trap with an open door?"

"You don't think we *can* leave?"

"I think we need to find out."

"He's right," Charlie says. "There's only one road in and out of town. Should be easy enough to check."

"Then let's do that," I say. "Right now."

"I'm not sure that would be wise," Cassiar says. "What if the safeguards that prevent you from leaving are lethal to those close to you?"

Damn it, he's right again. Just like Cassius—always two steps ahead. "So trying to escape with either of you could result in your death? Yeah, that sounds like exactly the kind of nastiness Ahaseurus would have set up. Which means I go alone."

"No way," says Charlie. "Not safe. Jimmy Zhang's still out there, remember?"

"Oh, I'm not going alone," I say. "But you two are staying here. You still got that streetsweeper?"

Charlie nods. "Yeah, but I don't see it doing much good against a vampire."

"Oh, it won't. In my experience, guns are useless against the supernatural. Ammunition, on the other hand . . ."

Charlie leaves the room. He comes back with a shotgun in his hands—specifically, a Mossberg Over/Under and a box of shells. I ask him for some tools, a funnel, and a few other odds and ends.

"This has to be the strangest load I've ever assembled," I mutter as I tinker. I put Charlie to work helping prepare the contents, while Cassiar watches from across the room.

"Something's just occurred to me," Cassiar says, getting to his feet. "This local boy you told me about on the way over, the one that's just been arrested. He can't possibly be the Gallowsman—and since Stoker is a member of the cult, he knows that. So why arrest him at all?"

"Good point," I say as I work. "But I don't see how it's relevant. Terrance seems to be a proxy for someone in my life named Tair, a homicidal thrope I helped put behind bars. His being arrested here mirrors what happened on Thropirelem."

"But it still makes no sense," Cassiar insists. "I think we should investigate further."

"Go right ahead," I say. "But me, I'm getting the hell out of Dodge."

"If you can," Charlie says.

"If I can," I admit. "But I won't be gone for long, Charlie. I'll come back. Azura and I will figure some way to defuse this. I'm not—"

"Abandoning me?" He shrugs. "I should be so lucky. . . ."

Charlie lets me use his car. I bring the shotgun with me.

There's only one road out of town, the one that connects to the highway. I take it. I see a few people on the streets as I drive, though most folks seem to be indoors; it's not that late, but Thropirelem tends to be pretty quiet after dark. The thunderstorm overhead is still threatening to break loose.

Dark, empty fields on either side. Two-lane blacktop, the occasional flash of lightning, and me. I think less about where I'm going than where I've been.

So I'm Alice, and this is the other side of the looking-glass. A distorted, warped version of my life, with familiar faces playing new roles. A remake, I guess. Can't say I'm a fan, so far.

Certain patterns seem to hold true, though. Charlie's my main ally. My dog's really smart. Cassius is an authority figure with vital information at his fingertips, and Tair's a jerk in trouble with the law.

Those are my friends—all the friends I can remember, anyway—and Tair's more of a part-time ally than a friend.

Then there are my enemies.

Isamu. Zhang. Maureen Selkirk, whom I knew as Maureen Selkie, an Irish witch with a talent for shapeshifting magic and a member of the terrorist group called the Free Human Resistance. Father Stone, whom I encountered as Brother Stone, a suspect in a series of bizarre murders.

I suddenly realize something. My clearest recollections are of people who are now dead: Stone, Isamu, Selkirk. My memories of Zhang are murkier, almost dreamlike. Must be Ahaseurus's spells, eroding. Makes sense, I guess; with the subject of the illusion gone—and no one to reinforce it—the spells are dissipating on their own.

That's not why I remember Charlie and Cassius and Tair and Galahad, though. It's because they're all important parts of my life, in ways both good and bad. Bad guys come and go, but some people will always stick around. Whether you want them to or not.

Patterns, patterns, patterns . . . what else holds true? Well, both Zhang and Isamu were pires, and both of them became neckbiters here. But Cassiar's not a pire, and Charlie's not a lem. Is Terrance a werewolf? Possible, but unknown. Maybe that's what he wanted to talk to me about—

There's a flashing orange light in the middle of the road.

I slow down, then stop. A traffic barricade straddles the blacktop, and on the other side there's a two-foot drop onto rough gravel. I can see the hulking shapes of roadwork equipment, backhoes and steamrollers and dumptrucks, plus a number of construction trailers. The sign on the barricade reads ROAD CLOSED just to make sure I get the point.

I park and get out of the truck. Study the situation. As I'm standing there, a door opens in the nearest trailer and a man walks out. Big guy, dressed in dirty orange coveralls, work boots, and a yellow hardhat. He's got a large mug in one hand, giving off steam, and he carries it carefully so as not to spill it.

He walks over and stops just short of the barricade. Looks at me with about as much expression as a prison guard.

"Evening," I say.

"Evening." He doesn't sound happy to see me. He's got a square, blocky face and the name JOE stitched over his right breast.

"Didn't know there was any roadwork going on out here," I say.

"Yes, ma'am. For some time now."

"Looks extensive."

"Yes, ma'am."

"Is there an alternate route to get to the highway?"

"Not that I'm aware of."

"Kind of inconvenient."

"I suppose."

"I guess I could just walk across the fields."

"That's not a good idea, ma'am."

I smile. "Why not?"

"Storm coming. Lightning strikes are a definite hazard."

At that precise moment, an immense blue-white bolt rips out of the sky. It smashes into an oak tree with a sound like the Jolly Green Giant hitting a home run with a telephone pole and a bowling ball, splitting the tree in two; both sides crash to the ground a few seconds later. The afterimage of the strike is burned into my retinas, a jagged glowing ghost I try to blink away; flames flicker redly at the base of the tree.

Joe takes a sip from his mug. "See?"

I nod. "Uh-huh. Yes, yes, I do. Think I'll head back into town, now."

"Probably a good idea."

I head back toward the truck, then turn back. Joe's still watching me, over the rim of his steaming mug. "You always wear a hard hat after hours, Joe?"

"Safety first," Joe says.

Looks like leaving isn't an option. I spend a minute wondering if that applies only to me, or if other people can come and go, then drop it—it doesn't really matter. There's nobody else on this world I can go to for help, anyway. This is my fight.

But at least I have allies.

My phone lets me know I have a call. It's Cassiar. "Jace, are you still within town limits?"

"Yeah. And for the forseeable future."

"Then you should come down to the police station. I've talked to a deputy here, Mr. Silver, and he has some interesting information."

"I'll be there in a few minutes."

I pull up in front of the police station, but don't go in right away. I'm still thinking about patterns; they're always—*always*—the most important factor in solving a case. What's bothering me right now are all the ways things are almost-but-not-quite matching up.

If Azura is right and the only other people Ahaseurus brought to this dimension with him—other than me—are one pire and one thrope, then who are all these other people that seem to be from my life?

Fakes, I think. *Real people, but not supernatural ones. Human beings with implanted memories hidden inside their*

heads, little ticking time bombs. Until they get bitten by the
genuine article—at which point they become incredibly
strong, very hard to kill, and remember just how much they
hate me.

Except some of them don't, right? Some might be poten-
tial allies. But I don't know which are which . . . and therein
lies the fun.

But the worst part of all, the part I don't want to think
about, is the single, most obvious, glaring fact of all.

Charlie Aleph, my partner, is a golem. Not a pire, not a
thrope. Ahaseurus didn't bring any lems with him—so this
Charlie is just another fake. And knowing Ahaseurus, he's
probably the most dangerous trap of all.

So why do I still feel like I can trust him?

I shake my head, then get out of the truck. I can't explain
why I feel this way, I just know that I do. And at this point, I
have to trust someone.

Deputy Silver must have been waiting for me, because
he steps out and hurries down the steps to meet me. "Jace,"
he says. "Hi. I think we should talk."

I let him steer me down the sidewalk, away from the
station. "Where's Cassiar?"

"He left. Said he had some things to get. Said you'd understand."

I probably do. I've got a shotgun, but I'm sure a monster-
hunter like Cassiar must have a few survival strategies of his
own up his sleeve. "What's going on, Quinn?"

Silver looks troubled. "I don't know, Jace. Two deaths in
twenty-four hours is bad enough, but . . . things are getting
worse. You heard we arrested Terrance Adams for murder?"

"I heard something about it, yeah."

"But I don't know *why.* We don't have a case—or if we
do, the sheriff won't talk to me about it. Keeps saying he has
his reasons, but won't explain. I tell you, it don't make any
sense." He pauses. "Thing of it is, he's got an alibi, a pretty
damn solid one. Sheriff says he's lying, but I can't see how.

So when this Cassiar fellow came by and asked to talk to the boy, I thought I'd let him, just to see what would happen."

"And what did?"

Silver frowns. "Sheriff just about blew a fuse. Told me nobody was allowed to see him until he gave the say-so, not even a lawyer. Then he threw this Cassiar out—but not before he threatened to arrest *him*, too. It's not like the sheriff to act like this, and I just can't figure it out. Mr. Cassiar said you might be able to shed some light on it."

Me? I'm dumbfounded. Why the hell would Cassiar dump this in my lap, then disappear? What, am I supposed to bring Silver into our little counter-conspiracy? And why would Cassiar think I was any more credible than he was? Not that anything in our story is even remotely believable, anyway. . . .

I give Silver a brilliant smile. "It's actually really simple. Sheriff Stoker has . . . a secret." I pause.

"A secret?"

"Yes. Haven't you noticed how *private* the man is?" I'm making this up as I go along, which feels a lot like tap-dancing on a high-wire while wearing a blindfold. "How he comes and goes sometimes with no explanation? Mysterious errands and so forth?"

"Well . . . come to think of it, he has been kinda withdrawn lately. On edge, too."

"Uh-huh. Exactly. Well, Terrance knows what's going on. And he's threatening to spill the beans all over the cat he's going to let out of the bag." I'm on a roll now. "So the sheriff's trying to convince him otherwise. Get him to see reason, show a little discretion, clam up. Understand?"

"Not really. What's this big secret he's trying to cover up?"

"Oh, I can't tell you that. Are you trying to get *me* locked up, too?"

He looks at me like he can't decide which one of his legs I'm pulling, and how hard. I drop the smile and stare back impassively.

"Look," I say in a low voice, "don't take my word for it. Do a little checking around—especially on the connection between Stoker and Old Man Longinus. You'll see what I mean."

"Longinus? What's he got to do with—"

"That's all I can say." I hope it's enough; I want to get his interest, but not tell him anything that could get me locked up. Having a cop on our side would be one helluva plus—if nothing else, it might help keep Stoker off our backs.

My phone chimes and I quickly dig it out, glad of the excuse to end the conversation. I'm hoping it's Cassius, but it isn't. It's Gretchen Peters, the librarian. *Wait. Librarian?*

"Hello, Miss Valchek? I've been looking through the town records, and I've uncovered some very unusual facts. I really think you should see them." She sounds a little nervous. "And as quickly as possible."

"I can be there in a minute."

"That's fine. The library is closed, but I'll unlock the door. I'll see you shortly." She hangs up.

I've walked a few steps away from Silver, the way you do when you've taken a call on a cell phone, and now I just keep walking as I hang up. "Gotta go!" I toss over my shoulder. "Remember what I told you!"

"But—" he says. I'm already halfway across the street.

The door to the library is open, just like she said it would be. I pull it open and go in.

My brain is trying to get my attention. Something about Gretch. *Gretch? That seems awfully chummy. Since when do you call Miss Peters Gretch? She can hardly stand you.*

Most of the lights in the library are off, but I can see a dim glow coming from the end of a long aisle. I head that way.

I don't think I've ever been in a library after hours. It's a little unsettling, having a mundane, normally well-lit environment turned into something full of towering shadows. The passage seems awfully narrow, the shelves pressing in on me from both sides; I become uncomfortably aware that someone one aisle over could be watching me over the tops of the books. Someone could even reach through that gap with one long arm and grab me . . .

I make it to the far end without being ambushed. The light is coming from the open door of an office with a small plastic sign next to the jamb reading HEAD LIBRARIAN. I stick my own head in. "Gretch—uh, en?"

She's seated at a cheap chrome and fiberboard desk, with a green-shaded lamp on it spreading a pool of light. Beneath it is a large metal tube, three feet or so in length, with roughly the diameter of a Mason jar.

"Good evening, Miss Valchek," she says. "Please, sit down."

I pull up a plastic-framed chair and do so, feeling absurdly like I'm about to be reprimanded for smoking in the girls' room. "You sounded a little upset. Everything okay?"

"Yes, yes. Everything's fine. But what I've discovered—well, it's quite the find. I simply had to show you, straight away." Her face seems a little flushed, and her eyes are practically shining; the look of an academic who's successfully stalked and captured a prize piece of information.

I point at the tube. "I guess this is it?"

"Oh, yes. Just wait until you see." She unscrews the cap on the end and carefully extracts a long, rolled-up piece of paper. Parchment?

She unrolls it, using four felt-padded clamps to secure it to the edges of the desk. I peer at it curiously. "What exactly am I looking at?"

"A very old map, Miss Valchek—can I call you Jace? Yes, a map made when this town was barely more than a few log cabins and tents. Hardly anything here at all . . . which is why this is so fascinating."

It looks to me like someone's gone to the trouble of marking out a bunch of streets, far more than you'd need in a settlement this size. Thinking ahead, I guess, or maybe just someone with grandiose ideas.

But then I notice something else: The streets aren't exactly straight, nor are they arranged in an orderly grid. Some of them seem to run right through existing buildings. "Wait a minute," I say softly. "These aren't streets—"

"No. They're *tunnels.*" I can almost taste her excitement. "Very, very old tunnels. In fact, I believe they were already here when the town was founded."

I study the parchment a little closer. There are numbers marked here and there, and I realize they must be depth indicators. There are other marks, too, that I can't decipher—but I recognize them just the same. They're in the same unknown language Longinus's book is written in.

Déjà vu surges through me, but not because of the symbols. It's this situation: sitting in a room with this woman, studying vital yet arcane information. I know I—*we*—have done this before. "Any idea why the tunnels are there? What they were used for?"

She glances up, her eyes bright. She doesn't seem quite so spinsterish any more. "That's the intriguing part. They approach almost every structure in town—gathering places, residences—including the sites of buildings that didn't exist yet."

"So, a way to travel undetected from house to house? Secret entrances in basements, that sort of thing?"

"You'd think so, but no. They almost always stay below the level of the foundations, and when they do near the surface they skirt the buildings instead of going under them. It's as if whoever roamed those tunnels wanted to be in close proximity to the residents, but not *too* close."

I see what she means; the tunnels snake around Thropirclem like an invisible anaconda, but I don't see any places where they intersect with the upper world.

Except one.

I tap the paper. "Look. The tunnel dead-ends right here. And the depth marking is only eight feet; that's shallow enough to connect with a basement."

She leans over to look herself. "I believe you're correct. How odd that I didn't notice that myself . . ."

It's funny, how smells can trigger memories. When she bends her head, some stray air current in the room carries a trace of her perfume to me. I remember it well, because I asked about it once and Gretch told me she had to have it imported from a little aromatherapy shop in London. . . .

Gretch.

I remember.

"I'd like to describe someone to you," I say. "Someone I think you may know."

Her head is still down as she peers intently at the map. "Mmm?"

"She's one of the smartest people I've ever met, an intelligence analyst for the National Security Agency. Born in London. Dry, razor-sharp wit. She has a child, Anna, whom she loves more than existence itself. She'd kill for Anna—in fact, she has. I was there."

No reaction. She doesn't even look up—but she's suddenly very, very still.

"The father of her child was killed by a lunatic who nearly killed Anna, too. I prevented that. We've had a special bond ever since, which is probably why I'm Anna's godmother.

"That woman's name is Gretchen Petra. She's a vampire. She's *you,* Gretch."

"I know," Gretch says softly. She raises her head and smiles at me with two long incisors. Her eyes are as red as blood. "But that's who I *was,* Jace. Not who I *am.*"

And then she has me by the throat.

ELEVEN

I can feel my trachea trapped between Gretch's fingers and thumb, her fingernails cutting into the skin of my throat. It's a hold that can let her rip out my windpipe with one quick squeeze and pull, a very professional immobilization technique. Not the kind of skill possessed by most librarians.

"Glurk," I say. I can still breathe, but just barely. I grab her wrist with both hands, more from reflex than anything else. She has me cold.

"Eloquent as always," she says. She *sounds* like Gretch, too, that combination of quiet amusement and self-assurance. "You have no idea how much I missed that. Which is to say, not at all."

"Guh?"

"Oh, don't sound so bewildered. You don't really think I ever found you witty, do you? I'm British, dear girl. Your japes were never anything to me but the crude vulgarity of an unsophisticated and ill-tempered brat."

"Nuh!"

"But I suppose I do owe you a debt of thanks. If not for you, I would never have known *this* world, never have known the freedom it confers. Being a pire here is very different,

Jace; it's stronger, wilder, less cerebral. My blood is practically *singing*. I must confess, I feel a bit giddy."

She looks it, too. I've never seen Gretch drunk—though pires on her world can and do consume alcohol with the aid of a little sorcery—but she's definitely under the influence of something. I know what, too.

She leans across the desk, pulling me a little closer. "I feel like I could do *anything*," she whispers. "I could tear off a man's head and bathe in the spray of his arteries. I could kill an army. I could conquer a *world* and drink the blood of its *children*."

I believe her. Unrestrained by moral boundaries and with no real supernatural opposition, Gretch could probably turn this whole planet into her personal blood bank within a generation or two. Welcome to the new British invasion.

"You have no idea how *glorious* it is, Jace. My chains have been broken, my soul released; I'm free of the cloying morass of petty human considerations like compassion or pity. No inhibitions, no restrictions—"

I let go of her wrist with one hand. I give her a look that says, "Yeah, but . . ." and hold up my index finger.

She frowns. Emotional repression, when finally released, produces emotional lability; she's riding high right now, but look out for those mood swings. "Oh? Very well, then—tell me what one thing still holds me back."

She releases my throat, letting me talk. I gasp, then stumble back a step. It's a temporary reprieve, I know; Gretch is at least as dangerous as Zhang or Isamu. Probably more so, because she's smarter than either of them. And she's fast enough to take me down before I get anywhere near the door.

I take a second to get my breath back, then say, "Precon—" *cough* "—preconditions."

"*What* preconditions?"

"You're not here to rule the world, Gretch." My voice is hoarse and it hurts to talk. I keep going, though, because it's the best weapon I have right now. "You're a booby trap. Sorry."

Her frown deepens. I don't have to explain it to her—all I needed to do was stall out her emotional surge, then point her in the right direction. I just hope that Ahaseurus's spells have degraded enough to let her mind become aware of them; her own ferocious intellect should take care of the rest.

"My . . . consciousness has been tampered with," she murmurs. "I'm not *whole*. Access to memories is incomplete. Emotional responses have been significantly altered. . . ."

NSA training on Thropirelem—the *real* Thropirelem—includes anti-brainwashing techniques. Gretch helped develop some of them. Right now she's evaluating how bad the damage is, attempting to isolate the worst of it with psychic firewalls, and activating deep-structure mnemonic repair protocols—

"Oh, dear," she says mildly. "That's a shame."

"What?" I manage.

"I hate you."

"No, you don't. You just think you do—"

She gives her head an impatient shake. "No, you don't understand. I really, truly, do hate you. I'm incapable of doing anything else. My entire emotional baseline has been subverted and slaved to that one response. Quite an impressive job, really. I hate you so much I'm incapable of killing you. Making you suffer is far more important."

"You—you can beat it, right?"

Her smile returns. "I'm afraid not. But there is good news: I'm not actually *me*. I'm a crude imitation, created through stolen memories implanted in a woman only recently turned into a pire. I can't tell you by whom, though; those memories are missing as well. You're absolutely correct about me being a trap: I'm here to make you doubt yourself, make you hesitate in crucial situations and/or wallow in guilt. Instead, I'm going to give you a single word of advice."

"Which is?"

She opens a drawer and pulls out a pencil, then meets my eyes with a steely glare. "*Don't.*"

She stabs herself in the chest.

With perfect precision, of course. The pencil slides under the breastbone and directly into her heart. Her body bursts into flames, just like Isamu's did, and she slumps forward.

Onto the map.

I'm so horrified that I just freeze up. By the time my brain kicks into gear, it's too late; I manage to find a fire extinguisher on the wall, but by then the map is gone. Whatever makes vampires self-immolate in this reality, it generates a lot of heat in a very short period of time.

Once I'm sure the fire's out, I go out into the darkness of the library. I slump down at the end of a row, put my head in my hands, and let the tears out.

I know it wasn't really Gretch. I know she did the best, smartest thing she could have. But right now, I don't care; I *miss* her. If anyone could have found a way to get me out of this damn place, it was her, and now she's gone.

Congratulations, Ahaseurus; guess this round goes to you.

I go home. I'm tired and depressed and all I want is a bottle of scotch, my dog, and a little TV. If Jimmy Zhang is hanging around waiting for me, I'll get the chance to see how effective my improvised shotgun loads are.

But the only thing that greets me is my dog's excited barking. I go in, pack a bag, then take Gally out to the car and leave. As much as the comforts of home are calling, this isn't home. It never was.

I drive straight to Charlie's place.

He's already at the door when I jump out of the car. "No good, huh?" he says.

"No. See that storm cloud overhead? Apparently it's keeping an eye on me. I try to leave and I turn into a lightning rod." Galahad bounds out of the truck and follows me up the steps. "Cassiar talked to Terrance, and he's got a solid alibi the sheriff is ignoring. Deputy Silver verified it, and it's confusing the hell out of him. Cassiar back yet?"

"Not yet."

We all go inside. I toss my bag down on the sofa and dig out my DVDs. I probably only need the one, but I brought them all just in case. "Oh, and Miss Peters, the librarian? She showed me an old map of a tunnel system beneath the town she found in the archives. Then she grew fangs, threatened to take over the world, and killed herself."

Charlie looks at me blankly, then slowly shakes his head. "That's it. You're not allowed to go out anymore."

"Buckle up, Charlie. This ride's barely around the first curve. . . ."

I put the DVD in. I don't know if Charlie's TV will work like mine, but now's the time to find out. I go to the scene menu, looking for the one with the Sword of Midnight, and find a scene that wasn't there before: It's titled *Azura*, and has a picture of her face. I select it and hit PLAY.

The image fills the screen but stays frozen. "Azura?" I say. "You there?"

"Maybe she's in the john," Charlie says. He's eating an apple, which Galahad is regarding with the same kind of expectant admiration he shows all food. "Sorceresses do that, right?"

"I don't know. Let me check my recently unlocked memories for detailed information on magic and/or peeing and get back to you."

The image abruptly stutters and comes to life. "Jace! I was starting to worry."

"Starting? Better put it in gear, Blondie—you're about three crises behind on the it's-time-to-freak-out train." I let her know what's happened since the last time we spoke.

"Too bad," she says when I tell her about Gretch. "She could have been an important ally. But on that front, I have some good news."

"The last time someone said that to me, she committed suicide with a sharpened number two pencil. Don't do that, okay?"

"You have my word. I have a much better idea, anyway. How would you like a few old friends to drop by?"

"Oh, sure. Because the *last* person to visit really cheered me up—"

"I'm talking about the real deal, Jace. It's tricky, but it's still a lot easier to send a mental link across the dimensional divide than a person. I can manage three, in fact."

"Wait. Three people? You can put me in touch with three genuine, not-mentally-screwed-with people from Thropirelem?"

"Better than that. I can link those people to their counterparts where you are, put them in control. You won't be alone anymore."

I'm thinking hard. "Which three?"

"Well, they have to have a counterpart there, of course, so your friend Gretchen is out. I don't know everyone who's available, either—you'd have to choose."

Great. Azura doesn't know enough about my life to throw any names at me, and my memory's still too spotty to trust. I'll have to go with what I know. "Charlie, for sure. Cassius would be good, but I'm pretty sure he's already here—"

"I'll work on that. It might be possible anyway."

Who else? I try to think and realize I can only come up with one other name. "Tair. But he'll be playing for the other side."

"Mmm. A shame your Doctor Pete isn't there, instead."

"But . . . he is. He's Tair—I mean Terrance's—twin brother."

She gives me a "you're kidding" look. "Truly? That's somewhat inspired, from a purely evil point of view . . . Doctor Pete and Tair are a single being, Jace. Doctor Pete was your friend and a fellow member of the NSA, while Tair is—well, an altered version of the same man. He's the sorcerous equivalent of an alternate reality counterpart, a Doctor Pete who made some very bad choices early in his life. The ruthless criminal you know as Tair had much the same thing done to him as Ahaseurus attempted to do to you; his memory was manipulated with sorcery, giving him a history that never actually occurred."

A magic-induced multiple personality—but here, each personality had his own body. Twice as many chances for Ahaseurus to mess with me. Maybe I can make that work for me, instead. . . .

"Think you can link to Doctor Pete and not Tair? Bypass the bad and plug in the good?"

She looks doubtful. "It's possible, I suppose. You'll have to get him to cooperate, though, and things could prove somewhat difficult on this end. The real Tair—the one that's still here, not there—is in control of the original body, correct?"

"From what I remember, yeah. And that body was in jail."

"Oh, good. I haven't broken into a jail since the last time we got together."

"Sounds like fun. Wish I could remember it."

"You will, Jace. You will."

"Uh, excuse me," Charlie says. "Did I hear right? The plan is to take some other guy's brain in another dimension and plug it into mine? 'Cause I gotta say, I don't know how I feel about that. Oh, no, wait, I do. No goddamn way."

Uh-oh. "That's understandable," Azura says. "In fact, that's exactly what Charlie Aleph said you would say. So he told me to convey a private message from him to you. Jace, would you back away, please? And Charlie, would you lean in close to the television, as if I were going to whisper in your ear?"

I shrug and do as she asks. Charlie looks a little more hesitant, but he steps forward and bends down.

There's a brilliant white flash.

Charlie hurtles backward and lands on his back on the coffee table. It's a sturdy thing, made of thick, polished wood, and it doesn't collapse.

"Aaah," Charlie says. His eyes are unfocused, but he blinks a few times, then sits up.

"Charlie?" I say. "You okay? Azura, what the hell did—"

"The message," Charlie says, "was real simple. *I know you'll never go for this, you stubborn gorilla, so let me explain it to you from the inside of your skull.* I think he got it."

"*Charlie?*" I repeat.

"Yeah. Hey, toots, nice to see you. Man, is this what it's like to be made out of meat? Feels *weird.*" He pokes at his own face with a forefinger.

"*CHARLIE!*" I whoop, and tackle him.

Okay, it was meant more as a hug, but we wind up tangled together on the floor with me on top. I push off him and look down at his face with undisguised glee. "*Damn,* sandman, am I glad to see you."

He glares up at me. "I can tell. I've had genitals for all of thirty seconds, and you're already kneeling on them."

I roll off him and spring to my feet. "This is fantastic! Charlie, you—"

I stop. Charlie's still flat on his back, and his eyes have rolled up in his head.

"Charlie? Charlie, that's not funny. Get up, or I'll show you what it's like to have shins, too."

"*Jace,*" Azura says, her voice urgent. "He's not pretending. Something's gone wrong with the link—I think it's the difference between lem and human minds, I don't know—"

"Fix it!"

"I'm trying, but—I need your help, Jace. If the link breaks up, we could lose both their minds between dimensions."

"Tell me what to do!"

"Kneel down. Cradle his head in your hands. Yes, just like that. We're going to do something similar to what you and I did when we accessed your memories of a man named Gibby. Do you remember?"

"What? No!"

"It doesn't matter, I'll guide you through it. We're going to access a powerful memory of Charlie's, one that will resonate at a deep emotional level. It'll act as an anchor, bonding his mind—temporarily—with that of Mr. Allen. Just close your eyes and repeat the words I say."

I close my eyes, concentrating on her voice. She starts to speak, alien words with odd syllables, first gutteral then sibilant. I've always had a good ear, and I repeat what I hear as exactly as I can.

The darkness behind my eyes begins to swirl, and then I'm someplace else.

It's 1962. My name is Amy Jorgunsen, and I'm seventeen years old. I know this because Charlie knows it, and he knows it because Amy just told him. He's sitting across from her in a booth in the Olde Tyme Soda Shoppe, dressed in his neatly pressed army fatigues. He is exactly two months old.

"So," I say, taking a sip of soda water. "I always kind of figured you'd be green."

Charlie looks confused. "Green? Why?"

"My brother has these green plastic army men. You're sort of made from plastic, and you're in the army."

"Oh, I get it. No, I'm kind of special. They call me an enforcement lem. Black volcanic sand instead of the regular kind. And I'm charged up with something unusual, too."

"What?"

"The spirit of a dinosaur. *Tyrannosaurus rex*—you know what that is?"

"Sure. One of those big meat-eating ones."

"You sure all you want is a soda water? I could buy you a malted or even a sundae. I don't eat myself, but I hear they're pretty good."

I shake my head. "No, thanks. This is about all I can have, really. Have you seen the menu?"

I point at the sign over the counter. A, O, and AB blood-shakes. Blood ice cream in flavors ranging from porcupine to baboon. Sundaes with anticoagulant syrup.

Charlie frowns. His smooth, glossy black face looks different, somehow—even though lems don't age the way humans do, he still seems younger. More innocent. "Don't they have anything for nonpires?"

"Why should they? The whole town's gone pire. That's why my family moved here in the first place."

I hear snickering behind me, and glance over my shoulder. It's a group of local teens, every one of them pale skinned and red eyed. They're looking at me with the malicious pleasure teenagers get from singling out the isolated and vulnerable. Charlie gives them a hard stare and they shut up.

"You got any nickels?" I ask him. "They've got some good dance songs on the jukebox."

When he nods, I get up and pull him to his feet. He joins me at the jukebox, though he protests he doesn't know anything about music or dancing. I tell him I'll teach him; my father taught me when he got back from the war.

Like all new lems, he learns fast. By the second song he's got the fundamentals down, and by the third he's pretty good. It's swing music, of course, stuff that was popular twenty years ago. There's no rock and roll on the jukebox at all.

Afterward, we go for a walk. Even though it's well past sundown, the main street is lit up as brightly as a baseball stadium during a night game. Huge banks of lights on tall posts stand sentry on each corner, illuminating every square inch of ground.

"Those are some lights," Charlie says as we stroll.

"Aren't they? I hear they got them from a studio in Hollywood. They play recordings of birds, too. You know, to make it feel like it's really daytime."

The cars on the street are all at least ten years old: Studebakers, Chevrolets, Edsels. Men and women are dressed in fashions from the 1940s. I don't see anyone I recognize as a thrope or a human, though I do see a few more lems in army uniforms.

"So, is basic training as hard as I've heard?" I ask. "My father complained a lot about it in his letters."

Charlie shrugs. "I don't know. My sarge says I'm a natural. It comes pretty easy to me, but I don't have anything to compare it to."

We stop in front of a haberdasher's shop. There's a double-breasted dark gray suit in the window, with a matching fedora. "You'd look good in that," I say.

He studies it seriously. "Really? It seems sort of . . . expensive. I understand clothing that protects you, but other than that—"

I laugh. "You can't wear an army uniform all the time. Besides—what else are you going to spend your money on?"

Charlie looks thoughtful. "I don't know. Those nickels I put in the jukebox were the first time I ever spent money on anything. Other than your soda, I mean."

"Well, being generous is nice, but you're going to have to think of yourself, too, you know. You can't rely on other people to do that." My own voice sounds a little sad, but Charlie doesn't seem to notice.

"Amy, I was wondering something. Why did you want to do . . . well, *this* with me?" He sounds genuinely puzzled.

I smile at him. "Because we both stand out, I guess. You're the first black lem I've seen in town, and I'm practically the only human. The only one who isn't ancient, anyway."

"You think we're alike?"

"Maybe. I wanted to find out."

"And?"

"You're a pretty good dancer, but we've *got* to do something about your fashion sense."

He walks me home. I live in a little white house with a white picket fence—though the pointed tops of the boards have all been rounded off. We stop outside the front door. "That was fun," I say. "We should do it again."

"Sure. But I don't know when I'm shipping out—they say I'm going to a country called Vietnam."

"Well, call me if you get another pass," I say. "Or you can always write me from Vietnam, if you like."

"I'd like that."

I give him an impulsive kiss on the cheek. "Good night."

When I close the door, I vanish. These are Charlie's memories, after all.

The next time I see him is the following week. We dance some more. We go clothes shopping. We even get to spend a little daylight time together, when I sneak out of the house after everyone else has gone to bed.

We stroll down the middle of the street, hand in hand. Charlie's carrying a basket of food I packed. There's no one on the streets, and every window has its curtains drawn. Heavy steel shutters cover glass storefronts and doors, a barricade against the relentless sun. Post-apocalypse small-town America, before any decay has set in.

We spread a blanket on the grass of a small park, next to a statue of a Civil War general. The general's riding a horse and holding some sort of battle-axe.

I see the way Charlie keeps looking around, and chuckle. "Don't worry. We won't get in trouble. It's just that everyone's asleep."

Charlie shakes his head. He's wearing the suit I picked out for him, an olive green number with wide lapels. "Even your folks?"

I look away. "Especially my folks. They're both pires."

"But you're not. How does that work?"

"My dad got turned against his will by a rogue pire. My mom decided to join him afterward, so they could be together. My brother's older, but he decided he'd rather be a thrope. My parents weren't happy about that—they haven't talked to him since."

"So what about you?"

I shrug. "I'm just waiting until I get a little older . . . eighteen, maybe. Then I'll kick daylight." I lean back on my elbows, close my eyes, and bask in the sun. "I won't get to do this anymore, but it still sounds like a pretty good deal. Immortality, right? Never get old, never get sick, never have to worry about my figure."

Charlie doesn't say anything for a moment. "Aren't you afraid you'll . . . miss something?"

I laugh. "You mean like food? Sure, I guess. But they're doing all kinds of things with blood now. I heard they're even working on potato chips!"

"That's not what I meant. Human beings are . . . well, you're *complicated*. You change as you age. You have all this biology that affects who you are, what you do."

"And what would you know about human biology?"

I swear he looks embarrassed. "They teach us many things. If golems are going to live in this world, we need to know how other beings think and act."

"I'll bet they didn't waste much time on *us*, did they? Not much point." I don't sound bitter, more like amused. "We're almost obsolete."

"You shouldn't say that."

"Why not? It's true. Anyway, it's just another change—isn't that what you were just saying, that change is good?"

"But it's not change, Amy. It's stopping at one point in your life and staying there forever. All those things you get to avoid—maybe you shouldn't avoid them. I haven't been around long, but I've learned a lot since I came into this world. Both good and bad. And I know you can't just pick one and ignore the other."

I smile at him. "Wow. You're quite the philosopher, Charlie Aleph. I'm impressed."

He looks down. "You're a good friend, Amy. I just want what's best for you."

"Don't worry about me, Charlie. I'll be *fine*."

*   *   *

My POV changes suddenly. I'm looking out of Charlie's eyes now, as he reads a letter.

> *Dear Charlie:*
>
> *I miss you, and I hope you're okay. I watch the news about the war every day and worry about you.*
>
> *It was hard for me to write this letter. What you're going through is so much worse than my little problems that I feel guilty even telling you about them. But I promised you I'd be honest when I wrote, so you're getting the unvarnished truth.*
>
> *School has been bad. I still don't have any friends. I have to bring my own lunch because the cafeteria only serves blood, and somebody keeps stealing my food. I'll find it on my desk with a note on it saying* This is Disgusting; *or even worse, I'll find out everything's been soaked in blood.*
>
> *I get a lot of insults thrown at me, of course:* blood-bags *is the new favorite, replacing the old standby* snacky. *Lots of offers to turn me, most of them lewd.*
>
> *Even the teachers treat me like I'm some kind of idiot. I'm not stupid, I just find it hard to concentrate on trigonometry at 2 AM. The other kids don't have that problem, of course; they were all born pires. They'll keep aging, just like me, until their parents decide they're old enough and cancel the enchantment. But in the meantime, they're stronger and faster and tougher than I am.*
>
> *And they belong.*
>
> *I'm tired of it, Charlie. Tired of being on the outside. I get up at noon, when I'm supposed to be asleep, and just walk around the town. It's quiet and empty and lonely, just like me. I sure wish you were here.*
>
> *But you're not. You're out there fighting the good fight, and I'm stuck in Nowheresville, America. I kind*

of envy you; at least you have other lems around that
you can count on. I'm on my own.

I'm going to do it, Charlie.

I just can't wait anymore. I want to have friends, I
want to do what everyone else is doing. My parents
still want me to wait, but once it's done, what can
they do?

There's a boy at school. Not one of the ones who
bully me—he just watches. There's something in his
eyes . . . the bullies are all cowards; I don't think any
of them would actually bite me, but I think this boy
would. We'll see, I guess.

Please don't be angry at me. I hope I'll see you
soon.

Yours,
Amy

Charlie puts down the letter. He's in a foxhole. I can hear
an odd noise in the distance, multiple snaps followed by a
sort of low thrumming. I look up and see a thousand arrows
falling toward me, filling the sky. As they get closer, they get
bigger; they're the size of spears, then flagpoles, then lamp-
posts, tipped with triangular heads as big as traffic signs. In
a world without guns, this is what passes for artillery. They
slam to earth all around, a rain of timber that shakes the
ground.

Charlie ignores it. He reads the letter again.

I come back to myself, kneeling on the floor, Charlie's head
cradled in my lap. I almost expect to feel the smooth glossi
ness of plastic skin, but no; it's warm and hair-covered and
human, Charlie Allen as opposed to Charlie Aleph. But who's
underneath?

Charlie winces and sits up. When he turns to face me, I
know.

"You wondering what happened to her?" he asks.

"It's none of my business, Charlie."

"It is now. You gonna go traipsing around between my ears, you get the full tour."

"Fair enough."

"She did it, just like she said. Wouldn't tell anyone who had bitten her, just that it was her choice. Took her a while, but she made friends, got accepted. By the time she graduated, she was almost popular." He looks down.

"And then?"

"Then I did some traveling. Fought in a few wars. Came back to visit, now and again. Grew up a lot. She didn't."

I don't say anything, because I don't have to. I get it. Whatever Amy did with her life, whatever she became, part of her would always be a seventeen-year-old girl. An unhappy seventeen-year-old girl.

"I just thought it was a shame, you know?" Charlie says quietly. "Maybe it doesn't matter. Maybe it does. But I'll never know—and neither will she."

"You still see her?"

He shakes his head. "Not so much. Turns out we don't have a lot in common, after all. . . ."

TWELVE

"How are we fixed for weapons?" Charlie asks. He's on his feet, flexing his arms, studying them as critically as a swordsman would study a blade.

"Shotgun with loads that may or may not be effective. Some homemade stakes. Not much else."

He nods. "This Allen guy—he work somewhere?"

"Owns a bar in town."

"Good. He'll have something stashed there. Bar owners always do."

I glance over at the TV. The DVD player has turned itself off, and all I see is a blue screen. I try to get Azura again, but she isn't taking my calls—I can't get her face to come up on the scene menu. Guess she's busy on her end, too. "Wait a minute, Charlie. Aren't you in Allen's mind? Can't you just remember whether or not he's got weapons at the bar?"

Charlie shakes his head. "No can do, toots. I'm me, and he's him, and it don't look like either of us can peek through the other guy's window. Which is fine by me."

I sigh. So now that I've got my partner back, it turns out he's even more clueless about this place than I am, is unarmed, and can no longer bench-press a truck.

Damn, I'm glad to see him.

What Charlie *does* know, however, is a bunch of the stuff that's still locked up inside my head. "Okay, I'm assuming Azura briefed you. As far as allies go, Gretch isn't available. Cassius—called Cassiar here—is. Who else should we be looking for?"

"You got a guy named Eisfanger?"

That surprises me. "Yeah, kind of a computer geek. Albino, stays inside and online most of the time. I know him?"

"You're colleagues. He's a forensics shaman—could come in handy."

"Not here. Different reality, different rules. And I don't think he'd be much good in a fight."

"Tanaka?"

"Ex-boyfriend. Hates my guts."

"Nice to see you haven't lost your touch."

I glare at him. "I wouldn't know."

"Guess you'll have to take my word for it, then."

"Terrific."

We decide our best move is stay together, keep moving, and hit the bar for possible supplies. "If nothing else, we should be able to find something flammable," Charlie says as we head for the car. "Fire work against supernaturals here?"

"Not sure. Pires tend to burst into flames when they die, so probably."

"Probably," Charlie growls as he gets into the driver's seat. "That *ain't* one of my favorite words."

"Neither is *ain't*. Or it wasn't before. You used to be quite the philosopher, from what I saw."

"People change," he says as he starts the car. "Some of us, anyway."

I try to get Cassiar on my cell phone as we drive. It goes right to voice mail. "We need to meet," I tell him. "Call me back ASAP."

"He remember who he is?"

"No. But he's on our side, anyway. I think."

We pull up at the bar. "The Quarry, huh?" Charlie says, looking up at the neon sign. "I like it."

"Gee, what a surprise."

When we walk through the doors, we get another one: The place is full of faces I don't recognize. Big, rough-looking guys in denim and plaid, wearing muddy, steel-toed work boots. One or two are wearing reflective orange vests, and a few have hard hats on the table beside their mugs of beer.

"Uh-oh," I say.

"Situation?" Charlie asks.

"Not yet. . . ."

We walk over to the bar. Not everyone in the place is watching us, but more than one pair of eyes track our path. Charlie doesn't hesitate, just goes right around the bar and into the back. I follow. The relief bartender, Bob, is too busy to even notice us.

We do a quick search of the office. Sure enough, I find a loaded Glock in a desk drawer. "Huh," I say. "Never figured you for a Glock kind of guy."

"More like a rock kind of guy?"

"Watch it. You're stepping on my material."

There's a crash out front. Loud, angry voices. I look at Charlie and he looks at me. "There a back door out of this place?" he asks.

"Yeah, but Bob's out there. Bob's a decent guy. Not really fair to him—or the guy whose body you're wearing—to let the bar get wrecked."

Charlie shrugs. "Hey, for all we know Bob's really a mafia thrope who wants to eat your liver. But you're right: it'd be a shame to ruin a good bar."

I shove the gun in my belt and we go out front. There's an angry confrontation going on between a group of road workers and a knot of locals: I spot Don Prince, Vince Shelly, Ken Tanaka, and Brad Varney. They don't normally hang around together, but it seems like they've found some kind of common ground—ground that seems to be composed of the mud the road workers tracked in. There are a lot more road crew members than townies, but that doesn't seem to bother the townies. In fact, they seem almost eager to get the snot kicked out of them.

And then I feel it. In the air, all around me. More than just testosterone or adrenaline. Sorcery. I don't know how I can tell; I just can. And when I glance at Charlie, I can see that he feels it, too.

"Something's gonna blow," Charlie mutters.

Don Prince, the dapper, silver-haired Italian owner of the hardware store, is getting into a road worker's face. "You think can just walk in here and talk to one of us like that? You have no idea who you're insulting!"

The road worker—not Joe, but someone who could be his brother—stares down at Prince with a sneer on his lips. It might be a trick of the light, but his eyes seem to have a weird blue glow to them. "I know. I just don't care."

Brad Varney, the transvestite mailman, looks about ready to throw someone through a window. "Take it back," he growls. *Literally* growls; his voice has dropped at least two octaves and acquired a rumble.

"It's coming apart," I murmur to Charlie. "The spell." It's just intuition, but I know I'm right; this whole place is aimed at *my* head, after all. If it goes off the rails, I'm going to be the first one to notice.

The road workers' eyes aren't the only ones starting to look strange. There's a yellow tinge to Don Prince's, and his fingers are curled into claws rather than fists. Varney, always scrupulously clean-shaven, is looking a good twelve hours past a five o'clock shadow. Both Tanaka and Vince Shelly have their upper lips bared in all-too-canine snarls.

"This place won't last," the road worker says. "Not once the new highway goes through. It, and all of you, are just gonna fade away and be forgotten—"

That's when Tanaka cold-cocks the guy.

It's an impressive punch. By that, I mean it lifts the guy right off his feet. And through the air. And into the wall ten feet away. I remember what Mayor Leo's punch did to that dumpster, and by this point I'm pretty sure I know where he got his strength from.

The other road workers don't seem impressed. They're all grinning, and their mouths don't look quite right; a little too wide, a few too many tiny, sharp teeth. Their eyes are giving off that blue glow, too.

And then the fight kicks off with a roar.

Bodies fly through the air. Furniture smashes and glass shatters. Howls of rage and angry cursing compete for volume. The townies are badly outnumbered, but for four middle-aged guys they're doing all right. Bob hunkers down behind the bar, and I can't say I blame him.

Maybe Charlie and I should sit this one out. That'd be the smart thing to do. Let the two sides pummel each other for a while, then wade in and break things up. Maybe learn something from watching, or from whichever side we decide to help.

There are three things wrong with that plan. First, if this goes on for any length of time there won't be a bar left; second, it's the *smart* thing to do. My reputation would suffer.

Third, Tanaka's in the middle of it.

I shouldn't care. He treated me badly. He's the sort of ex who leaves you with a general mistrust of the opposite gender, and I don't owe him a damn thing.

Except I do.

I have to. Ahaseurus wouldn't have stuck him in here, wouldn't have made him part of the grand design, unless he meant something to me. Something that the wizard could twist and distort, turn into something ugly. Which means, by simple and brutal logic, that the jerk I used to date and now hate is more than likely a decent, honorable guy who I might have even been close to.

"Let's get in there and help," I snap.

"Sure. Which side?"

I demonstrate, vaulting over the bar and kicking a road worker in the belly. He doubles over, and I straighten him up with a knee to the face.

"Oh," Charlie says, and then he's right there beside me.

I could use the gun, I guess. Fire a few rounds into the ceiling, shout for everyone to stop. But I don't think that would work—both sides are in the grip of something elemental, the ferocity of a barroom brawl amplified by out of control magic. I can feel it myself: I don't want to shoot anyone, I want to *hit* them. Hard. Many, many times.

So that's what we go with.

The road crew obviously aren't human, but they're not pires or thropes, either. Some kind of demon is my guess, something Ahaseurus was using as muscle. He's employed both lems and zombies in the past, so demons shouldn't come as much of a surprise.

But they don't belong here, in the town itself. I know it and so do the four neo-thropes fighting alongside me. These mooks are just here to have a little fun while the boss isn' looking.

I smash a chair over one guy's head. It leaves me holding two chair legs, one in each hand, which suits me just fine. I'm trained to fight with batons. I proceed to demonstrate on anyone unlucky enough to be within six feet of me.

None of the townies have gone thrope. That means none of them have experienced their first full moon yet, and thus none of them are the alpha. At least I've figured that much out.

And then one of the demons decides to kick it up a notch. He's got one of those SLOW signs with him, the kind you usually see in the hands of a blonde in sunglasses and a hard hat—I read somewhere people are more likely to respond to a blonde directing traffic—and he starts swinging it like a club. Not much of a weapon, really, just a lightweight piece of sheet metal on a stick. He smacks Tanaka in the head with it, and about all that accomplishes is getting his attention.

The demon's grin gets wider. He turns the sign edgewise for the backswing, and aims a few inches lower. The strike is almost too fast to see.

There aren't many sure ways to kill a thrope or a pire, but decapitation is one of them.

In the frozen instant before his body slumps to the ground beside his head, I remember who Tanaka really was and what he meant to me. It's no coincidence—it's one of the spells woven into the fabric of this place, doing what it was designed to do. Make me hurt.

Kamakura Tanaka. Proud member of the last samurai clan in the world. Security liaison between the NSA and the Nipponese Shinto Investigative Branch, until he was forced to choose between his country and me. My first supernatural lover. An honorable man who betrayed his own beliefs, and never forgave himself.

I'm supposed to blame myself. And maybe, if the spell were working properly, I would—but it's not, and I don't. I know that's not really Tanaka, just someone with a head full of implanted memories. Probably not even real memories, either; the fact that Tanaka's already dead is a little detail I doubt I'm supposed to recall. Or maybe I'm supposed to believe this is some sort of second chance, that he's not *really* dead—but whoops, now he is.

The body hits the floor.

You'd think that somebody getting their head chopped off in the middle of a bar fight might have enough shock value to bring the whole thing to a halt, but no such luck. People continue to curse, punch, kick, and throw things. I've laid out more than a few demonic road workers, and Charlie seems to be doing fine with just his fists. And feet. And knees. And elbows. And anything else that comes to hand.

What does stop the melee is the roar of a gun.

Everybody freezes and looks toward the door. Sheriff Stoker and Deputy Silver stand there, Stoker with a double-gauge to his shoulder and Silver with a drawn pistol.

"That's enough," Stoker growls. "This is *my* town. Any of you think you're tough enough to take a load of buckshot to the chest?"

Apparently these demons aren't as invulnerable to harm as some supernaturals, because they all lower their fists or release whomever they're holding. The townies still look mad enough to eat razors and crap barbed wire, but they back off, too.

"They killed Tanaka!" the mayor says.

"Yeah?" Stoker replies. "Where's the body?"

I look down at the floor. Sure enough, both the head and the rest of the corpse is gone. There isn't even any blood.

Mayor Leo glowers at him, but doesn't reply.

"R and R is over," Stoker says, addressing the road workers. "I think you all have a better place to be, don't you?"

One of them steps forward with a slight smile on his face. "Sure. Okay. Thanks for the dance."

Without a word or a grumble, they grab their hard hats and file out the door in a straight line. Their faces all wear that identical slight smile, which is about as eerie as it sounds.

"The march of the wooden soldiers," Charlie murmurs behind me.

"Something tells me these guys aren't nearly as flammable, though," I murmur back.

Mayor Leo, realizing how absurd his claim is with no proof to back it up, strides up to Stoker and glares at him. "You're just going to let them go?"

"I've got more important things on my plate than bar fights and wild accusations. They'll go back where they belong, and so will you. Understand?"

Something passes between them. "Yes," Leo snarls. "And I hope you do, too."

He stomps out, Varney and Prince behind him.

"Why am I not surprised to see you here, Valchek?" Stoker says.

"Your surprise gland isn't responding to the medication?"

He sighs. "You going to tell me you saw a murder, too?"

"Not me. I was busy dancing."

"Uh-huh. Charlie, you might want to think about finding a different dance partner."

"I like this one just fine, thanks," Charlie says flatly.

"Well, I'm getting tired of the whole do-si-do," Stoker says. "Because every time I hear the music start up, guess who's first out on the floor. One Miss Jace Valchek."

"That's because it's all about *me*, Sheriff. Haven't you figured that out yet?" Still charged up with adrenaline, I spit the words at him—then realize I've gone too far. He stares at me with a new expression on his face as a realization of his own hits him. If, as Cassiar claims, Stoker's the new leader of the cult, then he knows exactly why I'm at the center of all his problems. But until this minute, he didn't know *I* know, too. Good job, Jace.

"What I've figured out," Stoker says, "is that maybe you need to stop roaming all over town looking for trouble."

"I've looked into having it delivered, but I can't find a rate I like—"

"Maybe a nice cell would firm up the decision-making process."

"I doubt that," I say carefully. "Trouble stalks me like an old boyfriend with OCD issues and a pair of night-vision goggles. You can lock me up, sure—but that just means trouble will have to go through *you* to get to *me*. Right?"

He thinks about it. I don't know how informed he is as to Ahaseurus's plans, but he has to know I'm basically cursed. Cursed in such a way that the collateral damage surrounding my immediate presence can get pretty lethal. Presumably he thinks he's protected against such things—the whole purpose of the cult is supposedly to summon the Gallowsman so that he and his friends are happy and safe while others suffer—but by now he knows something's gone terribly wrong.

"Let's take a little ride down to the station and discuss it," he says finally.

"Is she under arrest?" Charlie asks. His voice is very calm, which sets off all sorts of alarms in my head.

"Charlie, relax," I say. "Sure, Sheriff. Can we turn on the lights and siren, too? I love that."

Stoker lowers his gun. "We'll see."

I can see Charlie's vehicle through the back window of the police car, following us. I hope he's not planning anything stupid; he seems to have taken an instant and extreme dislike to the sheriff. That's not a good sign, but I don't have the chance to question him about it.

Sheriff Stoker doesn't have the chance to question me, either. We're only halfway to the station house when his radio crackles and the dispatcher tells him he's needed at the bed and breakfast. Immediately.

"What's going on?" I ask from the back seat.

"Don't know yet," he says tersely. "But at least for once *you're* not involved."

"Not yet, anyway."

I have a sick feeling in the pit of my stomach. I think I know why Cassiar hasn't been answering my calls.

We pull up outside the B & B. Stoker gets out but leaves me locked in the back. Deputy Silver parks behind us, and Charlie behind him. Silver follows Stoker into the house, and Charlie strolls up to the sheriff's vehicle.

"What's happening?" Charlie asks.

"Let me out and I'll tell you." He opens my door. "Stoker got a radio call to come here. That's all I know."

Charlie looks grim. "Look, about Stoker—"

Which is when we hear a hoarse scream.

We bolt for the house. Through the door, up the stairs, straight for Cassiar's room. Deputy Silver's standing at the top of the stairs, holding back Silas Bloom, who's pale and

shaking and saying, "Oh my God, oh my God, oh my God."
I realize it must have been him who screamed.

I can see the interior of Cassiar's room through the open doorway. There's blood—a *lot* of blood. And what's barely recognizable as a human form lying on the bed.

But it's not Cassiar. It's Therese Isamu, the wife of the pire I killed.

THIRTEEN

Therese Isamu. Real name Teresa, real identity the curator of the Human Achievement Museum. The sight of her corpse floods my mind with memories, followed closely by a surge of grief. *Get ahold of yourself. This isn't really her.*

No, it isn't. This is the woman who greets me at the beginning of every shift with a friendly smile, who gives me meals on the house, who loves dirty jokes. This is—was—my friend.

"What's going on here?" demands a voice from behind me.

I turn. David Cassiar stands on the steps below me, looking puzzled.

Oh, boy.

"That's a very good question," Sheriff Stoker says, stepping out into the hall and pulling the door shut behind him. "Mr. Cassiar. You and I need to speak."

"Certainly," Cassiar says. "Would you care to step into my room, since you've been inside already?"

"That, that, that," says Silas. He looks like he's about to cry. "That's Therese, isn't it? I mean, *some* of her, right?"

Stoker frowns. "Quinn, take Silas downstairs and get a statement, all right? Jace, downstairs and get back in the car—you and Charlie shouldn't even be present. Mr. Cassiar, I'm going to need to talk to you right here."

Deputy Silver escorts Silas down the stairs, past me, Charlie, and Cassiar. I stay right where I am, and Charlie doesn't budge, either. He climbs a step and whispers to me, though. "Jace. Let's go. I need to talk to you."

Maybe I should listen. Maybe I should do what I'm told. Maybe I should leave the bloody crime scene to the professionals—oh, wait. That's *me*.

"Cassiar's not your guy," I say. "Give me two minutes with you in that room and I'll prove it. And I won't touch a thing."

"Excuse me?" Cassiar says. "Prove what, exactly? And who is Therese?"

Stoker stares at me. I meet his gaze levelly.

"*I* must be the crazy one," Stoker mutters at last. "Mr. Cassiar, don't go anywhere. Valchek—you got two minutes."

I nod, and wait for him to open the door again. He pulls out a pair of latex gloves and puts them on first.

We go inside. He shuts the door again.

My first good look at the body triggers another cascade of memories, but this time they're more professional than personal; forensics training, mostly. I try to focus on that.

"The amount of blood suggests she died from exsanguination," I say. "There's a blood trail from the window, but it's not extensive—probably from a minor injury as she was dragged to the bed. Blood spatter indicates arterial spray from a neck wound; her throat was torn open while she lay on her back."

"Torn?" Stoker says.

I point. "Look at the edges of the wound. Ragged, not straight. A knife or other sharp implement would have done a much cleaner job."

"What else?"

"Major organs are missing: heart, liver, lungs. Flesh on her upper thighs. If this body was found in a forest, it would be a clear case of animal predation."

"But she isn't out in the woods. She's in a bedroom."

"Yeah. Not *her* bedroom, either. That's because she was brought here and killed—by someone who leaped up to the second-floor window while carrying her. Probably by the throat so she couldn't scream; that would explain the blood trail, too."

He looks at me with no expression at all on his face. "Uh-huh. So an animal did this."

"I didn't say that. What I am saying is that Cassiar didn't. If he were going to do something as stupid as taking a woman back to his room to kill her as messily as possible, why would he go to the trouble of entering through a window on the second floor? Makes no sense."

"One little problem with your theory. This much blood and a wild animal? There'd be tracks all over the place."

"I never said it was a *wild* animal, either. But whoever or whatever did this, it didn't leave tracks coming in because of how the body was carried; the blood dripped to the side, not where it was stepping. After it was done, it leaped from the bed to the windowsill. Never touched the floor at all."

Stoker glances at the window. It's closed.

I smile and walk over to it. "Look at that. Somebody closed it. Must be a very *civilized* beast. But look at the sill."

Stoker does. There's a smudge of blood, one that runs underneath the window itself. Stoker opens the window—and there, on the sill, are what look like several very large paw prints, outlined in blood.

"Agile, too," I say. "Perched on the sill and closed the window from the outside. You'll find some blood transfer on the exterior wall, I'm sure. Maybe even some fur."

Stoker studies me dispassionately. "Any theories as to why?"

"Oh, that's obvious. This is a message. A warning."

He nods. "Looks like someone isn't fond of Mr. Cassiar."

Or maybe it's just the company he keeps. "You're going to take him in anyway, right?"

"Of course. If nothing else, for his own safety. And to find out who exactly is trying to scare him off, and why."

"I can help. Let me talk to him."

Stoker frowns. "You know I can't do that. This is a murder investigation, and he's in the middle of it. I shouldn't have let you in here in the first place."

"But you did. And I did what I promised, didn't I?"

He considers this. "All right. But I talk to him first, alone. Then we can talk to him together."

Not ideal, but it's the best I'm going to be able to do. "Okay. But I'm going to need Charlie to get me something."

I can tell Charlie is desperate to talk to me, but Stoker doesn't give him a chance. Stoker takes me to the station in his car, while Silver takes Cassiar in the other. We have to wait for the county coroner to arrive first, but seeing how that's Doctor Pete, it doesn't take long. I'm cooling my heels in the back of the sheriff's car, and give the doc a little wave when he looks my way. He seems more bemused than anything.

At the station, I get put in a cell to wait while Stoker questions Cassiar. Charlie tries to get in to see me, but Silver tells him he can't. He does, however, relay my message about the errand I need Charlie to run. I can hear a muffled argument through the door, but apparently Charlie thinks better of storming the place. I hope it's the right decision.

An hour later, Stoker unlocks my cell and escorts me to the interview room. Cassiar's there, looking completely unfazed for a man who's just been told a woman was brutally murdered in his bed. Or maybe Stoker's keeping him in the dark about that, though I can't see why. Maybe he wants me to tell him and gauge his reaction.

The only thing in the room besides us, the table, and two chairs, is a television on a rolling stand. It's got a DVD player built right in.

"Charlie get you that thing I asked for?" I say.

Stoker hands me a brown manila envelope. "You want to tell me how *this* is going to help?"

"Oh, you'd be surprised," I say.

This is a big risk. I *need* Cassius, and that means that whatever voodoo whammy Azura pulled on Charlie, I need her to do the same with Cassiar. Cassiar in jail doesn't help me at all; Cassius—in or out of jail, with or without the use of his eyes, ears, or limbs—is an invaluable asset. I need to get him into the game, and do it *now*. That means showing my hand to Stoker—but hey, that's going to happen sooner or later anyway. Maybe it's even a good thing; if Stoker is someone from my other life, maybe he'll turn out to be an asset, too. Just because he's an evil cult member in this reality doesn't mean he's some sort of monster in his original incarnation, right?

Right?

"Jace," Cassiar says. "Are you under arrest, too?"

"I told you," Stoker says. "You're being detained as a material witness. You're not under arrest."

"And neither am I," I say. "I just wanted to speak to you."

Cassiar frowns. "Privately?"

"Afraid not," says Stoker.

"But first," I add quickly, "I need to show you something. Bear with me, okay?"

Cassiar understands as soon as I slip the DVD out of the envelope. He glances at Stoker, then back at me. He gives me an "it's your funeral look" as I turn on the set.

Azura pops up in the scene menu, which I hope means she's accepting calls. Her image flickers to life, but before she can speak I quickly say, "This is the interesting part, Mr. Cassiar. It's very small, but if you get close to the screen you'll be able to make it out."

Cassiar does so. Stoker frowns, sensing something's wrong. "Hey!" he snaps. "Get away from—"

I slam my body into him as hard as I can. Stoker masses a lot more than I do, but I've got desperation and surprise on my side. We both smack sideways into the wall, but Stoker shoves me away an instant later. I go careening into Cassiar, knocking him away from the TV. Not good.

I grab Cassiar by his lapels, spin both of us around, and get us headed back toward the television. "Azura, *now*!" I bellow.

White light.

It's not like it was with Charlie.

I'm hanging in some sort of void. Blank nothingness, like having your eyes closed but more so. And then I hear Azura's voice in my head: *Uh-oh.*

Uh-oh? What do you mean, uh-oh? I demand.

I'm not getting a connection to Cassius. Dimensional harmonic's all messed up.

Can you fix it?

I'll try. A pire as old as Cassius has a really strong psychic signature, which helps. I think all the illusion spells in your area are distorting things, but I'm compensating for that now . . . got him!

The nothingness goes away, replaced by—

Warm, golden light. The kind of buttery sunshine I associate with early summer mornings, before the day gets too hot. The light isn't coming from overhead, though—not exactly.

My hand is warm in his, but it's not him I'm looking at. I'm gazing in rapt awe at my surroundings instead. We're in a lush, tropical jungle, palm trees and thick foliage all around us. Bright blue and yellow parrots preen themselves on branches or call to one another. The air is humid, warm and heavy and rich. We're also indoors, the plant canopy reflected upside down off the glass panes overhead. This is an artificial environment filled with real life, a carefully tended biosphere inside a transparent shell. During the day the sun shines through the roof and walls, but right now it's the middle of the night.

Not that you'd know it. The whole place is illuminated as

brightly as it would be at noon, and not from electric lights, either. No, the light seems to be coming from *everywhere*, almost as if the air itself is glowing.

"How are you doing this?" I ask, wonder in my voice. I know he's responsible, I just don't know how.

"Magic, of course," he says.

I turn to look at him. He's dressed like a Roman gladiator: sculpted golden body armor, a leather kilt, and sandals, all of it over some kind of bodysuit. His whole outfit is glowing with the same soft light. I can't see his face—he's also wearing a crested helmet with a visor that mostly conceals his features—but I'd know those blue eyes anywhere.

"David?" I say wonderingly. "No. No, you can't be—"

He flips the visor up, showing me I'm right. "Now you know why the Solar Centurion never lets you get too close, Rhiannon. You're too sharp to fool."

The Jace part of my consciousness remembers exactly who the centurion is: a member of the Bravo Brigade, legendary heroes who fought an evil cult back in the fifties. I have no idea how long Cassius has owned the armor, though, so I still don't know what decade this memory is from.

"So the sunlight the centurion armor emits," I say. "It doesn't hurt you, even though you're a pire?"

"That's right. I can make it do things normal sunlight can't, too—like light up this greenhouse."

He reaches up and takes off his helmet. His blond hair is charmingly tousled. I should be angry at him deceiving me, but I'm not. I came to terms with the fact that it's David's job to keep secrets long ago, and eventually realized just how heavy and lonely a burden that job is.

Now what I feel is gratitude and sorrow. There are things David knows that he wishes he didn't: things that someone *has* to know, things that can't be changed. Only endured.

I reach up and put a hand against his cheek. I love him so much, but I can't live in his world. Not anymore. Not the way he does.

"So this is it?" I say. "Your final attempt to change my mind? To show me that even pires can enjoy daylight, now and then—or at least they can if they have a magic-powered suit of armor?"

He puts his hand on top of mine. "No. I know your mind is made up. I simply wanted to fulfill a wish of yours. You said once you'd like nothing better than to just take a walk in a garden with me on a warm summer afternoon. This is the best I could do."

I smile at him, tears in my eyes. "Thank you," I say simply. I pull his hand down, clasp it in mine, and pull him forward down the path.

We have the place all to ourselves. The perfume of a dozen kinds of exotic flowers fill the air, mingling with the smell of sun-warmed leaves and moss. I look around, drinking it all in, but searching for something, too.

I finally find it beneath a tree dripping with crimson blooms. I stop and turn to face him. "I have a question. Two, in fact."

"Yes?"

"First of all, does the sorcery just protect your face?"

"No. My entire body is immune to this particular wavelength of light as long as I wear the armor."

"Which brings me to my second question. How much of the armor do you have to keep on for it to work?" I give him a mischievous smile. "Because there's something else I've always wanted to do with you under the sun. . . ."

As it turns out, the breastplate and gauntlets are the important parts of the ensemble; the helmet works with them, but he can remove it as long as it remains nearby.

We kneel on the moss together, and I push him onto his back. The leather kilt comes off first. It takes some ingenuity and patience to get the bodysuit off while keeping the armor on, but I'm in no hurry. I want this to last.

Finally, with more than a few giggles during the process, I have my centurion the way I want him. Then it's my turn.

I strip for David slowly, turning in the omnipresent sunlight, bathing in its glow, letting it warm every inch of me. I want to give that warmth to him, to press the heat of my skin to the coolness of his. I want to burn in his arms like a star.

But practicality gets in the way. Even while David uses magic to grant his lover's wish, hard reality won't be ignored. The armor that covers his chest and belly isn't made to be embraced; it's a reminder of the barriers between us that we can't remove, no matter how hard we try. Even while he reveals as much of himself to me as he can, some layers of protection can't be removed. That's just how things are.

But that doesn't mean I'm going to give up.

I get on top. An embrace is nice, but sometimes you just need to go for a long, hard ride. . . .

I don't experience her orgasm, of course, any more than I remember Amy's parents. These are Cassius's memories, not Rhiannon's, and though I'm seeing it through her eyes it's being filtered through his mind.

But that doesn't mean the intensity of the moment doesn't affect me. Even though I'm in Rhiannon's head—or some kind of magic/memory analog of it—my own memories are starting to intrude and overlap. The way he manages to brush his thumbs over my ribs without tickling. The firm grip of his hands on either side of my waist. His rhythm. And, oh God, the way that man can use his *mouth*. . . .

It goes on forever, and it's over too soon. I slump onto his breastplate like a marathon runner collapsing onto a metal deck, surprised to find the sculpted surface pleasantly cool.

"Thought . . . it'd . . . be . . . *hot*," I pant against his chest.

"Funny, no one ever complained before."

I raise myself up on my arms and give him a ferocious grin. "Your *armor*, idiot."

"Ah, now I see. I was expecting a different sort of comment."

"Well, I was also going to point out how . . . *rigid* it is."

"My armor."

"Yes."

"I see."

"Honestly, how are we supposed to snuggle like this? It's like lying on top of a rock."

"I refer you to my initial statement vis-à-vis complaints."

I laugh and roll off him. We both sit up, him with his arms behind him and his hands flat against the ground, me with my knees drawn up and my arms wrapped around them. We regard each other, our eyes full of emotion, not speaking. There's too much between us for the moment to last, though, the silence filling up with the memory of arguments past and consideration of those in the future.

"Don't," I say softly. "Don't start."

"Then don't end," he says.

"That's what human beings do, David. We're not meant to last forever."

"Then become something else. I did."

"I'm not you."

"And pretty soon you won't be anything."

I shake my head. "You know better than that. I just won't be *here.*"

He sighs, and stares up at the foliage. "I'm so . . ."

"Angry?"

"*Tired.* Tired of saying goodbye to the people I care about." His voice is bitter. "I should know better by now."

"You really should," I say.

His gaze snaps back to me.

"But you keep doing it, over and over," I say. "I don't know why, not for sure. Maybe you need to feel something vicariously through those that you've lost. Maybe you're addicted to the bittersweet intensity of inevitable loss. Maybe it's just a pattern you're locked into and don't know how to stop."

"What do you mean?"

"The dying are always beautiful, David. I can't remember where I heard that, but it's true. And it's a kind of beauty you find irresistible."

"You weren't dying when I met you."

"Sure I was. Human beings are dying from the moment they're born. Most of us try to ignore that fact, but to someone who's been walking the earth for a few thousand years it's glaringly obvious. You've known I was going to die from the second we met. I think part of you even looks forward to it."

And now he looks shocked. I've never seen Cassius look shocked before; I didn't know it was even possible. It makes him look *alien* somehow.

"I don't have a lot of time left to me," I say. "You know that. It brings things into sharper focus, really makes me aware of my priorities. Being tactful, I've decided, isn't one of them. You've seen a lot of women you love die, but I don't know if you've ever been with one like me—one who *knows* she's going to die, and soon. Have you?"

"No," he says quietly.

"Then maybe I can give you something none of them did. Some perspective, from a person about to cross that line you can't." I meet his eyes and hold them. "Maybe you have an unhealthy obsession with death. Maybe you're punishing yourself for things you've done or haven't done; maybe you're just afraid of committing to anything past a few decades. Well, whatever the reason, here's my big insight: *It doesn't matter.*"

He frowns. "How can you say that?"

"Because it's *true,* you big dope. Not that love doesn't matter; it's the *reason* for the love that doesn't. I don't care if you love me because you think I'm temporary or because you find wrinkles sexy or because I'm a dead ringer for someone you knew in Pompeii before it blew up; what I care about is the fact that you *do*. Right here, right now, *you* love *me*. I know that's real. And that's all that matters."

David looks troubled. And then he looks hazy—there's something wrong with my vision. Everything goes sideways before going away completely.

That's it? Seems like there should be more, somehow.

Sorry. Azura's voice, in my head. *There was some kind of consciousness spike and I lost the connection. I don't know if it was enough to kick his real memories loose, either, but it'll have to do—there's so much dimensional interference now I can't possibly get through. Even talking to you is—* She cuts off abruptly, and I'm suddenly aware of my own body again. "That's it," I mutter. "I'm switching dimensional carriers first thing in the morning. I have *had* it with dropped calls." I open my eyes.

Which is when I see the werewolf.

FOURTEEN

I've seen plenty of lycanthropes before, of course. But some-how, this one is scarier than any of the others.

It must be nine feet tall; even crouched over, the tips of its ears brush the ceiling. Its fur is midnight black, its eyes a blazing yellow. There's blood on its long, curving claws, and its lips are drawn back in a snarl.

It seems really, really angry.

The shock of going from an intimate post-passion scene to one where I'm confronted by a gigantic, hairy monster is enough to lock up my brain. I can't even take my eyes off the thing; its presence fills my whole world, a pure incarnation of savage rage trembling with barely suppressed violence. Any second now it's going to—

It slashes at me.

I hear my clothes tear, feel the claws cut through my skin. Once again—what is this, the third time in twenty-four hours?—I'm dead.

The beast pulls back and stares at me with its inhuman yellow eyes. I think, absurdly, of the golden light given off by the Solar Centurion's armor, and how different it is. I look down, expecting to see my own guts hanging out of my belly.

But no—there's some blood, but no gaping wound. The thing cut me, but didn't kill me. Why?

It's obviously asking itself the same thing, because it cocks its head to the side like a puzzled cocker spaniel and its growl shifts higher to a whine.

Which is drowned out a second later by gunshots. Can't see where they're coming from, so I dive for the floor out of instinct.

When I look up, the thrope is gone.

The room is trashed. The TV lies on its side, the screen smashed. The table is a pile of splintered wood, and the door's been ripped off its hinges. Stoker's sprawled on the floor with what looks like one helluva developing black eye, his gun in his hand.

No Cassiar.

"What the hell just happened?" I ask, getting to my feet.

"You tell me," Stoker snaps. He doesn't lower his gun, either.

"Hey, I just woke up, okay? At least I *think* I'm awake. . . ."

"And just what *was* that, anyway? The screen flared white, then both of you hit the floor."

"Can the explanations wait? I'm bleeding all over your nice interrogation room."

Stoker climbs to his feet, keeping his gun on me the whole time. "How bad is it?"

I eye him, considering possible responses: *Not too bad, as werewolf-inflicted injuries go*; *Ask me again when the moon is full*; *I'm fine, but the livestock in this county is in a lot of trouble*. "Not life threatening, as far as I can tell. Hurts like a bitch, though."

He studies me, then slowly holsters his gun. "Where'd Cassiar go?"

"You're asking *me*? Where'd the giant hairy monster come from?"

He approaches me slowly, pulls my arm away from my

belly. Examines the wound. "It busted in here a few minutes after you passed out. Gave me a good smack, turned my lights out. When I came to, I opened fire. Cassiar was already gone—he must have ducked out during the attack."

Which raises even more questions: Why would Cassiar run? Why would the thrope let him? Unless . . .

Stoker touches his eye and shakes his head, then winces. I realize he's still a little woozy. This might be my best shot at escaping myself.

"*Damn* it," Stoker blurts, then turns and sprints out the door. Having no immediate plans myself, I follow.

We find Deputy Silver lying beside the front desk. The thrope wasn't as lenient with him as it was with me; Silver's throat has been ripped open.

"It killed him," Stoker says. He doesn't sound nearly as upset as I thought he'd be; more annoyed than anything. "That unholy thing killed him."

"I'm sorry," I say. I feel a little dizzy, not from the sight of blood but from losing too much of my own. I stagger and lean against the wall.

"You need medical attention," Stoker says. "I'd take you myself, but with Silver dead I can't just leave. Get Charlie to drive you over to Doctor Pete's."

"You sure? You're not afraid I'll just take off the way Cassiar did?"

He gives me a cold, flat glance. "I don't believe you will. After all, where would you go?"

I don't know how to answer that, so I don't. I dig out my phone and call Charlie instead.

"Stoker's a *what*?" I manage as Charlie speeds me toward Doctor Pete's offices.

"Serial killer. Terrorist. Bram Stoker's great-great-grandkid. Genius-level psychopath who tried to end the world. Take your pick, then add all the others and mix well."

I stare out the window and try to stay conscious. "So

that's what you've been trying to tell me since the first time you saw Stoker."

"Yeah. I was about ready to tie notes to rocks and chuck them through your window."

I think about what Charlie just told me, trying to trigger a memory cascade, but all I can call up is the look on Stoker's face as he stood over the dead body of his deputy. The coldness in his eyes, the irritation in his voice. Not like a man who'd just lost a friend and colleague; more like a chess player whose opponent just took a valuable piece.

But something else is nagging at me, and I realize it's the deputy's name. Quinn Silver. Quicksilver. *The Quicksilver Kid.* A lem bounty hunter Charlie and I have run into once or twice. "Didn't recognize him," I say groggily. "Looked different with a metal face."

"Stoker has a metal face?"

"No, the Kid did. Quicksilver Kid. Didn't think Ahaseurus was using lem counterparts, too."

"I'm here, ain't I?"

I frown. "Can't transform, though. Not like pires and thropes. Not like you can bite someone and turn them into sand. You know, like a . . . a sandpire. Or a were-rock thing."

Charlie shoots me a worried look. "Yeah, we need to get you to a doctor. . . . I heard the gunshots from across town. Funny no one else came running."

"More magic, probably. If Ahaseurus can whip up a spell to make everyone on the planet not take firearms seriously, he can make a few townspeople ignore gunfire."

Charlie glances at me. "You remember the anti-gun spell? That's a good sign—you're getting more memories back."

"What I remember is that I used to have a gun myself. A really, really, big one." I sigh. "I miss my gun."

"Wouldn't be much use without the right ammo." On Thropirelem—the world, not the town—I had silver-and-teak bullets specially made.

We pull up in front of Doctor Pete's place, a two-story

brick building with a clinic on the main floor; he lives on the second. There's a buzzer beside the door for emergencies, and Charlie runs over and leans on it.

I feel oddly calm for someone who's just been clawed by a thrope. I look down and see that the front of my shirt is soaked through; guess I'm bleeding worse than I thought. Things start to get a little blurry.

Then Charlie's helping me out of the car, and Doctor Pete's asking questions, and there's the smell of antiseptic and bright lights and somebody sticking poky things in different parts of my body. My arm first, then my stomach. Doctor Pete is asking more questions and Charlie's stone-walling him.

Good ol' Charlie. I have to remember to hit him with that one later, the one about the stone wall. That's what he is, y'know. Not the kind that blocks you out, the kind that holds stuff up. The kind that protects you. The kind you can lean on . . .

Things go away right about then, but I'm not out for very long. I can tell, because when I open my eyes Doctor Pete's only halfway through stitching up the six-inch-long gash just above my belly button. I'm flat on my back with my shirt off and there's an IV in my arm, feeding me plasma to replace what I've lost.

Doctor Pete notices I'm awake. "Hey. How are you feeling?"

"Still a little woozy. How's the embroidery going?"

"Coming along fine. You lost a fair amount of blood, but the cut doesn't go all the way through the muscle. No sit-ups for a while, though."

"I'll keep that in mind." I look around. "Where's Charlie?"

"Guarding the door. Seemed a little concerned that whoever did this might come back to finish the job."

He goes back to work. There's something different about him, something I can't put my finger on.

He notices me studying him and raises his eyebrows. "What?"

"Aren't you going to ask me how I got this newly minted scar?"

"Not my business. If I was going to hazard a guess, I'd say it was a knife wound."

"Sure, let's go with that. I was cleaning my Ginsu and it went off."

"So this is self-inflicted?"

I hesitate before answering. "Not so much."

He keeps working. He must have given me a local, because I can't feel a thing. "You getting into fights again?"

"I wouldn't really call this a fight. More like an animal attack."

"Is that a put-down of the person who did this, or a joke I don't get?"

"If it's a joke, it's on me." As in, I'm the one who's going to howl about it . . . but maybe I'm not the only one. "Say, doc—you get any others like this?"

"What, knife wounds?"

"No. Animal-inflicted injuries—bites or claw marks."

Now he looks at me and frowns. "You're saying this was *literally* done by an animal? Because it doesn't really look like it. There's no way it's a bite mark, and claw wounds tend to come in multiples."

"Humor me and answer the question."

He shakes his head. "No. Not like this. If this did come from an animal, it'd have to be a big one, and there's nothing like that locally. Not unless somebody's got a Bengal tiger that I don't know about locked up in their barn."

So nobody else has been bitten or clawed. There's a pire on the loose biting people and activating implanted false memories, but no thrope equivalent. So how did Mayor Leo and the rest get infected? Is Doctor Pete lying to me?

Suddenly I realize what's different about him.

"So," I say. "Am I keeping you from something important?"

"What? No, I was just watching a movie."

"Uh-huh. Better get back up there before she eats all the popcorn."

"Excuse me?"

"It's almost midnight. Your hair is less shaggy than usual, verging on actually being combed. Those pants are new and even a brand I recognize. You're on a date."

He shakes his head. "Sorry to disappoint you, but it's just me and an old cowboy flick. I do buy new clothes and occasionally comb my hair, you know."

I give a discreet sniff. No cologne or lingering traces of a woman's perfume. Doesn't mean anything, though; lots of people don't use either one. "Well, okay," I say. "Guess my radar's not as sharp as it usually is. Must be the loss of blood."

"I think you're just mixing me up with my brother. He's the ladykiller, not me." He pauses in his work, then says, "I understand you were down at the station. How's Terrance doing?"

"Couldn't tell you. Stoker won't let anyone see him."

He nods, as if that's exactly what he was expecting. "Well, he's been arrested before."

"And that justifies being held incommunicado? Stoker hasn't even let him talk to a lawyer."

"I'm sure there's a good reason for that. If it's true."

"What, you think I'm lying?"

"Not at all. I just think you might not have all the facts." He finishes his stitching, ties a neat knot, and trims off the extra thread. "Done," he says. "Don't put any stress on it for at least a week. No stretching, no heavy lifting, no getting into bar fights—with extra emphasis on that last one. Understand?"

"Sure. Can I get out of here now?"

He stands up and checks the IV drip. "Not yet. I want

another bag of plasma in your tank before you leave. Otherwise, you could find yourself getting lightheaded again."

An idea strikes me. Probably a bad one, considering what happened last time, but it's worth a shot. "So I'm going to be here awhile?"

"At least an hour."

"Boring. Can't I watch some TV?"

"I've got a tablet with Wi-Fi. Will that do?"

I shrug. "Don't know. Depends on what I can find on the Internet." I grin. "And how good your connection is."

My plan is simple: download a copy of the same *Bloodhound Files* episode I played at the police station, use it to contact Azura, then get her to pull the same stunt she did on Charlie and Cassiar. I don't know if it'll work—maybe I need the actual DVD to contact her—but it's worth a try.

Too bad I don't get the chance.

The first part works just like I planned. I call Charlie in and chat with him inanely while I find and download the episode. Doctor Pete offers to make us some coffee, which I gratefully accept. While he putters around in another room, I fill Charlie in on what I want to do. He agrees we should give it a shot.

And then we hear the noise from the other room.

A surprised cry, quickly choked off, followed by the crash of a struggle. Charlie sprints out the door. I rip the IV out of my arm and run after him as quickly as I can.

Vampires. Werewolves. Demonic road workers. After the near-constant barrage of attacks, I've forgotten all about the Big Bad this town was built for in the first place.

The cord of the coffeemaker is wrapped around Doctor Pete's neck. It's tying itself into a hangman's knot, the plug whipping around at insane speeds as it darts and loops.

But that's not the only thing happening. Other cords are wriggling toward Doctor Pete from all over the office like a bunch of revenge-minded snakes converging on Saint Patrick: power cords, computer cables, lengths of transparent

IV tubing. When they come into contact with each other they twine together, a self-braiding, plastic-skinned python getting longer and thicker by the second.

I look around wildly for a weapon—one that chops, preferably. Charlie's already got a knife in his hand, something long and vaguely military. I spot a pair of scissors on a desk and grab them—by that point the python has reached the coffee pot cord and interlaced itself. Doctor Pete's face is turning red and his tongue is sticking out.

We jump in and start hacking. I can't get the scissors between the cord and Doctor Pete's throat; it's sunk too deep into his skin. Charlie's sawing away at the base of the hangman's knot, but it's too thick to get through easily.

I hear the crash and tinkle of breaking glass. The other end of the boa construct has been busy too, knotting itself into a lump and punching a hole through the window. It slithers through until it can't go any farther, its length snapping taut between the window and Doctor Pete's neck.

Slowly, it starts hauling Doctor Pete backward.

We switch tactics, both Charlie and I grabbing the cable-snake and pulling it away from the window. It doesn't work. Two of us, putting all our weight into it, straining every muscle, and it still manages to drag Doctor Pete across the floor inch by inch. If only Charlie were in his regular body—golems are strong enough to lift cars. But he isn't, and it looks like we're going to lose this insane tug-of-war.

We get right up to the sill. Doctor Pete's gone limp, his face purple, but he's still alive. I think.

I look out through the window to where the snake-thing is taking Doctor Pete and see that the cable simply disappears into the ground.

A tremendous yank pulls him right through the window, showering Charlie and me with glass. Doctor Pete's limp body slides across the dew-wet grass, then disappears head first into the ground like a swimmer diving for the bottom.

The ground swallows him in a second, legs grotesquely pointing straight up just before they sink into the earth.

Charlie and I stare through the broken window.

"Should we get a shovel?" Charlie asks.

"Waste of time. He's in the tunnels by now . . ."

"You're not going to turn into a werewolf," Charlie tells me.

We're driving back to his place, trying to regroup. Cassiar's AWOL, Silver's dead, and Doctor Pete's gone, all in the space of a less than an hour. I'm feeling a little shell shocked; at this point, any good news is welcome. "What do you mean?"

"You got clawed, not bitten, right? You've got an immunity to that."

I think about it for a second. "I *do*, don't I? I remember. I got slashed once before and survived it. Cassius did some kind of pire voodoo and managed to save me. Said I'd be safe from that particular danger in the future—but only from thrope claws, not fangs."

"Yeah. So you got lucky, there."

Did I? I'm not so sure it was luck. The werewolf that clawed me did so very deliberately, like it knew what it was doing. Or maybe like it had done it before . . .

"The thrope that clawed me the first time," I say. "It was Tair, wasn't it?"

"That it was. During a jailbreak."

"Huh. Maybe the thrope that attacked the police station didn't bust in from outside. Maybe it was already there."

Charlie glances at me. "Could be. But I don't think it's a good idea to go back and ask if Terrance is still locked up."

"No. Probably better if we avoid Stoker for now."

My phone rings. Unknown caller: I answer it anyway. At this point, talking to anyone, even a telemarketer, who isn't trying to maim or mutilate me would be a relief. "Hello?"

"Jace."

It's Cassiar—or is it Cassius? Did the memory treatment work? "What happened to you? Where are you?"

"I'm not sure what happened. There was a flash of light and I lost consciousness. When I regained my senses I was outside and several blocks away. Are you still in custody?"

Damnit, it doesn't sound like he's remembered a thing. "No. Charlie and I are on our way back to his place. Listen, I need to bring you up to speed on a few—"

"No time. Come to the parking lot beside the grocery store." He hangs up.

"Change of plans," I tell Charlie. I give him directions, and we're there in moments.

Charlie's headlights fall on two figures next to the brick wall of Zhang's store. One's sprawled unmoving on the ground; the other's crouched beside it. Cassiar straightens up as we park. The look on his face is grim.

Charlie and I get out of the car, but he leaves it running and the lights on. We look down at the figure on the ground.

It's Vince, our friendly neighborhood alcoholic, and he's taken his last drink.

I kneel by the body. Cause of death isn't hard to pinpoint; he's got something slim and metallic sticking out of his chest. "Looks like someone raided the good silverware drawer," I murmur. "It's sunk in pretty deep, but I think the murder weapon's a fork."

"Silver," Charlie says. "Think he was a thrope?"

"Or someone wants us to think he was. I need to take a closer look at the body."

"Forensically, you mean?" Cassiar asks. "I didn't know you had the skills—"

"Well, I do," I snap. He should know that, and the fact that he doesn't is pissing me off. "Charlie, think you can get us inside the store? Zhang's truck isn't here, so I know it's deserted."

"I'll check my trunk," Charlie says.

I'm not too surprised when Charlie produces a pair of

bolt cutters—both the human and lem versions of him like to be prepared. He snips through the lock on the loading bay door and Cassiar helps me carry the body inside. Charlie grabs the shotgun and does a quick recon, making sure Zhang hasn't returned to his nest. He's back in a moment and gives me the all-clear.

We put Vince's body on a big wooden table in the back room and turn on an overhead light. I remember the last time I was here, and Zhang's sibilant voice hissing from the shadows. Yeah, perfect place to conduct an impromptu autopsy.

"What are you hoping to learn?" Cassiar asks.

"Whatever I can," I mutter.

I rummage through Zhang's tiny, cluttered office and find a pair of scissors and a box cutter. I use them to cut Vince's clothes off his body, then examine every square inch of skin.

Once again, the death of one of Thropirelem's citizens triggers a memory cascade; I remember who Vince represents. He was a rich and powerful man when I first met him, a shaman who specialized in a very particular kind of magic: Kamic books, which looked just like the comic books from my reality but were actually powerful, reality-altering magic items. Ahaseurus must have harbored some severe professional jealousy to have stuck him in the body of the town drunk, close to the lowest rung on the social ladder—which, of course, was me.

Charlie's on guard over by the back door, but Cassiar is hovering at my shoulder, clearly intrigued. "Well?" he asks.

"He wasn't killed in the parking lot."

"How do you know?"

"There was very little blood on the ground—but there's very little left in his body, either. He was exsanguinated, postmortem and in another location." I point to wounds on both wrists. "From the flushed color of his face, I'd say he was hung from his heels and bled."

"Somebody drained the body of blood?"

"Yes. I can't be one hundred percent sure of why, because

the rules are different here—but the pires I'm familiar with prefer blood from a living victim, and wouldn't drink the blood of a thrope, anyway; that suggests the killer's motivation wasn't hunger."

"Then what was?"

"Same as whoever killed Therese Isamu and left her body in your bed. To send a message."

"But to whom?"

"Each other. Two different killers with two different modus operandi, but each saying the same thing."

"Which is?"

I look up from the corpse, having found the confirmation I was looking for. "This is *our* town. Get out or die."

He thinks about it, then nods slowly. "We're not the ones being targeted. The werewolves are threatening the vampires, and the vampires are responding in kind."

"Yes. Therese Isamu was killed because she was married to a pire. Vince here was killed because he's been infected by a thrope. The killer's species was made obvious in each case."

"Good lord," Cassiar says softly. "This town is on the verge of a war."

"One between pires and thropes. And guess who's stuck right in the middle. . . ."

FIFTEEN

We leave the body where it is and go back to Charlie's place. We're pretty subdued on the way, all of us lost in thought. It's late, and I'm exhausted and more than a little overloaded. I'm trying to think of this as just another case, but I'm not having much luck. This isn't something I can solve so much as something I have to survive.

Charlie recons the outside of the house before letting us in. Cassiar and I sink into chairs in the living room while Charlie roams from room to room, exploring his territory like a cat in a new home. Galahad follows him, trying to figure out what the rules of this new game are.

I explain to Cassiar what Azura and I were trying to do to awaken his memories. "Sorry I couldn't give you a heads-up, but I didn't know how Stoker fit into all this or how he would take it."

Cassiar nods. "So you had no luck accessing my mind?"

"Oh, no—I was in there, all right. You're exactly who I said you were. But some kind of dimensional interference was causing problems. Azura said it might be all the illusion spells embedded in this place, or maybe it's just that your mind is so powerful Ahaseurus had to go to extra lengths to brainwash you."

Cassiar nods, steepling his fingers in front of his face. "I see. You understand that I'm still having trouble with the idea that I'm not really me, don't you?"

"Sure. So did I, at first."

He stares at the tips of his fingers. "And yet . . . I'm starting to think you're right. No, I'm starting to *feel* that you're right. Every time I look at you, that feeling gets stronger." He glances at me with those blue eyes I know so well, bracketed now by crow's-feet that look all wrong.

I want to go to him, kiss him, do my best to drag his soul out from under the layers of lies Ahaseurus draped over it. But I can't; the look he's giving me is still wary and unsure. Shocking him didn't work last time, and I'm afraid trying it again will just push him further away.

"It's all right," I say. "It'll come back to you. Don't rush it."

He nods, but says nothing.

It's been a long night, and we all need to get some rest. We work out a rotation for standing guard with Charlie taking the first watch, and then Cassiar and I try to sleep. I take the couch, he takes the bedroom.

It seems like I just closed my eyes when a pounding on the front door jars me awake. I raise my head and look around blearily. "Charlie? Cassiar?"

Charlie steps out of the bedroom, wearing only boxers. Galahad starts barking excitedly. "Where's Cassiar?" Charlie asks.

"You tell me—I just woke up. Is that him outside?"

Charlie looks out the spyhole. "No, it's—hey, I recognize her. It's Xandra."

The name means nothing to me. "Well, the sun's up, so I guess she's not a pire. Let her in, let's see what she wants."

I get to my feet as Charlie opens the door. Alexis charges in, teary streaks of mascara trailing from the edges of her black-rimmed eyes. She's all punked out today: ripped jeans with fishnets underneath, combat boots, Sex Pistols T-shirt, denim vest covered with band buttons and held together with safety pins. "Jace," she says, her voice a sob, "you gotta help me!"

I shoot Charlie a quick glance. "Find Cassiar. And put some clothes on." I motion for Alexis to sit.

"This guy doesn't *own* any," Charlie growls, and stomps off.

"What's wrong?" I ask her.

"It's Neil," she says, sniffling. "The sheriff arrested him. They think he *killed* somebody!"

"Who?"

"I don't know! Stoker just came and dragged him away in the middle of the night! And Neil—he just—" She breaks down again. I let her cry it out a little before I sit down next to her on the couch and put an arm around her. "What about Neil?" I ask gently.

"He's been acting so *weird*! He just—he won't eat, he sleeps all day, he's so pale . . . I thought he had some kind of drug problem, but he doesn't even seem high!"

"How *does* he seem?"

She shakes her head miserably. "He hardly touches me. He disappears in the middle of the night. And he's . . . *meaner*. It's not like him at all—he's such a nice guy, you know? But that's not the worst part. The worst part is *crazy*. I don't even know if I should tell you."

"It's okay. I know crazy, remember?" I give her what I hope is an encouraging-and-not-crazed smile.

"It's what happened when Sheriff Stoker came to arrest him. He just laughed and said he wasn't going anywhere. I thought the sheriff was going to threaten him with his gun, but he didn't. He threatened him with something *else*."

"What was it?"

"A cross. He pulled this stupid silver cross out of his pocket and held it in front of him, and backed Neil right into a corner. Neil looked angry and terrified and—and his eyes went all red, and the sheriff made him put the handcuffs on himself, like he didn't want to get too close to him—" She bursts into tears again. "I don't *know*," she wails. "I mean, I know how it sounds, but that's *crazy*! And I didn't know what to do or where to go and something made me think *you* could help, I don't even know *why*—"

"Take it easy," I say. "Look, you're not going to be able to help Neil if you're this upset, right? So just calm down."

It takes a minute, but she gets herself under control. I find a box of Kleenex and hand it to her, and she wipes her eyes and blows her nose.

"I get it," I say. "You're confused and scared and want to know what the hell is going on. Well, what's going on is so convoluted and bizarre I can't really explain it, but here's what you need to know. Yes, Neil is . . . exactly what you think he is. And he's not the only one. You know what I'm talking about, right?"

"Vampires," she whispers.

"Yes. And—believe it or not—werewolves, too. Which, once you've wrapped your head around vampires, isn't that much of a stretch, right?"

She's staring at me, not blinking, trying to see if I'm kidding or out of my mind. I meet her gaze as evenly and sincerely as I can. "The two groups are about to go head-to-head, Alexis. Two gangs, same turf."

"So Sheriff Stoker's a *werewolf*?"

"I'm not sure." I consider telling her about the cult but decide it's too much to hit her with all at once. "He's in the middle of things, but I don't know whose side he's on. What you need to know is that this town is now very, very dangerous; the best thing you could do would be to leave."

"I can't. The roadwork crew has the highway shut down and nobody can get out."

Charlie returns, now dressed in khaki pants and a white button-down shirt. "Cassiar's gone. Must have taken off during his turn standing watch."

"Who's Cassiar?" Alexis asks.

"A friend," I say. "I hope."

"Let's say I believe you," Alexis says. "If Neil's a vampire, who turned him into one? And who's a werewolf?"

"We don't know for certain," I admit. "Except for a few people. Jimmy Zhang and Phil Isamu, for instance—they're both vampires. Well, Phil *was,* anyway."

"He got better?" she asks, a pathetic gleam of hope in her eye.

"He got deader. Believe me, that's a good thing."

"Who else?"

Charlie's giving me the "are you sure you want to do this" look, but I plunge ahead regardless. "Brad Varney and Don Prince are both going to be hairy and howling at the first full moon. Vince Shelly and Ken Tanaka would round out their little unbarbershopped quartet, if both of them hadn't met unfortunate accidents involving things that are either very sharp, very silver, or both."

"Uh-huh." She looks a little overwhelmed, and I've only touched on the actual situation. "So all of these people were bitten?"

"That's the traditional way, yeah—"

"So why don't I *know* about this? How can all this *biting* be going on without anyone *noticing*?"

"Because it's not being done in the traditional way—not the werewolf part, anyway." I point to one of her exposed shoulders. "That little red dot on your arm—you got an innoculation recently, didn't you?"

"What? Yeah, I got a flu shot from Pete—my dad made me go. The whole family got them—"

Her eyes go very, very wide. "Oh, no," she whispers.

"I'm sorry," I say quietly. "I think Doctor Pete was infecting his patients with the lycanthrope virus. Vince Shelly had a mark just like it on his shoulder."

Oddly, the news that she's now a werewolf-in-waiting calms her down. "This is why he was acting so weird toward me," she says wonderingly. She touches the innoculation mark with a single index finger, like it's an on/off button she

can press. "I was feeling it, too, only I thought I was just angry at him. . . ."

"Pires and thropes don't generally make good couples." *At
least not where I'm from.* "But there's a solution. Kill the
alpha wolf—the one that's doing all the infecting—before the
first full moon, and none of the people bitten will transform."

"Kill Pete? But he's *family*!"

"It may not come to that. Doctor Pete might be the alpha
wolf, but he might not." I'm thinking of the attack in Doctor
Pete's clinic—if he were the alpha, why didn't he transform
and defend himself against the Gallowsman? No, it makes
far more sense for somebody else to be the alpha, somebody
with a more aggressive, take-charge personality. Don Prince
fits that description, as does Mayor Leo, but both seem too
obvious to me. I've got someone else in mind, someone who's
only a minor thug here but a lot more ambitious in his natural habitat.

Tair.

If so, then he's really here in the flesh; he's not just a
memory-implant imposter. But if the person I know as Terrance is actually Tair, then who is Doctor Pete? Did Ahaseurus manage to isolate each personality in a different body?

That actually makes sense. Tair as the alpha—powerful,
aggressive, ruthless—with trustworthy-but-thoroughly-
brainwashed Doctor Pete secretly infecting people until he's
dragged into the bowels of the earth by the Gallowsman.

Sure. Unless Ahaseurus decided to be tricky and set
things up the other way around. Hide the alpha inside Doctor Pete's unassuming, helpful facade, while parading Terrance around as a big fat red herring. That works, too.

Either way, they may have both been taken off the board:
one locked up by Stoker, the other abducted and possibly
killed by an evil creature the cult summoned.

I just don't know.

"We need to search Doctor Pete's place," I say.

"I might be able to get us in there," Alexis says. "I know

where he hides a key. He'll be working in the clinic down-stairs, though—we'll have to be real quiet."

"I think we can handle that," I say. No way am I going to tell her about what happened to Dr. Pete, not unless I have to. She's got enough to deal with already.

"All right," says Charlie. "We search the doc's place. Then what?"

"Depends on what we find. If he's the alpha, there have to be traces of thrope presence around. If not—" I shrug. "Then we go to plan B."

I leave Charlie with Alexis, out in the parking lot of the clinic. She tells me where to find the key—under a cement planter beside the front door—and I let myself in. Even though it'll screw up my plans, part of me is hoping I'll find Doctor Pete inside.

No such luck. His apartment is empty, the movie he was watching still on pause: an old western, just like he said.

But he was lying about something else.

He has a woman living with him. Hard to believe he managed to keep that a secret in a town this size, but any-thing's possible if you're motivated enough. I find high heels in the closet—more than one pair—along with women's clothes and some accessories. From the styles I'd guess she's going straight to work from here; from the sizes I'd put her at around six feet tall and maybe a hundred and forty pounds. A big girl.

The medicine cabinet is more revealing. She takes good care of her skin—lots of creams and lotions, all of them nat-ural and unscented. No sunscreen, though, which seems odd considering the weather we've been having lately. She favors pads over tampons. She shaves her legs on a regular basis.

And she's a werewolf.

The fridge is what clinches it. Meat, meat, and more meat, with nary a fruit or vegetable to be found. It pretty much tells me that they're both thropes, or at least they're eating like they are. It could be that one's the alpha and the other's merely been bitten—the carnivorous urges kick in even before the first transformation. It's also possible neither one's the alpha and both of them are just bitees, since I don't find anything like telltale bits of fur or claw marks on the furniture.

I wonder who the woman is. The last female I saw Doctor Pete with was the new school teacher, Athena Shaker, but none of these clothes would fit her. I don't find a comb, but there's a brush beside the bed; the hairs caught in it are distinctive and easily identifiable. She's black.

Sure. Except there aren't any black women in town.

I go back downstairs and get in the car. "So?" Charlie asks.

"So Doctor Pete has an African-American girlfriend. Or maybe just African, I don't know—but whoever she is, she's practically moved in with him." I realize I sound a little jealous, which is embarassing and irrelevant. I move on. "She might be the alpha, or it could still be Doctor Pete. No hard evidence either way."

Alexis looks disappointed. "So what do we do now?"

"Plan B," I say. "We break Terrance out of jail. Assuming he's still there . . ."

"Tell me again," says Charlie, "why this is plan B. Because it seems like it should be considerably further down the alphabet."

"Because," I say, crouching down in the backseat, "we need Terrance for the *second* part of the plan. Even if he isn't the alpha, he's still Doctor Pete's identical twin."

"And if he *is* the alpha?"

"Then we've got him exactly where we want him."

"Sure. Because cozying up to a killer thrope is much better than leaving him behind bars."

"He's not doing us any good in there, is he?"

"He's not doing us any *bad* in there, that's for sure."

"He may not even *be* there. Which is something we need to know, and anyway, shut up."

We're not in Charlie's car anymore. Too conspicuous. Instead we're in Isamu's junky old Toyota, which was parked next to the diner with the keys in it. We're across the street from the police station with the engine running, while Alexis is inside trying to see Neil. There's no guarantee that Stoker will let that happen, but the fact that Alexis is the mayor's niece gives us a little leverage; I'm hoping that the threat of a major, dramatic breakdown will be enough that he'll give in just to keep her happy. I coached her carefully beforehand, and she seemed to understand exactly which buttons she has to push. I have faith in her.

We've been waiting for half an hour. Enough time for Alexis to cajole, threaten, and sob her way inside, enough time for her to talk to Neil and get him up to speed. His relationship with Alexis may be rocky, but I'm willing to bet he'll kiss and make up awfully quick to get out of a jail cell.

Charlie and I are here to make sure he's got somewhere to go. It's mid-morning now, the autumn sun bright and warm overhead, not exactly what a pire wants waiting for him. The thunderstorm that threatened my life yesterday is still there, lurking on the horizon and flickering with the odd flash of lightning. I'll bet if I tried to leave town it would get a lot closer real quick.

The door of the police station—hastily repaired with plywood and two-by-fours—opens, and Alexis comes out. She doesn't walk directly to the car, going the opposite way instead and circling around the block. She jumps into the back seat a few minutes later.

"He's in there," she says "Terrance, I mean. In the cell right next to Neil."

I turn in my seat to face her. "How'd it go?"

She looks troubled, but better than I hoped. "About how you guessed. Stoker was a real hardass at first, but halfway through my meltdown he started to reconsider. I saved Uncle Leo for the closer, and he went for it."

"What about Neil?"

"He's . . . he's with us." Now she looks more sad than anything. "Except he's not really *him* anymore, is he?"

"No," I say. "He's not."

Who he *is*, though, I'm not exactly sure. Someone from my past—but an ally or an enemy? Alexis showed Charlie some pictures, but he didn't recognize Neil from them. I guess we'll find out, though. . . .

Stoker's down a man and his station has been damaged. That gives us an edge, though not much of one. The main thing is that he can't be in two places at the same time, and he can't secure his building very well while he's gone.

Charlie sighs. Again. "Damn shame about the car, though."

"It's sacrificing itself for a noble cause." I rigged a simple bomb in Charlie's car by lugging a propane cylinder from a barbecue into the back seat, opening the valve all the way, then tossing a kitchen timer wired to an electric lighter in the front. The interior fills up with gas, the timer runs down, the lighter sparks, and *KABOOM!* Stoker should easily be able to hear the explosion from the station.

I check my watch. "Here we go. . . ." The timer's only about thirty seconds off, and the *boom!* is satisfyingly loud. A cloud of black smoke blooms into the sky, and a moment later Stoker steps outside to shade his eyes against the sun and study it. He goes back in again, but only for a minute; when he returns, he locks the door behind him, strides down the steps, gets into his car and drives off.

"You're sure nobody else will get hurt?" Alexis asks.

"We parked it in a field at the edge of town," I answer. "And anyway, how many people have you seen on the street this morning?"

Alexis glances around. "None. All the businesses are closed, too. It's creepy."

It is, but I'll take deserted over filled with bloodthirsty supernatural beings any day of the week.

"Let's go," Charlie says.

We don't have time for subtlety. Charlie pulls up on the

sidewalk, and I leap out with the tow chain we scrounged from his garage. One end gets hooked to the recently repaired station doors, the other to the front of the Toyota's chassis. Then I get back in, Charlie throws the car in reverse, and we yank the plywood out by the nails.

I look around as we all get out of the car, but nobody so much as peers out a window. Not that I can see, anyway.

I unhook the tow chain from the car, and all three of us dash inside. There's another locked door between us and the cells, but that's operated by a buzzer under the front desk. We get into the holding cell area and peer through the small, wire-reinforced glass windows set into each door. Terrance is in the first cell, Neil in the second. Even though Neil apparently just woke up, he's still wearing sunglasses and a leather jacket. He'd look incredibly cool if it weren't for his hair, which seems crazy enough to require a straitjacket. Even vampire musicians need combs, I guess.

"Morning, sunshine," I say.

"I'm not mourning anything, actually," he says with a smile. He seems to have acquired a British accent along with his fangs. "I just woke up from the most *amazing* dream. Very educational, among other things."

"Terrific," I mutter. All about how I killed your pet bat and you swore undying revenge on me, right? "We'll have you out in a minute, okay?"

I don't wait for his reply, moving on to Terrance's cell instead. He's already at the little window, staring at me. "Jace," he says. "What the hell's going on?"

"Checkout time," I say. "You could sleep for another hour, but then you'd be charged for an extra day. Or, you know, murder."

"I didn't kill anyone!"

"You did where I come from," I say under my breath. "Take it easy, all right? We're getting you out of there."

"How?"

"Like this," I say, holding up the shotgun. "Better stand to the side, away from the lock."

I've replaced the special loads I built with standard buckshot, and it pretty much destroys the lock at close range. The door swings open and Terrance steps out, looking a little wary. "Not that I don't appreciate it, but why exactly are you breaking me out of jail?"

"I'll explain once we're someplace else. Hold on."

I tap on the glass to Neil's cell and let him know what I'm about to do. He doesn't bother getting out of the way; the second after I blast the door he strolls out of the cell with a friendly nod. "Cheers."

"Don't try anything," I tell him, and motion toward Charlie. "*His* gun isn't loaded with buckshot."

Neil nods at Charlie, too. He looks like he's enjoying himself. "You have a plan for getting me out of here unsinged, I hope?"

"Yeah, but you're not going to like it," I say. Alexis steps forward with a large canvas duffle bag we found in Charlie's garage. "You're getting in that. We're going to carry you out and stuff you in the trunk until we can get you indoors again."

"I see. Well, not exactly first-class accomodation, but the devil drives when needs must." He climbs in with Alexis's help. She looks a little sick.

"I hope you're not planning on stuffing *me* in a sack," Terrance growls.

"No, but you can help carry him," I say. I switch guns with Charlie, and he grabs one strap of the duffel. After a second, Terrance grabs the other and we hustle back out toward the car.

We stash our cargo, get in, and take off. Our destination isn't far: the church. With Father Stone and Maureen Selkirk dead it'll be empty, and it's a good place to hole up with a vampire I don't trust. Lots of windows means lots of sunlight, too—I plan on keeping Neil in that bag as long as I can. It's not like he's going to suffocate.

We get to the church without any problems. We get inside the foyer—Charlie and Terrance carrying Neil again—without a hitch; it's not even locked. I send Alexis to hide the car and tell her I'll call her when it's safe to come back.

Then we haul Neil through the inner doors, and I notice a slight flaw in our plans.

The stained-glass windows have all been covered by heavy black curtains. The large cross behind the pulpit is upside down. And lashed to it with heavy-duty wire is Jimmy Zhang, red eyes glaring at us, fanged mouth gagged with what looks like a large chunk of wood.

"How about that," Charlie says. "Two for the price of one." He and Terrance drop the sack to the floor and step up beside me.

"What's he trying to say?" Terrance asks. He moves a little closer, trying to hear.

There's a sharp *thrum,* and an arrow appears in the center of Zhang's chest. He bursts into flames with a sharp crackle, like ripping cloth.

Then I hear a polite cough behind me, and I realize that no, that actually *was* ripping cloth. Canvas, to be exact.

We all turn. Neil grins at us with very sharp teeth, his no doubt very red eyes hidden behind his shades. "I think he's trying to say *look out for that tripwire.* Pity—but all the more for me, I suppose . . ."

SIXTEEN

"You're going to *eat* us?" I say.

"Drink, actually . . ."

"After we broke you out of jail?"

Neil shrugs. "It's awkward, I know. But I'm not really who you think I am."

Charlie brings his shotgun up. "An impending homicide victim?"

"Charlie, Charlie, Charlie . . . first of all, technically I'm already dead, or at least not living. You can't kill a corpse. Second of—"

And then he's gone.

One of the things I've apparently forgotten is just how fast pires can move. Neil hasn't. In fact, his assured tone of voice seems to indicate that he's adapted rather quickly to his new circumstances.

"—all, I'm rather quick," Neil continues. His voice is coming from somewhere in the pews, but I can't see him, and the echoey acoustics make it hard to pinpoint the sound. "Third, I'm more than simply undead; I know a little about magic, too."

I look around. The trap that killed Zhang was most likely a crossbow, and the direction it came from means it must be in the upstairs gallery. The cross is throwing orange light and flickering shadows across the pews, but the fire doesn't seem to be spreading. "Terrance," I whisper. "Get upstairs. We're going to need all the weapons we can get." I hope he doesn't just bolt, but I'll have to take the chance.

"I won't have to worry about competition now, in either category," Neil says. "In the instant before Jimmy died, I could tell he was once a reasonably competent shaman; whoever brought us here must have blocked that knowledge from his brain, of course. I can tell my memory's been tampered with, too." I think he's moved since the last time he spoke, ducked down between the pews. "But the kind of sorcery I practice has always had very porous borders— harder to quantify than many kinds of magic. Oneiron-mancy tends to shift and flow, depending on the situation and the one dreaming it. . . ."

A shaman. Oh, this just keeps getting better and better— the word *better* in this context meaning "well and truly screwed." But he hasn't actually tried to kill me yet, so that's something. . . .

"Uh, Neil?" I say, moving toward the windows on my right. "You seem fairly rational . . . this doesn't have to be confrontational. We're all stuck in the same situation and trying to figure a way out of it, right?"

Charlie sees what I have in mind and edges toward the other side of the church.

"Absolutely," Neil says. "Tell you what: both of you go stand in the center aisle, away from the curtains covering the windows, and I'll take that as an indication of good faith."

I freeze. So does Charlie. After a second, I walk back toward the middle of the room and a little way down the aisle. Charlie shakes his head but joins me—I can always count on him to back my play.

"Excellent. I just needed a minute to finish the conversation I was having with the floorboards of this church. . . ."

I'm remembering how shamans do magic. They talk to

the spirits that live in everything, from inanimate objects to rivers to weather systems, and convince them to act in a particular way. From the creaking and groaning all around the room, it seems Neil is very persuasive.

The wood of the floorboards underneath the windows sprout rapidly thickening stalks. They grow within seconds into tall, straight shafts, sending out branches to the sides that link to one another and turn the whole thing into a grid. Every curtained window is now trapped behind a thick-barred wooden mesh.

"A little insurance," Neil says.

"Understandable," I say. "And impressive." For a pire to get wood to listen to him, he must be pretty damn powerful.

His chuckle echoes around the room. "Oh, it's not as difficult as all that. Buildings dream, too, you know. Especially ones that have had ritual magic performed in them."

Ritual magic. I remember what Stoker told me, that Father Stone and Maureen Selkirk spent a lot of time with Old Man Longinus. They were also the first three murder victims; I've assumed Stone and Selkirk were part of the cult ever since, and this seems to confirm it. But Longinus's basement was clearly used for ritual purposes—why two locations?

Maybe because this one has a lot more room.

"So this is the headquarters of the cult, huh?" I say. "Yeah, I know about that. Funny, I could have sworn I heard actual hymns being sung here on Sunday mornings—well, that one Sunday morning I got up before noon to walk Galahad."

"Oh, that was real." I realize he's standing behind the pulpit, the burning upside down cross behind him. "This place is fully consecrated. Before this cross was turned into a funeral pyre, it was mounted in the standard position. The heavy black curtains covering the windows, now . . . well, I can't say for certain without interrogating them directly, but I believe they're a fairly recent addition. Seems someone was anticipating some changes around here."

Could that be it? Was Stone prepping his church for a new congregation, one that consisted of pires instead of cultists? Was that why Ahaseurus was murdered—because Stone was planning some sort of takeover? It almost makes sense. . . .

I wonder if Terrance has made it upstairs, or if he's just taken off. I realize now the crossbow won't do much good, not unless there's a handy cache of arrows right next to it.

Neil vaults over the pulpit. He's going for Charlie, who lets off a blast from the shotgun but misses; guns aren't his strong suit. Neil clocks him with an uppercut that lifts Charlie off his feet, and he comes down in a boneless heap.

"Charlie!" I yell, and bolt toward him. He's not far away, only the width of the aisle, but Neil manages to get between us before I reach him.

"Sorry," he says, picks me up like a doll and tosses me down the aisle.

I slam into Terrance going backward. My skull hits his and the world explodes in an instant fireworks display of pain—then everything gets very dark before I have a chance to applaud. Good night, brain. . . .

I hate the disconnect that happens when you get knocked out. The first thing you say—the first thing *everyone* says—when you wake up is "How long was I out?" It's as if everyone has the same secret fear, that they've slipped into a coma and missed the last fifty years.

Not me, though. First, there are things that scare me way more than that; and B, I hate being predictable. So—considering how often I seem to get my lights turned out—I decided a while back I wasn't going to utter that particular phrase ever again.

"How long," I mutter groggily, "is a football player."

"Excuse me?" Neil says.

"Howie Long. Football player. Did a bunch of commercials for Radio Shack with Wonder Woman."

"I think you mean Lois Lane, not Wonder Woman. The Terri Hatcher version, as opposed to Margot Kidder."

I sit up, still woozy. Neil's crouched beside me. The cross is no longer on fire; the light in the room is coming from candles. I'm still in the center aisle of the church. Charlie and Terrance both lie a few feet away, trussed up side by side with rope.

"Are they all right?" I ask.

"So far. Both unconscious, but breathing. I'm still working out what to do with them—and you."

"You have anything you're leaning toward, or are you just spitballing? 'Cause I'd love to jump in with a few ideas I think you'd find really exciting—"

He holds up a hand and I stop. "Well, on the face of it things seem quite straightforward. I drain one of you—I'm *parched*—turn the other two, then use this church as a base to take over the rest of the town. Exponential infection rates mean it's all over in a night. But something's stopping me. A spell—or, more accurately, a series of them."

"They were cast by Old Man Longinus," I say. "He's dead now. They're degrading."

He nods. "Yes, I can feel that. But only some of them; the deeper ones are long-lasting. And the one that's causing me to hesitate is definitely one of those. Unfortunately for you."

I nod, then wish I hadn't. Ouch. "Let me guess. You really don't like me, do you?"

He smiles and shakes his head. "If only it were that simple. You see, at the very core of my being, there's a motivating force. Regardless of what trappings might be layered over this force, it's really what defines me. And that force is concerned with only one thing: making *you* very, very unhappy."

"What a surprise. Know what I *really* hate? When the bad guys do something totally unexpected, like letting me and my friends go instead of throwing us into a deep—well, you get the idea."

He studies me. I wish he'd take those damn sunglasses

off. "I do indeed," he says softly. And then he drags me to my feet by one arm and pulls me toward the back of the church.

"Hey!" I say. "Where are we going?"

"This is a very *old* church, Jace. I like old things. They've always got such interesting things hidden away in their depths."

He takes me through a door and down a hall. "I have memories of this place from when I was a teenager. Of sneaking in through unlocked doors late at night to indulge in a cigarette, of creeping around exploring. I'd like to show you one of the things I found."

And now I start to fight back in earnest. Kicking, flailing, biting. Neil ignores all of it, of course.

We come to a door that looks ancient, made of thick wooden planks held together with strips of hammered iron. He yanks it open, and I see a flight of stone steps leading downward. I redouble my efforts to get away, but he's got a grip on my right wrist that's unbreakable. He goes down the steps and I'm forced to go with him. The door slams shut behind us.

It's very dark down there. The air smells musty and dank.

"Everyone has things they're afraid of." Neil's voice is quiet, almost a whisper. "Oneiromancers are very attuned to that. It's because we deal with nightmares so often, of course. . . . "

He's right. Dark, earthen cellars held a special terror for me, for many years. I used to have bad dreams about them all the time, and Neil can sense that.

"This must be especially terrible for you. Standing here in the pitch black, not knowing what's around you."

"I know where *you* are just fine—"

He releases my wrist. Hurray, except I'm still trapped underground in complete darkness, with a vampire sorcerer who's been *marinated* in hatred for me. Nice going, Jace.

"I'm quite enjoying this," Neil says. His voice is somewhere to my right. "Not that I have any choice, of course. But one takes pleasures where one can. . . ."

There's an old trick I know. If you're going into a place where there's very little light, close your eyes as tightly as you can. Keep them that way. Your pupils will expand in response to the darkness behind your eyelids, so when you open your eyes they'll already be adjusted for low light.

I've had my eyes squeezed shut since the top of the stairs. Pires can see in the dark, so Neil can see me just fine. I've tried to keep my face turned away from the sound of his voice—the flailing helped cover that up—and now I open my eyes and turn toward him. I stretch my arms out like a blind woman, but in fact there's a tiny bit of light in the cellar, coming through the crack beneath the door at the top of the stairs. It's just enough to let me see Neil's outline, and a few vague features of the room around me: stacks of boxes, some shelves, an ancient furnace turned off for the summer and not fired up yet for the fall.

And there, in the northwest corner, is a rounded, waist-high structure made of stone.

"You—you don't have to do this," I say. There's a little tremble in my voice, which is mostly faked. Mostly.

"Yes, I really do," he replies. "I understand your strategy: this is the part where you try to convince me that I'm the one in control, not the spell, that I can overcome my implanted urges. It's what the heroine always does in situations like this, isn't it? But you shouldn't bother, Jace; it won't work, and I'll tell you why. First and foremost, I'm not the person you think you know. I'm a hybrid, a former human being who grew up on this world and had his own life and dreams, combined with the selected memories and persona of a vampire from another reality altogether. These two elements are being held together by the same spell that makes me want to hurt you; should I manage to undo or nullify that spell, I'll come apart like a rag doll ripped in two. I'll cease to exist. Now, I may be a fairly new entity—and not an entirely original one, I'll grant you—but I *do* know that existing is very much something I would like to continue doing.

"And second—as I said earlier—I'm quite enjoying this . . ."

He backhands me casually. He's not moving at superfast pire speed, so I've got plenty of time to get out of the way—but that would let him know I'm not as sightless as I seem. I take the hit instead, letting the impact send me staggering in the direction I want to go. I fall against the stone lip and scrabble around until I find a handle, then yank upward and whirl around. I've got a shield now, a wooden disk about three feet in diameter.

"Oh, well done," Neil says. He's constantly moving as he talks, circling, darting back and forth, trying to keep my sense of where he is confused. "You've *armed* yourself. What is that, a serving tray? My doom is *sealed*."

He plucks it out of my hands like a parent taking a frisbee away from a toddler, and tosses it aside.

I back up. I stop when my butt hits the lip of the stone structure behind me. "Got it all figured out, huh? Funny, Father Stone thought the same thing, and look how he ended up."

"Oh, I don't think the Gallowsman will come after me. You can't hang a pire, after all."

"No, but there are other ways to deal with them. Stone knew that. That's why he prepped this church. See, Stone belonged to the same cult a bunch of the people in this town do, a cult that's supposedly all about using the Gallowsman to inflict despair and bad luck on others. But it turns out the cult was just a cover for Old Man Longinus to transform this town into the Let's Torment Jace theme park—and when Stone found out that part of the plan was to fill the town with werewolves and vampires, he wasn't happy about it. That led to him getting killed, but not before he'd made a few preparations of his own."

Neil takes a step closer to me. "What sort of preparations are you talking about?"

"Here's something you might appreciate. Isn't it funny

how people can compartmentalize their lives? As a profiler, I run into that all the time. Guy's a devoted dad and proud member of the community five days a week, and a serial killer on the weekends. Father Stone belonged to an evil cult, sure . . . but every Sunday he still gave a sermon praising the Lord and all his saints. I'm talking about the Catholic kind, not the sports team."

"Your point being?"

"What makes you think I have one? I'm just tired of hearing you monopolize the conversation. Blah, blah, blah . . . if you're going to bite me, *do* it already. You were an irritating wannabe poser musician when you were following Terrance around, and now you're an annoying supervillain wannabe with a pretentious accent. Also, I got over the whole I'm-scared-of-root-cellars thing a long time ago, so this lame attempt to terrorize me is more pathetic than anything else—"

And then his hand is around my throat, cutting off my air. That particular move seems to be genetically ingrained into every new vampire's brain, and my windpipe's still sore from last time. "Urk," is about the only sound I can manage in response.

He leans in close. "I think I know what I'm going to do to you. I'm going to turn you, then chain you up down here forever. You won't die, but there are all sorts of things I can think of doing to make your existence extremely unpleasant. Garlic stuffed down your throat. Wooden stakes driven through your limbs. Something clever and intricate involving tiny little mirrors and sunlight."

"You . . . forgot . . . one," I manage to choke out.

"Really? *Do* tell."

Showing is always better than telling. I bring my legs up, clamp them around his waist, and throw my weight backward as hard as I can. We both topple over.

And into the well.

Ever seen what happens when you throw a chunk of raw sodium into water? It catches on fire. That's apparently the same thing that occurs when you dunk a vampire into a well full of holy water.

Neil screams when we hit, and bubbles explode from every submerged inch of his body. He shoots up to the surface like a rocket, with me still wrapped around him. I can feel the heat through my clothes, but the water is having an insulating effect, leaching away some of the thermal energy at the same time it's causing it. Supernatural chemistry 101.

I grab his tousled hair, take a deep breath, and yank both of us underwater again. It's like holding on to a giant Alka-Seltzer tablet. He fizzes and flails, but he's in too much agony to fight back coherently, and after a few seconds he stops. I surface, treading water, and see that the only thing left of him is some glowing, sudsy-looking bubbles.

I've done some rock climbing, and the shaft is narrow enough to wall-walk up. I put my feet flat against one side and my back against the other, and start the process of inching my way to the top.

I've been cursing my memory since this whole affair began, but I'm ready to forgive it now. I remembered the well from looking at the blueprints Gretch showed me, which were quite detailed about underground structures.

But it was the water font near the door that made me realize this was a Catholic church, and the covered windows that convinced me Father Stone was preparing a trap of his own for the impending invasion of pires. Lure them in, then hit them with sunlight; and if that doesn't work, you've got a well full of holy water stashed in the basement.

I make it to the lip of the well and tumble over it to the basement floor. I lie there for a moment, getting my breath back and thinking about what I'm going to do next.

Then I get to my feet and head back upstairs.

I know who the real monster is. Time to go prove it.

SEVENTEEN

When Athena Shaker answers her door, her green eyes go wide and her pale skin flushes. It's a natural enough reaction; we've got the unconscious body of her boyfriend's brother propped up between us, his limp arms draped over our shoulders.

"Oh! What—what happened?"

"Can we come in?" I say. "It's not safe out here."

"Yes, of course!"

She stands aside and we haul our comatose cargo in. We put him on the couch in a sitting position, his head leaning back like he fell asleep studying the ceiling.

"Here's the deal," I say to Athena. "First off, this isn't who you think. It's Peter, not Terrance. I know, his hair's too long and those tattoos don't belong, but that's illusion magic for you; it can fool you right down to the level of bad teenage judgment."

She frowns, clearly confused. "I don't know what you—"

"Stop. We don't have time for the wide-eyed innocent act. You and Doctor Pete are a couple. You've been keeping it a secret, but that's not the only one."

Now she looks less confused and more angry. "That's hardly any of your business—"

"We don't have TIME for this!" I shout. I take a fast step forward, getting right in her face. "We were jumped by a pack of vampires on the way here! I know this looks like Terrance, but it's *not*. It's his brother—*your lover*—and he knows where the master vampire's lair is. He was kidnapped and dragged away before he could tell me, then brainwashed with sorcery and swapped with his brother; they thought the last place I'd look for him would be in a jail cell."

She meets my eyes coolly. The pretense of ignorance is gone. "What do you want?" she asks me flatly.

"We need help. I know a magic ritual that'll unlock Doctor Pete's mind, but I need somewhere to do it, and I'll be helpless while it happens. We can't use my place or Charlie's—they've both been compromised."

"Vampires. You know how crazy that sounds?"

"About as crazy as werewolves, but less hairy?" Her only reaction to that is a single blink, but that and the second of hesitation are enough to tell me I'm on the right track. "I know *you* know," I say. "About Doctor Pete, and what he's going to become the first time the full moon rises. He's being forced to do something he doesn't want to do, and I know you want to help. Don't you?"

And now her lips quiver. Tears rise to her eyes, and she turns her head to look at the still body on her couch. She sinks down beside him, and takes one hand in hers. "Is it—is this really him?"

"Yeah," I say quietly. "It really is."

"I'm so confused," she whispers. "I couldn't believe it when he told me. He said there was going to be a war, and we had to choose sides if we wanted to survive."

"So you chose the one you love. But this is about more than a battle for turf in a small town, Athena; it's going to spread. If we don't stop it here, right now, the mystical fence that's keeping the situation contained is going to break down. You know what you've got then? Two viruses competing to outbreed each other. And both of them will spread faster than the black death in the middle ages, because thropes and pires can travel a lot farther and faster than rats."

She shakes her head, now crying openly. "What can we do?"

"We need to find the identity of the master vampire. Take him out and we eliminate one side entirely."

"And what about the other side?"

"We'll worry about that later. One thing at a time."

She sniffles, then nods. "Okay. Whatever you're going to do, just . . . just do it. Do you need anything?"

"Just your TV and DVD player," I say.

It doesn't take long to get set up. I position myself next to our subject on the couch and call up Azura with the remote. "It's time," I tell her.

She nods. "I hope you know what you're doing."

"Me, too."

There's a flash of white light.

The memory is from before Tair and Doctor Pete diverged into separate personae. I thought it might be the actual moment itself, but I'm wrong.

I'm tied to a chair. A youngish Peter Adams—not yet a doctor, not yet a monster—is staring at me in consternation. I can feel a trickle of something wet down my face, but it's not a tear; it's blood.

He's dressed in a white lab coat over a T-shirt and jeans, but there's no name tag. We're in a small, dingy room with newspaper covering the windows, trash in the corners, and a desk missing two of its drawers. Pete's leaning against the desk, his arms crossed.

"Who are you?" I ask.

"I'm—" He catches himself and shakes his head. "No. The question is, who are *you*?"

"Someone who could use a painkiller or seven." I wince. "Clocked me pretty good, didn't you? That's a helluva bedside manner you've got."

"You're the one who broke in."

"Did I? Well, you can't blame a girl for trying to make a buck, can you? Not exactly easy for someone like me to get by in this world anymore."

"A human being, you mean?"

I give him a nasty smile. "Don't you mean an OR? That's the clever, ironic term all you toothy types are using these days."

"I guess I'm not that clever. I don't know what—"

"Original Recipe."

He looks a little disgusted. Good. I can use that.

"I don't think that's clever or ironic," he says. "It's just cruel."

"Oh, I've heard worse. *Breather, bloodbag, midnight snack, throatwich* . . . but really, my favorite's always been *tampon slurpee*. Not as widespread as some of the others due to exclusive pire usage, but crude, evocative, and demeaning all at once. Has a certain rhythm to it, too, you know? Makes it easy to chant."

He uncrosses his arms. "Look, I'm not a speceist. I don't use those terms, and I'm sorry you've been given a life that's not exactly fair—"

I snort. "Given? Nobody *gave* me anything, hairball. I had things taken *away*. Dignity. Respect. Any chance at making a decent life for myself or anyone I care about. But what does that matter, right? My puny seventy or so years is barely a quarter of *your* time on Earth, and an eyeblink to any pire."

"The fact that we live longer is hardly our fault."

"No, but everything else *is*. You killed us by the millions and then took over when there weren't enough of us to fight back."

He sighs. "Oh. You're one of those. Look, I may not be a doctor yet, but I'm in medical school. And I can tell you that the plague that hit the human population after World War Two wasn't caused by pires *or* thropes."

I laugh. "Sure. Only conspiracy fanatics believe that, right? And the whole pire pregnancy spell that just happened to come along right after that was a *total* coincidence. Absolutely."

I can see by the look on his face that I'm losing him. "Wait a minute, just listen to me. I'm not someone who believes whatever she's told. I've been *shown,* okay? I've seen actual hard evidence."

"By whom?"

I hesitate. "People who know. *Serious* people."

"What makes them so serious? They tell you all these things in a really sincere tone of voice?"

There's more amusement than mockery in his voice, but it pisses me off all the same. "These are people who do more than just talk. They *do* stuff. Stuff that gets *noticed.*"

That gets his attention. "Wait. Are you talking about the Free Human Resistance?"

I don't answer.

"You are, aren't you?" The frown on his face deepens. "You can't trust people like that. They're *terrorists,* for God's sake."

"No, they aren't. They're *freedom fighters.*" I can hear the passion in my own voice, but the feeling belongs to someone else. "They want to *change* things."

"How? By murdering people? That's not change, it's just mayhem."

"No. Some people *have* to die. That's just how things are. It's how things have always been."

"I'm sorry, but I don't believe that. I believe in life. In fact, I'm thinking of studying human medicine—"

"Sure you are. That's why you're working in a gray-market lem factory."

That stops him for a second. "One has nothing to do with the other."

" 'Course they don't. One's about studying a soon-to-be-extinct species, the other's about creating slaves."

"Isn't it better to be a slave than have no life at all?"

I shake my head. "That's how you justify it, huh? Well, I don't agree. If it thinks and feels, you can't simply use it up and throw it away. You're not giving them life, you're just giving them existence. Big difference."

He looks away, not sure how to answer that. Which is when the door opens and his boss walks in.

His boss is a thrope too, but only in the sense that a Doberman pinscher and a poodle are both dogs. This guy is a card-carrying member of *La Lupo Grigorio,* the Gray Wolf Mafia, and looks it—from his greased, jet-black hair to his hand-tailored Italian suit. Thick gold rings adorn both hairy hands, and the expression on his bulldog-like face is one of annoyed contempt.

"What?" he says to Pete. "*This*? You call me for *this*?"

"I caught her breaking in downstairs—"

The mobster waves away his explanation with one meaty hand. "Yeah, you already said. She got an eyeful, huh?"

"I'm not sure how much she saw—"

"I saw enough," I snap.

"Shuddup," Pete's boss says casually. He's looking at me with less contempt now, and considerably more interest. "You didn't mention she was human."

Pete frowns. "What difference does that make?"

"She's a federally protected endangered species, that's what difference it makes." He glares at Pete. "The last thing we need is the feds sniffin' around. You did right after all. I'm going to have to take care of this myself."

"What are you going to do?" Pete asks.

"Get her out of the country. Keep her on ice for a while until this batch is done—we were gonna move to a different location, anyway. Then whatever she knows don't matter."

It's a plausible enough story, but I don't believe it for a second. Mr. Wolfioso is a professional criminal, one who crosses swords with the federal authorities all the time; violating my protected status doesn't mean anything more to him than breaking any other federal law. He's feeding Pete just enough misinformation to keep him quiet, but once he's got me out of here—

"Bullshit," I say loudly. "C'mon, you really think he's going to go to all that time and trouble? He'll be on his phone to the nearest yakuza blood farm the minute after he locks me in his trunk."

Pete glances from me to his employer and back again. He knows I'm telling the truth, but he doesn't want to. He wants to sink back into his nice warm web of rationalizations, the one where he's just making a little money under the table by bending a few rules. All his boss has to do is feed him a few more sugar-coated lies—lies Pete will swallow as fast as he can choke them down—and the status will return to quo.

But that doesn't happen.

The Gray Wolf's face hardens. Maybe Pete's phone call interrupted something important; maybe he just had a big deal go sour. Maybe someone higher up the food chain is squeezing him, or previous encounters have left him with a grudge against human beings. It doesn't matter. What matter is that he holds my life in his hands, he doesn't give a damn what Pete thinks, and I've just pissed him off.

"You goddamn slice of *lunch meat*," he growls. He stalks forward and grabs me by the arm, which is pinned behind my back by the ropes. He hoists me one-handed into the air as easily as a man picking up a sandwich. My own weight threatens to dislocate my shoulder, and I yell in pain.

"Hey!" Pete says, taking a step forward.

His boss ignores him, taking me through the open door and onto a small landing overlooking the main floor of the warehouse. For a second I think he's going to throw me down the stairs or over the railing, but he doesn't. He just shoves me forward and says, "Take a look, girlie. Take a long, *hard* look, and tell me what you see."

What I see is an illegal lem production facility, what's called a gravel pit. Pens full of goats and pigs, all of them oddly quiet. Crude ritual altars made of wooden tables, crusted with dried blood. A gigantic yellow-brown pile of sand in one corner, almost reaching the roof. Racks full of empty golem skins made of thick, transparent plastic, like the ghosts of blow-up dolls waiting to be filled with breath and life. And trundling along with wheelbarrows and shovels, brooms and buckets, are quite a few of the finished product.

The Gray Wolf doesn't wait for my answer. "What you see is an efficient operation. Nice, tidy, profitable. Runs like clockwork—in fact, I *could* run it twenty-four/seven, except for one little problem: I don't got enough activators. Like your new friend, the one who's so concerned about you."

And now Pete steps out to join us. "Take it easy. You don't have to—"

"I think I do. And I think what *you* need is a little dose of reality." He points at the lems. "See, what you're looking at is a significant investment of time, effort, and money. But it didn't come easy, oh, no. I got all kinds of things to worry about: supply chains, distribution, production deadlines. I got lots of people I have to keep happy, and even more I got to keep quiet. It's a juggling act."

And suddenly he lifts me, chair and all, over the railing. The concrete floor is a good thirty feet below me.

"Don't!" Pete says.

"Sometimes," the Gray Wolf says, "it's all I can do to keep all those different things in the air. And you, Mr. Peter Damien—or would you prefer Doctor Damien?—are one of those things. An important thing, one I don't wanna drop . . . but I can only do so much, y'know? Sometimes, with so many things goin' up and down, I gotta make a decision. I gotta let something go, so I can keep everything else moving."

"Please," I say. I want to be brave, I want to be tough, but my voice betrays me.

"Killing her doesn't—you *can't*—"

"Oh, I can. It solves all kinds of problems. But I *won't,* and you know why?"

When he answers, his voice is dull. "No, I don't."

The Gray Wolf chuckles. He knows a lie when he hears it. "Because you didn't bargain. You didn't say, *if you kill her, I'll quit.* That tells me a lot, right there. It tells me you understand things, and where you fit in. It tells me you know where the line is, and not to push me past it. That's good. That'll keep you alive."

I swallow, and try to keep the quaver out of my voice. "What—what are you going to do with me?"

"You?" He laughs, pulls his arm back, and sets the chair down on the landing. "You got lucky, kid. Normally, I'd just make you disappear. But that would upset my activator here, and I want to keep him happy. So—today only—you get a pass."

"I—I'm free to go?"

He smiles. "Not just yet. We're going to have a little talk in my car, first. *Then* you can go." He turns to Pete. "That okay with you?"

Peter Damien—soon to be Doctor Peter Damien, then Doctor Peter Adams—blinks. His face is pale. The lie his boss is offering is as thin and fragile as tissue paper, but he wants to believe. Believing means he isn't condemning me to a horrible death. Believing means he doesn't work for a monster. Believing means he still has a soul.

"Yes," he says faintly. "That's fine."

"No," I say, as the Gray Wolf carries me down the stairs, still bound to the chair. "No! He's lying! *He's lying!*"

"She's pretty upset," the Gray Wolf says. He's got me slung over his back one-handed, like a jacket. I can see Pete's pale face in the shadows of the landing above, slowly receding as we descend. "I'll keep her restrained until we get outside. Don't worry, she'll calm down."

Pete doesn't say anything. He just stares.

We make it down to the floor. The lems stare at me with curious eyes, then quickly look away.

"No!" I scream. "No, you can't let him do this! He'll kill me! *He'll kill me!*"

"Ssshh," the Gray Wolf says. "Everything's fine. Everything's going to be *okay.*"

"He won't let me go! *He told me your real name, you bastard!*"

And then he drags me through the door and out into the alley.

That's where the memory ends.

EIGHTEEN

Now that I've done this a few times, I come back to myself fairly quickly. My eyes snap open and I check to see if the rest of the plan is working.

Athena Shaker lies in the middle of the floor, wrapped in chains; her eyelids flutter as her own consciousness returns. Charlie stands over her, his arms crossed, looking pensive. I turn my head to the side and see Doctor Pete, already awake but looking groggy. But is it really him?

"What was—what was that?" Athena says. "I thought you were going to . . . what's going on?"

I shake my head, trying to clear the last of the muzziness out of it. "What's going on is the old switcheroo, Athena. I took a chance that the alpha werewolf wouldn't be able to resist discovering the identity of the master vampire, and you went for it. We both got sucked into the memory sequence, and Charlie wrapped you in a few dozen feet of tow-chain while you were drooling on the carpet. Didn't want you to wolf out and gut us as soon as you woke up and discovered you'd been suckered."

She glares at me from the floor. "You're making a mistake. I'm not—"

"You *are*. But you know who isn't? This guy." I aim a

thumb beside me. "Sometimes a good old-fashioned lie works just as well as an illusion spell. We used Terrance to fake you out and throw you off balance. It's the kind of thing he's good at."

Terrance—or maybe someone else—gives me a look of consternation. "Jace? Damn, this is messed up. . . ."

"Let me clarify things for you," I say. "Doctor Pete was shacked up with the alpha werewolf, who was using him to infect the townspeople with her own blood via phony innoculations. She may look like a petite redhead, but that's more illusion magic; you just can't trust appearances in this town. I even briefly considered that she might be a he, but the local transvestite is the wrong shade—the alpha wolf is not only tall, she's black. Her real name is Catherine Shaka, AKA the African Queen."

She doesn't bother to deny it. "I *knew* he smelled wrong," she growls. "I should have killed all three of you the second you walked through the door."

"The woman I knew wouldn't do that," I say. "Not without a good reason, anyway. After Longinus snatched you, he must have tampered with your memory. What do you remember?"

"I had returned to my homeland, traveling in secret, to meet with a shaman who said he could return my throne to me. He told me of you, and what you had done to my people, and where you were hiding. Then he brought me here." Her tone is savage. "This place of evil will be redeemed through your suffering. My bloodline will spread throughout the population, giving birth to a world of foot soldiers. Then we will return to my country to reclaim it."

I sigh. More wrongheaded, hate-filled propaganda—but this time, it hasn't been pumped into the brain of some hapless alternate-world civilian. This is the genuine article, a royal woman warrior I've fought alongside—and she is *not* someone I want as an enemy. Even without the ability to turn into a nine-foot-tall hairy monster, the African Queen is a legendary heroine, one whose fighting prowess, battlefield experience, and skill with a bow make her lethal at any distance.

"You've been brainwashed," I tell her bluntly. "With powerful sorcery that's slowly eroding. You're one of the most single-minded people I've ever met; if anyone can beat a spell into submission through sheer willpower, it's you—"

"Excuse the hell outta *me*," Terrance interrupts, "but I'm still a little confused. I seem to remember something about being in a jail cell, but there was this little blonde in there with me. Only I *also* remember being in a cell—a *different* cell—all by myself. And then there's *her*." He points to Shaka's bound body and shakes his head. "I kind of remember being *with* her, you know? And giving shots to people. Was that me?"

I study him carefully. "On Thropirelem, Azura's a damn fine illusionist herself. She used her abilities to infiltrate the federal prison where you were locked up, then convinced you to help us. That is, she convinced *Tair* to help us." What I don't tell him is that because more than one mind was involved, there's a possibility that either persona could surface, or parts of both—leading to a confusing mix of memories in Terrance's head.

He frowns at me. "I . . . I don't think my name is Tair. That doesn't *feel* right."

I grin. "Maybe not," I say. "And that's fine by me."

I turn back to Shaka. "How about you, Catherine? You feel any more like yourself, or do you still think I'm the Antichrist?"

Her response is to bare her teeth, which are a lot longer and sharper than they were a minute ago. Her auburn hair darkens, and coarse, jet-black fur sprouts from every inch of her skin as her frame reshapes and contorts. Her eyes glow bright yellow; her fingernails lengthen and curve into razored weapons. She's hoping to burst her bonds through brute, physical-law-defying force as her mass increases and her body expands.

All I can do is stare. I have one of those moments of sudden clarity brought on by intense emotion—in this case, terror—as the real, true horror of what Ahaseurus planned for me becomes evident. The snarling monster straining at her chains in front of me is exactly one-half of a pitiless equation, the other half being her vampire equivalent. Together, they spell the inevitable, bloody demise of every human being sharing this particular version of Earth; those who aren't turned into creatures like this will become food, slaves, or both.

And all of it will be my fault.

The chains hold. She howls and writhes and bucks, but we keep well away from both claws and jaws. I try to communicate with her using thrope sign language—it's how beings with a muzzle for a mouth communicate—but she doesn't seem to understand me. In the end, we grab a dangling length of chain and drag her into the garage, where the trunk of her late-model sedan is just big enough to cram her into. It's like wrestling a grizzly with rabies—I may be immune to scratches, but one bite and it's Full-Moon City, final stop on the Fur-Ball Express.

She keeps hammering away on the inside of the trunk, but I'm not too worried; as long as the chains hold she's not going anywhere. One monster down, two to go.

"Pretty worked up, isn't she?" Terrance says.

"It's this place," I say. "Or maybe this world. Pires and thropes aren't the same, here. They're—more *basic*, somehow. Wilder. Less evolved, maybe—"

"Nah," says Charlie. He's inspecting a row of tools on the garage wall. "That ain't it. You don't want to say it, but you know exactly which word to use."

"Primitive?"

"*Evil*." He picks up a pair of gardening shears and studies the cutting edges critically. "I can feel it, and so can you. They ain't like the pires and thropes back home—these are bad-to-the-bone *killers*. I don't know why, and I don't much care. They get in our way, they gotta go down and never get back up."

I want to argue. I want to tell him that these are—or were—ordinary people, before Longinus got ahold of them. Maybe some of them could have made better choices in the religion department, but none of them asked to be turned into bloodthirsty creatures of the night.

But I don't say a thing . . . because he's right. I could hear it in Zhang's hungry whisper drifting out of the shadows; I could see it in Isamu's cruel eyes. Even Neil, with his soft-spoken musings on the tortures he planned to inflict, practically radiated it: evil. The real thing, fully self-aware and predatory, utterly without mercy and deriving immense satisfaction from the suffering of others. An implacable, elemental force, indulging in destruction for destruction's sake.

"Yeah, okay," I say wearily. "They're the bad guys. No problem. Never mind that some of them look like people I care about, or remember chatting with in a supermarket line, or maybe even got naked with. Nope. Just line 'em up and I'll take 'em down. . . ."

We troop out of the garage and back into the house. We make it as far as the kitchen, then collapse into chairs around the table. Terrance has been pretty quiet up until now, no doubt trying to sort out the conflicting things his brain is telling him. I haven't had a chance to ask him about the memory he relived, and even with all the other craziness he's been thrown into, it must be eating at him.

"Hey," I say. "You all right?"

He doesn't look at me when he answers. "Getting there. I know what we have to do next."

"Oh?"

"Go after the Gallowsman. He's the key to all this."

That's more coherent than I was expecting, but good news; it means Terrance is adapting. "You think?"

"Yeah. I—Terrance, I mean—was just screwing with you

when he told you that story, but you're the one the Gallows-man is focusing on."

Interesting; he seems to have the memories of Terrance, Tair, *and* Doctor Pete, or some combination thereof. "I thought it was supposed to possess the body of a suicide and then target the ones who made the victim's life miserable."

"That's what Terrance said, yeah. Because that's what he was *told* to say."

"By whom?"

"Whom do you think? His father. Mayor Leo knows all about the cult, though he isn't a member. That means he took orders from the *real* town leader—Longinus."

"More smoke and mirrors," Charlie grunts.

"So what's the actual story?" I ask.

Terrance frowns. "The Gallowsman is some kind of bad luck and despair vacuum. Sucks it up and hands it over to a specific target—in this case, you."

I nod. "That much we know. And with me primed by your little urban legend, presumably I was eventually supposed to go out to the woods to off myself in the hopes of a little postmortem payback."

It's Charlie's turn to frown. "But you aren't supposed to *die*—just suffer, right?"

"Sure. Which means any attempt to kill myself wouldn't work—Ahaseurus wouldn't leave an obvious escape clause like that in place. It's just another way to demoralize me; after all, once you've tried to kill yourself and failed, you've pretty much hit bottom."

Unless, you know, you're then responsible for the slaughter of your entire race. That might just depress you a touch.

"Terrance doesn't know a lot about the cult, but one of his friends does," Terrance says. "Zev. He's the one who told Terrance about the tunnels."

Zev? Now the name sounds familiar, in that double-resonance sort of way that means I must have known him before Ahaseurus stuck me here. "So why does the local bad

boy's sidekick know more about the town's secret history
than the mayor's son?"

Terrance shrugs. "Same reason everything happens
around here, probably; something to do with you, and screwing with your head. But there are two facts I *am* sure of. The
first is that the Gallowsman is at the center of this, magically
speaking. Eliminate him, and all the spells woven through
this place fall apart."

"And the second?"

"That Zev's loyal to Terrance, and he's the only one in
town who knows about the tunnels but isn't a member of the
cult. If I ask him to help, he will."

I study Terrance's face. What he's saying rings true, but
at this point I suspect everyone and everything. "What's the
first thing you gave me when we met?"

He looks blank for a second, then smiles. "Oh. A mug of
Urthbone tea, to help with your Reality Dislocation Trauma.
You wanted coffee, but I insisted you drink the tea first."

I sigh in relief. Doctor Pete seems to be the one in charge
of the brain. "Okay. Well, we should either go after the Gallowsman or the master vampire, and at least we know where
the Gallowsman is likely to be—plus, we have someone to
play tour guide. If you think Zev will go for that."

"Oh, I think he will. In fact, I won't take no for an answer."

"Then let's pay him a visit," I say, getting to my feet.
"And, Doctor Pete? Welcome to the party."

He hesitates, then gives me a smile in return.

"Terrific," Charlie mutters as we head for the door. "For
once, I was hoping we'd get the ruthless killer instead of the
medic. I just hope we don't need him. . . ."

We take Athena Shaker's car—with her still in the trunk—
down a dirt track to a spot just outside of town, where there's
a little wooden shack hidden by a stand of birch trees between two wheat fields. I tried calling Alexis before we left,

but got no answer. That worries me, but I can't waste time looking for her.

Doctor Pete informs us that this is where Terrance and his little gang like to hole up and drink cheap beer when they can't afford the Quarry. Zev's inside—and he isn't alone.

I can hear the noises from inside the shack as we get out of the car. Neither of them are exactly trying to be quiet, and I recognize Sally January's voice almost immediately.

From the look on Doctor Pete's face, so does he. ". . . the hell?" he mutters, strides forward, and yanks the rickety wooden door open.

"Ah," says Charlie as we follow. "The distinctive yet oddly disturbing sound of two biological entities trying to smush themselves together to make a third. No wonder it's the inspiration for all the great art of the ages."

"Sounds more like they're trying to invoke a deity," I remark. "The God of Oh, I think."

That's as far as we get before Zev comes flying through the open doorway. From her surprised shriek, I guess Sally wasn't expecting her current boyfriend's sudden arrival. Neither was I, frankly, but it looks like Terrance still has some influence in the decision-making process.

"Terrance and Sally had a thing," I tell Charlie as we look down at the naked man sprawled at our feet.

"Looks like Zev has one, too," Charlie observes. "Guess Sally wanted to compare."

Zev grins, then bounds to his feet like a chimpanzee. "Buddy!" he says as Terrance steams outside, a naked Sally trying to hold him back. "Come on, man—it's not like you were *serious* about her—"

I step between them. "Cut it out," I snap. "Hey, Doc—remember who you are."

That stops him. He blinks, breathing hard, and forces the scowl off his face. "Sorry," he mumbles. "You're right. I don't even know this woman."

"Doc?" Sally says. She looks Doctor Pete up and down, notes the tattoos and absence of haircut or shave. "You're not . . . what the hell's going on?"

"Long story," I say. "Both of you get dressed, then get back out here. Zev, we need your help."

Zev shrugs. "Okay. No hard feelings, right?" He claps Doctor Pete on the shoulder as he strolls past.

"Loyal to the end, huh?" Charlie says.

They're back out in a few minutes. "We thought it was the apocalypse," Sally blurts out. "All the crazy stuff happening? That freaky storm that won't let anyone leave? And—and what happened to *Alexis*—" She breaks down and starts to cry. It looks like she wants to fall into Terrance's arms, but Terrance isn't here anymore. Doctor Pete regards her with all the warmth of a snowman in midwinter—as opposed to a new man in January.

"What happened to Alexis?" I ask.

"She called me," Sally sobs. "She was driving. Said she had to get out of here. I told her she *couldn't*, that the lightning would get her, but she wouldn't *listen*. I heard it strike, and she *screamed*, and then there was this horrible *buzzing* noise. . . ." That's as much as she can get out; her sobs become wails, and it's Charlie who grabs her before she can hit the ground.

Doctor Pete looks grim. Zev looks unimpressed. "Zap zap *zap*, right off the *map*," he says. "At least it was quick. One tap of the cosmic cattle prod and you're burnt toast—not even time to do the Frankenstein Shuffle." He mimes a stiff-legged sleepwalker pose, then jitters violently from side to side.

I deck him. It's a carefully calculated blow, delivered with my elbow and not my fist, and while it may loosen a few teeth or crack his jawbone, it won't actually kill him. His head snaps to the right, he spins halfway around and then drops bonelessly into the dirt.

"Damn it," I mutter. "Now we have to wait for him to wake up. . . ."

We stick him in the rear seat between Doctor Pete and Sally, while Charlie drives and I ride shotgun. We head back the way we came and keep going, all the way through town. It's still eerily deserted, no one on the streets at all. This may not be the end of the world, but you can see it from here. . . .

Zev didn't tell Terrance much about the tunnels, and they're too extensive for me to recall them in detail from the brief glimpse of the map I got—but I remember a few things. One is the well beneath the church; the other is an entrance located in a basement.

The basement of the Longinus house, of course.

We park outside. The constant thumping from the trunk has stopped. Sally's so overwhelmed she hasn't even noticed it, and Zev is still unconscious—until Doctor Pete does something medical involving a nerve cluster and a sharp pinch. Zev snaps awake with a howl of pain.

"Rise and shine," says Doctor Pete.

"Where are we?" Zev asks, rubbing his jaw.

"Old Man Longinus's house," I say. "He asked me to water his plants while he's out of town, but I can't find the darn watering can. You're going to help me look."

"Yeah, sounds like a real party, but I think I'll pass."

"He said something about it being in a tunnel."

Zev's eyes get wider and he barks with laughter. "Oh! I get it. You want to get *down* and *dirty* underneath the *streets*. I can dig *that*."

"I don't want to do any digging, Zev. More like a little hunting."

"Yeah? You planning on throwing together a rat stew? 'Cause that's about all that's down there—" He stops as he realizes what I'm talking about, and a smile spreads across his face. "Oho. I gotcha. What the hell, why not? Go after the Gallowsman before he comes after us. Hope you got a really *big* pair of scissors, though."

I show him the shotgun. "This'll have to do."

"Got one for me?"

"Sorry, no. You'll have to rely on your razor-sharp wit."

"Hey, story of my life."

We get out of the car. Sally looks around nervously. "This is crazy. I must be *crazy.*"

"Well, you slept with *him*," I say, jerking a thumb in Zev's direction. "Not exactly a ringing endorsement of clear thinking . . . but crazy? Nah. I know crazy. This is dangerous and possibly a horror-movie cliché, but there's a lot to be said for a preemptive strike—not to mention the element of surprise. If the victims in all those slasher films tried running *at* the killer instead of away, they'd probably stand a lot better chance of surviving."

We step onto the porch and I try the door. Still unlocked. I open it and lead my little band inside. The house has that empty feel, but I stay alert as we head down the hall and into the basement.

The room with the altar is just like Charlie and I left it; if someone's been here they haven't moved anything. I kick a black pillow out of my way and stand in the center of the room, doing my best to remember what I saw on the map. The entrance had been close to the south wall, but not on it—which would mean . . .

I walk over to the altar. It looks like a single chunk of solid stone, but my fingers find a very faint seam an inch or so below the top.

Zev steps forward. "It's on a swivel," he says. He puts his hands on the edge and pushes; the top of the altar grates to one side in an arc.

"How'd you find out about this?" I ask him, peering inside. A wooden ladder descends into darkness.

"Let's just say that some middle-aged married ladies in this town like to drink wine in the afternoon with irreverent young stud muffins," Zev says. He fumbles with the underside of the lid, then produces two flashlights, one a small LED and the other the old-fashioned kind with the long, rubberized grip. "Ladies who like to show off how sophisticatedly *perverse* they are. Not much compensation for all the sagging flesh, but better than dressing up in a clown costume and calling her Mommy. . . ."

He gives the small light to me, and keeps the other for himself. "After you," he says.

I hand the shotgun to Charlie, turn on the flashlight, and shine it down the hole. The ladder goes down about twenty feet and ends in what looks like stone. I hold the light between my teeth and clamber down, hoping I won't run into any booby traps along the way.

I get to the bottom and look around. The tunnel's like something you'd find under the streets of Paris, or maybe Rome. An arched roof overhead; flat, smooth floor; everything made of mortared stone. The tunnel goes straight for about thirty feet and then branches.

"All clear," I say. "Come on down."

Doctor Pete, Zev, and Sally follow, with Charlie bringing up the rear. He tosses the shotgun to me first, and I snag it out of the air one-handed.

"Okay," I say once Charlie steps down. "You're the expert, Zev. How well do you know these tunnels?"

"Oh, pretty damn well," he says. "Mrs. Johnson took me here on many a dreary afternoon. Gave her a real thrill to do it below the grocery store or post office, thinking about everyone going about their business with no clue what was happening right under their feet. . . ."

"So where do we look for the Gallowsman?"

He chuckles. "Follow me."

He doesn't wait for any further questions, just struts along the tunnel as confidently as an usher in a darkened theater. If this *were* a horror movie, he'd be the wise-ass who dies halfway through cracking an offensive joke, a role that otherwise might have been played by me.

Makes me glad he's the one in the lead.

We have to hurry to catch up with him. "How about a little more information?" I hiss.

"What, and ruin the surprise?" He doesn't turn around, but I can hear the grin in his voice. "Just chill out, okay? You're in good hands."

"I'd prefer your hands where I can see them," I mutter, but there's not much more I can do at this point other than trust him. I don't, but I do have a shotgun pointed at his back, which is the next best thing.

He takes the tunnel that goes left, then another that forks right, then another right. He seems supremely confident of where he's going, never hesitating or slowing down. I keep expecting iron spikes to shoot out of the wall and impale him, but nothing like that happens.

We come to an intersection with shafts branching off in three directions, and he finally stops. Looks around, plays the beam of his flashlight down one way, then another. "Hmmmm. Okay, I'm pretty sure it's this way." He leads us ten feet or so down the center tunnel, then stops. Looks up at the roof. "Damn. Okay, just stay here for a second, I need to check something. . . .

He pushes past us and back into the intersection.

His flashlight goes out.

"Zev?" I call. "You all right?"

No answer. Of course not. This is the part of the movie where the wise-ass decides it would be funny to pretend the killer got him, and then jumps out from the shadows and makes everyone scream.

Then again, these days directors like to play with your expectations. It's just as likely that his severed head will suddenly drop into our laps, or even that he'll pull his little joke and then get chopped to pieces a second later. Whatever it takes to make the audience jump—

Sally screams.

I spin around. Sally's eyes are wide and terrified, and she's pointing farther down the tunnel. "I saw it! I saw its *eyes*!"

I shine my beam in that direction, but there's nothing there now. "Charlie? Doctor Pete? You see anything?"

"Thought I saw a flash of red," Charlie says.

"No," says Doctor Pete. "Yellow. Definitely yellow."

"It was both," Sally whispers. "Two glowing eyes—one red, one yellow."

There's a moment of silence while we digest that, and then I hear the chuckle. Zev's chuckle, coming from somewhere ahead—he must have gone up another tunnel and doubled back. "Red and yellow," he says, his mocking voice echoing off the stone walls. "But no green and no go. Stop dead or stand and yield."

"Uh-oh," Charlie says.

"Y'think?" I snap.

"Oh, this is going to be *so* much fun," Zev says. "*My* turn for a little roughhousing, right? Let's see: My former best friend threw me around and gave me a nasty little pinch, but Ms. Valchek elbowed me in the face. Charlie's thrown me out of his bar on more than one occasion. Which should it be, I wonder?"

There's a dull crack, like wood breaking, right beside me. Sally crumples to the ground. I swing the light in the other direction, but Zev's already gone.

Doctor Pete's kneeling beside her. Blood spreads in an ever-widening pool under her head, and her eyes are wide open. He looks for a pulse but I can tell he isn't having any luck.

She's dead.

NINETEEN

I bend down and turn Sally's head to the side. There's a large, ugly hole in the back of her skull, and something perfectly round with a little nub in the center is barely visible under the welling blood.

"Assault with a battery!" Zev crows, somewhere in the darkness. "Didn't see *that* coming, did you?"

"No," I say. "I must have missed that movie."

I fire the shotgun down the tunnel. I don't have a prayer of hitting him, but I need to make him hesitate while we get around a corner to cover. On the world of Thropirelem, thrown weapons—spears, knives, ball-bearings—dominate, largely because supernatural strength and accuracy can turn almost any projectile deadly. Zev's just demonstrated that with an Energizer D-cell . . . but the question now is, which kind of supernatural being are we facing?

And why the hell did I trust him in the first place?

I motion to Terrance and Charlie, and we sprint up the tunnel in the opposite direction of the battery's trajectory. We duck to the left, up another shaft, then around a corner to the right. I know we don't have a prayer of outrunning or losing Zev—pire or thrope, he knows these tunnels and can see in the dark regardless—but I need a moment's respite to just *think*.

We flatten ourselves against the wall. "What the hell *is* he?" Doctor Pete hisses.

"Good question," I hiss back. "Shut up and let me figure it out, okay?"

There are two main kinds of spell woven through this town: illusion and memory. One screws with my perception, the other with my mind. But the memory spells are like deadfalls: A big chunk of information is held back until I stumble over the tripwire, and then I get clobbered by a cascade of information.

And they're set up that way for a reason. Maximum torment. I don't remember an ally until they die, because that's what hurts the most. And I don't remember an enemy until they have me at their nonexistent mercy, because that produces the most terror.

But.

The spells are degrading. Triggering earlier. Which means I might be able to break through to my memories *before* Zev's about to rip my throat out. I close my eyes and try.

Zev. Sounds like an abbreviation. Short for what? Not a lot of words start that way.

Brute force it. Go through the vowels. Zeva. Zeve. Zevi. Zevo—

Zevon.

That's it, but I still don't know what it means. I try free associating. Only Zevon I know is Warren Zevon, the musician. Big hit was a song called—

"Werewolves of London."

Zevon. British accent. Red hair? Or was it white? Had to have been a thrope, but that doesn't seem quite right, either. And the voice—that had been a fake accent, hadn't it? And not the only one . . .

And then I have it. The goofy sense of humor, the thrope connection, the voices.

I sigh. "Charlie, you never met him face to face—not in

his real form, anyway—but this guy is based on a trickster spirit. The *kitsune* in Vancouver, remember?"

"But it's not him, right?"

"I don't think so . . . but I'm not sure. Azura said only three entities were brought over the dimensional divide— me, the alpha wolf, and the master vampire—but she didn't mention the Road Crew from Hell, so I guess this could be the real thing. I doubt it, though; Zevon worked for an actual deity, and I don't think she'd take kindly to someone poaching him."

"I know what a *kitsune* is," Doctor Pete says. "Not usually this bloodthirsty, are they?"

"Depends on how funny the carnage is," I say. "Which gives me an idea. . . ."

I call down the tunnel. "Hey! Funnyboy! Want to hear a joke?"

No answer.

"What do you call a half vampire, half werewolf with a grudge?"

Now I hear an echoey laugh. Closer than he was before. "Who says I have a grudge?"

"Oh, you've all got a grudge—they hand 'em out for free when you enter city limits. But yours doesn't make much sense, does it?"

"It does to *me* . . ."

"I don't think so. Old Man Longinus may have been able to steal or duplicate the memories of some of the people I know, but the personal assistant of a goddess was out of his reach. So he just *made them up*. The real giveaway is the half-thrope, half-pire thing—that's just not *possible*."

"Oh, I don't know." His voice is an amused whisper. "This town is weirdsville squared, right? All *kinds* of bizarre shit is possible here."

"Not this. The supernatural viruses that cause vampirism and lycanthropy don't get along, and here they're magnified—so much so that a war's about to break out between their hosts. Both viruses in one body would rip you apart—which means you don't contain *either*."

"Is this going to be one of those long, pointless setups with a lame punchline? 'Cause I really *hate* those."

"You want a punchline, Zev? Here it is: *You aren't real.*"

Silence. Is he thinking about it, realizing that what I'm saying makes sense? Can he *feel* that it's true, or is he incapable of that? Just how much crazy did Ahaseurus pour into Zev's skull when he made him, and how crazy has he become since Ahaseurus's spells started to fall apart?

I get my answer by way of a low chuckle. A chuckle that grows into full-throated laughter, then up the register to pure, hysterical screams of glee; the sound bounces off the stone walls, reverberating through the damp, chilled dark like the howls from a basement full of lunatics deprived of their meds.

He knows I'm telling the truth. He just doesn't care.

"Nice," Charlie says. "Knocked him right off his rocker. He'll be *much* easier to deal with now."

"Oh, absolutely. Trapped underground with a monster who's equal parts pire, thrope, and mental patient—we've got him right where we want him."

"You're smiling," Doctor Pete says to me. "Why are you *smiling*?"

Charlie glances at me, then him. "Because that *wasn't* a joke . . ."

"Stay close," I say, and take off at a run.

I know crazy. And I know monsters. I know where we are, what Zev was designed to do, and where I'm supposed to go. This is a maze, with a rabid animal at one end and me at the other. He'll pursue, but he won't try to take me down until we reach the end—the longer the chase, the higher the level of terror.

But I'm not terrified. I'm *pissed off*.

This isn't a maze. This is my life. Dead ends, blind alleys, being manipulated to go one way and then another . . .

I feel like all I ever do is react to one crisis after another, an endless cycle of what's-going-to-screw-with-Jace-next. What I really want to do is stand and fight, but that's just not a smart move at this point. Whatever Zev is, I'm guessing he doesn't have the traditional weaknesses of pires or thropes, which means the custom loads in my shotgun are useless.

But I know something that might—should—work. Every maze has a piece of cheese at the end, and I have a pretty good idea what this particular slice of fermented curd must be. Not just something I want, but something I need. Something I'd be willing to venture into the Gallowsman's lair for, something Ahaseurus was going to tempt me with but never got the chance. There are two possibilities, actually, but I know which one I'm putting my money on.

So if the entrance under the altar is the start of the maze, where's the logical end—and how do I find my way there without a guide?

I skid to a stop, and so do Charlie and Doctor Pete. "Doc," I say. "I need your nose."

"Okay, but—this body isn't a thrope. It's been bitten, but it's never transformed."

"I know that, but even before the first full moon there are changes. Your strength and senses are still heightened. It should be enough for you to follow a trail."

I hear Doctor Pete inhale deeply through his nose. "What am I looking for?"

"The smell of old rope. Hemp, probably. With maybe just a touch of decay."

The monster's lair. It's always in the monster's lair. But where does a creature like the Gallowsman call home?

"I've got something," Doctor Pete whispers. He frowns, his face shadowy above the glare of the flashlight. "That way." He points.

We follow. I've got the shotgun ready, and Charlie's got his Glock, but I know neither will do much to Zev except maybe slow him down.

And then I see it. Two little winks of light in the darkness ahead of us, one red and one yellow.

"Down!" I yell, and we all hit the floor. Something whizzes past overhead and smashes itself to pieces against the far wall: another battery, no doubt. I fire down the tunnel, but he's already gone.

"He just *appeared* in the middle of the tunnel," Doctor Pete says. "I was looking for those eyes, but I didn't see them until the last second—"

"That's because he kept them closed until he was ready to pitch," I say grimly. "You're not the only one who can navigate with his nose, Doc. And I bet his is a lot sharper. Next time he may decide he doesn't need to open them at all."

"He got ahead of us, too," Charlie says. "Must know these tunnels as well as he said he did."

"He's only got one battery left," I say. "After that, he'll have to take us on face-to-face. Stay sharp and keep moving. Doc, same plan as before, but stay between me and Charlie. We can't afford to lose you."

I take point. I know Zev won't kill me from a distance; that would put an end to his game far too quickly. *Maiming,* however, is a definite possibility. I'll just have to risk it.

We make it to the end of the current tunnel, which branches off to the right and left. "Left," Doctor Pete says.

"Any idea where we are?" I ask.

"Not really," Doctor Pete says. "Somewhere under the middle of town, I think. But I could be wrong—"

And then we see the noose.

It hangs straight down from the center of the ceiling, the loop at head height. I play the flashlight beam over it; the rope is dirty white and hairy, like ancient twine furred by tiny, broken strands. I follow the cord up to the roof, where it goes straight into a crack between two mortared stones.

I get closer so I can take a better look. Even though it's braided and tied in a perfect hangman's knot, it's not rope at all; it's a root. The little strands on it are tiny rootlets, searching blindly for sustenance in the air.

"Is this it?" Charlie asks.

"I don't think so," Doctor Pete says. "The trail keeps going, past it."

"It's a focal point," I say. "A charging station. He stands here with the rope around his neck and draws despair and bad luck down into himself. We must be under somewhere people gather—the supermarket, maybe, or the hardware store."

We skirt the thing, careful not to touch it. I get a powerful image as I edge past it, and realize I was wrong; the Gallowsman doesn't stand here, after all. Not after the first few seconds. That's when the root tightens around his neck and pulls upward, just enough to let his feet dangle over the floor. . . .

It's the first one we encounter, but not the last. They're all the same, eerie albino ovals hanging down as straight as stalactites. I wonder what kind of plants are on the other end, or if there even are any; maybe there's only a system of roots, reaching out under every corner of town like pale, hungry fingers. . . .

I try not to look at any of them for too long.

The Gallowsman must roam through all these tunnels, but in this case the relative weakness of Doctor Pete's tracking ability should be a plus; what he's picking up will be the thing's home, the place it spends its time when it's not sucking down depression and ill fortune. That's the theory, anyway.

"It's getting stronger," Doctor Pete says. "I think we must be close."

And Zev still hasn't made his move. Which means he won't go after Doctor Pete, because he *wants* us to make it to our destination.

"Charlie, switch places with the Doc—"

Too late. There's a *whump,* not as sharp as the crack that signalled Sally's death but just as sickening. Charlie curses and staggers, but doesn't go down. He gets off a shot, and I hear a yelp; sounds like he made Zev pay for what he got, anyway.

"How bad?" I ask Charlie, blocking his body with my own.

"Leg. Missed the kneecap, but the shinbone's broken. Damn stupid things, anyway." He sounds more angry than hurt.

"What, batteries?"

"Bones. Why stick something under all that meat if it's just gonna break? Crappy design, if you ask me. . . ."

We make it to the next intersection, Doctor Pete supporting Charlie, and me ready with the shotgun. I make sure I recover the battery from the ground first; no way am I going to let Zev use it against us twice.

"Aw, you're all out of ammo!" I call down the tunnel. "Too bad you don't have the *cojones* to do this up close and personal!"

"Jace," Charlie growls. "You really sure you want to taunt the psychopath with the claws and fangs?"

"I know what I'm doing," I mutter. I hope.

"We're here," Doctor Pete breathes.

I shine the flashlight around. The tunnel we're in leads to an arched doorway inscribed with arcane symbols. Steps go down into a large, round room, easily fifty feet across. It's filled with . . . well, junk. Junk carefully arranged on make-shift tables, old bookshelves, in the open drawers of rusty filing cabinets.

But this junk isn't random. It's the debris of dreams.

A wedding dress, covered in brownish-red stains. A cardboard globe with *NO* spray-painted across it in ugly black letters. A row of stuffed animals and dolls, every one ripped or burned or beheaded. A dusty manuscript on top of a battered typewriter, with a butcher's knife stuck deep in the pile of paper.

I can almost taste the sense of loss in the room. Many

serial killers take trophies, but what the Gallowsman takes is sorrow itself. Shards of pain from failed plans, from adventures deferred or goals unrealized. The contents of the room are a monument to surrender, to simply giving up and settling for what you have as opposed to what you really want. The Gallowsman collects them, leaving contented, worry-free townspeople in his wake. No despair, no bad luck, just good crops and a serene population—all except for the one poor soul who gets all this gloom and regret dumped on his or her head so everyone else stays happy.

Me.

"Jace," Charlie says. "I don't know if you should go in there—"

"Yeah, yeah," I say tiredly. "Frying pan, fire. The lady or the tiger. Damned if I do, damned if I don't, *et* goddamn *cetera*. C'mon, let's get this over with. There's something in there I need."

We help Charlie down the steps, then park him on an old wooden stool where he can watch the door. I hand him the shotgun—it's better than his pistol—then start rooting through the Museum of Lost Chances. Charlie gives the pistol to Doctor Pete.

"Where are we?" asks Doctor Pete, looking around.

I glance at the roof, where there's a perfectly round, dark hole in the stone about six feet in diameter. "Pretty sure we're underneath the church. See that hole? I figure that's where the congregation threw their offerings. A payoff for the Gallowsman's services."

"What are you looking for?"

"Something that doesn't belong here. I didn't find anything like them when I searched Old Man Longinus's house, so I figure he gave them to his pet monster. The more I think about it, the more sense it makes; these items were given to me by someone who died, someone I cared about. I haven't been able to hold them since then without thinking about him. About what could have been."

"I'm guessing handcuffs," a voice says. Zev—*and he's already in the room.*

I whirl toward the voice. He straightens up from where he was crouched behind a hulking, rotted desk; he's got something in his hand.

A baseball.

He throws it too fast to see, his arm blurring like a special effect. Beside me, Doctor Pete snaps off a shot with Charlie's pistol. I hear a double *thump,* one close and one far: the baseball, ricocheting off Doctor Pete's skull and into the far wall. That's good—it means it didn't strike straight on, and the Doc has a fair chance of surviving a glancing blow. I dive to the ground, already scrambling for the pistol in Doc's hand as he topples over, and hope that the blast from Charlie's shotgun will buy me enough time to grab it.

But the blast doesn't come.

What does arrive is Zev, leaping through the air and landing in a crouch right in front of me. His appearance isn't what I expected.

He's half thrope and half pire, but those halves aren't distributed evenly and don't stay the same from second to second: Fur sprouts, then grows backward into his body; fangs get longer, then shorter, in a mouth that shifts between muzzle and jaw; the skin of his hands pales then darkens, while claws twitch and lengthen sporadically. He grins at me with a lopsided, deformed mouth and says, "Hey, Jace. Miss me? I've been waiting *forever.*"

I've got the pistol, but he swats it out of my hands before I can bring it to bear.

"Uh-uh," he says cheerfully. "No gunsies. I'm not packing anymore, so neither are you." He raises his voice. "Hear that, Charlie? Give up the boomstick or I'll rip her head off."

I glance over. Charlie's not where I left him.

"Uh—I think we've got bigger problems," I say. "You know where we are, right?"

Zev cocks his head to the side, just like a curious dog.

"Relax. Home is where you hang your hat; work is where you hang someone *else*. Right?"

I takes me a second to digest that. "You think we're safe here because this is where it *lives*? You think this thing punches a clock, comes home, and puts its feet up?"

Both of Zev's eyes are blazing red and fur covers the lower half of his face, but when he talks I can understand him perfectly; seems his mutating state is at least partly under his control. "Why not? Morning Ralph morning Fred, night Ralph night Fred. Hey, you think that sheepdog is a vampire?"

The backhand comes out of nowhere. It connects with the side of my head and sends me sprawling with fireworks of pain behind my eyes, but I can tell he's holding back.

"Strike one!" Zev calls out. "Fouled it down the third-base line—next time, for sure!"

He's trying to draw Charlie out. But it's not Charlie's style to lay low and wait for the right moment; he's more a "charge straight ahead damn the torpedos" kinda guy. Which means—

No. No, I don't believe it. Not Charlie.

I get to my feet. "You get one for free," I say. "Next time you pay."

"Can I run a tab?" He tries something a little more flashy, a side-kick from a hairy leg and clawed foot.

Mistake.

He's fast, but I'm ready for him. I pivot, let the leg snap past me, then grab his ankle with both hands. I shove the leg down, bring my knee up sharply, and snap the joint like a piece of kindling.

Zev howls in pain, but I'm not done. I keep his leg up in the air and kick him in the crotch. Twice.

He finally manages to wrench his limb free, but he's off-balance. I step in and nail him with an elbow strike to the face as hard as I can manage. That turns out to be a mistake, because it sends him staggering backward out of range for a second.

That's apparently all Zev needs to recover, because he immediately goes on the offensive, lunging forward on his one good leg and slashing wildly with his claws. I dodge or block most of them, but he gets under my guard and rakes my belly.

My turn to stagger backward. He laughs. "Strike two!" he shouts. "Looks like a triple to me!"

I can't spare the attention to check how bad the wound is, but my intestines still seem to be on the right side of my skin. "Charlie?" I say. "Charlie, now would be good. . . ."

No response. And Zev's reaction to his broken leg is to make sure it's straight before shifting its morphology from thrope to pire, the fur replaced by pale white flesh. White, *undamaged* flesh; you can't break a pire's leg. Not unless you use silver or wood.

"Well, it's been fun," Zev says. "But pitch number three is about to go over the plate. Hey, I don't make the rules." He pauses, then giggles. "Okay, I guess I do. Same difference either way—"

And that's when the shotgun goes off.

The blast catches Zev in the neck. It's good strategy; most supernaturals are susceptible to decapitation. But the shotgun load is a mix of oak splinters carved from a table leg and silver shavings painstakingly scraped from the back of an old mirror. It's enough to hurt something with a pulse, and probably cripple a pire or a thrope.

But Zev's something else entirely.

The shot tears away most of his flesh, leaving his spinal cord intact. He stares at me, his mouth moving soundlessly. That'll happen when your larynx is abruptly removed.

And then the bloody knobbed column between his skull and his shoulders starts to sprout ribbons of meat. Nerves, muscles, tendons. A thrope can't regenerate that fast without some kind of mystic boost, but Zev isn't a thrope. He's a trap, just like everything else in this town, designed to prey not only on my pain but on my assumptions. Of course he isn't going to be easy to kill; he's a wild card, a joker in both attitude and application.

In a moment he's got his pipes back. He turns around and smiles at Charlie, who's stepped out from behind the bookshelf he was hiding behind. He meets Zev's eyes and shrugs. "Hey. Had to give it a shot, right?"

Charlie hops forward, dragging his broken leg behind him. He's still got the shotgun aimed at Zev. "Maybe I should give it a few more. See how many times you can do that little trick."

Zev chuckles. "Go right ahead, tarbender. But now that I know it's coming, don't expect me to just sit here and take it."

He leaps onto a bookshelf, then crosses to another, moving as swiftly and surely as a wild animal. I can't beat Zev toe-to-toe, and Charlie won't be able to do more than graze him if he's on the move.

And now he's got a golf ball in his hand. Great. Somebody's lifelong daydream of being the next Tiger Woods is going to get one of us killed.

"I'll give you a choice, Charlemagne," Zev says. "Put down the Elmer Fudd Penis Substitute and I'll kill you quick. Touch that trigger and I'll make you suffer."

I'm still trying to figure out our next move when the unthinkable happens.

Charlie drops the gun.

"Charlie, what are you *doing*?" I blurt.

"Only thing I can," Charlie says. "No-win situation, Jace. What's the point in beating our heads against a brick wall? Take a look around." He gestures with one hand. "All this junk is stuff people gave up so they could be happier. Worked, too. Sometimes . . . sometimes you just gotta know when to let go."

I can't believe it. I *won't* believe it. "*Charlie*. You said it
yourself—look around. It's this place, all these pathetic little
mementos . . . it's doing something to you. Don't let it—"

But it's too late.

TWENTY

Zev springs from his perch, landing in front of Charlie. He casually kicks the shotgun out of reach. "Okay," he says. "A deal's a deal—and hey, you did sell me an awful lot of beer back in the day. But before I kill you, can I ask you something?"

"You can ask."

"What the hell *am* I?" There's a note of genuine frustration under the manic glee in his voice. "I'm not a werewolf, I'm not a vampire. I don't think my real name is even Zev. Everything keeps sliding around in my head, and it's getting *worse.* About the only thing I *am* sure of is that it's *all her fault,* and you two seem to be real close. *So what am I?*"

Charlie regards Zev calmly for a second. "What are you? That's easy." He leans forward an inch or two, locks eyes with Zev, and says, "You're *done.*"

The noose drops over Zev's head as silently as a snake, and tightens its grip just as fast. It yanks him straight up through the hole in the ceiling and into the darkness beyond.

Charlie and I stare up at the black mouth of the opening for a second. Then we *move.*

I dive for the spot Charlie gestured to when he gave his little "I give up" speech. Charlie scrambles after the shotgun, breaks it open, and reloads it with standard shells.

I find the case peeking out from under a stack of old fashion magazines, almost invisible unless you've got your face pressed to the floor; that's how Charlie must have seen it. I yank it out, undo the clasps, and rip it open.

Hello, my lovelies.

Twin *escrima* sticks nestled in black foam. Eighteen inches of polished ironwood tipped with silver spikes, each with a folding silver blade a foot long that snaps out and locks at a forty-five degree angle.

My scythes.

I yank them out, pop 'em open, and stand up. I wouldn't say I feel invulnerable, exactly, but an enraged grizzly could walk through the door right now and I'd tell *him* to run. One look in my eyes and he'd do it, too.

Charlie snaps the twelve-gauge shut. "How's the Doc?"

"Twitching and groaning," I say, glancing over at him. "Probably has a concussion—we'll ask him when he wakes up."

"If that isn't soon, he'll miss the good part."

Above us, absolute silence.

No growling, no thrashing, no curses or howls. The shapeshifting thing that seemed unkillable a minute ago isn't looking so invincible anymore. And any second now we're going to come face-to-face with the being that just ate it whole.

"How'd you know it would attack Zev?" I ask, my eyes fixed on the ceiling.

"That thing's attracted to despair. Nobody makes as many jokes as laughing boy did unless they're hurting inside. Bad."

I blink. "And what if it had come after you, instead? You know, to make *me* despair?"

"Then I'd feel pretty stupid. For a few seconds, anyway."

"You know that hole is also our exit, right?"

"I wasn't planning on stumbing around in these tunnels until it found us, no."

"Ideas?"

"Lot of this stuff looks like it might burn."

A natural chimney and plenty of fuel. Problem is, the top of the chimney is no doubt covered, and that means we could find ourself not only trapped underground but blind and asphyxiated. "I don't think so. You have these things in your chest now, called lungs; they wouldn't appreciate suffering from smoke inhalation."

"Then I guess we go up there and introduce ourselves."

I have this sudden strong mental image of what we'll find halfway up: the Gallowsman, perched in a crazy-ass web of cables, ropes, and wires like a four-legged spider, with Zev wrapped in a cocoon of the same stuff. The Gallowsman's head will be tilted all the way to one side, lying flat on his shoulder like it was glued there. His eyes will bulge from their sockets, as big as hard-boiled eggs, his black, distended tongue lolling from his mouth like a dead eel. . . .

"Sounds like fun," I say. "How about we take a look, first?"

"You're the one with the sharp things. Cover me." I walk over and give him the flashlight. He hops closer to the hole, holding the shotgun with one hand, and shines the beam upward.

"Huh," he says.

I'm ready to chop to pieces anything that might drop out of there. "What do you see?"

"Not much. Empty. Ends in a trapdoor, looks like. And there are rungs carved in the side of the shaft."

So that's why we didn't hear Zev struggling—it dragged him up and out. "Think you can climb with that leg?"

Charlie grunts. "I'll manage. You and the Doc might have to give me a hand."

Speaking of which, Doctor Pete is now sitting up and clutching his head. "Goddamn it," he says. "This is—ow! This is not acceptable. Concussion damage in human beings is cumulative."

I walk over and help him to his feet. "If you can utter that sentence without slurring your words, you're probably okay. But Charlie isn't—his leg's broken. Take a look."

Doctor Pete automatically shifts into professional mode—I knew he would—and examines Charlie's leg. We rig a makeshift splint, and then Doctor Pete and I start piling up enough furniture to get us closer to the ceiling.

I go up first myself, with one scythe closed and stuck in my belt, and the other open and clenched between my teeth. Charlie's below me, shining the flashlight beam up. When I get to the top of the shaft I have a moment of panic when I think the trapdoor is locked—then I realize it's on springs, and I have to pull down to open it, not push.

Of course. Very like a real gallows, only this one closes automatically after use. More like a doggy door, really.

That makes me think about Galahad, but I don't have time to worry about him right now. I cautiously stick my head through the opening, holding my scythe in one hand, but nothing drops around my neck or tries to throttle me. The trapdoor's set into a round, raised stone platform in the middle of a dark room, the beam of the flashlight from below showing me only vague shapes. I climb out and tell Charlie to come up; he manages pretty well, even with one leg in a splint.

In a few minutes we're all above ground again. The flashlight reveals a room very similar to the one in Longinus's basement: black draperies on the walls, lots of candles. The door isn't obvious, but with a little searching we find it; it opens into the apse of the church, behind the altar.

I can smell burnt flesh as soon as we step out. What's left of the cross Jimmy Zhang was lashed to hangs from the back of the door, and his ashy remains now lie scattered at my feet. Something's been dragged through them and up the aisle.

"Gone," Charlie says.

"Yeah," I say, frowning. "The Gallowsman must have

taken him somewhere else to string him up. Makes a certain amount of sense; Father Stone was probably killed right here in the church, but the body was left outside for everyone to see."

"Why?" Doctor Pete asks.

It's a good question, and I think I finally have an answer. "The same reason Athena Shaker killed Therese Isamu and left the body in Cassiar's room. Same reason the master vampire killed Vince Shelly with a silver fork and bled him like a slaughtered pig. Same message, too: *This is my town now.* I've been thinking of this as a war between pires and thropes, but it's not; there's a third element, with its own agenda."

"The cult?" Charlie says.

"No. The first two victims, Father Stone and Maureen Selkic, were both members of the cult. No, I think the third element is the Gallowsman himself. Now that Ahaseurus is dead, he's not under anyone's control. He started off killing cult members—his former masters—but he's escalated since then. He took down Doctor Pete—the townie version, I mean—and now Zev. He's staking his own claim on this place."

"Three-way war," Charlie says, nodding. "Two ways to play that."

"If you're smart, yeah. You can either join forces with one side to gang up against the other, or wait on the sidelines until one side beats the other and then attack the survivor while he's still weakened from the fight."

Doctor Pete sighs and sinks into a pew. "So which side is going to do what?"

"Well, assuming the African Queen is still stashed in the trunk of her car," I say, sitting down beside him, "we've already taken one side out of play. If we get the master vampire, we're handing the town over to the Gallowsman; if we take out the Gallowsman, by tomorrow night the whole town will be vampirized. So I'm going to suggest we go back to

Charlie's, regroup, maybe drink a gallon or so of high-octane coffee, and then do something daring and stupid."

"As usual," Charlie says. "Wait. Did you say 'do something stupid' or 'work with someone stupid'?"

The walk across town is a long one. The streets are still deserted, and the storm that surrounds the place like a fence has gotten bigger, darker, and angrier; lightning the color of blood arcs and flashes constantly, but there's no thunder. The silence makes it feel like the storm is a million miles away and bigger than the world.

We get back to the Longinus house without incident, me and Doctor Pete helping Charlie hobble along, and retrieve Athena's car. The thumping from the trunk tells me she's still in there, and Galahad's frantic barking when we pull up to Charlie's place tells me he probably needs to be walked. He doesn't rush to the door to greet me, though, which is odd—

Sheriff Stoker is sitting on Charlie's couch, a riot shotgun across his knees. Galahad's wearing his leash, and the other end is tied to the leg of my kitchen table. He's managed to drag the table up to the kitchen doorway, but it's gotten jammed there.

"Come in and sit down," Stoker says. "We need to talk."

I'm too exhausted to say anything clever. I go over to Galahad and assure him I'm all right, then lean against the wall. Charlie lowers himself carefully onto a chair, and after a second so does Doctor Pete.

Stoker's face is impassive. "So. To save time, I'm going to assume you pretty much know what's going on. If that's not true, ask me whatever you need to and I'll do my best to fill you in. Let's keep this discussion short, though—things are going south fast."

"Did you kill Ahaseurus?" I ask him.

"So he *is* dead. No. I've been running things since he disappeared, as best I could."

Doctor Pete glares at him. "That include locking people up for murders they didn't commit?"

"I needed leverage to keep a lid on the war. One from your side, one from theirs. Hostages to fortune, I believe it's called."

That brings a tired, humorless smile to my face. "But what you got was misfortune. Funny, I thought being the Gallowsman's pal was supposed to prevent that."

Stoker stares at me coldly. "He's supposed to do all sorts of things. What he's not supposed to do is kill the people he was brought here to serve."

"You can't control him anymore, because Longinus was the man with the plan. So what's next, Stoker? Every human being in this town is going to be pale, hairy, or swaying at the end of a rope inside of twenty-four hours—and we can't *leave*, either."

"I know." He pauses, then looks away. "I'm here to offer an alliance. Way I figure it, we're about all that's left to mount any kind of resistance."

"What, you can't convince any of your cult buddies—"

"*There's nobody left, Jace.* I've been to house after house. Empty. I don't know which side got them, either. Maybe they were eaten or drained, maybe the Gallowsman dragged them into the tunnels, maybe they're all hanging upside down in somebody's backyard shed waiting for nightfall. But I *do* know this: It all started with you. And that's how it's going to end, too."

I stare back, then nod slowly. "Yeah. You're right. Now here's a few things you don't know: First, we've got the alpha werewolf locked in the trunk of the car outside. Second, I know who the master vampire is."

"You do?" says Doctor Pete. He sounds surprised.

"Not only that, I know *where* he is." I pull out my phone, put it on the coffee table, and slide it over to Stoker. "Take a look."

He picks it up, studies the screen. "What am I looking at?"

"Figure it out for yourself."

He thinks for a second, then hits a few buttons. He's found the video file—

There's a flash of white light.

Sucker.

Every induced-recall experience so far has had me playing the role of a woman from someone's memory, Doctor Pete's or Charlie's or Cassius's. Stoker's no different—except that this time, I seem to be almost completely passive. I'm lying down, I'm naked, and it's very hard to focus my thoughts. I realize I must be drugged, or maybe brain-damaged. My arms and legs are restrained—to keep me from hurting myself? There's an IV in each of my arms. I must be in a hospital.

But why am I in a box?

It's made out of glass, or maybe thick plastic. I can hear sounds, but they're so muffled that I'm not sure what's causing them. Machinery? People talking? I finally make out a few words, but I can't understand them; they're not in English. Something Asian?

There's a smudge on the glass ceiling of my box. I stare at the smudge for a few years, struggling to focus beyond it. When I finally manage to, all I see is a plain white surface a few feet above me. It's not nearly as interesting as the smudge, and to alleviate my disappointment I decide to embark on an ambitious, multistage project: turning my head.

Whew. It's a long road, filled with toil, heartbreak, unexpected surprises—I never saw that second smudge coming, for instance—and eventual success. I can't take all the credit, though; gravity did give me some assistance in the final phases, and it'll definitely receive a big thank-you in the acknowledgments.

There's another glass box beside me, with a man in it.

Stoker.

His head is shaved, and he looks younger. Just as massive,

though: his muscular arms are pressed up against the sides of his container, as is the top of his skull. He's got twice as many tubes stuck in his arms as I do, and three of them are bright red. I guess he's getting a transfusion.

It takes a while for the facts to coalesce into a realization.

I'm not in a hospital. Those tubes aren't giving Stoker blood; they're taking it away.

I'm in a yakuza blood farm.

I should be horrified, but I don't seem to remember how. It's more than drugs, it's magic; the part of me that's still Jace remembers the blood farm Stoker and I took down in Stanley Park, where the victims had all had their brains wiped by sorcery.

That's not the case here, though. I can still think, still feel, however distantly. So can Stoker; he manages to turn his head to look back at me, and his dark eyes hold more than numb acceptance. They hold rage—rage suppressed, rage that's been smothered and chained but still glows with stubborn heat. It warms me, too, quickens my sluggish pulse, melts a few of the cobwebs wrapped around my brain. I struggle to say something, to tell him this, but the best I can do is to soundlessly move my lips.

He nods, ever so slightly. His own lips move while his fingers twitch, but he isn't speaking to me. He's reciting a spell.

His eyes clear. He glances to the side, studies the tubes draining his blood away, and leans forward as far as he can. He gets his teeth on one of the tubes and yanks it out with a twist of his head. Blood starts to leak from the end and pool on his stomach. He puts his head back down, stares blankly at the ceiling, and waits.

It doesn't take long. Somewhere, a little sensor tells a technician that valuable product is being wasted. Before very long, an Asian man in a white smock is peering into Stoker's cubicle. Stoker's face is as empty as a discarded wallet. The technician unlocks the lid and lifts it up, then leans in to re-attach the tube.

Stoker clamps onto the technician's windpipe with his teeth, and rips it out with a yank of his head.

He must have silver or wood implanted in his teeth; it's the only way he could inflict a wound like that on a pire. Blood gushes everywhere, but only for a moment—it's a fatal wound, and as soon as the pire's body figures that out his immortality vanishes and he pays off his time debt to the universe all at once. Flesh and blood turn instantly to dust, and the technician's bones clatter down the stepladder he'd been standing on and onto the floor.

Stoker grits his teeth and starts yanking on the restraints. They're designed less to physically imprison than to keep arms and legs from thrashing about, and he manages to rip both his arms free in about thirty seconds. He unbuckles his legs, tears the other tubes from his arms, and leaps out of his cubicle.

That's the last I see of him for some time. I hear what might be shouting, somewhere.

I sort of drift away in the interim. I should feel relief, I suppose, but I don't. If I feel anything at all, it's a kind of regret.

Eventually Stoker comes back. He opens the lid to my own glass coffin and stares down at me. He's covered in gray and white dust, like he's been rooting through the remains of cold campfires. Even with the lid up, it's very quiet.

He stares down at me for a long time.

"I should just leave you here," he says finally. I feel no surprise at this, just a twinge of shame.

"I understand why you did it," he says. "I make a better martyr than a leader, and me dying in one of these places would make great propaganda for the Resistance."

He shakes his head. "But you fucked up. Even now, after all this time, you don't understand these bloodsuckers. You think they can be reasoned with, negotiated with. Maybe they can—but not by us. You don't negotiate with livestock. That's all we are to them, and that's why they stabbed you in the back and took you, too. Your little power play is over, and you lost. Me, I was prepared—an antihypnotic spell and silver crowns over my teeth, painted white."

I know I should say something in my defense, but I don't. Maybe I'm unable to speak, or maybe I just have nothing to offer.

"You did get one thing right. Us dying in service to our cause will be good for recruitment. So that's what's going to happen: from this moment on, both you and Aristotle Stoker are dead. I'm going underground, so deep no one will find me—but I'm not giving up. Oh, no."

He leans in, only inches from my face. "I had a revelation recently. In order to fight these monsters, you have to *become* a monster. Something as big and scary and inhuman as they are. That's what I'm going to do—reinvent myself as a creature even they'll be frightened of. I've even thought of a name: the Impaler. What do you think?"

I do my best to nod. He seems to understand.

"No one will know who I am, or where I came from. Not even the FHR. I will be invisible and lethal, a murdering ghost. And it will be their turn to be afraid."

Something touches the inside of my thigh, very quickly and lightly, and then warmth gushes down my leg. Femoral artery.

"Good-bye, Linda," he says softly. "You'll be remembered, and revered, and missed."

He stays with me until the end.

I'm grateful for that.

Azura and I had set up the trap beforehand. I knew that sooner or later I'd have to use the memory trick on the sheriff, and since Azura had already broken into prison to get access to Tair, it made sense to use the opportunity to swap this fake Stoker for the real thing. If, you know, your definition of sense is trading an officer of the law for a convicted serial killer and terrorist.

But then, by the time he wound up behind bars, Stoker wasn't quite the killer he used to be. In fact, I hadn't captured him; he'd turned himself in, claiming the mystic artifacts he'd been using had affected his sanity. He swore he was through with murder, and had a grandiose plan to save the remaining human population that didn't involve eliminating all the supernaturals on the planet.

I wasn't entirely convinced. But Stoker hadn't given us any trouble since surrendering, though he refused to volunteer information on his former associates in the FHR. His days of ruthless slaughter might actually be at an end. . . .

Sigh. Just when I *need* a singleminded killing machine, he goes and reforms. I can hear the universe—several of them, in fact—sniggering behind my back. Real funny, guys.

I open my eyes. Stoker does the same. We stare at each other for a moment, and then he smiles and glances around. "Huh. Now *this* is what I call a jailbreak."

"Oh, you've just exchanged one cell for another," I say. "This one is slightly larger, but a lot more dangerous. Azura filled you in?"

Stoker nods. "Anything new since the last time you two spoke?"

I tell him about Athena, and the tunnels, and the Gallowsman. He takes it all in stride. I hate to say it, but I'm actually glad he's here; no matter how capable or competent this reality's Stoker is, he hasn't spent his entire life training to fight supernatural beings. Mine has.

He's examining his own arms critically as I talk, but I know he's paying attention. "Hmmm. Not in peak shape," he murmurs. "Fewer scars, as well. Guess it'll do. What's our plan?"

"We take down the master vampire," I say. "Then figure out a way to deal with the Gallowsman."

Charlie clears his throat. "You keep calling him that. The master vampire. Why don't you use his name? We know who it has to be, right?"

I hesistate. "Yes," I admit. "It's Cassius. I don't know how he ignored my cross—maybe it's because he's from a reality where religious symbols don't affect pires—but it has to be him."

But it isn't really Cassius, I want to say. It's a magnified, distorted version of him, warped by this reality's rules and Ahaseurus's magic. A Cassius with his ethics gutted, a centuries-old pire stripped of any morality or empathy and filled with a bottomless loathing for yours truly. Yeah, I have no trouble facing the truth of that at all.

"You know where he is?" Stoker asks.

"No. But I know where he'll be."

"Where?"

"Wherever I am. He knows I've got Ahaseurus's spell book, and Cassius is no slouch at magic himself. It's his shot at taking control. He's probably searched my place already."

"But it's not there?" asks Doctor Pete.

"No, I brought it with me and stashed it here."

"Maybe we should have a look at it ourselves," Doctor Pete suggests. "I may not be a high-level shaman, but I know my way around a book of spells."

"I know a few things myself," Stoker says, giving the Doc a curious glance.

"I'll get it," I say.

I hid the thing in Charlie's garage, under a stack of old motorcycle magazines. It's still there. I pull it out, then pause for a minute before going back into the house.

Something's not right.

Charlie's garage is neat, tools all hung in their places, floor swept, boxes on shelves properly labeled. But still, I have this sense of something being out of place.

I look around. It takes me a moment, because it's right under my nose; it's the stack of old magazines I used to hide the book. It's the only thing here that's not neatly organized— the magazines are just in a pile on a bench, not even properly aligned with one another. I frown, then look under the bench; there's an empty cardboard box there labeled MOTOR-CYCLE MAGS 1992–94.

I start looking through the pile. I find what I'm searching for in the middle, where the casual sloppiness of the magazines has been used to hide a slightly larger object. It wouldn't have meant anything to me a few days ago, but now I realize what I have in my hands . . . and what it means.

I go back inside, holding it in one hand and the spell book in the other. I'm not sure if it's safe to let them touch.

"Jace?" Charlie says when I walk in. He can tell right away that something's up, without me saying a word.

"I thought there was only one book," Stoker says.

"So did I," I reply. "I was wrong. This is the missing piece of the puzzle. I know who killed Ahaseurus now, and I think I know why."

"Who?" Charlie asks.

"You," I tell him.

TWENTY-ONE

"Well, ain't that a kick in the pants," Charlie mutters. "You wanna back that up and try again, or should I just let you slap on the cuffs?"

I hold up what I found in Charlie's garage. "See this? *The Wonderful Wizard of Oz*. I was giving Charlie a hard time about reading it at the bar."

"Yeah, that really clears things up," Charlie says. "I knew a guy once who went on a killing spree after an all-night binge of *The Wind in the Willows*."

"This isn't just a book, Charlie." I toss it on the coffee table. "It's an illustrated version, what's called a graphic novel. In other words, a *comic book*."

Comic books. Harmless hobby of kids and middle-aged geeks, right? On the world of my birth, sure . . . but not on the version of Earth I call Thropirelem. There, shamans use comics' combination of words, images, and imagination to turn them into powerful mystic totems, so dangerous that they've been outlawed since the nineteen-fifties.

Doctor Pete leans down and picks it up. Studies the cover, but doesn't open it. "Yes. I can feel the mystic potential being routed through it. Is this what Longinus was killed for?"

"I think so—but that was only part of it. See, everything

in this town was carefully manipulated to make my life a living hell . . . but you can't really suffer pain unless you have a little pleasure first. In the end, it gives you even more to lose. That's why Charlie Allen—the Charlie of this reality—really was my friend. He was someone I could trust, someone who really and truly was on my side. That way, whatever horrible thing Longinus had planned for him was guaranteed to cause the maximum amount of anguish."

Stoker nods, his gaze on Charlie. "So he recreated Charlie as closely as he could, right down to his loyalty. Big mistake."

"Yeah," I say. "I should have suspected something when Charlie offered to help me get rid of the body so quickly. He had no idea I'd be the one to discover the corpse—and once I did, he figured the best solution to keep me from being locked up was to sanitize the crime scene."

Charlie looks thoughtful. "So this version of me figures out that Longinus is behind you having such a craptastic life. He goes to Longinus's house, confronts him, maybe catches him in the middle of some kind of ritual. He kills Longinus and steals the mystic artifact he was using, then stashes it while he tries to figure out what to do next, not wanting any of the other cult members to get their hands on it."

"Yeah. He leaves in a big hurry, then can't go back for fear of being discovered. Until I force his hand."

Doctor Pete is turning the graphic novel over in his hands, studying the back as well as the front. "So this is, what—the mystic center of all the spells woven through this place?"

I nod. "Has to be. Think about it: a girl, ripped out of her own world and thrown into another. When I first got my memory back, I compared my situation to Alice's in *Through the Looking-Glass*, but this place is a lot more like a warped version of Oz: I was taken from a supernatural world *into* a small town in Kansas. There's a storm that *prevents* me from going anywhere. The beasts are anything but cowardly, the tin man's heart is too large for his own good, and the guy with the big brain is an albino afraid of burning in the sun. I've even got a faithful *dog*, for Christ's sake."

"And at the middle of it all," Doctor Pete murmurs, "A genuine wizard who specializes in illusions. Yes, that's exactly the kind of resonant structure that would work with this kind of sorcery. Preestablished patterns waiting to be mystically energized . . ."

"Right down to the Yellow Brick Road," I say. "Once again, its purpose is inverted: it leads out, not in. The highway."

"And the Gallowsman?" Stoker asks. "Who does he represent?"

"He's the Wicked Witch," I say. "No flying monkeys, just a hangman's rope. Makes a backward kind of sense, I guess; you find both in trees, but one defies gravity while the other uses it to kill."

"Classic black magic," Doctor Pete says. "Turn a cross upside down, perform a holy ritual in reverse. Turn a work of joy and wonder into one of despair and terror." He taps the cover lightly with one finger. "But poor Charlie Allen had no idea what to do with this. It would take someone trained in shamanism to properly utilize it, especially now that the one who cast the initial spells is dead."

"Somebody like Stoker?" I ask.

Doctor Pete hesitates. I know what he's thinking: *Oh, sure, as long as you're fine with placing the mystic equivalent of an atomic bomb in the hands of a professional terrorist.* Okay, Doctor Pete wouldn't make the bomb reference—they don't use them where he's from—but otherwise that's got to be what's bothering him—

"I don't think so," Doctor Pete says carefully, then says something else. It's a short phrase, not in English, and sounds less like language than a series of growls and whines.

The book becomes *more*. That's the only way to put it. The colors on the cover get brighter, the lines crisper—not just the lines of the illustration, but the lines of the book itself, its outline in space and maybe time. It's more *book-like* than it was before, making it both more real and more unnatural simultaneously. It's almost like a hyperrealistic, three-dimensional drawing of itself.

"Doc?" I ask. "What's happening?"

"For everyone's safety, please don't come any closer," Doctor Pete says. "It's not unusual for an artifact like this to be mystically encrypted or booby-trapped. I'm doing my best to interrogate it without setting anything off. . . ." He mutters a few more animalistic words, and it feels like the air in the room gets thicker.

"Uh-oh," says Charlie.

"That wasn't an exploratory incantation," Stoker says.

"No," agrees Doctor Pete. "That was to ensure nobody does anything rash, like try to grab me. Though only you, Mr. Stoker, would have the acumen to understand exactly what I'm holding and just how useful it's going to be."

"You want to explain that, Doc?" Charlie says.

"Of course, Charlie. This book is a focus for more than illusion and memory spells; it can concentrate and magnify a variety of occult forces, much like the Gallowsman does. But what he does with misfortune and despair, the book does with more potent supernatural energies: the pure essence of a lycanthrope or a hemovore, for instance. It can channel that energy, pump it up, and return it a hundredfold—turning an ordinary pire or thrope into something much more. It's why the supernaturals here seem less human and more predatory."

"Good thing we're all human, then," I say.

Doctor Pete chuckles.

When I hear that sound, I don't need to hear any more. I know who I'm talking to now.

"Not exactly true," Tair says. "I—this body, I mean—has been bitten by a thrope. Tiny little bits of werewolfy virus are coursing through my bloodstream, just waiting for the first full moon to explode into furious activity."

"Was it you all along?" I ask. "Or did you just hitch a ride and lurk in the background until you saw an opportunity?"

"A little of one and some of the other, actually. You brought both of us across—the Doc and I each have that particular memory you accessed—but I've managed to impose a state where we're both present at the same time, though not in equal amounts. Basically, one can passively watch and the other can act. I've resisted acting until now—you're too smart to fool for long—but this is too good to pass up. And don't think the Doc is coming back, either; I just used the book to give him a little shove through the extradimensional door. He's back in his own body, back in his own reality, back in his own prison cell. And me—I'm *here*."

"For now," I say. "Until we eliminate the alpha wolf. Then you and everyone else she's infected go back to normal."

Tair shakes his head. "Oh, I'm aware of the situation. But let's reason this out, shall we? To dewolf everyone, you have to kill the African Queen. Can you do that? Ruthlessly execute a former ally, someone you've fought alongside? Yes, she's currently locked in the trunk of her own car, but this is more about willpower than opportunity."

I don't answer that, so he keeps on talking. "And anyway, there's very little point in returning the status to quo. Most of the wolf-bitten are probably already dead, or will be soon. No, I doubt very much that you'd execute Ms. Shaka just to cure me of lycanthropy."

"You've got it the wrong way around," I say. "Now that Doctor Pete's not a factor, the only one I *need* to execute is you."

He smiles, but I can see in his eyes that he realizes he's made a tactical error. I smile back. "Anyway," I say, "I doubt if I have much to worry about from you, anyway. You're not even a lycanthrope anymore, just a guy who got a hickey from the real thing—and this is all going to be over long before the next full moon."

"You're right about that," he admits. "The last thing, I

mean. But obviously you haven't been paying close enough attention; see, I'm holding the mystical equivalent of a full moon right here in my hands. . . ."

He says something else in that guttural language, and this time I can identify at least one word: *Luna*.

And then he begins to change.

I've seen thropes transform before, too many times to count. But this is different; this is the very first time the body Tair's stolen has been through this, and it's not ready— it's being forced to change, the flame of lycanthropy inside him getting sprayed by arcane gasoline. Fur erupts from Tair's skin, bones loudly crack into new configurations, fangs and claws snap out like spring-loaded knives. It must hurt like hell, but his mouth and throat are transforming so fast he can't even howl.

Or talk.

The thickness in the air that's preventing us from moving evaporates. I'd like to say that I'm the first one to react, but that distinction goes to Stoker. He lunges up from the couch, driving his shoulder into Tair's gut and knocking him backward. *The Wonderful Wizard of Oz* drops to the ground.

"Get the book!" Stoker yells.

I scoop it up. It doesn't do me any good, though; my knowledge of shamanism is strictly informal and second-hand. The only people in the room with any training are currently locked in hand-to-hand combat.

And what a fight it is.

Stoker shouldn't stand a chance. He's big and muscular and experienced, but Tair's a supernatural being. In their own world, Tair would disembowel him and throttle him with his own intestines.

But that's not where we are. And Stoker seems to be adapting a lot quicker than Tair.

Stoker's strategy is simple and brutal: cause so much damage that all Tair's resources will go into fixing it, while inflicting massive amounts of pain to keep him off-balance and confused. Tair's already in agony; Stoker intends to keep him there while turning up the volume.

It's ugly and vicious and cruel—but from a purely technical point of view, it's a thing of beauty. An elbow strike to the muzzle that breaks Tair's jaw and sends newly minted fangs flying, followed by a knee to the ribs and an elbow to the temple and a punch to the snout, blow after blow after blow. Stoker's not holding back, putting everything he has into offense and nothing into defense; he's got bloody knuckles from hitting Tair in the mouth and at least one set of clawmarks on his chest. He ignores them and what they mean; this isn't *his* body he's fighting with, after all.

I think it's the first time Stoker's ever been able to really cut loose. An ordinary human taking this sort of beating would have been unconscious or dead in the first few seconds; a pire would have been annoyed, but unhurt. But right here, right now, Stoker can unleash all the rage and hatred that's been burning inside him his whole life and not care about the consequences.

Some people think werewolves are invulnerable to being hurt by anything other than silver, but that's not how it works. They can be hurt by anything, they just heal really fast—and Tair is healing even faster than that.

Stoker uses it against him.

He hammers at Tair's upper arm until it breaks. Then he bends it in a direction it was never meant to go—and holds it there until it heals.

That only takes a second or two, but it's long enough for Tair to regain a little composure and launch a less frenzied counterattack. He's down on the floor by now, and he slashes at the back of Stoker's ankle, trying to hamstring him. Tair's claws rip through Stoker's boots with ease, but the heavy leather provides enough protection that Stoker escapes being crippled.

Stoker releases Tair's arm and jumps back, out of range. He's lost the momentum of his attack, but managed to take one of his opponent's weapons out of commission; Tair's arm is a weird L-shape now, almost impossible for him to use effectively.

"My turn," Charlie says.

He opens up with the shotgun. The blast catches Tair in the eyes.

While the thrope can shrug off the damage caused by the bits of wood in our improvised ammo, the silver shavings are another matter. They blind him, and not in a temporary way.

I pull one of my scythes from my belt and snap it open. Tair snarls, recognizing the sound. I know him well enough to predict what he'll do next: try to run. Hide somewhere, fix his arm, regroup. He's smart that way.

Not this time.

"Sorry, Tair," I say. I'm between him and the nearest window or door. "End of the line. You gambled, you lost."

He understands. He crouches there, his right arm at that disturbing angle, and tries to shift back to human form. It almost works: his fur shortens, his frame shifts, his claws retract. But only for a moment; having let the wild genie out of its bottle, he discovers he can't just stuff it back inside. His fur and claws lengthen, and his muzzle returns—though his eyes don't. He growls in frustration, shaking his head like a dog with a flea in its ear. A gigantic, rabid dog on the verge of losing control . . .

Stoker plucks the other scythe from my belt and snaps it open with a single flick, almost as easily as I would.

"No!" I shout, and then Tair leaps for my throat.

Stoker and I strike at the same time. I duck, swinging up as Tair passes over me and slicing open his belly. It's a nasty wound, especially with a silvered blade, but I've seen Tair survive worse. It's designed to hurt him badly enough to end the fight and force him to listen to reason.

Stoker isn't interested in a conversation.

He shows this by aiming for Tair's neck. It's an easy hit; Tair's blind, in midair, and Stoker has plenty of time.

But it's still a shock when Tair's head thumps onto the floor next to me. I hear the body slam into the front door.

He transforms back into human form; that's what thropes do when they die. His skull and face reshape themselves, until I'm looking at Doctor Pete's familiar features instead of the head of a monster. His eyes are still ruined.

I stare down at him. Tair was an egotistical, arrogant bastard, one who screwed me over more than once, but he had style and his own peculiar brand of honor. Ultimately, he was a collection of bad choices, rage, and self-interest . . . and that's why I felt sorry for him. We're all one ill-considered decision away from a different life, but we never get to see what that life might entail. Tair did. I couldn't even blame him for those bad choices, because he didn't really make them—they were created by sorcery, an artificial history as fake as anything Ahaseurus imposed on the citizenry of this town.

"You didn't have to kill him," I say, glaring at Stoker.

"Yes, I did. He wasn't trying to escape, Jace; he was in a killing rage. The lycanthropic essence he'd charged himself up with was overpowering his mind. He wouldn't have stopped until all of us were dead or he was. I made the only choice."

I wish I could argue with him, but I suddenly just don't have the energy. I should be happy—Doctor Pete is finally free of Tair, and once that's been verified by the prison shamans I have no doubt he'll be freed.

But it doesn't feel like a victory.

It's much darker outside than it should be at this time of day. It's the storm, filling the sky overhead and looking less and less natural every minute. Crimson lightning dances through the black and gray clouds, which are churning and boiling more like smoke from a volcano than anything generated by the atmosphere; it wouldn't surprise me if they began to belch poisonous toads on our heads.

Stoker's been studying both the spell book and the graphic novel for the last half hour. I'm so burnt out from near-constant betrayal that I don't even care if he decides to Benedict Arnold me; I'll just let Charlie shoot him and soldier on. When the only person you can trust turns out to be the perp you were chasing all along, you kind of have to give up and go with the flow.

We moved Tair's body out to the garage. His head, too.

"I think I know a way out of this," Stoker says at last.

I'm curled up on the sofa, working on my third cup of coffee. Charlie's staring out the window with the shotgun in his hands.

"Go ahead," I say.

Stoker taps the spell book with one finger. "I recognize some of these. Gateway spells. There has to be a door into and out of this place, and this is the key that unlocks them."

"So where's the door?" Charlie asks.

"It's not a door, it's a road," I answer. "The highway work site, the one guarded by the road crew. That's where it has to be."

"So let's go." Stoker gets to his feet.

"Not yet," I say. "We've got unfinished business."

"Cassius."

"Yes."

"Planning on capturing him the way you did the alpha wolf? That's not going to work."

"I know. I'm hoping I can talk to him."

Stoker shakes his head. "That's exactly what Ahaseurus would want you to do. He's already scripted the inevitable confrontation between you two, and all possible endings are bad ones: He betrays you. He doesn't betray you but dies in your arms. You kill him. He turns you. He turns you and *then* you kill him. You kill him because you *think* he's going to betray you, and then you discover his innocence. You *know* this—you've run all these possibilities already. What possible outcome could you even hope for?"

"The one where he doesn't father a race of evil vampires that turn this planet into their own private blood reserve. You know, the kind of horrific nightmare you've spent your entire existence fighting."

He meets my angry gaze calmly. "Good. I know what the stakes are; I just wanted to make sure you do, too. Because I *know* how clever Cassius is. If we don't take him down fast and hard, he'll game us. You know he will. And there's nobody better."

"I'm aware of that." I keep my voice cold, my body language tense. Considering the situation, it isn't difficult. "But he's working at a disadvantage. He doesn't have access to his usual intelligence network. This isn't his world. Ahaseurus will have altered his mind, just like the others—but this is Cassius we're talking about, a pire thousands of years old. He's developed techniques to store and retrieve his own memories that make him much more aware of his own mental processes. The psychic blocks Ahaseurus will have been forced to use will be equally powerful, which puts Cassius at a further disadvantage. If we were going up against him at his full strength, we'd already be dead—but he's being forced to play this damn game too, which handicaps him. And that's the *only* thing that gives us a fighting chance."

"She's right," Charlie says. "You know what our best weapon against Cassius is? Himself. We gotta break whatever chains Ahaseurus wrapped around his brain. He must be fighting to get loose already. With the local magic starting to fray at the edges, maybe we can finish the job."

"Too risky," Stoker says. "He could mislead us. We can't gamble with the future of every human being on the planet—"

"I'll do what I have to," I say.

"And so will I," says Cassius.

He's standing in the hall that leads to the garage. He must have come in through the side door.

And he's holding a really big gun in one hand.

* * *

"Charlie?" Cassius says pleasantly. "Put the shotgun on the floor, please. Sheriff, do the same with your weapon. And step away from the spell book—if you so much as utter a single arcane word, I'll be forced to shoot you."

He doesn't mention me or my scythes. Why should he? They're only a threat in hand-to-hand combat, and he's got a gun—*my* gun, a Ruger Super Redhawk Alaskan chambered with .454 rounds that can be used to hunt moose. It looks very, very odd in his hands, like a battle-ax being wielded by an astronaut.

Charlie and Stoker do as he says.

"Where'd you get my gun?" I ask.

"Longinus, of course. He had no use for it, and seemed to think it was funny to give it to me."

"How much did you overhear, just now?"

"Oh, pretty much all of it, I think. Intriguing, but about what I was told to expect."

"Whatever Longinus said to you, it wasn't the truth."

"Oh, I'm aware of that. I'm in the intelligence field, after all; I understand compartmentalization and plausible deniability. Longinus told me as much as he could, and lied to me when necessary. Even so, I have a firm grasp of the situation."

He sounds very sure of himself—but then, Cassius always does. "Yeah? Can you explain it to me?"

"I'll do my best. Whether or not you believe me is up to you. Please, all of you, sit down—Charlie, I'm sure your leg must be bothering you."

We take seats on the couch. He picks up the spell book and graphic novel, and moves both of them out of reach before he begins.

"None of this is real, Jace. Oh, yes, we're physically here, events are occurring—but not for the reasons you think. This town isn't what you believe it to be."

"Oh? And what is it?"

"A training exercise. One being run by the intelligence

agency both you and I work for. They do this sort of thing every few years, pushing agents to their psychological limits; illusion spells and memory implants are used to manipulate both the present and past, to see how we'll react as things gradually get worse and worse."

"You said *we.* Surely they don't subject the director of the NSA to this—"

He cuts me off with a harsh laugh. "Director? Jace, I'm a field agent, just like you—or Zhang, or Tanaka, or Isamu. We all have our little dramas we've been programmed to play out, and it's all smoke and mirrors. Nobody actually *dies,* it just appears that they do."

I study his body language, his eyes, his phrasing, looking for signs that he's lying. I don't find any. He seems to really believe what he's telling me, as preposterous as it sounds.

I guess it makes a sort of sense, from a brainwashing point of view; if you want to convince a spook of something, appeal to their paranoia. Spin a web of conspiracy and half-truths, a structure complicated enough to occupy their attention while obscuring your real intentions. It's almost credible. . . .

Unless you're a trained psychologist.

"So this is all a carefully crafted scenario?" I ask. "Designed to see how field agents react to escalating stress through gradually increasing chaos and persecution? Okay, that's a viable explanation for some of the insanity around us. But in order to make that explanation work—to properly explain away a hundred possible tiny discrepancies and contradictions—it's necessary to use false memories and illusion spells, correct?"

"That's the procedure. I know your memories feel like they really happened, but—"

It's my turn to laugh. "No, that's not it. It's a basic problem in logic. You can't mess with people's thought processes on a physical level—including memories—and get any kind of useful data about their genuine reaction to a given situation. It's like the old joke about the scientist who teaches a frog to jump when it hears a bell, then immerses it in boiling water and notes that it no longer jumps when the bell sounds."

"I don't see—"

"He concludes that boiling water makes frogs deaf. We're the frogs, Cassius; Ahaseurus can get us to jump or he can boil our brains, but *he can't do both*."

He frowns. I can see him struggling with what I just told him, and I honestly don't know how he's going to react.

"This is unacceptable," he says flatly.

He points the gun at Stoker and fires.

TWENTY-TWO

The Ruger makes one hell of a bang when it goes off. And one hell of a mess.

The impact blows a hole in Stoker's chest, bounces him off the back of the couch and forward onto the coffee table.

Cassiar eyes the body calmly. "Too much chaos," he says. "Unmanageable. This is much better."

My ears are ringing and my stomach is in free fall. I don't know if Cassiar is going to shoot me next, or execute Charlie. I'm afraid to even open my mouth.

But I do, anyway.

"You're right about one thing," I say. "Your memories *have* been tampered with, even more than you know. You're not a field agent."

His face is the careful blank of an assassin. He doesn't remember being the director of the NSA, he doesn't remember being my lover. Most likely he doesn't remember the centuries of his undead existence before we met, or any of the human women he fell in love with and watched die.

I'm going to do my damndest to reach out to him, to touch that part of him that loves me.

I'm going to fail.

And then I'm going to kill him.

That's the script that Ahaseurus wrote: Cassius dies at my hand, without remembering me. Heartbreaking and tragic, no?

No.

"Have it your way," I say. "This is an intel-ops scenario. What's the objective?"

"Survival, containment, and recruitment. Disseminate the pire virus as widely as possible while eliminating all thrope vectors."

It's a plausible enough explanation; intelligence agencies are always running worst-case simulations, and a thrope/pire conflict over the colonization of an alternate Earth is unfortunately all too possible. In fact, since the huge power requirements necessary for dimensional transfer make a large invading force impractical, the best way to do it would be exactly what Cassiar is describing: send a lone agent and get him to turn as many of the locals as possible. Of course, then you have the problem of controlling them . . . but the last time I raised a logical objection, Cassiar shot one of my allies. I need to choose my words carefully. "How are you planning to disseminate anything when we're trapped inside the town's borders?"

"With these." He points to the two books. "Obviously, this is more than a simple infiltration scenario. The storm, the Gallowsman, and his soldiers represent this reality's mystic opposition, their attempt to keep the situation contained. Those aspects weren't in the initial briefing, but obviously we were meant to figure that out for ourselves."

"Soldiers?" I ask.

"The road crew. In order to successfully carry out the mission, we need to overcome them and use the exit. Once free of the town's confines, I should have no problem triggering a rapidly spreading pandemic."

I can't let that happen. But he's the one with the gun, the

vampiric reflexes, and the two powerful mystic artifacts. I've got a bartender with a broken leg. That, and . . .

I notice something then. It doesn't make sense for a second, and then it does. *No,* I think to myself. *No, you can't do that.*

But I have to. It's my only chance, even if it breaks my heart. I make a vow to track down Ahaseurus in whatever hell he's currently burning in, and make sure that no matter how much he's suffering, it gets worse. "You've missed one important factor."

"Which would be?"

"The spell book. It's the right weapon to use against the Gallowsman, but only if you know how. You just killed the guy I was going to use. How's your shamanistic training?"

I hold my breath. The Cassius I know would be able to use that spell book, but I'm pretty sure this version can't. Ahaseurus suppressed Jimmy Zhang's sorcerous expertise, and would have done the same to any other shaman.

"I'm not a shaman," Cassiar says. "But your friend Azura is."

I let a glance flicker toward the bedroom door, ever so briefly. "True. But the only way to contact her is through a certain DVD—one that's safely hidden away."

He smiles. I can almost see the hook go through his lip. "I'm sure it is. But I have my suspicions about where it might be . . . let's go into the bedroom, shall we? I'll take the weaponry and books with us so Charlie won't be tempted to get up to any mischief—not that he can move very fast with that broken leg."

I keep my face resolutely neutral while Cassiar unloads the shotgun and pockets the shells, then sticks my scythes—closed—in his waistband. He keeps the books in one hand and my gun in the other, and motions me toward the door. About as good as I can hope for.

I pause with my hand on the doorknob. God, I hope this works.

I open the door, walk through quickly, take two steps and turn. Cassiar is keeping a certain professional distance—you never get too close to someone while holding a gun or similiar ranged weapon on them—but he can't let me get too far away in case I'm planning on doing something stupid.

But I'm not the one he should be worried about.

Cassiar steps into the room. That's when my brave, loyal, incredibly smart dog—who hasn't made a single sound since Cassiar showed up—lunges from where he's been waiting and locks his jaws around Cassiar's wrist. Pires are strong but Saint Bernards are heavy, and Galahad has the advantage of both surprise and leverage; he hauls Cassiar's gun hand down so it's no longer aimed at me.

I lunge forward, grab a scythe from Cassiar's wastband and yank it free.

Cassiar recovers. Rather than try to shake his attacker off, he uses his other hand to bring a fist down on top of Galahad's head. I'm going to have nightmares about the sound it makes for the rest of my life.

There's no time for anything fancy. There's a small silver cone at the top of each scythe, actually the short end of the swiveling blade; when the scythe is open and the blade locked into position, the cone juts out the opposite side at a forty-five degree angle. But when the scythe is closed, like it is now, the cone turns the handle into an eighteen-inch iron-wood stake with a silver tip.

I drive it through Cassiar's heart.

His eyes go wide in disbelief. There's an instant that lasts forever while I wait for him to explode into very, very fine dust.

He bursts into flames instead.

I yank the stake out, ignore the burning body, and kneel over my dog. "Galahad? Gally?" I say.

He raises his head groggily from where he's lying, and a surge of relief goes through me. *He's okay. He's going to be okay.*

But then I see the blood running through his fur, and I realize how wrong I am.

Charlie's already managed to stump his way over, and the first thing he does is use a blanket to douse the fire. "Oh, hell," he says. He's not talking about Cassiar. "Oh, fucking hell."

Galahad looks up at me with those big, red-rimmed brown eyes, his tongue lolling out the side of his mouth. He tries his best to lick my hand.

And then he dies.

People who have never lost a dog don't know what's it like.

I'm not going to be crass and compare it to losing a child. As an FBI profiler, I dealt with people who had lost children, often in horrible ways, and that's a very particular kind of torment I don't want to get into here. No, losing a dog is simpler and more selfish than parental grief, because it doesn't have all the what-ifs attached: what they could have done, where they could have gone, who they could have married. When you grieve for a human being, you're mourning the loss of many things, both for them and for you.

But a dog doesn't have that kind of unused potential waiting for him. He's just a dog, and he's perfectly happy being exactly what he is. A dog has few, if any, regrets. What he mainly has is love—love for life, for food, for playing. And most of all, for you.

That's what you're mourning, more than anything. That pure, unselfish love. That trust. That loyalty. When your dog dies you feel like a failure, because he trusted you and you let him down.

And even though you did, he still loves you.

I know this wasn't really Galahad. He was just some big Saint Bernard that Ahaseurus found and implanted with stolen memories, like most everyone in town. I don't care. Wherever he came from, he was just as brave—and nearly as smart—as my own Gally, and I won't ever forget his sacrifice.

He was a good dog.

* * *

When I'm done crying, I stand up and stick the scythe in my belt. Charlie hands me the other one, having rescued it from the corpse before it could burn. "So," he says. "Not Cassius, huh? How'd you know?"

"Couple things," I say, wiping my eyes. "First, I couldn't believe Cassius could ever be brainwashed into believing a cover story like that; too many holes in the logic. He would have unraveled it in no time, especially with the spells degrading. This guy believed it wholeheartedly.

"Second, Cassius wouldn't throw away a possible asset like Stoker in a situation like this, not unless he was an immediate threat. And third, he wouldn't have fallen for an obvious ruse like my glance toward the bedroom, not even if he was blind drunk and brain-damaged. When I put all that together, I could see that it was just another Ahaseurus mind game."

"So Cassius—"

"Oh, Cassius *is* here, and he *is* the master vampire. Cassiar was just a proxy, a pire created by Cassius's blood, his vampiric essence amped up through *Wizard of Oz*ry—that's how he could ignore the improvised cross I shoved in his face. He was a stand-in, a stunt double; the fact that he burned instead of dusting proves it. Kill the real Cassius and there'd be nothing left but free-floating pire molecules."

Charlie's rearmed himself—he even grabbed the shotgun shells from Cassiar's jacket pocket before they cooked off—and now he hands me the spell book and the graphic novel. "So where's the real thing?"

"I'll show you."

We go outside and get in the car, me in the driver's seat. The storm overhead is finally making noise, but not thunder—it's more like the pop and hiss of static, a bad connection threatening to turn worse. As we drive through the deserted streets, I've got the uneasy feeling we're being watched, but not from any of the buildings.

From overhead.

When we pull up in front of the house, I expect Charlie to say something like "Oh. Really? Guess that makes sense." But I don't get any reaction at all, because of course it's Charlie Allen that would recognize where we are, not Charlie Aleph.

We get out, walk up the sidewalk. I knock on the front door. There's no immediate answer, but I didn't expect one. We wait.

He gets to the door a few minutes later, blinking in mild surprise and confusion. He doesn't get many visitors, and this is the second time I've been here in the last few days. "Jace? Hi! I was wondering when you'd come by with your laptop—"

"Hi, Damon," I say. "Can we come in?"

He invites us inside, clearly happy I'm there and utterly oblivious to what's been happening in the town. He spends most of his time on the Web, I'm sure; the outside world isn't nearly as important—or demanding of his attention—as the electronic one. It keeps him busy, distracts him, focuses his intellect on solving puzzles in games or code. I'll bet that in some of those games he's an ancient vampire, and in others he's the head of a vast spy network. Because that's how you manipulate the mind of someone as old, as smart, as experienced as Cassius: you don't suppress it, you redirect it. Bombard it with familiar stimuli that you control. It's far easier to install mystic filters on a Web server than a living mind, because a computer won't fight back. Cassius hasn't had his memories blocked so much as repurposed.

As a geek, he avoids human contact. As an albino, he avoids sunlight. That leaves one piece of the puzzle unsolved.

"Can I get you guys something? A cola, maybe?"

"I'm a little dry," I say. "Not sure what I want, though. Mind if I see what you have?"

"No, no, help yourself."

I go into the kitchen, open the fridge. Not much on the

top shelf—some half-empty jars of condiments, a six-pack of generic cola in cans. But the lower two shelves are crammed with flats of protein shakes in rectangular waxed cartons, the kind with a little screw-cap on the top. I take one out and look at it. Strawberry. I open it and take a sniff. Smells authentic, in a chemically kind of way. I get a little dab of it from the underside of the cap and taste it.

That's not strawberry.

Looks like the illusion spell masking the flavor has degraded enough to let the taste of blood through—either that, or Ahaseurus never bothered to conceal it from anyone but the pathetic geek who lives here all by himself. Or maybe the sorcerer just convinced him that this is what strawberries taste like; it's been a few centuries since Cassius ate one, after all.

I put the carton back and close the fridge. "Guess I'm not as thirsty as I thought," I say.

I return to the living room, where Damon and Charlie are sitting across from each other. Charlie's studying him with a thoughtful look on his face, and Damon's blithely ignoring him.

"Huh," says Charlie. "Really?"

"There's a little video I'd like to show you," I tell Damon, pulling out my phone. "I tried to send it to you earlier, but it didn't go through. Went to someone else entirely, actually—they had a very similar address."

"Oh. Okay, sure." His eager smile almost breaks my heart. I could tell him I was here to burn down his house, and he'd probably hand me a book of matches.

I call up the video—not so different from placing a call to Azura herself, now—and I'm relieved when she pops up and says, "Jace! What's going on? Tair just woke up, only it's *not* Tair; he claims he's Doctor Pete. I don't know how much longer I can stay hidden from the prison guards, either—my masking spells are good, but they do random mystic sweeps every few hours."

"I'll make this quick. I need you to do the memory thing one more time."

She sighs. "I'm in a prison cell, remember? About the only person I can link you up to is Doctor Pete or myself—"

"We're doing Cassius remotely again. It didn't work last time because I had the wrong guy. This is the real thing."

She frowns, then nods. "That would explain the link going down—we didn't have it plugged into the right socket. Okay, just say when."

"Now would be good." I hold the phone up for Damon to see. He's been following our conversation with a puzzled but intrigued smile.

There's a flash of white light.

TWENTY-THREE

This time is different from the others. It's a much newer memory, and for the first time I'm playing myself.

I'm sitting in a chair, but I can't move anything below my neck. Magic restraints. Cassius sits next to me in a similar chair, and I can tell by his posture that he's in the same situation. We're in some sort of cave, with torches flickering on the walls.

Standing in front of us is Ahaseurus.

He studies me coolly, with that undertaker's face of his: long, bony, hawk nosed. "One of the fascinating things about an extended lifespan—as I'm sure you'll agree, Mr. Cassius—is watching certain patterns arise and take root. Clichés, for example. When a particular phrase, persona, or event becomes popular to the point of overuse, it's not, as some people claim, due to creative laziness, or even a cultural tendency to conform. No, such patterns repeat themselves for the same reason a particular configuration of DNA does: because it's successful. A catchphrase is no different from a stubborn species of fungus that grows upon a boulder and refuses to die."

"Not sure if you're comparing yourself to a fungus or a cliché," I growl, "but either one works for me."

He continues as if I hadn't spoken. "For instance, the antagonist of a drama explaining his master plan to the protagonist when he has her captive. A tiresome device, no? Always leading to this information being used against him at the climax, after her inevitable escape. Why does he do it? Hasn't he ever seen a spy movie?"

He smiles and shakes his head. "I know why, because I have been doing this very same thing for a very long time—long before it ever became a cliché. In fact, I may have been the one who started this particular phenomenon . . . except that none of my captives have ever escaped to use this knowledge against me. *Not ever.*"

"Chassinda did," I say.

Chassinda was the first woman Ahaseurus ever killed. He enjoyed the experience so much that he brought her back to life as a zombie, then kept her around as an undead trophy for hundreds of years. But even though he'd sewn her lips shut, Chassinda found a way to give me vital information—information I used to defeat her owner.

Ahaseurus is still smiling, but his eyes are cold. "You mean the escape of the grave? I stand corrected. If that is your definition, then *all* of my captives have found freedom. All . . . except you."

"Yeah, I'm not much of a follower."

"Ah, but you followed *me,* did you not? Seeking to rescue your lover, you came all the way to the Dark Continent . . . where, despite the assistance of the African Queen, all three of you wound up my prisoners."

He sees the look on my face and chuckles. "Yes, I captured her as well. No last-minute rescues for you. Now, where was I . . . oh, yes, clichés. The reason the antagonist reveals his machinations to the protagonist is simple: because it provides him with a great deal of enjoyment. It allows him to demonstrate how clever he is. To preen and strut before his possession. To see the hope die in her eyes as she realizes—as she truly *knows*, for the first time— that these are the last moments of her life. It's *this* moment that those who take life live for, not the act itself. I could no more deny myself this pleasure than I could deny myself breath."

"Good," I say "That's *my* job."

"Not for much longer. You're about to enter a new profession—one that you won't enjoy very much, I'm afraid I, however, will get a great deal of satisfaction out of it."

"You know, I just made a decision," I say. "I'm going to *end* you. Up until now I thought I'd just have to capture you, because you're the only one who can send me home without me turning into an old homeless woman—but *fuck* that. I'm just going to kill you, the first chance I get." I let out what's supposed to be a melodramatic sigh of relief, but it feels more real than I expected. "Whew. That's going to make things *so* much simpler."

"Oh, but I'm going to make them simpler still. You see, there's yet another reason I can divulge my plans to you: You aren't going to remember them. In fact, you aren't going to remember who you are, or what you do, or the fact that I even exist. You're going to be my plaything, in a very special place I put together just for you."

That scares me, worse than any threat of physical torture. The sharpest weapon I own is my mind, and he's just told me he's going to blunt it. It makes me feel sick, and angrier than I've ever been.

Cassius has been silent until now. He doesn't believe in threats or posturing—I know he's been spending the time studying the situation, evaluating every aspect and considering possible courses of action. "I have taken precautions in the event of my death," he says to Ahaseurus. "I presume this is not a surprise to you."

Ahaseurus favors him with a cold smile. "Of course not. It's what I would do."

"Then you don't intend to kill me."

"Not unless I have to."

"Then know this. The price of tampering with Jace's mind is your own soul." He says this in a flat, matter-of-fact voice; it's not a threat, simply a reminder.

Ahaserus's bushy eyebrows go up. He appears to be slightly taken aback. "I don't think that's a claim you can—"

"It's not a claim, it's a vow," Cassius says. His voice has gotten softer, almost casual. "I don't undertake them lightly. In two thousand years I've only made such a thing once before. It remains unbroken. Beings such as you and I tend to view mortals as ephemeral, not worth serious consideration. They simply don't endure, do they? But hatred does."

His voice has an edge to it now, one I've never heard before. An amused, bitter tone. "Pledging another's destruction can give purpose, direction, to a life that stretches across the long, dusty years. You know this all too well. So do I. And I'm telling you that, should you violate Jace's mind, you will become my purpose. My direction. My reason for continuing to exist. All the many, many years I have spent learning to survive, everything I know of war, every bit of knowledge I possess concerning the profession of tracking, hunting, and destroying other beings—all of it will be brought to bear on ending your extremely long life."

Ahaserus stares at him. So do I. It's an all-or-nothing declaration, one with only two possible outcomes: Either the wizard lets us go, or he kills Cassius.

And he's not going to let us go.

After a moment Ahaserus lets out a rueful little chuckle. "So be it," he says softly. "But you will not perish just yet. You have a role to play in my little drama, a very important one. You will be the father of a new race of vampires, Cassius. Your blood will unleash them on a world where they are only stories, and the African Queen will do the same for thropes. There will be no slow assimilation, no gradual decline of the human race this time; it will be fast and brutal and relentless, driven by a war between the two supernatural species that will demand each propagates as quickly as it can. You will both watch this happen, helpless to stop it, and only when you are drowning in guilt and despair will you finally die."

I shake my head. "Why? You'd murder a whole *planet,* just to make me suffer? Talk about overcompensation—I mean, honestly, after the first million casualties or so, I'm going to be done. Anything past that is just make-work."

He turns back to me. "Oh, it's not just about you. Or even the one Earth. That's the problem with you mortals: you have such tiny, limited perspectives. An immortal such as myself thinks on a far grander scale; using genocide as a psychological weapon against an individual is simply one gambit." I didn't think it was possible to utter a line like that without irony, but, all I hear in Ahaseurus's voice is arrogance.

"I find it hard to believe even you could top that," I growl. It's a lie, but I need to know what else he's planning; it's the sunshiny optimist in me beaming through.

"I recently discovered a very interesting alternate Earth, with the unique quality of being a sort of natural gateway; it's much, much easier to cross the dimensional divide to any number of alternities from there, though getting to it in the first place is proportionally more difficult. I'm in the process of solving that problem, though, with the help of my new lieutenant. He's a collector of negative forces—forces I'm using to break down the barrier between this world and the reality I just mentioned. Once he's established an entry point under my control, I believe his world will make a fine capital for my empire."

His empire. A network of realities, all of them under Ahaseurus's thumb. It won't be just the sorcerer jumping from world to world anymore, it'll be him and a supernatural army. . . .

Which is when I start to laugh.

Ahaseurus watches me, smiling indulgently. He thinks

this is a ploy—maybe I'm stalling, maybe I'm just trying to provoke a reaction. But he's wrong. This is real, genuine enjoyment.

I get myself under control. "You've been out of touch, haven't you? Sure, holing up in another dimension means you're hard to find, but it also means you're out of the loop. Haven't been able to check your e-mail lately."

"There's nothing I need to check—"

"You were putting together an army of damned souls—actually, you subcontracted the job, since you were busy with your transdimensional shortcut project. Well, guess what, Sparky? Before I came here, I stumbled across your little project . . . and oops, clumsy me, I sorta broke it."

The look on his face tells me he thinks I'm guessing. I grin and start firing details at him. It may be the last chance I ever get to piss him off.

It takes all of thirty seconds before he lets loose a roar of pure fury. His eyes flood with an unearthly blue light, and he points a hand crackling with the same energy at me.

The world fills with lightning, then disappears.

Reality, such as it is, swims back into focus. I immediately look over at the paunchy albino I knew by the name Damon Eisfanger.

He's perched on the edge of the recliner, his back straight, his shoulders squared. His features haven't changed physically, but he's wearing an alert, focused expression that's light-years away from Eisfanger's eager cheerfulness. He considers his own pale, pudgy hand.

"I see," he says.

He clenches his hand and stares at it. The flesh begins to shiver, then blur into translucence, revealing another, firmer fist beneath it. He moves his gaze along the arm, the effect traveling with it; it's as if he has some sort of Reveal Vision, invisible beams from his eyes burning off the illusion wrapped around his body.

I know that's not it, though. It's just sheer willpower, focused by an experienced shaman, peeling off a layer of decaying magic like a sunburn victim stripping dead skin. I wonder what he's going to do when he gets to his face.

He asks for a mirror, of course. As a vampire, Cassius doesn't show up in it, but the illusion does—for a second or so, anyway. Then it just dissolves, leaving him staring at his nonexistent reflection.

He puts the mirror down. Glances at Charlie. "Jace. Charlie?"

"Got it in one, boss."

He nods. "Good to see both of you. Sitrep."

That's op-speak for *situation report,* the kind of shorthand you use in the field when you don't have time for multiple syllables. I break it down for him, as quickly and succinctly as I can; right now, we're not lovers, we're two professionals in a very bad and dangerous place.

But even while I'm running down the insane events of the last few days, I can't help noticing that I'm suddenly feeling a lot better.

He asks one or two relevant questions, but otherwise doesn't interrupt. When I'm finished, he thinks for all of three or four seconds, then says, "I'm sorry you had to go through all that. However, you needn't worry about my going feral. I can feel the primal power of this reality—it's similar to that of Azura's world, though not as strong—but my memories weren't supplemented with artificial hatred the way the African Queen's were. Once her own memory implants degrade, she should be able to regain control as well."

"Good to know," I say. "Maybe we should go check on her. We could use another ally."

Cassius is already headed for the door. "After which we should proceed to the highway site. We need to get through it as soon as we can; it's our ticket home, and with Ahasuerus dead it won't stay open forever."

I hesitate. "Are you sure we should run? Ahaseurus's plan—"

"Was to overrun this world with pire and thropes, yes. You've taken care of the thrope problem, and my status as the so-called "master" vampire should give me a psychic link to any other pires created from my blood. I don't sense any; whomever my doppelgänger turned, they must have been destroyed."

Well, that's good news, I guess, though I'm starting to feel sorry for the townspeople caught up in this. Okay, a lot of them belonged to an evil cult, but some of them were probably innocents victimized by Ahaseurus, hapless extras suddenly cast as players from my past.

I shake off the surge of guilt. Wrong time, wrong place. I'll revisit the feeling later, with a good bottle of scotch, some solitude, and a very dark room. Right now, we have to move.

We march out to the car. There's something in the rear window that catches my eye, though it takes me a second to recognize it: fluffy white stuffing from the back seat.

"She's free!" I shout, pulling my gun. Charlie has the shotgun up and ready, while Cassius spins around and looks back at the house—which, it turns out, is exactly where she is, perched on the edge of the eaves. She launches herself straight at Cassius, knocking him over with her momentum.

"Go!" Cassius yells as they grapple. "I'll meet you there!"

And then they're tumbling across the street, Shaka doing her best to claw his head off, Cassius cooly and methodically using kicks, punches, elbows, and knees to inflict as much damage as he can. Our guns are useless; there's too big a risk of hitting the wrong target.

I swear, then jump in the front seat of the car. Charlie joins me. I start it up, gun the engine, and swerve onto the road. I have to trust Cassius; as long as he protects his neck and keeps Shaka from getting her paws on anything pointy and wooden, he'll be okay. By the same estimation, he probably can't kill her—not unless he finds some silver or manages to decapitate her. Fighting her is a strategic move, designed to stall her while we get away; he'll disengage as soon as he can, follow our trail out of town—

Something smashes onto the roof of the car.

For a second I think we've been hit by a falling tree or a meteorite—hey, in this town either one is possible—but then a pale hand gropes over the windshield from above. "Keep going!" Cassius yells.

I glance in the rearview. An extremely pissed-off werewolf is loping after us. Through cunning or dumb luck—and knowing Cassius, I'm pretty sure it's the former—he's gotten his opponent to *throw* him at us. Or maybe she just hit him so hard it launched him like a missile in the right direction.

Either way, I'm not going to look a gift pire in the fangs. I stomp on the accelerator, wondering if it's possible to outrun her.

The answer is: yes and no. In town, where I have to contend with corners, I can't get up enough speed; she's gaining on us steadily. On the highway I'll stand a chance, but I have to get there first.

Charlie smashes out his window with the butt of the shotgun, leans out, and blasts away in the African Queen's general direction. I guess he must have tagged her, because she starts to zig and zag, bounding off mailboxes and vehicles more like an ape than a canine.

It buys me enough time to get to the main road, the one that connects to the highway. I floor the gas pedal and Shaka finally falls behind in the rearview mirror.

And then I see what's waiting for me, just outside of town.

The road is lined on either side with bizarre, stunted trees shaped like giant candy canes. Each is about eight feet high, composed of different-colored strands wound around each other; the strands start out thick at the base and grow increasingly slender, the whole structure curving over at the top and tapering to maybe half an inch in diameter—the thickness of a piece of rope.

Rope that ends in a hangman's noose.

A body sways from the curved tip of every tree. I recognize Zev first, not from his distorted features so much as the clothes he's wearing. His toes almost brush the ground, creating the illusion that he's standing on his tiptoes, maybe about to do a pirouette.

But he's only the first. I see Don Prince, the owner of the hardware store.

Brad Varney, my transvestite mailman.

Mayor Leo.

And many, many others . . . people I knew or thought I did, all the familiar faces you see day after day in a small town. Men, women, children. My paperboy. The guy who drives the snowplow. That plump woman with the five kids. The old couple who always smile when they pass me on the street and apparently don't know a word of English.

All dead. All dangling at the end of rope-trees that apparently sprouted overnight: bastard hybrids composed of roots, underground wires, telephone cable, garden hoses, bright orange extension cords. Strangled by the mundane, by the sinews and tendons that hold together modern existence. Crimson lightning dances overhead, now the only source of illumination in a black sky. I feel like I'm driving into hell.

But I'm not. I'm driving *out* of it. I keep telling myself that as I check the rearview mirror nervously. The African Queen is barely visible behind us, now in full wolf form and tearing after us as fast as she can. I assume Cassius is still on the roof, though I can't really tell.

There's a single traffic barrier across the road ahead, a yellow and black–striped sawhorse with a blinking orange light mounted on it. It looks absurd and out of place, like a BACK IN FIVE MINUTES sign on the Pearly Gates. Beyond the barricade is . . . nothing. No bulldozers, no backhoes, just a vast, yawning pit that the storm seems to be belching out of like smoke from an active volcano.

I screech to a halt, grab the spell books and jump out of

the car. Cassius leaps down from the roof and joins me; it takes Charlie a few seconds longer with his bad leg. We've got maybe thirty seconds before the furious werewolf catches up with us; I toss the spell books at Cassius, then brace my gun arm on the hood of the car and aim down the road. "Read *fast*."

Charlie is right there beside me, the shotgun snugged to his shoulder. "Scattergun will work best if I try to take out her legs," he says. "You've got the pistol; aim for her center mass."

I narrow my eyes and flick a glance at him. "That's awfully knowledgeable for someone who just learned how to handle a gun." Charlie, like everyone on Thropirelem, doesn't know squat about guns.

"I'm a quick study."

"Not that quick. Some of Allen's memories must be bleeding through—maybe because the magic around here is unraveling."

He hesitates. "Could be."

I know my partner. I know when he's not telling me something. And at times like this—all my senses heightened by adrenaline, my instincts going full throttle in sheer survival mode—I know a lot more. Without really thinking about it, I realize exactly what it is he's hiding from me.

"You love me," I say.

He doesn't meet my eyes, doesn't so much as twitch. He could be made of stone.

"Charlie Allen, I mean. *He* loves me. He loves me and you can tell and *you're not mocking me*." I say this last phrase in total disbelief, because it implies a whole world—a whole universe—of consequences that I am simply not prepared to think about at this point in time.

"Maybe later," Charlie manages. "If we're both, you know, still alive."

Cassius intones three words, none of which I can spell

or even pronounce. There's a noise behind me like a rope snapping taut. I risk a glance.

Twenty feet away, the Gallowsman hangs suspended over the pit, the rope around his neck extending straight up into the storm itself. He looks much as I imagined him, a long, lean figure dressed in rags, but his head is erect instead of lolling to the side. The noose is sunk deeply into his flesh, and every inch of skin above it is a horrible mottled green and purple, as if his entire face were a single bruise. His eyes bulge from their sockets and his lips are grotesquely thick and distended, like blisters about to pop. His hair is long and black and greasy.

"Thank God," I say wearily. "I thought you were going to look like my fifth-grade math teacher or something."

"*I am not your nightmare,*" he hisses. "*I am everyone's.*"

The sound of Charlie's shotgun going off interrupts our witty banter. I snap my head around just in time to see the black, lupine form of the African Queen hurtling straight at us. She springs—not for Cassius or me or Charlie, but over our heads and at the Gallowsman himself.

She never makes it.

From my perspective, it's like she leaped into an invisible wind tunnel, a blast of air so powerful that it not only makes every strand of fur on her body stream backward, it also stops her in mid-leap.

The Gallowsman is pointing a single, outstretched arm at her; scarlet electricity crackles down the rope from the storm above, dancing around his neck like a second noose.

The Queen's fur isn't streaming backward anymore; now it's all pointing straight up, like an angry black cat plugged into a wall socket. Fur is nothing but tiny little strings, after all, and that's what the Gallowsman controls. He's got her by the short hairs, the long hairs, and all the hairs in between.

She snarls, writhing and twisting in midair, and I can see huge tufts of fur pulling right out of her flesh, some of them still attached to patches of skin. Must hurt like hell, but it won't kill her; she might even have a shot at freeing herself. I make a silent vow never to complain about waxing my legs again.

Cassius is chanting now in a low, sonorous voice. The Gallowsman gestures with his other hand, and I hear something ripping itself free under the hood of the car. A multi-colored rope made of fan belts, electrical harness wiring, and brake cables snakes its way from beneath the vehicle and slithers toward Cassius. I shoot at it, but it's hard to hit.

The African Queen is ripping free of her own pelt in a frenzy, spattering blood everywhere. I shield my mouth and eyes; a previous thrope experience may have left me with an immunity to the virus that lives on werewolf claws, but I still have to watch out for other modes of infection.

The fur that's no longer attached to the Queen isn't just dropping to the ground—it's weaving itself into a long, thick black rope in midair. At the same moment that it loops around the thrope's neck, the autoconda wriggles up Cassius's body and around his throat. Both yank tight; Cassius's incantation stops.

"You fight a war for no purpose," the Gallowsman intones. *"He who summoned me is gone. I care not for his plans. You may go."*

He flicks his wrist. The African Queen, her body now covered in more blood than fur, falls to earth. The black rope begins to haul her toward the edge of the pit; she fights it every step of the way.

I can't worry about her, though, not when Cassius is being throttled. I know a sharp blade can sever a pire's head from his body, but I'm unclear on the rules about garroting. Cassius doesn't need air to breathe, only to speak—but a cord can cut through a neck, too, given the application of a strong enough force, and the Gallowsman seems to have plenty of that.

I snap a scythe open as I sprint. Cassius isn't even trying to free himself, just focusing on the spell book and the graphic novel; he's got one open in each hand, and his lips are still moving.

I get the point of a scythe between the cable and his neck and cut through the strands. They immediately reweave themselves, and I have to cut through them again—this time, I yank the cable free and pull it as far as I can from Cassius's neck; it wriggles and squirms, trying to get back to its objective. It's like wrestling satanic kudzu.

I hear a howl of anger and desperation behind me, one that quickly fades away to silence. I look back. The African Queen is gone.

I chop at the cable-snake. It reforms again and again, but I'm buying Cassius time. Charlie fires the shotgun, putting round after round into the Gallowsman's chest. Cassius resumes chanting, but I can't hear him over the roar of ordnance.

Which doesn't seem to be affecting its target at all. More crimson lighting arcs and crackles down the rope that leads from the Gallowsman to the storm, and I realize what's going on: Ahaseurus turned the Gallowsman into a battery for mystic energy, but with the sorcerer gone he's started tapping into that energy for himself. He may not have the kind of world-conquering ambition the Big A had, but he's now just as powerful . . . and he's plugged into a dimensional nexus that will let him travel to any number of alternate worlds.

Where he'll do what? Why, the same thing he's always done, but on a bigger scale. He thrives on bad luck and despair, so the more there is the more powerful he becomes. I have a brief, intense vision of the President of the United States, weeping in suicidal remorse as he enters the nuclear activation codes. . . .

"*You,*" the Gallowsman says, turning his attention to Charlie. "*Puppet man. I see the strings that run from you, that stretch across the dimensional divide. They are* here." He reaches out, makes a grasping motion in the air—then *yanks.*

Charlie lurches forward like he was pushed—no, more like he was *pulled*. He drops the shotgun. He staggers, catches himself, then shakes his head. "What? What's—what's going on?" He looks around in utter confusion, and I realize that my partner just got kicked off this dimensional plane.

Down to me. I've got to keep Mr. Dangly there busy long enough for Cassius to finish the spell, or it's all over. There's only one thing I can think of to do, and it didn't work out so well for the African Queen.

But I have an advantage that she didn't. My pelt comes off a whole lot easier.

I skin out of my clothes as fast as I can and throw them as far away as I can manage. They don't come to life and try to return, for which I'm thankful; either the Gallowsman hasn't figured out what I'm up to or he doesn't care.

Then I grab a scythe, clamp the handle between my teeth, and sprint for the edge of the precipice.

Everything seems to slow down as I run. My mind is perfectly clear, perfectly focused. Yes, I'm about to throw myself off a cliff, one that seems to be perched over a dimensional gulf. Yes, the being I'm aiming at has plenty of time to prepare and is vastly more powerful than I.

I launch myself into space, wondering if this is how I'm going to finally die: naked in midair, a silver-bladed, monster-killing weapon between my teeth. . . .

Nah. Not bizarre enough.

It's a long jump, but I've got momentum, adrenaline, and desperation on my side; it looks like I'll be able to reach him, barely—

My head comes to an abrupt halt. He's mystically latched on to my hair, yanking it back the way he did the African Queen's fur. But the rest of my body keeps going, just like I knew it would; my legs swing up, on either side of the Gallowsman's body, and wrap around his torso. It feels like clamping my legs onto a cold, damp burlap sack filled with bones.

I reach up and grab the handle of my scythe. My eyes are

no more than a foot from the Gallowsman's, which are very dark and very dead. This isn't a person; this is an elemental force given human form. It can't be reasoned with, it has no pity or mercy or compassion. It just is. The reason it was summoned was simple: to collect despair, and dump it into me. To make me suffer.

But not to kill me.

I see a look of consternation cross his face as the scythe begins its arc, not toward his neck but toward the rope above his head. He wants to strangle me, or maybe drop me into the pit the way he did the Queen, but something's stopping him. The rope around his neck isn't just a noose; it's a leash, one Ahaseurus placed there to ensure his attack dog didn't go too far. Killing me was a pleasure the wizard had reserved for himself.

It's also the conduit the Gallowsman's using to channel energy from the storm.

Sorry, baby. Time to cut the cord.

The blade bites into and through the strands. There's a brilliant flash of crimson, but I was expecting that. With my other hand, I lunge for the end of the rope I just severed.

My hand closes on it. Cut off from the mystic maelstrom that was feeding him, the Gallowsman drops straight down without a sound. In a second he's vanished into the darkness of the pit beneath us.

I put the scythe back in my mouth and grab the rope with my other hand. Twenty feet away, Cassius has stopped chanting and is now studying me quizzically.

"Libble helb?" I manage.

Rescuing me turns out to be easy; the storm, and the portal beneath it, are now under Cassius's control. He directs the dangling rope to move, and it deposits me on the edge of the cliff before zipping up into the clouds and disappearing. Whichever reality the Gallowsman disappeared into, he's no longer connected to a storehouse of mystic energy.

Charlie Allen looks the other way as I get dressed. Cassius doesn't.

"Okay," I say. "Now what?"

Cassius doesn't reply for a moment. When he does answer me, he sounds hesitant. "That's up to you, Jace."

I frown. "What do you mean?"

"When he brought you here, Ahaseurus eliminated the condition that would have prematurely aged you if you tried to return to your own reality. You've captured Stoker, fulfilling the terms of your contract. There's nothing to stop you from going home—and I can send you there from here."

I blink. The evil witch is dead, I've reached the end of the Yellow Brick Road, and I can finally get the hell out of Oz— or in this case, Kansas.

But do I want to?

I glance over at Charlie Allen. He stares back at me with a guarded expression I know too well. He's not worrying about himself, he's worrying about me. I know he's not *my* Charlie, but . . .

But he could be.

I look back at Cassius. His face, by contrast, isn't guarded at all; it's just sad. He thinks he knows what I'm going to choose, and he's getting ready to say goodbye.

I think about home—the one I was born and raised on, the one without thropes or pires or golems. The one that has butterscotch ice cream and shooting ranges and the house I grew up in.

I take a deep, deep breath.

And then I tell them what I'm going to do.

Don't miss the other novels in
the spectacular Bloodhound Files series by

DD BARANT

BACK FROM THE UNDEAD

BETTER OFF UNDEAD

KILLING ROCKS

DEATH BLOWS

DYING BITES

Available from St. Martin's Paperbacks